HIS MAKE-BELIEVE BRIDE

RAKES & REBELS: THE RAVENEAU FAMILY, BOOK 6

CYNTHIA WRIGHT

BOXWOOD MANOR BOOKS

~ BOOK DESCRIPTION ~

Guarded hearts...

A French pirate of smoldering passions, Justin St. Briac has vowed never to marry. However, when his manipulative mother beckons him to her deathbed in Cornwall, he succumbs to her plea that he take a bride —devising an elaborate charade to grant her dying wish.

Her days are numbered, after all, and soon he'll return to his life of unfettered romantic conquests and adventure.

A pretend marriage...

Mouette Raveneau, once the toast of the London ton, has been ruined by her dead husband's crimes. When she reluctantly takes refuge in Cornwall with her two adolescent sons, Justin hires her to help carry off his grand scheme.

Soon, however their "business arrangement" begins to feel like what Justin has avoided his whole life--a real marriage, one where he could lose something much more valuable than his freedom…he might actually lose his heart.

HIS MAKE-BELIEVE BRIDE is Book 6 in the
captivating series,
Rakes & Rebels: The Raveneau Family:

1 – SILVER STORM (André & Devon)
2 – HER HUSBAND, THE RAKE (André & Devon)
a sequel novella to SILVER STORM
3 – SMUGGLER'S MOON (Sebastian & Julia)
4 – THE SECRET OF LOVE (Gabriel & Isabella)
5 – SURRENDER THE STARS (Ryan & Lindsay)
6 – HIS MAKE-BELIEVE BRIDE (Justin & Mouette)
7 – HER IMPOSSIBLE HUSBAND (Justin & Mouette)
8 – HIS RECKLESS BARGAIN (Nathan & Adrienne)
9 – TEMPEST (Adam & Cathy)

CHAPTER 1

*I*t didn't help Justin St. Briac's mood when the gray sky began to spit cold raindrops at him. His knees ached, curse them, as he climbed the steep hillside path to his brother's manor house. Shielding his face with one hand as the rain fell harder, he looked ahead with his good eye and saw Izzie's painting cottage nearby, just as his brother Gabriel had imagined it a decade ago, on the eve of his wedding.

As that long ago night had worn on, the St. Briac brothers imbibed more and more cognac. Eventually, Gabriel had brought out a sheaf of sketches, enthusiastically describing his plans for a hilltop estate above Polperro, including a light-filled atelier where Izzie could paint. Justin had pretended to listen while silently scoffing at his brother's dreams. Even now, seeing the handsome manor house come into view, framed in an archway of rhododendrons, he thought that appearances were usually deceiving.

"M'sieur, how fine a home your brother has made," remarked his manservant, Baptiste.

Justin was so deep in thought he'd nearly forgotten Baptiste was walking beside him. "Fine enough, I suppose."

"But of course," Baptiste amended quickly, "it pales beside your mansion in Saint-Malo."

"Do not attempt to placate me as if I were an ill-tempered old man."

"Certainly not, m'sieur." The rail-thin Frenchman fell back into his habitual state of silence.

Built of mellow Cornish stone, the home Gabriel and Isabella called Elysium was simple yet handsome, lined with windows and fronted by neatly-trimmed boxwood hedges. Parkland and gardens spread as far as the eye could see. Justin found it odd to think of his younger brother as a prosperous landowner. Odder still was the notion of Gabriel as a contented husband and father who no longer cared for adventure.

It was Justin's experience that people didn't change. At least, not in ways that really mattered.

Reaching the house, they were greeted by a plump, ginger-haired housemaid who took Justin's greatcoat and Baptiste's hat. Unlike most servants who kept their eyes averted as if they weren't permitted to be human, this girl gave them bright, welcoming smiles. She was even bold enough to announce that her name was Claire.

Justin saw that the entrance hall was spacious, with a tile floor and walls paneled in carved walnut. Although the atmosphere was homey rather than impressive, he had to admit that the effect was not unpleasant. And there were tantalizing smells wafting toward them from a kitchen at the back of the house.

"*Mon Dieu,*" Justin said, inhaling appreciatively. "It smells like *Bretagne.*"

"Aye, sir," said Claire. "That be Madame Kerjean's fine onion tarte, made with onions brought from Roscoff." She turned her friendly gaze to Baptiste. "I'll ask that you wait here, please, while I take M'sieur St. Briac to my master. Then I'll bring you a large piece of Madame's tart!"

Baptiste, who was used to discreetly running a very grand household, bit his lip but allowed Claire to put him in a chair before she led Justin to a door at the back of the house. At first, as she opened it, it seemed they were returning outside, but quickly he realized that he was in a sprawling, open room with floor-to-ceiling windows on three side and a high, vaulted ceiling. Seeing rows of dwarf citrus trees in pots, Justin realized this must be his brother Gabriel's conservatory.

"There you are!" called a familiar voice, and he turned to find his brother, standing at a long, rustic table with two little girls. All three of them wore long aprons, doeskin gloves, and were clearly in the midst of transplanting what appeared to be an exotic cactus.

"Are you Uncle Justin?" asked the younger child, pronouncing his name with a flawless French accent. She walked right over and extended a gloved hand. "My name is Camille St. Briac. Louise and I have been waiting for you for the *longest* time."

Justin was instantly captivated. The child couldn't have been more than four years of age. Blessed with huge eyes of Parisian blue and gleaming tawny ringlets, Camille was already a great beauty.

"*Ma belle*," he said softly. "It is an honor to meet you."

Gabriel had put down his trowel, removed his apron and gloves, and now he took the hand of Camille's older sister. As they drew near, Justin saw that the other girl was a delicate, serious brunette, perhaps eight years of age, who wore spectacles like her mother. She regarded him with some uncertainty.

"How good it is to see you, *mon frère*," said Gabriel. Releasing Louise's hand, he embraced Justin, who tried not to stiffen. It had been a long time since anyone had touched him with genuine affection.

As greetings were exchanged and Louise bobbed a reserved curtsy, Justin observed that his brother was still fit and lean at forty-two, with only glints of silver in his chestnut hair.

"Grandmère says you are a wicked pirate," Camille declared, staring at Justin with frank curiosity. "It must be true. You wear an eye-patch!"

Gabriel shook his head. "Enough of that, *ma poulette*. It is midday and you two must be hungry." He gestured to Claire. "Go and see Madame in the kitchen."

Watching the girls leave the conservatory, Justin felt a momentary pang of regret that they didn't know him.

"I'm sorry that it took Maman's illness to bring you to our home at last," Gabriel said, as if guessing his thoughts. "I trust your Channel crossing was uneventful. Did you hire a conveyance?"

"No. Baptiste and I walked up from the harbor." The pain in his knee intensified as he spoke.

"Ah. I suppose I should have warned you about the steep lane leading up here from the village. Actually, there is a less precipitous drive that leads over to the main road, but no doubt my intrepid brother could climb a dozen hills like this one."

Justin looked around for a chair. "What sort of conservatory is this, without any seating areas for guests?"

"I like to keep it just for myself and the plants. It's much more convenient to be able to move in and out of the house, rather than working in an outdoor greenhouse. What's wrong? Do you need to sit down after your exertions?"

Before Justin could make a sardonic reply, Gabriel took his arm and led him back into the house.

They soon came into a library filled with books of every size and color, ranged along the floor-to-ceiling shelves and precariously stacked on a worn desk near the window. A cheerful blaze beckoned from the fireplace, where a pair of worn leather wing chairs waited for them.

"You'd doubtless like a bit of fortification before going up to see Maman." Gabriel said, pouring cognac into two crystal glasses. "Shall I order food?"

"Later, perhaps." As Justin settled into one of the unfashionable chairs, he found that it was surprisingly comfortable compared to those in his own magnificent, immaculate library. He was beginning to relax when his brother spoke again.

"What has happened to your eye?"

Justin wanted to flinch, but managed instead to shrug lightly. "Ah, just a misstep during a duel. I never think of it now." Deftly, he changed the subject. "Where is your beautiful wife? I would much rather greet Izzie than our mother."

He was gratified to see Gabriel's body tense. "Isabella is in London for a few days. She's gone to visit her friend Mouette Raveneau Brandreth. Perhaps you remember her from our wedding?"

"I believe I do." To Justin's surprise, a hot tide of memory swept over him at the mention of Lady Brandreth. He'd nearly forgotten her—until that very moment. "She is well?"

"Unfortunately, Mouette has fallen on hard times— but that's another conversation." Taking a drink of cognac, Gabriel added, "Isabella was happy that you were coming to see Maman and looks forward to seeing you when she returns."

"Unfortunately, I will not be here. I must return to France as soon as possible."

"You have just arrived but you are leaving?" Gabriel

murmured dryly.

"Correct." Unable to resist dangling a reminder of what his married brother was missing, Justin added, "A beautiful woman awaits my return, quite possibly in my bed."

"Indeed?" Gabriel showed no sign of envy. "Is it Azelma Marchand?"

Justin blinked at the mention of the woman he had dallied with years ago. "Are you in jest? Azelma is far too old for my taste."

"How fortunate that you alone, at forty-eight, have remained unmarked by age," Gabriel said dryly. "In view of your crowded social calendar, we are grateful you could travel to Cornwall, even for the briefest of visits."

Justin frowned. Was Gabriel mocking him? "If you imagine that I want to be with Maman any longer than necessary, you are mistaken."

"I trust you don't plan to tell *her* that."

"Do you blame me for feeling manipulated to make this journey? I have a busy life, as you know, with a great many responsibilities." Drinking his brother's fine cognac, Justin was relieved to feel the pain ease in his knee. "I came because you informed me I must, but after I see our parents, Baptiste and I will return to sleep on *Deux Frères* and set sail for France with the morning tide."

"I see." Gabriel leaned back in his chair and nodded in a way that Justin found extremely annoying. "You feel nothing when you consider the prospect that Maman may soon pass from this world?"

Justin couldn't suppress a harsh laugh. "Do you expect me to believe that she is truly at death's door? For God's sake, since the moment of my birth, I have been forced to watch her play out her little dramas and call the tune while our father danced—and you and I foolishly joined in. I vowed long ago never to join in her games when I was old enough to have a choice in the matter." Waiting in vain for his brother to agree with him, Justin reached for his snuffbox. "I will tell you plainly that I felt liberated when Maman and Papa decided to move their household to Cornwall after your marriage."

"Indeed?" Gabriel sounded unconvinced. "You could have come to visit. After you returned from your adventures with Surcouf in the Indian Ocean, our parents expected you to appear. Have you even seen their little home? It's quite charming."

"Leaving France was their choice. Can you blame me for being relieved that Maman would no longer be turning up on my doorstep, claiming to have run away from Papa?"

Gabriel's tone was maddeningly calm. "No matter their faults, they are still our parents. And it does appear that Maman is desperately ill. Before Isabella left for London, she insisted that they come here to stay, so that we could look after them."

"Maman is plotting something," Justin insisted.

"Ah yes, plotting. Perhaps a pastime that you yourself learned at her knee?" came his wry response. "Can you not suspend your judgment until you assess how ill she appears to be?"

"You seem to have fallen under Maman's spell, just like our father." When Gabriel only shrugged in response, Justin marveled again at the change in his brother. Arching a dark brow, he murmured, "Are you really happy, confined here in this conventional existence? Can you possibly enjoy—what, raising plants?— as much as planning a dangerous smuggling venture?"

Finally, he saw Gabriel's blue eyes flash. "You don't understand the first thing about botany, or the challenge of growing something new." He leaned forward. "As for this *conventional* existence, my days are filled with a treasure you have never known and could never gain through smuggling or any other reckless escapade." With soft emphasis he added, "Love."

Justin felt his nostrils flare. "Oh, please…spare me."

Gabriel pushed gracefully to his feet without any sign of aching knees. "Shall we go upstairs to see Maman? Clearly you are in a hurry to be on your way."

* * *

As Gabriel led the way down the wide upstairs corridor, Justin noticed the exquisite paintings that lined the walls and guessed they were the creations of his sister-in-law. One watercolor perfectly evoked his favorite view in Saint-Malo, of the isle of Petit Bé, as seen from the ramparts. A few were delightful portraits of his nieces, capturing them at the various ages he had missed, while one larger painting portrayed a family he didn't immediately recognize, seated on the wildflower-strewn Cornwall cliffs.

"That is Isabella's brother, Sebastian, with his family," Gabriel supplied, following Justin's gaze. "No doubt you remember him from his days as a smuggler? There is his wife, Julia, and their children, Cassandra and Lucas. They hosted our wedding, on their estate overlooking the River Fowey."

"But of course I remember the daring Lord Sebastian. I am very surprised that he continues to resist indulging his craving for adventure. Perhaps age and another decade of marriage have made him dull."

Gabriel seemed not to notice the bait Justin had cast

before him. Instead, he continued down the corridor, inclining his head at a framed sketch as they passed by. "Isabella framed a likeness of you as well."

Justin paused before the informal portrait made so long ago. In it, he was lounging in an elegant Sheraton chair, impeccably dressed, his favorite agate snuffbox in one hand as he flicked it open with his thumb. Seeing the faintly predatory expression on his face, Justin felt a pang. Was that the way he'd appeared to Izzie? Perhaps he had rather tricked her into being alone with him, but he hadn't truly meant any harm.

Gabriel, who had gone ahead, stopped before a paneled door and knocked. After a long moment, during which Justin came up beside him, the door opened a few inches to reveal their father's face.

"By all the saints," Xavier breathed, "it is you, Justin. You have come!"

It was a shock to see his father looking considerably older, his strong shoulders slightly bent, his weathered face careworn. Justin felt himself soften just a bit. "Of course I have come, Papa. What do you take me for, an ogre?"

Before Xavier could reply, his mother's quavering voice arose from the bed. "Justin? Can it be?"

A wave of emotion engulfed Justin, catching him off-guard. For a moment, he felt physically ill. "Papa, will you swear to me that this is not a trick?" he demanded in a harsh whisper.

Xavier recoiled. "Truly, you shock me. Age and hard living have made you more cynical than ever!"

Was that an answer? Justin supposed it would have to do. His heart was in his throat as he went forward, so preoccupied with the scene in the bedchamber and his mother's pale countenance that he forgot about his own quite drastically altered appearance.

"Oh, Justin, how I have dreamed of this moment," Cerise St. Briac began, extending a shaky hand in his direction. "My first-born son. So magnificent—"

As his mother spoke, she looked up at him, focusing in disbelief. Justin watched as the rest of the blood drained from her face. He looked past her, into a mirror on a stand near the bedside, and saw the reason for her shock.

No longer was he the daring, irresistible corsair who seemed only to grow more attractive with each passing year. No, the man who stared back at Justin in the mirror was dissipated from too much wild living, too many reckless brushes with death and, a soft voice whispered inside him, an aversion to love. His black hair was now streaked with silver, lines bracketed his hard mouth, and even his waist had thickened.

Worst of all, under the black eye-patch, his arresting face was now marred by a thin white scar that slashed down from his brow, continued through his left eye— or the place where it had once been—and ended below his cheekbone. Even the duel that had cost him his eye now seemed a taunt that he was no longer invincible.

Justin's heart pounded as he saw the questions in his mother's eyes. Dying she might be, but she was as shrewd as ever, her gaze peeling back his defenses until he was utterly exposed.

"What have you done to yourself?" she asked in a ragged voice.

Reflexively, he raised a hand to touch his eye-patch. It was fashioned of black silk, edged in the same dark plum as his waistcoat. As soon as the physician had told him that he could not save his eye, Justin had decided to turn it to his advantage. He would make every man in France want to wear a rakish patch over one eye.

"'Twas but a twist of fate, Maman," he replied,

adding more jauntily, "Do you not find me more dashing than ever?"

"Pray do not waste our time." Cerise patted the bed. "Sit down beside me. Each moment is precious, for there may not be many left to us."

Although Justin longed to resist, he obeyed, searching her face for signs of impending death. True, she was paler than usual, and appeared to be very tired, but if she only sat up and pinched her cheeks, wouldn't that make a difference? "Maman, I think that you may only need a nice bath, some good food, and your maid to dress your hair properly. What about a glass of champagne? I have seen that raise your spirits more than once."

She swatted at him weakly. "Pah. You are nonsensical, Justin. I am an old woman and my life is ebbing away as surely as the tide."

"Get up and walk with me. I will help you." He started to motion to his father and brother to join in his efforts, but Cerise gave him a sharp look.

"It is too late for that, don't you see?"

"Maman…" he protested. "There must be something I can do."

"You have come," she whispered. "That is a…beginning."

Justin was still absorbing her pronouncement when his father rushed over. Gently, Xavier lifted Cerise up from the pillow and held a crystal glass of water to her parched lips. Justin felt a sense of profound disbelief as he watched her attempt to sip the water, managing only a few drops before turning her face away. *Sangdieu,* how could he have allowed a full decade to pass without visiting his parents? Was it possible that his vibrant, maddening mother might actually die before he could mend things between them?

"Show me," she was saying now, watching him under her lids.

"What do you mean?" he asked warily.

"Show me your eye, *mon fils.*"

She was like a cat, he thought, seemingly somnolent yet fully capable of tormenting her prey. "I would rather not."

"I am your mother. I washed your private parts long before you knew what to do with them, so I can certainly view your injured eye. You must show me now."

This interview was excruciating. Better to get it over with! He leaned closer and slowly lifted his eye-patch so that she alone could see the wound—a wound that replaced an expressive black eye nearly identical to Cerise's own.

Just when he thought this ordeal couldn't get any worse, at the moment he was about to replace the covering and retreat to safety, his mother unexpectedly reached up and touched her fingertips to his scarred eyelid. To his further horror, she began to weep.

"Justin, do you not see that this is but a sign of your broken life? You are at an age when other men have raised their children and are enjoying their homes and families."

"I am not other men," he growled. "My life is not broken! On the contrary, it is what all men secretly aspire to."

"You are speaking to your mother," she said softly, staring at him in a way that made him feel like a child again. "I will not be fooled. It is time for you to put aside your games of adventure and take up the challenges of real manhood."

"Maman! Are you delirious?" He felt his brother and father watching them with interest, but forced himself to ignore them.

"If you want me to die a happy woman, a fulfilled mother, you must grant my last wish."

"Last wish?" What the devil was she talking about?

"You must take a wife…before it is too late, Justin! I cannot leave this world in peace unless I know you've taken a bride and are endeavoring to make a happy marriage." Glancing over toward Gabriel, Cerise turned the knife as only she could, "As your brother has done so *magnificently*."

For a moment, Justin couldn't breathe. A black curtain closed around him, but he fought it off. He wasn't about to let his mother of all people perceive how deeply he dreaded being trapped in the prison of marriage, without any avenue of escape.

Breathing slowly, he felt his head clear. His relationship with his mother had been disastrous over the years, Justin realized, and now it was nearly too late. If he could win bloody battles against pirates and the British Navy, could he not find a way to grant his own mother's dying wish?

On his own terms, of course.

"*Eh bien*. If that is what you want, Maman," Justin said in a low voice, reaching for her hand, "consider it done."

She blinked. "Oh, *mon fils*, you love me after all! Will you divulge the identity of your future bride?"

"Patience, Maman, patience."

Gabriel came up beside him and spoke to their mother. "You have had enough excitement for one day, and Justin must have food after his long journey."

As they left the oppressively warm bedchamber and emerged into the corridor, Justin inhaled the fresh air of freedom.

"Thank God you rescued me just now," he said.

"For the moment," his brother replied. "Come downstairs and have a large piece of Madame's onion tart. I can't wait to hear more about the stunning plans for your marriage."

"Oh, I'm not *really* getting married." Justin gave a derisory laugh, arching a brow as he added, "But what harm can it do to pretend to grant Maman's wish? I shall fool her into believing that she alone had the power to make me take a wife, when in truth I shall remain as untethered as ever."

CHAPTER 2

London, England
April 1818

ouette Raveneau Brandreth sat at a small writing desk in the window of her morning room, facing Bedford Square. Holding a quill pen poised above an inkpot, she waited for inspiration.

She was making a list of ideas for possible employment.

Governess, wrote Mouette. Seconds later, she crossed it out. How could she become a governess, living in someone else's home, when she had two sons? It might be slightly feasible if they were either adorably young or nearly adult, but Charles and Anthony were at the rather horrid ages of thirteen and nine.

Teacher, Mouette wrote more tentatively. Hadn't she been tutoring her own boys? Was it possible that anyone might actually employ her to educate their daughters? It seemed unlikely, for such positions were usually filled by men.

Mouette put down the pen and looked around the

room. Although very sparsely furnished, it was not as empty as the rest of the townhouse. Piece by piece, she'd sold off the stylish furnishings chosen with painstaking care during her decade-long marriage to Sir Harry Brandreth. She'd been comfortably ensconced in the *ton* during those years, but it had all come crashing down when Harry betrayed the trust of Mouette's father, André Raveneau, and even tried to kill him. Only a few months later, he had hanged himself in prison.

It seemed a lifetime ago rather than four years. Her parents had lovingly rescued her and the boys and taken them away to their other home in Connecticut, where they'd remained as the wars between England, France, and America raged on. But Mouette couldn't be satisfied hiding from life forever.

Although her entire adult life had been spent in England, now that she had returned, she found herself struggling to craft a future. Harry had left her debts rather than a fortune. All that remained were the lavish possessions accumulated during her years of striving to become a society hostess. She'd returned from America to find trunks of exquisite, if rather dated, gowns. Storerooms were filled with furnishings in the most recent Empire style, sets of china, paintings, and other treasured valuables.

Mouette had returned to this perfectly respectable home in Bedford Square, hired a staff, and waited for something to happen, for surely something *must* happen.

And yet, her circumstances had taken a turn for the worse.

Why had she imagined her old friends would welcome her back into their midst? Instead, Mouette felt tainted by events she'd been powerless to control. Her former friends held routs but did not invite her, or they pretended to not see her in a crowd. When Mouette did attend a social gathering, she began to notice the subtle cues sent her way: the angling of shoulders to shut her out, the glances that were exchanged when she approached. Was she to be ostracized for the rest of her life because her handsome, ambitious, charming husband had turned out to be the worst sort of villain?

Apparently so.

Staring down at the sheet of foolscap, Mouette picked up her pen and forced herself to write, *Seek out a protector.* It was the one option that had a real chance of success. However not only did her spirit rebel against such a notion, but the thought of giving her body to another man was abhorrent. Even with Harry, her own husband, she had had to force herself to submit to his desires.

Just then, the bell jangled inside her front door. She'd dismissed her servants one by one over the last year, and now only one kind-hearted housemaid came to assist her when she had guests. Mouette had learned to always plan well in advance for those occasions.

Gracefully, she rose from her satin-upholstered side chair and smoothed her skirts. Her heart raced as she glanced in the gilded mirror above the mantel. She'd hung the looking-glass here just last week, to replace a family treasure she had been forced to sell, a portrait of Mouette herself. Painted by Élisabeth Vigée Le Brun, it had been made to celebrate her engagement to Harry in 1804.

Now, instead of viewing her likeness in the portrait, made at a moment when she had been young and filled with hope, she saw her older reflection in the mirror. True, she was thirty-six years of age, but was she not still lovely? If one didn't look too closely, her gleaming ebony curls, azure-blue eyes, creamy skin, and fine figure, remained relatively unchanged.

The knock came again at the door and Mouette continued on toward the entryhall. Who could possibly be calling unannounced? If it was another bill collector, she would pretend to be her own servant and say that Lady Brandreth was away for the afternoon.

Opening the door, Mouette was utterly shocked to see her younger sister, Lindsay, standing on the front step next to her childhood friend, Isabella. Could they hear the pounding of her heart?

"Goodness! Whatever are you two doing here in London?" Surely they were wondering why she was answering her own door instead of a butler. Since she had been forced to let Steele go months ago, Mouette couldn't invite anyone to come to her home. "I—I'm quite unprepared for guests!"

"Unprepared?" echoed Lindsay Coleraine with a laugh. "We have come to surprise you, darling sister! Aren't you pleased?"

With a rising tide of panic, Mouette watched them enter uninvited. "Perhaps you were surprised that I opened the door to you myself!" She wanted to press her hands to her flushed cheeks. "Steele, you see, has gone to—to visit his aunt, who is very ill!"

"Surprised? It never entered my mind," Lindsay replied with a quizzical glance. Removing her bonnet to reveal upswept strawberry-blonde curls, she added, "Whatever is the matter? You're very flushed. Do you have a fever?"

Mouette quickly recovered her composure. "Of course not. I simply was not expecting guests. Do come into the sitting room and I will order refreshments."

With a flourish, she threw open the doors leading into her sitting room. This one room remained a vision of sheer perfection, the place where Mouette had fully exercised her talent for creating an artistic living space. She'd had the walls painted the warm, inviting color of beeswax and discovered just the right Axminster carpet. Its muted shades of blue and gold perfectly accentuated the upholstery. Every candlestick, every piece of art, every small ornament that graced the polished tabletops, had been carefully chosen and placed by Mouette.

"Oh my dear, what a beautiful room!" exclaimed Isabella St. Briac, her eyes shining behind her spectacles as she turned in a circle, staring. "Where is the portrait of you by Madame Le Brun? I have dreamed of seeing it again."

A wave of shame washed over Mouette. Her friend Izzie was an artist and Madame Le Brun had been her mentor. While the Frenchwoman executed the portrait, Izzie had practiced at her own easel, while Mouette's mother, Devon, poured tea. The memory of that long-ago, convivial day in Madame's light-filled London home, when the future held only promise, made her heart ache.

And she couldn't possibly tell her friend the truth, that she had sold the portrait to pay a particularly nasty bill collector. "I—I—" Wildly, Mouette searched her mind for a plausible explanation for the portrait's absence. "I loaned it to an artist friend who wanted to study Madame Le Brun's technique."

"Oh!" Isabella nodded, looking rather perplexed. "Well, your home is simply lovely. Clearly, your situation must be more agreeable than I had imagined."

"Izzie, don't you know that it's very bad taste to allude to one's financial resources?" Mouette scolded. They had been close friends for so long that she could speak to Isabella like a sister. "Is that why you are here? Because you two thought might I need rescuing from dire circumstances?"

Having taken seats in a lovely pair of Adam chairs, Lindsay and Isabella exchanged guilty looks. "As it happens," Lindsay said, "I have been wanting to visit again, ever since our brief reunion when you and the boys first returned from America. However, one can't simply pop in from Oxford—and I've been very occupied with baby Bridget."

Mouette knew a moment's shame that she hadn't made a real effort to meet her new niece. "I understand completely. I've been longing to see Bridget for myself —and of course, you and Ryan. The year has flown by since I returned to London."

"You will adore Bridget! She has my hair and Ryan's blue eyes and she is already a flirt."

"It sounds like Bridget is the image of our mother. I'm rather surprised that you didn't bring her with you today." As she spoke, Mouette watched her younger sister. It wasn't easy to be with Lindsay again, remembering the way their lives had been entangled during the weeks of Harry's descent into ruin. Once, Mouette had enjoyed a feeling of superiority. She had been a member of London society, with a grand home, two beautiful children, and a handsome husband.

Now, her flush deepened as she remembered how she had held herself up as a role model for Lindsay, assuming that her sister would covet her status and apparent wealth. It was humiliating to consider how their situations had become reversed, with Lindsay enjoying a rewarding life, married to her great love who was now a professor of astronomy at Oxford University. Mouette was alone and penniless, her pride in tatters.

Lindsay spoke, bringing Mouette back to the present. "You are right, Bridget does have Mama's coloring, even more than I do."

"Speaking of our mother," Mouette said very casually, "I was just thinking today of her ruby necklace. Do you remember it? It fit around her neck like a collar." Her heart began to race. "She never cared for it because it was incompatible with her reddish hair. Do you think she left it behind in the Grosvenor Square house?"

"Of course I remember it! But I believe Mama took all her jewels back to Connecticut." Lindsay leaned forward in her chair, pinning Mouette with her gray eyes. "What's wrong? You've gone a bit pale."

"I forgot to eat at midday. Tea will help," said Mouette quickly as she rose from her chair. "And some little cakes."

"Let me help you," exclaimed Isabella. She was beside her in an instant.

"No! My maid will prepare it. We will return in just a few moments." Of course, there was no maid, and surely they must suspect something was amiss, but Mouette turned away and hurried blindly from the room.

Traversing the corridor, she paused to close the doors to the now-empty dining room and library. It was a relief to reach the kitchen at the back of the house. Shame flooded her as she remembered her mother's necklace and the expression on Lindsay's face when Mouette had mentioned it. Did her sister guess that she had sunk so low she would consider selling some of their mother's jewelry to keep a roof over the heads of her little family?

She had just filled a kettle and put it over the fire when the sound of footsteps reached her ears, accompanied by the sound of doors opening along the corridor.

"Mouette? Where are you?"

With a shock, she realized it was Isabella, following her, looking into all the rooms she had emptied of their contents in recent weeks.

Mouette's stomach churned with panic. She wanted to open the back door and run out into the garden, but just then her best friend appeared in the doorway. Looking around the kitchen, she clearly saw that there was no maid, just as the rest of the house had been nearly bare of furnishings.

"I am worried about you," Isabella said solemnly. "Please, let me help you."

To Mouette's further shame, hot tears welled up in her eyes and spilled onto her cheeks. "Help me? Why, nothing is wrong." As she spoke, her voice became a sob and she covered her face with her hands.

"Oh, darling," exclaimed Isabella. She was beside her in an instant, gathering her near. "Whatever is troubling you, you must not be afraid to tell me."

Mouette wept on her friend's shoulder for a full, blessed minute before finally she could speak. She was older than Isabella by two years and had always held the balance of power in their relationship. Mouette's parents, André and Devon Raveneau had taken Izzie in when she had been orphaned. Mouette had blossomed into a swan, making an impressive marriage, while Izzie long remained a duckling, ill-at-ease with men.

Yet now the tables were turned. Isabella was a self-assured artist, married to a charming, handsome Frenchman who treated her like a princess. It was Mouette who no longer fit in. She was six-and-thirty, for pity's sake, with awkwardly adolescent sons. Those impediments, combined with the lingering stench of Harry's scandal, rendered her virtually unmarriageable. For a woman in this world, there were few options.

Even carrying on as a respectable widow seemed virtually impossible. As an American by birth who had infiltrated London society with beauty, charm, and connections, Mouette had to realize there was no place for her now that her titled husband had died in utter disgrace.

"I perceive that you are in difficulty," Isabella was

saying, patting Mouette's curls, "and I know that you have a great deal of pride. But pride must go out the window now, darling."

"I've been trying desperately to keep up appearances," Mouette admitted tearfully.

"I can see that." There was an undercurrent of gentle irony in her voice. "How are the boys? Do they realize the truth of your situation?"

Mouette straightened and wiped her eyes with a napkin. "Perhaps. A bit. Especially when I began to remove their bedchamber furniture to be sold." Despite her misery, she laughed a little, overcome with relief to be telling someone the truth.

"Clearly you were running out of things to sell. Was your mother's necklace going to be next?" Her tone was loving rather than judgmental.

Just then, Lindsay appeared in the doorway. "I grew tired of waiting and I confess I'm rather peckish. Where are those pretty little cakes you promised?"

Mouette's chin began to tremble again. "Oh, Lindsay, I have no pretty cakes. Nor is there milk for your tea. Your sister is a *fraud*!"

* * *

ISABELLA AND LINDSAY put Mouette in a chair as they made tea. Upon discovering some eggs in the larder, Isabella cooked them with a little cheese. Once Mouette had eaten, the two women led her into the sitting room and all three of them sat together on the beautiful blue-and-gold striped settee.

Mouette felt surrounded, yet it was a relief to be forced to address her problems head-on. She had no more energy for grappling with them alone.

"I don't really understand why you are struggling this way," said Lindsay. "You know that our parents will provide a home for you and the boys, forever if necessary."

Mouette frowned. "You don't understand. We spent three years living with Mama and Papa in Connecticut. At first, it felt wonderful to be safely in their care, given all that had happened—with Harry, you know." It hurt just to say his name. "But as time passed, I realized I had to make a life for myself. A future!"

"I see." Lindsay nodded slowly. "And I can imagine that it would be daunting to be in the company of our parents every day. They are so much in love, even after all these years..."

"Yes! In truth, I gave up long ago on any dream of achieving that sort of marriage for myself. If I could make my own way in the world, I would be quite content to manage without a husband. In fact, after Harry, I would prefer it."

Isabella was staring off into space. "There must be a way for you to support yourself, without selling your possessions..."

"Or Mama's jewels," Lindsay interjected.

Mouette felt her cheeks flame. Did they have to sit so close to her, watching her every reaction? "I only thought of it in passing since Mama was never fond of rubies." When Lindsay did not reply, she admitted, "But of course, you are quite right. I suppose I have become desperate."

"It is a shame you don't have a talent," said Isabella. "Like painting."

"Or teaching," added Lindsay, who had been a schoolteacher in Connecticut before coming to England four years ago.

"I have been making a list of possible professions," Mouette told them a trifle defensively.

"Our friend Natalya Beauvisage became a successful author," said Lindsay. "Even now, as Lady Hartford, she continues to write. Her novels are nearly as popular as those of Jane Austen!"

"I'm quite sure I haven't any talent for writing, and even if I did, the thought of turning my imagination toward *romance* makes me feel ill." Sinking back against the graceful settee, Mouette added with a sigh, "The only talent I have is for furnishing a home."

After a long moment of silence, Isabella sat up straight, her eyes sparkling. "Of course! That's it! Why can you not offer your services to wealthy aristocrats who need help with artistic home decoration?"

"Izzie, you may have hit on a solution," Lindsay said, tapping a finger to her cheek.

"It's very far-fetched." Even as she resisted, Mouette felt a little twinge of excitement. "How could I do such a thing? Knock on all the doors of the very people who have shunned me since my return to London? They would surely scoff at me."

"Wait." Isabella held up a silencing hand, smiling warmly. "I have a wonderful idea! Come home with me to Cornwall for a few weeks. I know you have always found it dreadfully provincial, but it is also a place of peace and beauty where you can rest and recover from this ordeal. We can go for long walks and make better plans for your new endeavor, and when you and the boys return to London, you'll be ready to plunge right in!"

Mouette's heart spun like a top as she remembered her last journey to Cornwall, on the occasion of Isabella & Gabriel's wedding a decade ago. An unexpected wave of anxiety swept over her. Although her friend's plan sounded inviting, she wasn't a bit sure she could bear to return.

Just then, through the wide bow window, Mouette saw Charles and Anthony walking across Bedford Square, accompanied by their fencing master who doubtless expected to be paid. The sight of her sons made her straighten her shoulders. More and more often, she had regrets about the sort of mother she'd been. She wanted her boys to have a proper future, to be educated as gentlemen, and to be proud of their mother.

It came to her that she couldn't go on this way. She must put her own reservations aside and do what was best for them.

"Yes." She looked first toward her concerned younger sister, and then met Isabella's eyes. "I shall come with you to Cornwall and devise a new plan going forward. I owe it to my boys to do everything in my power to make a new life."

CHAPTER 3

"**W**here are you taking me?" Justin said in a vexed tone. He and Gabriel were riding side-by-side down a narrow, winding lane closed in by tall, ancient hedgerows and a canopy of budding trees. "I feel as if we are descending into a rabbit hole."

"Ah, but that is part of the charm of Cornwall," his brother replied with a laugh.

Justin's eyebrow flew up. "Do not lead me too far into the wilderness. I have an appointment at the Old Ferry Inn in Bodinnick at three-o'clock. A fellow who lost to me at cribbage has offered his sister as a possible candidate for my *faux* bride."

Gabriel gave him a startled look. "I had forgotten how entertaining it could be to be a bystander in your life."

Just then, they rounded a bend in the road and saw the sky again. On one side of the lane, a drive curved up an open hillside to meet a plain double-pile stone manor house with a hipped slate roof. Gabriel reined in his stallion, Victor, and glanced over at Justin.

"I am almost afraid to ask this," said Justin, "but why are we stopping?"

"You should be thanking me. I've found you a house

to live in after you are married." His lips twitched. "I happen to know the owner. Reginald Pendudwell's wife died and now the gout has forced him to seek care with his son in Plymouth. Since Pendudwell Manor has stood empty all winter, I feel certain Reggie would be delighted to let the estate to my brother."

"You are enjoying this too much." Justin slid his gaze over the façade of the manor house as if it were an unattractive woman. "Besides, that old relic is hardly my style. It looks as if it belongs to a country squire who drives a gig and eats week-old mutton."

"What does it matter if it is all a charade? It's not as if you are really going to move in and make it your home." As Gabriel rode between the gateposts, Justin had no choice but to follow. "You ought to at least go inside and have a look around. That is, if you are serious about carrying off this pretend marriage."

Feeling cornered, Justin replied, "For God's sake, don't be so dramatic. It's only a little show to placate Maman." But of course he realized that Gabriel was right. Even in her weakened state, their mother was as attuned to him as a cat watching a mousehole. If she sensed he wasn't fully committed to his plan to marry, she would pounce. "All right. As long as we are here, I will go inside."

Dismounting, they tied their horses to a tree near the drive and Gabriel led the way to the front door. Everything about the house was plain and dull as far as Justin was concerned. His own grand mansion overlooking the sea in Saint-Malo, on the other hand, was boldly handsome in the simplicity of its exterior. The steep mansard roof, the arched green gate leading into the courtyard, the double flights of stone stairs that curved upward to the front door…all of it made a statement about Justin St. Briac, the reckless and wealthy smuggler, corsair, and seducer of women.

A faint smile touched his lips. Yes, that was who he was…but could he not put that to one side for a short time?

As they entered the house, Justin's distaste intensified. It appeared that the old fashioned, dust-coated furniture had been picked over, for there were gaping spaces in the drawing room and library that opened off the front entrance hall.

Gabriel shrugged as the two of them looked around. "Reggie's children have looted the place, I surmise, ever since their father decamped to Plymouth."

"Perhaps it's just as well, for I couldn't possibly live in a house with furnishings like *these*." His nostrils flared as if he'd caught a whiff of something rotten.

"Once the place is cleaned up, I'm certain you'll feel better," Gabriel said briskly. "And after all, it's not as if it's really your home, is it? I thought you meant to treat it as a sort of stage for the play you mean to perform for Maman."

"True, but a man must have standards, *mon frère*. Maman would be the first one to be suspicious if she thought I'd abandoned them." Strolling over to examine the starkly unadorned fireplace surround, Justin cringed slightly. "Look at this. What were they thinking? Was it made for a man of the cloth?"

"Pendudwell Manor was built more than a century ago, when plain bolection moulding was doubtless the height of fashion." Gabriel came closer. "There isn't time to build a house to your specifications, so I suggest you stop finding fault. That is, unless you aren't serious about this farce after all…?"

Justin stared around the room, jaw clenched. "All right. I'll take it. But I draw the line at calling the place *Pendudwell*! I'll think of something much better."

"I've no doubt of that," his brother replied dryly.

***

DURING THE JOURNEY TO CORNWALL, Mouette rode with Isabella in her friend's own landau. Painted a pretty shade of marigold-yellow, the conveyance boasted gleaming black wheels and a black folding hood on top.

But even a carriage as well-sprung as this one could not disguise all the bumps and ruts in the roads of Cornwall. They had just jounced over a particularly rough patch when Izzie apologized, "I'm sorry. I know you find it terribly rustic here."

Mouette knew a moment's shame as she remembered how quick she had been in the past to disparage the county her friend called home. "Oh, it's not so bad. I'll wager the boys are enjoying every bump!"

In the seat facing them, her sons nudged one another and laughed. "Look!" cried nine-year-old Anthony as they entered an especially narrow lane that was enclosed by high hedgerows and darkened by over-arching trees. "It's a proper tunnel! Perhaps there are fairies here."

"We do have our share of fairies in Cornwall," Isabella replied, smiling. "I think you'll find this is the perfect place to be a boy."

"Fairies aren't real," Charles said flatly. "Father said so."

In spite of herself, Mouette bristled. It was hard enough to be the widow of a miscreant, but since her older son had lately begun to worship his father's memory, she felt an urge to challenge the boy's every utterance.

Just then, the landau rounded a bend in the lane and emerged from the trees. To the south, Mouette saw a plain but imposing manor house perched on a hillside.

"Why, I believe that is Victor, my husband's horse,"

said Isabella. She pointed to the two fine horses that were tied to a tree outside the house. "We should stop. I confess that I've missed Gabriel quite desperately."

"Do you know who lives there?" asked Mouette. Her first thought was that Gabriel might be trysting there with another woman and she should protect her friend from such a horrific discovery.

"Of course I know. Pendudwell Manor belongs to an elderly gentleman who has gone to live with his sister in Plymouth," Isabella replied, distracted by her efforts to signal the driver to stop. "It is doubtless empty."

"My dear, are you certain this is wise?" Mouette asked, even as the horses turned through the gates to the manor house. If it were indeed empty, it would make an even better trysting place.

However, Isabella paid no attention to her. All Izzie's senses were focused on reuniting with Gabriel St. Briac, and Mouette prayed that her friend's heart would not be broken. The coachman, a Frenchman called Helivet, climbed down from the box to open the door and assist them.

Just as Isabella emerged first into the sunshine, her husband came through the front door of the manor house. Tall and broad-shouldered, Gabriel was even more handsome than he had been at his wedding a decade earlier. His face lit up at the sight of his wife, who was holding up her muslin skirts as she stepped onto the gravel drive.

"Can it be?" he exclaimed with a laugh. Clearly, he was mad for Isabella, and Mouette felt ashamed to have suspected anything else.

Isabella was transformed into a girl in love. When he caught her up in his arms, Mouette's own heart ached. Of course she was happy for her dearest friend, but the realization that no one would ever cherish her in such a way was painful nonetheless. Then she quickly reminded herself that another man was the last thing she needed—or wanted.

"What are you doing at Pendudwell Manor?" Isabella asked Gabriel as he set her slippered feet back on the ground.

"I brought Justin out to have a look around. He needs a place to live." Gabriel broke off, shaking his head ruefully. "A lot has happened while you were away."

"Justin is going to stay in Cornwall?" Isabella proclaimed, amazed. "I am eager to hear all about it. And as it happens, I also have news! Look who has come home with me for a holiday."

It was Mouette's cue. Taking a deep breath, she reached for the coachman's hand and came out of the landau. She had just summoned her widest, prettiest smile for Gabriel when another man emerged from the manor house.

"What's happening out here?" he demanded in a compelling French-accented voice.

The man was tall and arrestingly handsome, with glints of silver in his black hair. He also wore an eyepatch, giving him the rakish look of a pirate. Something in Mouette's very core awoke and took notice.

"Come and say hello to Isabella," Gabriel said while making a welcoming gesture to the man.

As he spoke, Gabriel came toward Mouette and lifted her hand to his mouth. "Bonjour, Lady Brandreth. How good it is to have you with us in Cornwall!"

In the next moment, all four of them were standing together and Mouette watched as Izzie embraced the man with the eye patch

"My dear," Isabella asked in concern, "what in the world has happened to your eye?"

"An unfortunate duel." He glanced away. "Merely a scratch."

Mouette tried not to stare. Part of her wanted to back away from the dark stranger, yet she was fascinated at the same time.

"Mouette," Isabella said, "do you not recall my brother-in-law, Justin St. Briac? You two met when you attended our wedding at Trevarre Hall."

"Oh!" The exclamation escaped Mouette's lips involuntarily. Of course, this man was Justin St. Briac, Gabriel's wicked brother, whom she had endeavored to block from her mind since their last meeting a decade ago. Mouette forced herself to take a slow, deep breath and murmured, "Oh yes, I do remember now."

Justin was staring down at her. As her heart began to race and hot blood crept over her cheeks, he slowly arched a black brow above his visible eye and smiled.

"Ah, Lady Brandreth, what a pleasure." To her further chagrin, he reached out, caught her hand, and raised it to his mouth. Mouette could feel the heat of his lips through her glove. "We meet again."

Scattered details of their past encounters, memories she had buried for years, returned in a wave. "So we do. *Bonjour*, m'sieur." Coolly, she attempted to extract her hand from his and after a moment he released her.

By this time, Isabella had turned to Gabriel and was happily telling him how she had managed to persuade Mouette to come home with her to Cornwall. "For a little rest," she explained. "So much has been happening and there are plans to be made about her future."

Charles and Anthony had appeared and, after introductions were made, they ran off again to explore the grounds of Pendudwell Manor.

"My sons are rather high-spirited," Mouette said to Gabriel. "I hope you won't object to their presence for a few days."

"Days?" echoed Isabella, laughing. "Don't you mean *weeks*? You must feel at home with us. We have children of our own, so we are used to their exuberance."

"But you have daughters," Mouette said, sighing. "They are quite different, I can assure you."

"We are very happy to have all three of you," Gabriel said firmly. "And you must stay as long as you like."

"It's lovely that Justin has come to Cornwall as well," Isabella said, while looking around at the old house and its grounds. "I'll wager Cerise's condition has already improved just having both her sons nearby. But I don't understand why Justin should want to live out here? Isn't Squire Pendudwell returning from Plymouth?"

"His son informed me that he plans to stay for several months." Gabriel glanced over at Justin, who suddenly wore a bad-tempered expression. "I am trying to convince Justin to live here for a few weeks, while he —well..."

"My brother means to say that I am forced to linger in Cornwall until our Maman breathes her last." To Mouette's consternation, he actually took out his timepiece and consulted it, as if counting the minutes until his mother's demise.

Isabella looked from one man to the other. "I see! As you said, so much has happened in my absence. Perhaps, since we are all here, we should go inside and have a look around?"

Mouette had no desire to spend even another minute in the company of Justin St. Briac. Shading her eyes against the sunlight, she gazed into the distance in search of a glimpse of her sons. "Perhaps I should remain outside and wait for you."

"The boys will be just fine," Isabella said, linking arms with her. "I shall instruct Helivet, our coachman, to keep Charles and Anthony in sight."

The St. Briac brothers led the way into the manor

house. Walking behind them, Mouette found it impossible not to notice how confidently Justin wore his impeccably-tailored clothing. The long muscles of his thighs were outlined against his buckskin breeches with each step he took, while a midnight-blue tailcoat accentuated the breadth of his shoulders. The silver in his hair was quite striking. And, in addition to the eyepatch he now wore, a thin white scar marked his tanned cheekbone.

At that moment, Justin turned his head and stared at her, as if he'd felt her gaze and guessed all her thoughts. Mouette quickly averted her face, but not in time to hide a traitorous blush.

"Oh my," Isabella was saying. She stopped in the middle of the drawing room, arms akimbo, and shook her head. "How can Justin possibly live *here*?"

"My sentiments *exactly*," Justin agreed, his voice low and sardonic. He stood off to one side, watching Lady Brandreth.

Mon Dieu, he'd forgotten how absolutely delectable she was, even though she must now be well past thirty years of age. Her skin was soft and creamy, her lips pink and inviting as rosebuds, her eyes sapphire-blue and fringed with thick lashes that matched the lustrous raven curls peeking from her fashionable bonnet. And her *figure*. Lazily, Justin swept his gaze over the lush curves of Mouette's breasts, hips, derrière...all alluringly outlined by the thin muslin layers of her gown. Hot blood coursed through his veins as he easily imagined stripping her bare and touching her intimately, bringing her to a state of arousal far beyond anything—

His reverie was shattered by the beauteous Lady Brandreth herself, exclaiming, "You are absolutely right, dear Izzie. This house is deplorable!"

Justin watched, utterly beguiled, as she wrinkled her nose for emphasis.

"You two are very harsh," Gabriel protested. "Pendudwell Manor merely needs attention. Here and there."

"Oh, much more than that!" Mouette, who had been nearly silent while they were outdoors, was now clearly in her element. "It requires new chandeliers, new dado rails and cornices, plaster repair, fresh paint..." Strolling over to the nearest wall, she leaned closer for a better view of the dingy color. "Really, one can't tell if it is merely dirty, or if some misguided soul actually meant to paint the walls this grimy shade."

"Exactly." Justin directed an accusing glare at his brother. "You see, I told you it was hopeless."

"Just look at this fireplace surround," Mouette said, waggling a finger in the air. "No, no! It simply won't do."

With a few unhurried steps, Justin was at her side. "I tried to tell Gabriel the same thing," he said. "He has apparently forgotten that I have very high standards."

Isabella, who continued to stand in the middle of the room, now addressed Justin. "If this house is so very deplorable, why do you want to live here? You are perfectly welcome to stay with us! Elysium is certainly large enough."

He took out his snuffbox and flicked open the lid, aware that all eyes were on him. "While you were away, our mother forced me to make a deathbed promise. It's the real reason that I must remain in Cornwall for the time being."

"A promise?" Isabella repeated in confusion. "What sort of promise?"

"Maman insists she cannot die in peace unless I am wed. In moment of weakness, or perhaps *madness*, I agreed." Arching a black brow, Justin added, "I cannot have a wife without a house, can I? And time is of the essence."

CHAPTER 4

$\mathcal{M}$ ouette stood at the window in her pretty bedchamber at Elysium, gazing out at the gardens that spread below in a colorful tapestry of flowers, trees, and winding pathways. Twilight was gathering. In the distance, she spied her sons, apparently enjoying a tour of the gardens in the company of Isabella's young daughters, serious Louise and precocious little Camille.

"I hope you will be happy while you are here."

Turning, Mouette saw Isabella standing in the doorway. "It's a very beautiful place." In truth, she felt increasingly untethered from her own life, but she would not say so to her friend. "I am grateful to you and Gabriel for welcoming us to your home."

"We are so pleased to have all three of you stay with us. And the girls are over the moon." She came to stand next to Mouette, adding, "I know that Louise and Camille are younger…"

"Louise is nearly the same age as Anthony," Mouette said with a shake of her head. "And your Camille is such a charmer, I'm certain they will enjoy her company." In truth, she wasn't a bit certain of that. Would Charles, at thirteen, tolerate a four-year-old for very long? She must add that to the list of items to discuss with him.

"What a drama we have come home to," said Isabella. As she spoke, she walked around the lovely room, clearly assessing that her servants had properly unpacked Mouette's clothing and had seen to her needs.

"I was rather surprised to discover your brother-in-law here," Mouette said tentatively.

"To be honest, so was I. I knew he was coming to see Cerise, but I expected him to be back in France by now. Justin has distanced himself quite effectively since the rest of his family settled in Cornwall." She paused. "I know that you two didn't get on very well when you met at our wedding. I hope this isn't terribly awkward for you."

Mouette pretended to look for something in one of her drawers so that Izzie couldn't see her telltale flush. "Awkward? No, not at all! In truth, I barely recall the man."

"I would have thought Justin was rather unforgettable." Isabella seemed to watch her for a long moment before adding, "Of course that was ten years ago. It is a long time."

"An eternity," Mouette agreed. She felt momentarily wistful, reflecting on all that had transpired in her own life since then. "Am I to understand that Gabriel's parents are also staying here?"

"Yes. They have a little house nearby, but Cerise fell ill before I left for London. I thought it would be best for them to be here, where Gabriel could look after them and our own physician is in the nearby village." She wore a perplexed expression. "It seems that her condition worsens by the day. I so wish there was something we could do for her."

"That's very sad. Have they considered repairing to

Bath? The waters there are said to have miraculous healing powers."

"Sad indeed," Isabella agreed. "Perhaps Justin hopes that, if he grants her wish and takes a bride, Cerise might rally and recover. However, he has always been completely opposed to the idea of marriage, so it is hard to believe that he might do something so momentous out of love for his mother." Meeting Mouette's eyes, she said more softly, "In truth, they have never gotten along. This entire situation comes as a great surprise to me!"

* * *

ALTHOUGH JUSTIN HAD FOLLOWED his brother's seemingly simple directions for reaching the riverfront village of Bodinnick, he still managed to take two wrong turns down narrow lanes darkened by hedgerows and the arching branches of ancient trees. Cornwall was a devil of a place, he decided, and it would be a great relief to end this pretense and return to the sweeping, sunny sea views of his beloved Saint-Malo.

When he finally bent to enter the low-beamed public room of the Old Ferry Inn, Justin was both tired and hungry.

"Greetings, sir!" chirped a buxom tavern wench. "Will ye have ale?"

"Brandy," he growled. "And food." He wanted to order a rustic Breton *galette*, stuffed with bits of ham, tangy cheese, leeks, and potatoes. Imagining the aroma and flavor, his spirits lifted—but then he remembered he was in England. It was the worst place imaginable for food. "What are you serving?"

"Shepherd's pie. Sausages. Pasty."

Justin winced. "All right then, bring me a pasty." It

was the Cornish specialty, he told himself. How bad could it be?

As the serving girl turned away, Justin saw a hand waving at him from the corner. It was Tom Johns, the fellow who had parted with his last coin during the previous night's games of cribbage. As his losses mounted, so had Tom's panic. Soon, he'd begun to extol the virtues of his sister, seeming to offer her for any purpose Justin might devise, no matter how shocking.

Justin made his way across the half-empty public room, casually appraising the pale, thin girl who sat beside Tom Johns. To his consternation, he saw her look up with an expression of revulsion as she focused on his eye-patch and scar. He began to deeply wish he hadn't come. What had seemed like a logical idea last night, after too much brandy and too many throws of the dice, now struck him as appalling.

Tom Johns was a farmer who liked to style himself as a "squire." His ill-fitting clothes could no longer comfortably stretch across his growing paunch, yet clearly he couldn't afford to visit a competent tailor. His weak chin was unshaven, and there were dark shadows under the young man's haunted eyes. In his right hand, he held an unlit clay pipe and sucked at it as if hoping to comfort himself.

"*Bonjour,* m'sieur," Justin said, disliking the way other patrons turned at the sound of his French accent. As he took his seat, he added, "I trust you are well?"

"No. Can't say I am." The Englishman looked as if he might be sick with nerves. Pointing to the girl who sat mutely at his side, Johns said, "This be my sister, Deb. Aren't she comely, just as I said?"

Justin's nostrils flared. He was offended by the man's treatment of his own sister, as if she were a piece of livestock he wished to sell. He extended a dark hand to her and offered, "Good afternoon, mademoiselle."

Deb made no reply. She kept her head down, stealing surreptitious glances at him, as if Satan himself had made himself known to her.

Meanwhile, the serving girl had returned. She set down a small glass of brandy before producing a plate with some boiled carrots and a cold pasty that resembled a brown shingle. Justin blinked.

"It be Mum's own recipe," the girl confided proudly, "and the local fishermens' favorite."

When she had gone, Justin broke the thing open with his fork and saw bits of fatty beef, cubed potatoes, sliced turnips, and a good deal of ground pepper. He set down his fork and suppressed a sigh.

"What ails ye?" asked Tom Johns, clearly offended on behalf of the cook.

"I'm sure it's fine. It's just that I never learned to like turnips." Justin felt trapped in a play where everyone else knew the lines except him. Taking a second look at Deb Johns, he realized that even if she had smiled at him and seemed willing, his shrewd mother would never be convinced that he could have fallen in love with this sort of female.

Never.

"Alas, the hour advances," Justin said with studied nonchalance. He pushed back from the table and rose to his full height. "You'll pardon me for rushing off, but I have just recalled another pressing engagement."

Tom Johns stared as Justin tossed some coins on the table. "But—but—what of my debt to you? I have no other means of payment *except*—" He nodded strenuously toward his cowering sister.

Disgusted, Justin raised a silencing hand. "Say no more. Our debt is cancelled. *Finis.*" Bowing he added, "I bid you both *adieu.*"

Before ducking under the lintel to take his leave, Justin glanced back to see Tom Johns devouring the awful brown shingle while Deb watched. She looked for all the world as if she'd just escaped the guillotine.

Outside on Bodinnick's steep main street, he inhaled the fresh spring air. How dare that girl, who hadn't the wits to polish his boots, behave as if *he* were the repellent one?

Down the hill, beyond the ferry landing, the River Fowey glimmered invitingly. Justin momentarily wondered what forbidden diversions might be found across the river, in the larger, ancient town of Fowey. The notion of escaping for a day or two held a powerful appeal, but in the end, Justin sighed and swung up onto his horse's back, guiding the stallion up the steep cobbled lane that would return them to Elysium.

That is, if he didn't get lost again.

* * *

Mouette and her sons shared a delicious early supper with Gabriel, Isabella, and their daughters. Only Justin was absent, apparently off on a mysterious errand.

"I heard that your brother Nathan was in London recently," Gabriel remarked as they all shared a bowl of raspberries from his greenhouse.

"Indeed?" Mouette's heart quickened. She knew that Nathan was due to return soon from the West Indies and had worried that he might search her out and discover her embarrassing circumstances. The prospect of him attempting to put her on his ship and take her back to Connecticut had filled her with dread. "I am sorry to have missed him."

Smiling, Gabriel poured her a tiny goblet of sauterne and said, "I know that life can not have been easy for you and your sons, Mouette. Isabella has worried about you, and now that you have come to be with us, I hope you will tell me how we can be of assistance."

Because the children had wandered off to engage in a game of Fox and Geese before going upstairs for the night, Mouette felt she could speak more freely.

"I confess that I have suffered a great deal since my husband's disgrace and death." Feeling tears sting her eyes, Mouette forced them back, determined not to cry again. "My parents were very comforting and helpful. I realized, though, after three full years, that I could not make a future there in Connecticut." She paused, thinking of the marriage her mother and father enjoyed, filled with passion and camaraderie. She had come to believe long ago that their marriage was nearly a miracle, a once in a lifetime occurrence, and thus she had settled for more practical qualities in her own husband: financial security, good looks, ambition, social standing.

"So you returned to London…" said Gabriel, nodding.

"My sons are British. England is the only real home we have ever known. And even though I was born in America, I've spent more than half my life either in my parents' Grosvenor Square house or the one I made with Harry."

"It's not easy for a woman alone to make her way in the world," Isabella said softly. She covered Mouette's hand and looked at her husband. "Together we will make a plan for my friend's future. She hopes to support herself by helping members of the *ton* to create beautiful homes."

Just then a deep voice interrupted from across the dining room. "*Mon Dieu*, I thought I would never get here. What is there to eat? I'm famished."

Justin St. Briac entered, a life force that charged the air with electricity. Mouette could smell the damp outdoors on his body as he drew near, pulling off his doeskin gloves and running a strong hand through his wind-tossed hair.

"It would have been good of you to arrive in time for supper," said Gabriel. "Our home is not an inn."

"Thank God for that," Justin retorted. "I've just come from one of those, where they tried to serve me an inedible piece of wood."

Madame Kerjean herself appeared, clad in her Breton lace cap and apron, and wearing an uncharacteristic smile. Since Gabriel had a wife, she seemed pleased to have another St. Briac male in the house who might need looking after. "Ah, m'sieur, you have returned. Allow me to bring you a plate. What would you like to eat this evening?"

"Madame, I beg you," interjected Gabriel. "Do not encourage my brother's bad manners. If he cannot bother to arrive in time to dine with the rest of us—"

"But you are very harsh!" The old woman silenced him with a quelling glance. "I am happy to attend to M'sieur Justin's needs, at any hour."

"Ah, madame, you are a wonderful woman," Justin said with an irresistible smile. "I can almost bear to be in godforsaken Cornwall thanks to you. Whatever you serve will be delicious and much appreciated."

As Madame Kerjean hurried away on her mission, Justin took a seat at the table with the others and said in a conversational tone, "Perhaps that good woman would prefer to work for me instead, at Frenchman's Lair."

Gabriel slowly turned and gave him a long, measured stare. "You aren't *really* going to call it that, are you?"

"Why not?" He helped himself to the last raspberries.

"If you don't know the answer, I can't help you. And no, Madame Kerjean will not leave Elysium."

"How do you know? Have you asked her?" Before his brother could answer, Justin turned to Mouette. "What do you think of the name Frenchman's Lair, my lady?"

"It is very…descriptive," she replied, avoiding his gaze.

"My point exactly."

Just then, Claire hurried toward them with a plate. On it was what appeared to be a large pancake, folded in at the corners and filled with vegetables, cheese, and ham. Even though Mouette had just eaten, the fragrance made her mouth water.

"Ah!" cried Justin, cutting a large bite. "Our Madame Kerjean is a sorceress. I was dreaming of a *galette* exactly like this one. Thank God I was late for the proper meal."

Across the table, Gabriel exchanged glances with his wife before asking, "How was your appointment in Bodinnick?"

"Horrible. Is there wine?" When his glass was filled, he drank half of it and turned to Mouette. "Before I entered the room, I confess to overhearing some of the trials you have endured, my lady."

She felt her face growing warm. "Did you overhear —or *eavesdrop*, sir?"

His visible eye, black as ebony, narrowed slightly. "Take your pick."

Mouette could feel the heat from his big, powerful body as he turned slightly in her direction. She wanted to jump up and go off in search of her sons.

"*Justin…*" Gabriel muttered in a warning tone.

"Why are my motives always in question?" Justin wondered. "I was about to beg Lady Brandreth to come to my aid at Frenchman's Lair. I am in dire need of someone to help with the refurbishment of my new home."

Isabella spoke up. "I was actually thinking the very same thing."

"You see?" Justin speared the last bite of *galette* before continuing silkily, "My lady, you can help me in my supposed quest for a bride—"

"*Supposed?*" Mouette and Isabella echoed in unison.

"*C'est vrai.* That's right." His grin flashed in the candlelight. "You didn't think I was really getting married, did you? I am merely pretending, since Maman insists this is the one thing that will give her pleasure during her final days." Justin now was looking only at Mouette. "As I was saying, I shall pay you a great deal of money for your help. Enough for you and your sons to enjoy a comfortable life for many years."

Her heart began to beat very quickly. Why did his offer feel so insulting? "I shall need time to consider your proposal, sir."

"Indeed? I fear that I cannot afford to wait. Neither, I should think, can you."

"What exactly do you mean by that?" she demanded.

"Only that you are not getting any younger. Sadly, women of your age have few options, wouldn't you agree?"

"You are a scoundrel, m'sieur!" Mouette jumped to her feet. It was only the sight of her friends, watching in apprehension, that stopped her from slapping his dark cheek. "And speaking of advancing years, what of yours? Are you not much older than I?"

Justin St. Briac gave her a wicked smile. "Perhaps I am, but you know how it is. Men improve with age, while women, well…the passage of time is not charitable to women."

"When I named you a scoundrel, I was being far too kind!"

To Mouette's further aggravation, he seemed to be

enjoying himself. "Just tell me if you will help me furnish that sad, neglected house."

She couldn't look at him. "Only because I must have employment, I will agree. However, we must discuss terms."

"Excellent. Here are my terms: you will be generously compensated for your skills, but I will expect you to be available at all times." Justin rose so that he was standing too close to her, his masculinity a potent force she could clearly feel. "We begin tomorrow."

CHAPTER 5

$\mathcal{I}$n the morning, Justin instructed Baptiste to pack a bag for him to take to Frenchman's Lair. He then walked down the corridor to his parents' rooms.

Standing outside their door, he listened to the sound of voices inside. His father was conversing with someone. Justin imagined that he heard a moment of soft, shared laughter. Could it be that his mother had revived enough to engage in lighthearted conversation? He knocked at the door and waited.

The voices softened to whispers. After a moment, his father exclaimed in French, "Who is it?"

"Papa, it is I. Justin. I must speak to you and Maman."

Now there were rustling sounds. "Just a moment!" cried Xavier.

"What the devil are you doing in there?" Justin was scowling. "Open the door."

"But, I must—find my breeches!"

"To greet your own son? Papa, just let me in, for God's sake."

Finally, the door swung open and Xavier peered out

at him. "What is it? Your maman is sleeping and cannot be disturbed."

"Sleeping? To whom then were you talking when I knocked?"

His father blinked. "No one. This door is very thick, nearly sound-proof." His eyes widened. "Perhaps you heard servants nearby."

"I know what I heard." Justin insisted. Walking past the elder St. Briac, he approached the bed where his mother lay with the blankets drawn up to her chin. "Maman?"

"Is that my son? My darling Justin?" Her eyelids fluttered. "Have you brought your betrothed to see me?"

He saw how pale she was and felt ashamed of his momentary suspicion that she might be pretending to be at death's door, just to trick him into getting married.

"Not yet, Maman. But I shall marry a fortnight hence. I have already found the house where we shall live, and now all that remains is to plan the wedding."

The sight of her weak, hopeful smile heightened his guilt. What a scoundrel he was to have so mistrusted his dying mother. Even he would probably be softer and kinder at the end of life.

"The wedding..." Cerise whispered, and looked toward Xavier. "You see, my love, we must do whatever we can so that I may live to attend Justin's wedding."

"Ah, yes!" he exclaimed and hurried over to stand next to his son. "I think I should take my beloved away to Bath. They say that the waters there are immensely restorative."

"To Bath? But I thought Maman was..." Justin bent near his father's ear and murmured, "dying."

"Indeed she is. All the more reason to repair to Bath

with all possible haste. We will pray that the waters will allow her to last until your wedding."

At something of a loss, Justin sighed and nodded. "Well, I would ask you to return before the fortnight is out. You wouldn't want to miss my wedding, would you?"

Outside in the corridor, Justin saw his brother emerge from his own rooms. They fell into step together and walked toward the stairway.

"Papa is taking our mother to Bath. For the waters," Justin said.

"Is he? He's become quite the nursemaid."

"Not only that, he told me they are *praying* that the water's restorative powers will keep Maman alive long enough to attend my wedding."

"Your faux wedding?" Gabriel parried dryly.

"Have you ever heard either of them talk of prayer? No, I thought not. Neither have I. Such moments of drama arouse my suspicions that Maman might be pretending."

His brother had the nerve to laugh. "Well, you are pretending yourself, so you have nothing to lose."

That was true! Justin breathed a little easier. "Yes, nothing to lose. Thank you for that timely reminder."

At the bottom of the stairs, Gabriel turned toward his conservatory, adding softly, "Of course, it is also possible that our parents have learned to pray now that they face the harsh reality of Maman's death..."

Justin stopped, conscious of a pain in the area where he supposed his heart must be. It came to him that he was more comfortable with his familiar suspicions than the notion of his mother being frightened enough to pray.

* * *

"MAMA," exclaimed nine-year-old Anthony, "only wait until you see the gardens. There is even a jungle!"

Following her sons through the conservatory and out into the sunshine, Mouette felt a gentle surge of elation. At first she couldn't identify the feeling, for she was far more used to being caught off-guard by waves of fearful anxiety. When she realized that all was well, she allowed herself to smile.

"Isn't it a beautiful day?" Isabella asked as they walked together toward a door in the high brick wall surrounding the kitchen gardens and greenhouses. "I would usually be painting in my atelier on a day like this, but I can't resist the urge to accompany all of you."

Louise and Camille St. Briac led the way through the door, into the mysterious gardens that spread over the hillside surrounding Elysium. Ahead of them wound pathways lined with giant ferns and palm trees, and when Mouette mentioned her surprise to see such exotic plants, Isabella told her that Cornwall was blessed with a tropical climate unique in all of England.

Mouette was pleased to see that even thirteen-year-old Charles seemed to be having a good time. In recent months, he had begun to look down his nose at Anthony and anything that he perceived to be "child's play." But today, his face was alight with pleasure.

"Mother," he informed her as she came closer, "Gabriel plans to build a hanging rope bridge over a ravine that's deeper in the jungle. He said we could help! Wait until I tell my friends in London. They'll be green with envy!"

Just then, a familiar deep voice broke in. "Lady Brandreth, I have come for you."

She felt her cheeks growing warm as she turned to face Justin St. Briac. He was walking toward them on the path, impeccably clad in a dove-gray cutaway coat, snug white breeches, polished top-boots, and a deftly-knotted cravat. Today, his eye-patch matched the slate-gray silk of his waistcoat, and the breeze ruffled his hair.

"Hello," Mouette said calmly. "Are you hurt, sir?"

He frowned. "I can't imagine what you mean."

"I'm quite certain I saw you limping slightly." She pointed to his left knee. "I thought perhaps you might have fallen and had come in search of assistance. Do you need to lean on Isabella and me?"

"That is ridiculous. You are imagining things, my lady."

As he swept her with his gaze, Mouette felt annoyed by his insolence yet secretly pleased that she was wearing such a becoming gown. Fashioned of clinging ivory muslin, it sported long, slender lavender ribbons that fluttered behind her, and she knew that her breasts were very fine for a woman her age.

"Justin," Isabella said, "are you really going to take Mouette away to that house so soon? If so, someone should be with her, you know, for propriety's sake."

This made him look stormier. "Darling Izzie, you know well enough how little patience I have for propriety. Your friend is perfectly safe with me." He turned to Mouette. "We have no time to lose. My parents depart for a fortnight in Bath, and I have promised Maman a wedding when she returns. I must search for a plausible bride while Lady Brandreth makes Frenchman's Lair fit for habitation."

Just then, Anthony Brandreth raced up to them, his dark eyes sparkling with excitement. "Hello, sir! Camille says that you are a pirate. Have you many chests of buried treasure?"

"More than you can imagine," he confirmed in faintly ironic tones. "I intend to give your mama one of them in return for helping me with my house."

"How very excellent! I hope it will be filled with pieces of eight!"

Before the Frenchman could reply, the boy ran off again, leaving a cloud of dust in his wake.

"I should join the children, just to be certain the boys don't trip over a tree root or fall into the ravine," Isabella said, looking from Mouette to Justin.

"Lady Brandreth is coming with me. We must walk through the house and make a list of repairs and the necessary furniture." The look he gave his sister-in-law said that his mind was made up.

"I had planned to watch the children while Izzie paints," Mouette said.

"That was a foolish promise to make when you know perfectly well we have an arrangement." Pausing, he reached for her arm. "I feel certain you recall the terms we discussed just last night."

Isabella had already started off in the opposite direction, waving goodbye as she went. "I don't mind a bit if you go with Justin! But I must hurry or I won't know which way the children went."

Tilting her delicate chin up at him, Mouette said, "I do recall you dictating terms to me, but I have no memory of a *discussion*."

"Time is passing," Justin said impatiently. "Any discussions you desire must happen at Frenchman's Lair."

* * *

"I APOLOGIZE FOR THIS MODEST CONVEYANCE," Justin said to Mouette as they traveled the bumpy road to Frenchman's Lair in Gabriel's two-seated gig. "I fear that we might lose a wheel at any moment."

"That scenario is a reminder of the first time I met you, sir," she replied.

Justin glanced over in surprise and saw the color in

Mouette's cheeks. She was like some delectable, beautifully-made dessert. Unfortunately, she had brought a periwinkle-blue shawl for their journey and used it to hide her breasts from his sight.

It didn't seem wise to let her know that he vividly recalled their first meeting. "I beg you to refresh my memory."

She wrinkled her delicate nose as if he'd insulted her. "I wouldn't want to bore you."

By God, now he had to hear her tell the story. "Don't tease me, my lady."

"Very well," she said primly. "I was traveling by carriage to Isabella and Gabriel's wedding, a decade ago. Charles was with me, only three years of age at that time."

"Your husband was still alive?" The things he'd been hearing recently about Sir Harry Brandreth now cast his past encounters with Mouette in a new light.

"He was alive, but far too busy to accompany me to the wedding of my dearest friend."

"Ah." Justin drew on the reins so that the horse would turn into the lane leading to his new home. Even though Mouette's tone was carefully neutral, he swore that the pain of Harry's snub was there, still lurking under the surface. "And what do you remember about our first meeting?"

"It really was too uncivilized to be called a meeting. Just a few miles from Trevarre Hall, we had an accident on one of these horrible Cornwall roads. We lost a wheel, as I recall. My coachman was unable to fix it alone, but then *you* came along." She narrowed her thick-lashed eyes just enough to let Justin know that she recalled every single moment of that encounter.

"Ah, yes. I was your knight in shining armor," he said lightly.

"Just the opposite, as I think you well know. You were arrogant. Over-bold."

Justin couldn't help laughing softly at that.

"And," Mouette finished, "no decent man would look at me as you did."

To his shock, her words brought him to sudden, full arousal. He nearly closed his eyes against the tide of hot desire that coursed through his veins. Instead, Justin looked at her and knew that she realized what was happening to him.

It was unsettling to have her bringing up their encounters at Gabriel's wedding. He'd done a good job of burying them in the same vault with every other romantic dalliance he regretted, and now he was determined to avoid the subject.

The horse came to a stop outside the house and they looked at one another.

"I perceive that you have memories enough for both of us," Justin murmured. As he gazed at her, he saw her nipples begin to harden inside her thin bodice, just before she remembered the shawl and covered herself again.

He could almost taste her on his tongue.

"Perhaps, if the encounter had been more pleasant, it would not stir up so many intense emotions within me," Mouette said. Her voice shook slightly. "Shall we go inside, sir? I am eager to be done here so I may return to my sons."

CHAPTER 6

s Mouette walked through the front door of Justin St. Briac's temporary home, she imagined she could feel his eyes on her derrière, stripping her gown away. How dare he tell her he didn't remember their first meeting—and then behave as if she should melt under his smoldering gaze?

Whirling around, she caught him in the act of lazily inspecting her backside. As if he could read her mind, Justin returned her stare, one brow arched above his piratical eye-patch.

"Have you forgotten something, my lady?" he inquired.

"I did. Yes! I forgot to discuss with you *my* terms for this business arrangement."

The corners of his lips twitched slightly. "Indeed? I am eager to hear them."

Mouette led the way to an old-fashioned rustic settle that crouched against the drawing room wall like an ugly beast. She sat as far to one side as possible, perching on the very edge of the dark wooden seat.

Justin joined her and flicked open his snuffbox. "I thought you were in a hurry." His voice had a decadent quality.

Sitting up perfectly straight, Mouette firmly criss-crossed the blue shawl over her breasts. "Apparently, I must make you aware that I am not a doxie who swoons in the company of men who style themselves as libertines and pirates." It pleased her to see him draw back slightly in surprise. "This must be a business arrangement. I am a professional and I insist that you treat me as such."

"A professional who has no other clients?"

Coolly, she replied, "I am exceptionally well-qualified in the field of interior decoration. The great Thomas Hope himself has remarked upon my abilities and it was your own sister-in-law who suggested I enter this profession. You are fortunate that I happen to be visiting Izzie, for once I return to London, I'll doubtless have far too many clients to bother with someone like you, in the hinterlands of Cornwall."

"Bravo, my lady." He tucked his snuffbox away and pretended to applaud. "I am duly chastened."

"Do not mock me, sir. I am deadly serious. Treat me with professional respect or this arrangement is ended."

Justin had straightened out his left leg and now he absently began to rub his thigh and knee. "I understand, but what did I do to earn this stern reproof? I haven't touched you." He leaned toward her slightly, adding, "And I am quite certain you secretly long for me to do so, or you wouldn't be in such a taking."

"Let us tour the house." Mouette stood and gave him a regal nod, hoping that her cheeks hadn't gone pink. "I will make lists and return tomorrow to enter the measurements and other details."

She tried to pretend he wasn't there as they walked through the rooms of the manor house. Mouette still thought of it as Pendudwell Manor, for the thought of calling the plain yet dignified house *Frenchman's Lair* was beyond imagining.

When they reached the top step, she gave a soft gasp at the sight of an impressive stairwell decorated with an elaborate mural depicting various figures from Greek mythology. Mouette guessed that it had been rather exceptional in its day, but now years of grime, candlesmoke, and neglect had darkened the paintings to the extent that the details were now difficult to discern.

"What an unexpected treasure!" she exclaimed. "I know someone who could restore this mural, but I seriously doubt he could be persuaded to travel to Cornwall."

Justin frowned. "You say *Cornwall* as if it were the back of beyond."

"As far as the London *ton* is concerned, it is," she said. "When did you say you plan to be married?"

"When?" It was a pleasure to watch him blanch. "The answer is *never*. I have told you that I am only pretending to marry, to satisfy my dying mother."

"But if that's the case, why are you so concerned about the appearance of this house? If your mother pays a visit, we could merely dress up the drawing and dining rooms and she would never know the difference." Of course, she was speaking from experience at Bedford Square, but he would never know that.

Justin shook his head, clearly appalled. "If you can say such a thing, my lady, you do not know me. I take great pride in my home and possessions. I am incapable of merely constructing a façade to fool Maman. If I am going to live here, even temporarily, I will treat this awful place as my own. When this masquerade is ended, I shall gladly return to my mansion in France." With a note of finality, he added, "If I never see Cornwall again, it will be too soon."

"I see." Mouette sighed. "And I must perform this miracle within a fortnight?"

"If you succeed, you will be rewarded well enough to live comfortably for many years."

"Will I be forced to deal with you during my labors?"

"Forced?" Justin put a hand to his heart and looked affronted. "I intend to live here now, so yes, you must endure my company. However, I have discovered that it isn't as easy as I had hoped to find someone to play the part of a make-believe wife. While you are making a masterpiece of this humble manor, I shall be otherwise occupied, interviewing prospective brides."

"My, that sounds like just the sort of pastime you would relish." Mouette was beginning to enjoy the feeling that she could say almost anything to this man without fear of censure. After years living under the constraints of society and then of widowhood, she felt a sense of liberation in her new situation.

He lifted both brows slightly. "I suppose it might *lead* to the sort of pastime I would relish."

Mouette turned away and entered one of the bedrooms. "I will inquire about a craftsperson who might restore the mural." She stopped at the sight of a heavily-carved tester bed, quite possibly a creation of Thomas Chippendale himself. The heavy, dark-red bedhangings were dusty where the outer folds were exposed to the light, but Mouette thought that they might be salvaged. Certainly it would be nearly impossible to have anything new made in less than a fortnight, especially in Cornwall.

Justin wandered over and fingered the silk brocade. "None of this is my style. I prefer something much more classical."

"It's a very fine bed," Mouette told him. "Can you live with it for now? It really does fit the tone of the house, and I think that the hangings, once cleaned, will do nicely."

"I suppose I shall have to make do, at least until after my wedding night."

Mouette knew he was baiting her and she was ready for him. "But I thought this was meant to be only a pretend marriage. Do you hope for more?"

"I suppose it depends on the bride herself. Perhaps she'll be carried away with her role." His smile was cool. "But don't worry, I won't be staying. Once the faux wedding is passed and Maman has gone on to her reward, I shall depart with all possible speed for France, never to return."

As they walked through the other rooms, Mouette took note of the furnishings she guessed might remain. She privately thought that it might be necessary to purchase only a few pieces, if Justin would agree to only decorate the rooms in which he would entertain his mother. It would have been easier to persuade him if she could relate her own story of closing off all of her house except for the grand drawing room, but she would never reveal so much sensitive information to Justin St. Briac.

On the main floor, they explored the morning room, where the deceased Mistress Pendudwell's writing desk and feminine settee remained.

"I'll have this room for my study," Justin said. "You can find me a proper desk and Baptiste will arrange to have the rest of this put in storage."

Mouette walked over to touch the rosewood writing table. "I must say, I find this quite lovely. It fits this room perfectly."

"I disagree. It couldn't be more wrong for a man's study."

"That must be one of the advantages of hiring a pretend wife," Mouette observed softly. "There's absolutely no need to consider her wishes."

He slanted a look at her but said only, "Let us survey the kitchen. I'll need a cook."

"Yes, I've thought of that," she said as Justin led the way. "I've spoken to Izzie and she thinks she can find you a few servants—temporary ones, that is—by making inquiries of her own staff."

"I'll consider that," Justin replied. "But in the meantime, Baptiste will cook for me."

Together they looked over the dark, old-fashioned kitchen and the scullery behind it. It would do, Mouette decided rather skeptically, but if it were her house, she'd make several renovations.

"I will go downstairs and inspect the butler's pantry and the wine cellar," Justin said.

Mouette made a mental inventory of the rather homely set of china and the various serving dishes that lined the shelves. Perhaps, if she didn't point them out, Justin wouldn't want to put them in storage with everything else.

"Those will have to go," he said from the doorway.

Mouette nearly sighed aloud, longing to tell him that his arrogance was wearing on her nerves. However she merely inquired, "Where exactly do you plan to store most of the contents of this house?"

"I thought we might convert part of the stables. I'll have Baptiste look into it." As he spoke, Justin held up a dusty bottle of wine, a small round of cheese, and an apple. "The wine cellar is well-stocked and there are a few items in the larder that are still edible. I've just realized that I'm so hungry even one of those horrible pasties sounds appetizing."

Mouette suddenly felt her stomach rumble. "Midday has come and gone."

"If you will bring glasses, a plate, and a knife, we

shall dine *al fresco.*" He gave her a look that promised adventure and Mouette felt her heart lighten.

Justin went on through the kitchen to the door that opened out onto the overgrown gardens, while Mouette gathered the other items on a silver tray and quickly followed. Finding him seated on a wooden bench against one of the cool stone walls, she sat down a safe distance away with the tray between them.

The air was cool and fresh, scented with rosemary and lavender that had just come into bloom. Mouette was pleased to see a kitchen garden laid out along the brick pathways. She daydreamed for a moment about what she would grow there before remembering that this entire situation was temporary at best. It would doubtless be ended before the first seedlings could emerge from the dark earth.

Justin poured dark wine into the crystal glasses and offered one to Mouette.

"*Salut,* Lady Brandreth," he said huskily, touching his glass to hers. "Here's to a mutually satisfying association."

Justin's gaze was so penetrating that Mouette found herself forgetting that one of his eyes was hidden from her view. She tried to swallow, but her lips were dry. A liberal sip of wine sent a current of warmth through her body and Mouette leaned back against the cool stone wall, letting her blue shawl slip away. "This is delicious."

"The squire seems to have better taste in wine than furnishings. It is a very fine Chinon vintage, one of my favorites. Do you perceive the essence of raspberries?"

Mouette sipped again, holding the wine in her mouth for a few moments before yielding to an urge to swallow and feel its warming effect. "Yes! I love it."

Her artless exclamation caused his cynical expression to relax. He reminded her of a big tomcat who now was pleased with the world and ready to bask in the afternoon sun. "Have some more," he invited, his French accent sounding especially seductive.

Mouette watched him pour the wine, knowing that she should refuse. But were they not outdoors in the garden, in full daylight? And she was hardly a young maiden whose virtue or reputation might be compromised!

"No doubt you have contrived a very shrewd plan to find a bride," she dared to say.

Justin began to cut small slices of cheese and apple, placing them on the plate that lay between them on the bench. He ate a piece of cheese before replying, "My plan is quite simple. I have come to realize that I must engage the services of an actress."

"An actress!" gasped Mouette.

"Have I shocked you? In a wilderness like Cornwall, it may be the only way to find someone who could convince Maman."

"Perhaps you are right. Such a woman would know that she is only playing a part."

"I will be quite busy, I think, interviewing potential brides. That's why I am putting you in charge of the renovations here at Frenchman's Lair, at least until I have settled on my counterfeit wife." He flashed a sinful grin.

Mouette's heart beat faster. Every so often, she felt a little frisson of memory and feared that it might be connected to their past encounter at Trevarre Hall, when she and Justin had both stayed there after Izzie's wedding. Even the act of drinking wine with him seemed to touch a long-buried memory.

"It is fortunate that we are so very clear on the business nature of our association," she said, sitting up straighter. "I must say, I completely understand your determination to avoid marriage."

"What do you presume to know about that?"

"Only what my own powers of observation tell me. You are quite advanced in years, and yet it seems you have never taken a wife." Now that he was on the defensive, Mouette selected an apple wedge and took a bite, waiting.

Justin's face darkened slightly. "I made a vow when I was very young that I would never marry. I will never relinquish my independence for a farcical marriage like the one my parents endure." He poured himself more wine. "Besides, I have a perfect life." He gave her a challenging stare. "Exactly as it is."

"Why do you say your parents' marriage is farcical?" Seeing his guarded expression, Mouette put a hand on his sleeve and added, "You needn't worry about revealing these things to me. We have a business relationship and when it is over, you'll never see me again."

Justin stared at her for a long moment, as if taking measure of her trustworthiness.

"It's not as if I want to marry you myself!" Mouette reminded him with a laugh.

"And why wouldn't you?" he demanded. "Because of my *advanced years*?"

Pleased to realize she had struck a nerve, Mouette continued. "I share your aversion to marriage, especially to an arrogant scoundrel. Like you, sir, I have taken a vow never to become ensnared in another marriage." She paused before adding softly, "So you see, your secrets are safe with me."

"*Eh bien*," he murmured. "After I tell you my reasons, you will reveal yours. Agreed?"

"Agreed!" Feeling a little giddy, Mouette extended her ungloved hand and watched as his strong male fingers closed around it. When he deftly caressed her palm with the pad of his thumb, a little current of electricity traveled directly to the intimate core of her, a place that Mouette had willed to go numb even before Harry's death. When she tried to pull her hand free, he tightened his hold for a moment before releasing her. A blush heated her cheeks and he responded with a knowing smile.

"You were saying?" Mouette queried in an unnaturally high voice. "About your parents' marriage?"

Justin shrugged. "My mother is expert in the art of manipulation. Napoleon himself could have taken lessons from her. She knew exactly how to get what she wanted from Papa, without any regard for Gabriel and me."

"What did she do?"

He looked into the distance. "There were frequent tantrums and full days of silence if Papa did not grant her every wish. My brother and I never knew which way the wind would be blowing in our home. But worst of all, when Papa dared to lose his temper, Maman would often run away from home."

"Run away?" Mouette echoed in disbelief. "When you were little boys?"

"*Oui*. When he discovered she was gone, Papa always panicked as if it were the first time. Feeling guilty, he would rush after her, out into the night, even it meant going to the far corners of France." As he spoke, Justin reached across the back of the wooden bench to touch one of the black curls trailing free from Mouette's Grecian knot. Absently rubbing it between his two fingertips, he continued, "There was always a servant to step in and look after us, but I confess that I was never quite certain if our parents would bother to return."

Tears stung Mouette's eyes as she imagined him as a little boy, falling asleep without parents in the house, worrying about the future. "That's terrible! I can't imagine how a mother could do such a thing to her children."

"Maman simply put us out of her mind." He shrugged again, but his face was shadowed. "Because I was six years Gabriel's senior, I felt responsible for both of us. I always kept a plan for how we would survive, if necessary, without parents. By the time I reached adolescence, I began to wish they would just stay away and leave us in peace."

He reminded her of a wild animal made vulnerable by pain, and Mouette knew an impulse to take him in her arms and gently soothe him. As if sensing her pity, Justin tensed his powerful body.

"So you see, who could blame me for choosing a life of freedom?" A muscle flexed in his jaw. "I make my own way in the world and owe nothing to anyone."

"No wonder you became a corsair," she whispered.

"Exactly so. Even after I grew to manhood, my mother tried to keep me tangled in her games by running away to *my* house. I finally devised a method to keep at her arm's length by saying as little as possible and treating her with polite indifference."

"You must have been relieved when Gabriel and Izzie settled in Cornwall, and your parents decided to move here, too."

Justin relaxed enough to smile slightly, as though impressed by her perceptiveness. "I've had a decade of blessed peace. Gabriel and Izzie came once to visit me in Saint-Malo, and the rest of the time I've been free of Maman and her wiles."

"And yet...she still has the power to stir up very strong emotions in you," Mouette dared to murmur.

His gaze hardened again. "My lady, if you imagine that you understand my inner workings, you are utterly mistaken."

Mouette watched as he drank the rest of the wine in

his glass, set it aside, and closed the space between them on the bench. What had happened to her shawl? She saw that her nipples had tightened visibly against her thin muslin bodice, and her heart began to flutter like a trapped bird. "I apologize, sir, if I have been rude. It's just that, well, you are a rather intriguing person."

"Am I?" Justin bent near, his breath warm and intoxicating on her cheek. He smelled of expensive soap, Chinon wine, and the spring sunshine. "Have I told you how beautiful you are, Mouette?"

She felt disoriented, falling back through time to another moment when it seemed he had spoken virtually the same words to her. Pushing the uncomfortable memory away, she made herself return his gaze. "I don't think it is wise for you to say such things…"

"We are both adults of a certain age," he said in a mesmerizing tone, just inches from her ear. "Why should we pretend otherwise?"

She felt giddy and queasy at the same time. And when she tried to speak, her heart seemed to lodge in her throat. "Sir, it would not be—"

"Justin," he interrupted, pronouncing his own name in the delicious French way. "We have embarked on a grand adventure together, have we not? You must call me Justin."

His strong arm stole around her back and she was swept by a mad longing to melt against him. "You must understand…although I have been a married woman, I do *not* yearn for other men. As I have told you, I have taken a vow never to marry again."

"Did I ask you to marry me?" Now his warm mouth grazed the delicate shell of her ear, sending warm, disturbing sensations skittering over her nerves.

"I am not speaking only of marriage," Mouette protested. "You see, I have never wanted to…even be *touched* by another man."

"Because you have enshrined the memory of your dead husband?" Justin's tone was sarcastic.

Just as she was about to tell him the truth about her awful marriage, Mouette realized that it would not be wise to share so intimate a secret with a rake like Justin St. Briac. Instead she replied, "I cannot speak about this."

"Ah." He drew back and studied her, his gaze predatory. "But you are a healthy and beautiful woman. Even though you may continue to feel loyal to your husband's memory, would it not be wrong to deprive yourself of the joys of—" his breath touched her ear again, and this time Mouette felt a little convulsive pulse at her intimate core, just as he murmured, "physical pleasure?"

How desperately she wanted to offer her parted lips to him, to feel the heat of his kiss! She was certain he must be a masterful kisser, whatever that might mean. When Mouette had married Harry, she'd expected to enjoy the physical side of marriage, for her parents clearly did. But Harry was as undeveloped a lover as he was a person. He disliked kissing or fondling, preferring to go straight to the "main event", as he called it. Eventually, Mouette had packed away her sensual longings, finding solace in pastimes such as decorating their home and treating herself to delicious desserts.

"A simple kiss," Justin promised in a low voice. "What harm can there be in that? I am the soul of discretion."

Her panicked urge to escape was as powerful as her longing to surrender. Drawing back, her cheeks hot, Mouette managed to scramble to her feet. "I should finish touring the house. My sons are waiting for me, after all."

She started to reach for the tray, but Justin waved her off.

"Allow me to make myself useful, my lady," he said, reclining against the bench and reaching for his agate snuffbox, as if nothing she said or did could possibly perturb him. "You clearly have more important work to do."

"That's true. I do!" Unaccountably, Mouette felt both agitated and annoyed. "And you, sir, should not take snuff. It's very bad for your health. Although you clearly believe otherwise, you are not immortal. Far from it!"

With that, she turned on the tiny heel of her slipper and walked briskly back into the house. Her head was high, but her cheeks burned with humiliation that she could have said such things.

What in the *world* had come over her?

CHAPTER 7

*J*ustin lay in his mammoth Chippendale four-poster bed, thinking about Mouette Raveneau Brandreth's inviting mouth.

The same mouth he had been just moments away from tasting yesterday, before she ran away.

He would have given her a kiss potent enough to erase the memories of Harry Brandreth—or any other man—that might plague Mouette. Deftly, Justin would have explored the surface of her mouth with his own, waiting for the inevitable signs that she was falling under his spell. Then, he would have gradually worked his tongue between her lips, slowly at first, exploring until he felt her moan in surrender, her hips arching against him…

Justin gave himself a mental shake. For God's sake, the last thing he wanted or needed was to be entangled in an *affaire du coeur*! There was no time for such a dalliance, even if Mouette welcomed it. And if she developed feelings for him—as his lovers invariably did—matters would be complicated beyond belief.

Throwing back the sheet, Justin rose naked from his bed and paused at the window, looking out at the very plainly-landscaped grounds. He had a busy schedule planned for today and could not afford to waste another moment brooding about Mouette.

The familiar fragrances of strong *café au lait*, buttery fresh-baked *brioche*, potatoes, and ham drifted up the stairs to tempt him. Baptiste was in the kitchen, Justin surmised, not only preparing breakfast but also reorganizing his new household empire.

The clock on the bedroom mantel chimed softly, eight times. How the devil could he have slept so late? Within an hour, he was due to greet and interview the first bride candidate with real promise. Thank God for Baptiste. Once the loyal servant had learned that there was a theatre troupe performing in Bodmin, it had been easy enough for him to inquire if any of the actresses might desire a role that would provide sufficient remuneration that the chosen lady need not work again for a full year.

Baptiste had instructed all would-be candidates to make appointments for interviews with St. Briac himself. The first of the aspiring brides would arrive that very morning.

Donning butter-soft buckskin breeches and polished top-boots, Justin stood at his shaving stand and poured water from a cracked pitcher into the matching chipped bowl. He scowled. Was this Pendudwell fellow completely lacking in pride? If the man was incapable of properly furnishing his home, couldn't he at least have replaced damaged crockery? It was one more thing to mention to Mouette.

Mouette.

As he shaved, Justin was annoyed to find himself thinking of *her* rather than the young actresses who were lining up to pretend to be his wife. He could doubtless have his way with any of those bits of muslin—even a few at once, for God's sake—yet his mind kept circling back to one middle-aged widow, saddled with children, who rebuffed him at every turn.

He studied himself in the mirror and decided that, even with an eye-patch, he remained a compelling figure of masculinity. Of course, it seemed to be a fact of life that men improved with age, while women slowly wilted on the vine. It was the reason why powerful, handsome men were permitted to discard their lovers, even wives, as the women grew older.

As Justin shrugged into a fine linen shirt and skillfully tied his own cravat, he made a mental note to tell Mouette that he must have a proper manservant. After all, Baptiste couldn't be expected to do everything.

Justin straightened his flawlessly-tailored frockcoat of midnight blue kerseymere as he descended the stairway. In the dining room, he found Baptiste serving breakfast at that very moment.

"How well you know me," Justin said, smiling.

"*Oui*, m'sieur. For many years, I have prepared your *café au lait* ahead of breakfast, knowing that the aroma will rouse you. Experience has taught me exactly how many minutes will pass before you appear for your breakfast." Baptiste pulled out his master's chair and shook out a napkin for him. When St. Briac had begun to eat, the servant said, "You will be happy to know I have made great strides towards organizing the kitchen. But I need a staff, m'sieur. I was hoping you might send for our favorite servants from the house in Saint-Malo."

Justin glanced up with a frown. "That's out of the question. You know very well that this is a *temporary* situation. By the time my Saint-Malo staff would arrive, we might be packing to return home." He sampled a bite of ham and grimaced. "God knows I hope that is the case. There is nothing like French ham."

From the doorway to the stairhall, a female voice

said, "You would be better served to give up ham all together. It is not kind to one's waistline."

Justin knit his brows as he regarded her. "Lady Brandreth, *you* would be better served to keep your advice to yourself. I believe I have done very well up to now, have I not, Baptiste?"

"Indeed. It is widely acknowledged that all other men wish to be *you*, m'sieur."

Crossing to sit down at the table a few chairs away, Mouette gave a soft disparaging snort. "Clearly Baptiste is well remunerated for his loyalty."

"What the devil are you insinuating?" Even as he spoke, Justin saw his servant backing away.

"Allow me to bring her ladyship a cup of *café au lait*," Baptiste mumbled, and then he was gone.

"Coward," Justin muttered under his breath before turning his attention to Mouette. "Are you in the habit of entering a private home unannounced? And how did you get here?"

She was untying the rose silk ribbons of a becoming poke bonnet. "Gabriel has allowed me to use his gig. I knocked, twice, but had to let myself in. Clearly, we must hire more servants. Even someone of Baptiste's talents cannot be your butler, chef, manservant, and footman."

"Indeed." Justin purposely took a larger bite of ham. "He has also been helping with my bride search. The first candidate is due to arrive very soon for our *private* interview."

Her eyes flashed, but she did not take the bait. "Where exactly do you plan to conduct these conversations? I had hoped to use the desk in the morning room—"

"You must be referring to my study."

Mouette narrowed her lovely, thick-lashed eyes. "Where may I work on my lists?" She indicated a slim leather case that appeared to contain papers and a book or two.

"*Eh bien.* I suppose you may use my study. This time. My guest and I will doubtless be more comfortable in the drawing room. Pendudwell left me at least one fine sofa, as I recall. It should do well enough for the purpose I have in mind."

This time she actually bit her lip and took a deep breath before replying, "Good. You see, last night I made a thrilling discovery in Gabriel and Izzie's library —a copy of Thomas Hope's 1807 masterwork, *Household Furniture and Interior Decoration!*"

"Indeed?" Justin put down his fork in surprise. "I relied upon that book while refurbishing my home in Saint-Malo! Hope's classical designs and Flaxman's excellent drawings were tremendously helpful."

"I am delighted that you are familiar with Hope's book!" In her excitement, Mouette seemed to forget herself. "Of course I have a copy of my own in my London house, but neglected to bring it with me. John Flaxman's line drawings are superb. And I will tell you in all modesty that I am personally acquainted with Thomas Hope!"

"I believe you have mentioned that," Justin said. Her cheeks were pink with emotion and he felt a sudden throb of arousal. Mouette was older than any woman he had ever made love to, yet at that moment, she appeared as enticing as a ripe and juicy piece of fruit. "May I peruse your book?"

She was already reaching for it, flipping it open to a page she had marked with piece of foolscap. "Look at this settee. Wouldn't this be an excellent piece for the drawing room? Perhaps as part of a set, with these curved armchairs."

Justin saw that she was pointing to a striking mahogany settee carved in the Egyptian style, the two ends decorated with reclining lions. Her taste was in perfect concert with his. "I would choose cushions in cobalt-blue," he mused, nodding.

"Perhaps." Mouette tilted her head, absently displaying the inviting curve of her neck to him. "Or emerald-green."

"No. Blue."

"With gold-embroidered laurel wreaths?"

"Hmm. You may contrive to persuade me of that," he allowed, unable to keep the wicked gleam from his smile, "though a thornier problem will be finding such sophisticated furnishings or fabrics in the wilds of Cornwall."

Before she could reply, Baptiste entered with a large cup of *café au lait* and placed it before Mouette.

"I believe your—um—guest has arrived, m'sieur," he said to St. Briac. "I just heard a carriage on the drive."

"*Bien.*" Justin stood and straightened his cravat. "It is a lovely day to choose a bride, is it not?"

Glancing back while striding from the room, he was gratified to see that Mouette's cheeks were even pinker than before.

* * *

MOUETTE SAT at the worn desk in the morning room, her Thomas Hope book open by her left elbow, her lists and measurements to her right. The sound of Justin St. Briac's deep, French-accented voice carried from the nearby drawing room, but she tried not to listen, telling herself that whatever the scoundrel was saying to his first *candidate* was none of her affair.

Instead, Mouette finished the *café au lait*, a concoction that tasted of France itself, and dipped the nub of her pen into the inkwell. Under the heading of

"Drawing Room", she wrote: *Pair of armchairs, adorned with griffins.*

Of course, St. Briac was right. Where in the wilds of Cornwall could they possibly find such exquisite pieces? Her gaze lingered on a finely-wrought line-drawing of a grand settee. The arms, embellished by inlaid scrollwork, curved gracefully outward. A carved frieze of twelve Greek and Roman gods marched above the upholstered back of the settee and the sight of it sent a familiar thrill coursing through her. Not so long ago, she would have made herself sick with longing to possess that magnificent piece, moving heaven and hearth to acquire it and place it in her own magnificent sitting room.

As Mouette closed her eyes, the years melted away and once again she was a new bride, furnishing her husband's elegant home in Bedford Square.

She had spent as freely as Harry had gambled, and together they'd dug a very deep hole, filled with excess, secrets, and shame. All of it had ended so badly—and for what? A title, possessions, and the acceptance of the *ton*—the same people who had snubbed her after Harry's scandalous downfall and death.

Feeling queasy, Mouette closed the book of Thomas Hope's decorating ideas. For heaven's sake, she told herself, this house could be furnished perfectly well without aspiring to the very pinnacle of design. Tomorrow, she would go to Truro and visit the shops. St. Briac might have to settle for something less grand, but after all this *was* only a pretend marriage. It would all be ended by summer, no doubt, and the furniture would be sold to the highest bidder.

"Exactly *WOT* are you suggestin', sir?" cried a female voice from the direction of the drawing room.

Mouette heard Justin's low voice making a reply, but was unable to make out what he was saying. Unable to help herself, she rose and went to the door, turning so that her ear was near the slight opening.

"I can assure you, you will be paid very well for your services, mademoiselle," St. Briac was saying. "May I assume that you are able to converse in a more refined—uh—accent?" He cleared his throat. "That is, you will be playing the part of a young lady of quality—"

"I kin be as quality as any," came the girl's reply. She had adopted a coaxing tone that immediately aroused Mouette's suspicions. "An' sir, you 'ave my leave to call me Sally."

Opening the door a few more inches, she was afforded a clear view across the stairhall and into the drawing room. Justin and the golden-haired young actress sat close together on the single upholstered settee. Sally was leaning toward him, her face turned up to his. Mouette couldn't help noticing the actress's deep décolletage and the way her barely-concealed bosom seemed to be brushing Justin's arm.

"I don't doubt your quality," Justin said smoothly.

From her distant vantage point, Mouette thought she saw him sweep his gaze over the girl's breasts. What an unscrupulous rogue he was!

"I nearly won the part of Fanny in *The Clandestine Marriage*," Sally boasted. "That be a quality play, y'-know. They said I were too pretty for Fanny, though."

Mouette had had enough. Unable to contain herself, she pushed the doors open and walked through to the drawing room. "Oh, hello! I completely forgot that you were conducting an interview this morning, m'sieur."

Justin leveled a dangerous look at her. "You *forgot?*"

She came closer, extending her hand to the flustered Sally. "It's lovely to meet you. I am Lady Mouette Brandreth."

The girl struggled to her feet, wearing a blush that

spread hot color from her brow to her breasts. "Oh! 'Ello!"

Justin rose to his feet, still glaring at Mouette, who merely smiled sweetly back at him. "Uh—Sally—" he began.

"Fitzroy," supplied the girl. "Sally Fitzroy."

"Yes, of course. Sally, allow me to present Lady Brandreth, my—uh—purveyor of home decoration."

"Yer *wot?*" the girl exclaimed in confusion.

Still beaming angelically, Mouette reached for Justin's arm. "You see, Miss Fitzroy, for all intents and purposes, I am in charge of Frenchman's Lair." Out of the corner of her eye, she saw Justin's brows fly up at her bold assertion, but her only response to him was a patronizing tap on his coat sleeve. "It's a pleasure to meet you. I hope you will forgive me if I beg a few moments of time with M'sieur St. Briac. A matter of business, you understand."

Sally's painted mouth formed a perfect O before she nodded.

"I will return shortly," Justin told the girl. Pausing at the cellaret, he poured a glass of sherry and handed it to her. "Meanwhile, you may drink this."

Mouette tugged at his arm until they were in the entrance hall, and then in the morning room. After closing the doors, she led him to the far corner.

"What the *devil* are you on about?" he demanded, towering over her.

It was extremely annoying that he seemed to be able to make himself twice her size when attempting to intimidate her. And even more annoying was her helpless feeling of intoxication when he stood so close, his male energy charging the air between their bodies.

Mouette took a deep breath. "See here, if I am going to be part of this charade, you must let me have a say in your choice of bride. After all, my professional reputation is at stake!"

"What are you talking about? No one remotely connected with your *so-called* 'professional reputation' even knows you are in Cornwall."

She nearly hit his chest with her fist. "All right then, I must have a say because I shall be forced to spend a portion of my days with your faux bride."

A maddening smile touched his mouth. "I take it you don't care for Sally?"

"No doubt she is a perfectly nice person, but she isn't right for this role and there isn't enough time in the world to effect such a transformation. It is a waste of time for all of us to keep her here any longer." Mouette paused, unable to resist adding, "And do not imagine that your efforts to ply her with wine, in the *morning*, have gone unnoticed!"

To her shock, Justin reached out and slid both hands around her waist, drawing her against him. His mouth hovered above hers, just out of reach, and Mouette nearly came up on tip-toe to reach him.

"My lady," he taunted softly, "are you certain you don't want me for yourself?"

Her heart raced. The feelings he stirred within her were foreign and frightening, yet almost irresistible. "Your conceit knows no bounds," she finally managed to say, sounding properly outraged. "Loose me, sir, so that you may send Miss Fitzroy on her way. In case you have forgotten, we have *real* business to attend to!"

*W*hen Mouette dressed in the morning, she chose one of her prettiest ensembles. The canary-yellow round gown with an ivory spencer and plumed French bonnet had been a birthday gift from her parents, two years ago. Whenever she wore it she thought of her father's approving smile.

It was a rare day that did not include a moment of longing to return to her parents' home, where she would feel secure and protected from the storm-tossed seas of life. During one of those low moments during the previous winter, when she had sold a cherished piece of statuary in order to pay her London butler, it had finally come to Mouette that if she gave up and went home to her family, she would be going backward. It was a coward's choice, and no Raveneau had ever been a coward!

Surveying her reflection in the looking glass, Mouette gave a little nod to loosen some of her glossy black curls. There was color in her cheeks and her eyes sparkled. Papa would still approve if he could see her now.

When she descended the stairs at Elysium, carrying her bonnet by its ribbons, Mouette expected to find her sons waiting for her. They usually shared breakfast, but today neither boy was anywhere to be seen.

Claire had just poured chocolate for her when Isabella peeked in.

"You should come outside," Izzie said, smiling broadly. "I have a little surprise for you."

"I'll bring your breakfast to the garden if you like, my lady," said Claire.

"That would be lovely." Mouette paused, adding, "Do you suppose I might have *café au lait?*"

Izzie was watching her as they walked together through to the side door leading out to Gabriel's conservatory and walled gardens.

"I remember very well the first time Gabriel made *café au lait* for me, in my brother Sebastian's kitchen at Trevarre Hall," Isabella said. "I'd tried it before, even during my journey to France with you and your family, but it had never smelled or tasted so delicious as that morning when Gabriel poured the hot milk and strong coffee together, mixing them with sugar." Isabella smiled dreamily at the memory.

"How very romantic," Mouette said without enthusiasm.

"My dear, I beg you not to become cynical. It is my ardent hope that you will one day love again."

"Love again? I am not a bit sure I have *ever* experienced true romantic love, except by observing my parents." She gave Isabella a meaningful sidelong glance. "As you know, they set a very imposing example when it comes to matters of the heart."

"I take your meaning, but I am certain that even André and Devon have had their challenges. And you look especially beautiful this morning. I think Cornwall agrees with you! Your project at Pendudwell Manor, in Justin's company, must not be as trying as you had feared."

Mouette wanted to confide all her feelings to Izzie, including her confusing responses to Justin's touch, but something held her back. Just then, the sound of her older son's voice provided a welcome distraction.

"Mother! There you are at last."

As young Charles rushed toward them, between the neat vegetable plots of the kitchen garden, Mouette was surprised again to see how tall he was growing. It seemed that he grew an inch every day. Soon he would be taller than she was.

"Dear son, that is hardly a proper greeting," she chided. Even though she felt guilty and ashamed that she was not a more consistent mother, she wanted her boys to grow into real gentlemen.

He stopped and wrinkled his nose before reciting in a monotone, "Good morning, Mother. I hope you slept well."

"Good morning, darling." Mouette beamed at him. "I did sleep well. Was there something you wanted to show me?"

"Yes!" He tugged at her hand. "Do hurry. That pirate, St. Briac, has promised to teach little Anthony how to duel to the death!"

* * *

AFTER BENDING to pass through the low door in the brick wall, Mouette and Isabella followed Charles along a curving path that led to the Italian Garden. In the distance, Mouette saw a lovely, shaded courtyard with a pool at its center. The focal point was a fountain crowned by a statue of a boy holding a goose, water spouting skyward from its beak. On the flagstones, her son Anthony stood facing a particularly dashing-looking Justin St. Briac, who had shed his coat.

"Now then, let us practice moving from the first to the second position," Justin told him.

Looking fierce, Anthony extended his wooden toy sword with his right hand. At Justin's command, he brought his left arm up in the air, his feet properly placed, knees bent outward. Justin, meanwhile, held a tree branch in his own dark hand.

"Remember," he advised Anthony, "you must make your chest as wide as possible, in order to dominate your opponent. *En garde!*" He struck a pose, looking graceful yet powerful in spite of the rather comical tree branch. "And now, the second position."

The toy sword, held outstretched in the little boy's right hand, had already begun to quiver. "*En garde!*" he echoed excitedly, moving through the two positions. "M'sieur, have you truly dueled with swords to the death?"

"Of course," Justin replied without hesitation, "but only with the very worst sort of pirates, in the heat of savage battle. In your refined world, my boy, swordplay should be only for sport. You know? Exercise."

Anthony's face fell. "But I don't want to live in a refined world. I intend to be a pirate. Like you!"

"Indeed? *D'accord*, if you mean to be a true corsair, you must learn all the tricks." One of his black brows arched up meaningfully. "If you take my meaning..."

"Tricks?" panted Anthony as he brought his sword close to his body, then thrust it forward, over and over again.

"These are secret techniques your London fencing master would not teach you, things no true gentleman would do to win..."

Mouette was aghast. What was that devil talking about? She watched her little boy shifting back and forth, leaning more heavily on his left foot, which had been slightly deformed since birth. Ever since he had been old enough to walk, she had worried about Anthony falling and injuring himself during just this sort of overexertion.

Walking toward them, Mouette held up a hand. "I am sorry to interrupt this very unconventional lesson, but I believe M'sieur St. Briac and I have an appointment in Truro."

For a moment, she feared Anthony might burst into tears. "Mama! You are cruel! M'sieur was just about to teach me one of his *secret techniques!*" His eyes flashed. "I must learn them, in expert detail, if I am going to be a pirate."

"The proper term is corsair," Justin corrected.

She narrowed her eyes at Justin, who had reached over to pluck his coat from one of the stone benches. Clad only in top-boots, snug buckskin breeches, a loose white shirt, and a fitted waistcoat, he was shockingly attractive. Mouette turned to her son. "Anthony, you may *pretend* to be a pirate, but I do not appreciate anyone implying that you might grow up to become one in reality."

Justin seemed to ignore her. Shrugging into his coat, he retrieved his tree branch and aimed it at Anthony. "If you are going to fence properly, you must spend a great deal of time doing exercises for strength. Like this." Bending one knee, he lunged lightly forward until the tip of his branch nearly touched Anthony. "You see? Back and forth." His powerful thigh contracted as he lunged forward again. "Now you do it. Show me, *mon jeune pirate.*"

Mouette wanted to intervene, to remind her son that his left foot would never be quite as stable as his right, but he seemed so happy as he mimicked Justin's movements that she hadn't the heart to stop him.

Justin ruffled Anthony's dark curls. "Well done.

Practice this, morning, noon, and night. Ten times. Can you do that?"

The boy beamed up at him. "Yes, sir! Will you teach me one of the secret tricks next time?"

"Perhaps." Justin glanced toward the disapproving Mouette. "If your beautiful mama allows it."

Louise and Camille were running down the pathway toward them, calling the boys' names, and Isabella went to meet them. "I may take all four children to visit Trevarre Hall later today." She looked back at Mouette. "My brother has been asking after you, my dear."

"You must relay my warm regards to Sebastian and dear Julia," Mouette replied. "I know my parents send love to them as well."

Isabella smiled. "Of course. You may recall that their son, my nephew Lucas, is nearly the same age as Charles. Also, my niece Cassandra, who will soon be eighteen, has been begging me to begin work on her portrait." She looked at the children. "Would you like to feed the baby lambs and goats?"

"I would rather not." Charles sniffed, looking bored. He turned toward Mouette. "Mother, I believe I should accompany you and M'sieur St. Briac to Truro. Is it not improper for you to travel alone with such a person?"

"Have I been insulted?" wondered Justin, looking on with a wry smile.

"You are very sweet to worry about my honor, Charles," Mouette told him, "but I need you to stay near your brother and make certain he stays out of trouble. Can I rely on you?"

"Yes, all right," the boy grumbled. "But I'm not looking forward to spending the entire day on some sort of *farm.*"

Isabella polished her spectacles with the edge of her shawl. "It's really more an estate than a farm, Charles.

And you know, there is a real smuggler's hole nearby. Perhaps Sebastian will take you all to see it!"

Amidst shouts of excitement, the quartet of children rushed off toward the house, followed by Isabella, who turned to wave at Mouette and Justin. "I wish you a successful shopping adventure in Truro!" she called.

Mouette suddenly felt shy as Justin took her arm and they began to walk together. Leaning closer, his warm breath teased her ear as he murmured, "Alone at last, my lady."

Gabriel had been good enough to loan Justin his fine open landau for the journey to Truro. In addition, they were blessed with weather that was particularly fine for Cornwall: more sun than clouds for a change.

Mouette leaned back against the soft leather upholstery and allowed herself to enjoy the outing. Her companion might be a sinfully handsome libertine, but did that mean she could not enjoy the stirring pleasure of his company? After all, her advanced age of six-and-thirty should at least grant her the benefit of greater freedom!

"How kind your brother was to loan us his beautiful carriage," she said with a sigh. "It allows us to ride in comfort, even on the wild roads of Cornwall."

Justin had just leaned forward to speak to Helivet, the coachman, but he straightened at her words. "Do you imagine that I cannot purchase an even finer equipage if I so choose? I can assure you that I do not depend on my brother's charity."

She widened her eyes, secretly pleased to have touched a nerve. "Of course not."

"Do not patronize me," Justin warned. "I can assure

you that I own carriages in France far grander than this one."

"Of course you do." Attempting to look proper, Mouette turned to gaze out at the gently undulating hillsides, comprised of various shades of green that made a striking patchwork pattern. It surprised her to realize that she was beginning to find Cornwall quite lovely, in part because of the very wildness she had previously disparaged.

Justin sat back against the seat and watched her from the corners of his eyes. Indeed, Mouette could have sworn that even the eye covered by a patch was tracking her carefully.

"I haven't forgotten our conversation," he said.

Her heart jumped. "Which one?"

"The one in which you promised to tell me your secrets. I believe that I revealed a great deal to you, my lady, but somehow you eluded keeping your part of our bargain."

"You make it sound so serious!" Mouette gave a little laugh. "Because I share your aversion to marriage, must it follow that I have secrets?"

"Perhaps not. Your own parents certainly can't be to blame," he agreed, watching her closely. "Their marriage appears to be the stuff of fantasy."

Mouette sensed that, in spite of his light tone, he was baiting her again…yet it was so tempting to confide in someone who might understand.

"A fantasy for the two of them, perhaps, but less so for their children." As the landau slowed to mount a gentle hill, she leaned back and closed her eyes, drifting back in time. "As you know, I was the first born. My parents loved to tell the story of my birth, during which Papa was away on a sea voyage. Although they enjoyed a tempestuous romance from the moment of their first meeting, they were unmarried and estranged when I was born. Mother had allowed her childhood suitor to come to her rescue, but Papa chased us down at sea and jumped onto the deck of his rival's ship, brandishing his rapier." She tried to smile, but felt the corners of her lips turning down. "How could a mere infant compete with such consuming ardor? No doubt I was quite forgotten."

"Ah, but surely, they adored you," Justin asserted. "Did you really feel it was otherwise?"

Mouette opened her eyes and caught him gazing at her with tender compassion. "Of course my parents love their children, but none of us have ever been able to hold a candle to the passion that burns between them."

"Shouldn't that be all the more reason for you to seek out a romantic marriage of your own?"

She shrugged, her heart aching. "I have never aspired to romance. I am not certain I believed it was possible."

"Ah." Justin glanced away and took out his snuffbox. "I see."

Mouette tried to explain. "I wanted something more substantial, less ephemeral."

"Are you speaking of wealth? An abundance of coin?" His tone was sardonic.

"I am endeavoring to be honest with you, m'sieur."

"My apologies. Am I to understand that your husband, Sir Harry, succeeded in providing you with something more...substantial?"

Her cheeks flamed. Why did it seem that he was mocking Harry's rather tiny manhood? "I do not claim that I was right to discount the importance of love, for wealth and position did not bring me happiness either," she said crisply. "In truth, I am suspicious of men and their intentions. That is why I wish to make my own way in the world, so that I never need to rely on a man to provide for me or make me happy."

Justin seemed to be listening intently, watching her. "Fair enough." Nodding, he added, "We are in complete accord. Everything you have said makes perfect sense to me."

As the landau crowned the hilltop, Mouette saw a grand estate spread across the valley below them. A drive wound through groves of trees to an austere manor house of gray stone, while the River Fowey sparkled in the distance.

"Oh my," Mouette exclaimed. "For a moment, I was transported. I wonder who could live on such a magnificent estate...here in Cornwall?"

Temporarily distracted from his probe of her childhood, Justin studied the estate as they descended the hill. "I believe it may be Leyton Court, the seat of Viscount William Edgecumbe," he murmured.

"How do you know that? I thought you were as unfamiliar with Cornwall as I am."

After glancing over in surprise, he finally flicked open his snuffbox and took a pinch between his strong fingertips. She swore he did it to give himself time to think of a response. "Unfamiliar I may be," Justin said at last, "but that does not mean I am ignorant. I am more astute than you may imagine."

He was plotting something. Mouette could feel it. As the landau continued down the road, they came to a crossing marked by a signpost. "Ah," she said, pointing to the sign. "Here is our turning for Truro."

"We aren't actually going there today," he informed her.

"What do you mean? Today was meant to be an outing to choose furnishings for Pendudwell Manor!"

"Have I not asked you to refrain from calling Frenchman's Lair by that horrible name?" he admonished. "As for our outing, I changed my mind. I met Lord Edgecumbe last evening, at cards, and was told in confidence that he must sell a quantity of family heirlooms in order to pay some debts. He has agreed to meet with us."

"He wants to sell his family treasures to *you*?"

Justin gave her a lazy smile. "You ask too many questions. Try to remember that you are in my employ."

"I most certainly am *not*," she exclaimed. "You insult me, m'sieur."

"I beg to differ. I am paying you to perform a service for me."

Mouette was grateful to be distracted by the sight of Leyton Court's dark granite towers emerging among the trees. The manor house, surrounded by ancient oak and yew trees, had a rather forbidding Gothic appearance. On a nearby raised terrace, Mouette saw an overgrown garden where a couple sat together at a small table. There should have been a small army of gardeners, trimming the shrubs and tending the flowers, but instead there was only one old man with a small tool-filled cart.

"How sad," she said suddenly. "Do you suppose that Lord Edgecumbe has been forced to let go of his staff?"

"I wouldn't doubt it." Justin tucked his snuffbox away. "Perhaps he should have thought of that before he began to gamble and drink excessively."

"Don't you see, clearly this estate has supported a way of life for entire families, perhaps for centuries! And now, because of one man's weakness and folly, it may all come crashing down. It is tragic!"

"Such tales are rife in England. But take heart. Perhaps by selling a few bits of old furniture to this wicked Frenchman, Edgecumbe will be able to steady the financial ship." He gave her a sardonic smile. "So to speak."

Mouette couldn't quite understand why she suddenly felt so emotional about the plight of Leyton Court, but her heart was beating fast and there were tears in her throat. However, they had already turned into the curving drive that led to the main entrance.

"We've arrived," said Justin. He straightened his white cravat and ran his gaze over Mouette. "You will behave yourself, won't you?"

It wasn't really a question, she decided. "Whatever that may mean."

A liveried footman had appeared under the portico to welcome them, and soon Mouette and Justin were out in the fresh, warm air with its scent of spring blossoms.

"Ah, there you are, St. Briac," said a voice from the shadowed doorway. "I haven't quite decided whether you are my enemy or my friend."

As Justin drew Mouette forward, he replied with a slightly wicked smile, "I hope rather to be your savior."

Now Mouette could see their host more clearly. He was exceedingly tall, with a prominent jaw and a thin mouth that looked incapable of smiling.

"Are you in jest?" Lord Edgecumbe inquired coldly.

Justin stared right back at him, clearly unfazed by the older man's pretentious manner. "You may hope that I am not, sir." He turned his attention then to Mouette. "Allow me to present Lady Mouette Brandreth, my purveyor of home decoration."

"Indeed?" His lordship looked highly skeptical of her job title. "I knew a Brandreth once, in London. A baronet called Sir Harry, as I recall. He came to a very bad end."

"Unfortunately, that was my husband," she confessed.

"Hmph." Lord Edgecumbe turned away and declared, "I have other appointments this afternoon, so let us carry on."

Justin clearly relished the opportunity to wander around Leyton Court and Mouette followed in his wake, drinking in the sight of priceless pieces of furniture and family portraits, many of which had been in place for centuries. She had the feeling that Justin would have purchased their host's pedigree if that were possible.

As they proceeded through the manor house, Mouette brought out a tiny notebook and pencil from her reticule and paused occasionally to write a description of a piece she thought was promising. Most of the furnishings were very old and thus, she realized, not to Justin's taste. However, she saw him pause before a particularly fine ebony-inlaid pedestal table that was similar to one they had both admired in Thomas Hope's *Household Furniture*.

"I agree," Mouette whispered to him. "For the drawing room, I think."

Justin nodded thoughtfully. "Or perhaps for my study."

She felt the energy emanating from his masculine body. "You must be referring to the *morning room*."

The corners of his mouth twitched slightly. "It is not a feminine piece. It belongs in a man's study." He gazed down at her. "And will you not agree that we could never have found this at some common *shop* in Truro?"

Although she couldn't approve of his methods for uncovering such treasures, Mouette smiled. "*Touché*, m'sieur."

"I suppose you are interested in that table?" declared Lord Edgecumbe as he bore down on them. "It is a particular favorite of mine."

"Worry not," Justin murmured with the air of

someone who knew he had the upper hand. "You shall be handsomely reimbursed. Have you any more Greek-revival pieces?"

Lord Edgecumbe led them up an Elizabethan staircase and down a long corridor to the most magnificent gallery Mouette had ever beheld. She could feel Justin's powerful, silent reaction as he stood next to her and inhaled appreciatively.

The barrel-vaulted ceiling of the long gallery was a masterpiece of the plasterer's art, decorated with intricate raised panels depicting scenes from the Old Testament. Light filtered in through tall windows that punctuated the carved, paneled walls.

"Its magnificent, is it not?" Edgecumbe queried in an imperious tone.

Mouette began to feel sorry for the poor man. He was clearly struggling to salvage some pride during this humiliating tour. How it must sting for Edgecumbe to have to relinquish his family treasures to an arrogant French corsair in order to replenish the coin he had foolishly gambled away!

"Your home is breathtaking," she said sincerely. "You must be very proud."

The exceptionally tall Viscount Edgecumbe threw back his shoulders and lifted his great chin. "Indeed."

The nobleman began to lead the way to a grouping of Greek-revival chairs across from the fireplace. However, when Mouette glanced back expectantly to gauge Justin's reaction to the stunning pieces, she saw that Justin had made a detour to stand before the imposing carved granite mantelpiece. Even from a distance, she sensed something akin to lust emanating from his powerful body.

"This is exactly what I need," he stated.

Edgecumbe thinned his lips. "You must be mad."

"Indeed, sir," Justin agreed with a laugh. "However, I

am in need of a handsome mantelpiece for my new home, and this one is perfect. It speaks my name."

"Out of the question." The other man vigorously shook his head. "That fireplace has been here since the bloody Restoration! It was built with stone carried down the road from Restormel Castle, which dates to Norman times."

"Nevertheless, I must have it."

Mouette was alarmed to see the viscount's face begin to redden, and when he raised a finger to point at Justin, his hand was shaking.

"You insult me!" cried Lord Edgecumbe.

"On the contrary, I have come to save you from ruin." Justin's nostrils flared slightly. "Name your price."

Mouette watched as the older man turned to stare at the mantelpiece that had been part of Leyton Court's history for over five hundred years. His eyes grew wet and her heart ached for him as she remembered the beloved pieces of furniture and art that she had been forced to sell from her London home, just to pay the bill collectors. One by one her prized possessions had disappeared, until her home and her pride felt like mere shells.

"M'sieur," she whispered to Justin. "Kindly stop this!"

But Lord Edgecumbe now wore an expression that mingled defeat with relief. "I shall consider your offer, St. Briac."

Just then, an ethereal figure appeared in the doorway to the gallery. "Oh!" cried the beautiful young woman. "Hello! I hope I'm not disturbing you."

It seemed to be the same young woman Mouette had glimpsed sitting in the garden with a thin, fair-haired gentleman. As she came forward, her eyes lighting on each of them with a mixture of curiosity and cleverness, Lord Edgecumbe went forward to greet her.

"This is my sister," he said, looking as if he wanted to pretend the visitors didn't exist. "Lady Daphne Leyton."

CHAPTER 10

$\mathcal{A}$s introductions were performed, Lady Daphne glanced briefly at Mouette before turning her entire body toward Justin and speaking directly to him.

"How lovely to discover someone completely new and wonderful here, in the wilds of Cornwall," she said.

"My lady, I couldn't agree more," Justin replied with a smile meant to elicit a certain response. *Lovely indeed*, he thought, quickly surveying her very slim, lithe figure. Lady Daphne also was blessed with high cheekbones and soft toffee-hued hair drawn up into a loose knot atop her head. Her high-waisted gown was the pinnacle of fashion: fragile jaconet muslin trimmed with lace and pale green ribbons.

"Of course, I don't live here myself," she informed them with a little shake of her head. "On the contrary, I have come from London only to visit my brother, to lend my support during this *difficult* time."

Lord Edgecumbe's cheeks went ruddy. "You exaggerate, Daphne."

"What good it is to attempt to hide our circumstances from this kind gentleman, since he has clearly come to help you, Edgy? We must take him into our confidence."

Justin noticed that a glass of whisky had appeared in their host's hand. "I have indicated to your brother that I will be pleased to purchase some of the pieces from Leyton Court, to furnish my new estate."

"Your *estate*...?" Daphne echoed.

"It's not really an estate," interjected Mouette. "It's a manor house with a bit of land. Perhaps you've heard of Pendudwell Manor?"

Before Daphne or her brother could respond, Justin said, "It's called Frenchman's Lair now. I mean to transform it into something very special."

"How intriguing, m'sieur," purred Daphne. Glancing toward Mouette, she added, "Do, please, refresh my memory. Who exactly are you, madame? An *American?*"

Seeing Mouette's cheeks flame, Justin stepped between the two women. "Lady Brandreth is my purveyor of home decoration."

"Indeed?" Daphne lifted her eyebrows. "I have a great deal of talent in that area myself, m'sieur."

"Your *talent* won't be needed," Mouette said in a low, faintly threatening tone.

"That's true," said Justin, even as his mind moved quickly to assemble a plan. "However, I may have need of other talents of yours, my lady. Would you be willing to walk in the gardens so that I might explain?"

* * *

THE LONE GARDENER stood on the path gravel, staring hopelessly at an overgrown magnolia tree.

"Hello, Mr. Bender," said Daphne as she and Justin drew near. "Are you quite all right?"

Justin thought that the bent, frail fellow looked to be close to ninety years of age. What the devil was he doing out here alone, holding pruning shears? "Can I help you, sir?"

"You can send me a few young men," grumbled Bender. "I can't do it alone."

Justin glanced at Daphne. "If your brother sells me the mantelpiece, he will be able to hire more workmen to assist your head gardener."

"I shall remind him of that," she replied, then turned to the old man. "Dear sir, I insist that you retire for the remainder of the day. Find some shade and put up your feet. You have earned it!"

As they continued on down the weed-choked path, Daphne sighed. "Of course, that is but the tip of the iceberg. Most of the house servants have been released as well. The whole place will rot away if something isn't done quickly."

"It would seem that your brother was unwilling to confront reality until now."

"How grateful I am that you can see my problem and speak to me frankly about it," she said. "I have felt quite hopeless since my arrival from London."

"Tell me, Lady Daphne, have you a husband?"

"Indeed not, m'sieur." She slanted a coquettish look up at him. "Why do you ask?"

"I have a business proposition to make to you, one that could very well benefit not only both of us but also your brother. You see, I am in need of a wife." He paused as her green eyes widened with surprise. "Not a real wife, you understand, but a make-believe one. If you and I can reach an agreement, I will reimburse you handsomely."

Daphne slowly nodded. "Yes, please do enlighten me. I find the prospect of becoming your wife, make-believe or otherwise, to be highly alluring!"

* * *

MOUETTE WAS the picture of serenity as she bade Lord Edgecumbe and his sister farewell. However, the moment the coachman closed her inside the landau with Justin St. Briac and they began to clatter away down the bumpy drive, she turned on him.

"You are exceptionally ill-mannered, sir."

"I'm desolated to hear it," came his laconic reply. "How have I mistreated you today? I thought you were enjoying your time at Leyton Court."

"You left me alone with Lord Edgecumbe, who is relentlessly morose, while you dallied in the garden with that horrid woman."

"Do you refer to Lady Daphne? She isn't horrid in the least. I found her to be decidedly young and lovely."

Mouette winced inwardly. How could men be so obtuse? Why couldn't Justin see what had been utterly clear to her the moment she laid eyes on Lady Daphne Leyton? "I thought you might be more discerning than other men, but clearly you are as blind as the rest. Your precious Lady Daphne is a schemer."

"Is she?" To Mouette's extreme irritation, he took out his agate snuffbox and flicked it open as if he hadn't a care in the world. "That was not what I noticed about her."

Mouette seethed. "When you described Lady Daphne as 'young and lovely,' were you making an indirect reference to my age?"

"Because you are so much older than she?" His tone was light, but razor-sharp. "I did not mean to do so, but clearly it is a sensitive point for you, my lady."

Stinging, she sat back against the leather upholstery and bit her tongue. Justin, meanwhile, looked out at the passing landscape as the landau jounced along.

At length, he gave a sigh. "I find it very sad to see a grand estate like this one disintegrate."

"I tried to say the same thing, earlier, before Lady

Daphne appeared and apparently caused you to feel more compassion for her family's plight," Mouette said. "Have you changed your mind about absconding with their ancestral mantelpiece?"

"Changed my mind?" He looked surprised. "Hardly. I still mean to have it, but I will not endeavor to take advantage of Edgecumbe's desperate situation. I'm now willing to pay a more generous price for his treasures."

They were back on the main road again, where meadow pipets chirped from the hedgerows. As the landau crowned each successive hilltop, Mouette beheld another vista of emerald-green meadows and farms, spreading southward to the English Channel.

Justin, meanwhile, had closed his eyes and appeared to be dozing in the warm breeze. A faintly roguish smile played at the corners of his mouth. Mouette frowned, wondering how to discover what had transpired between Justin and Lady Daphne during their interlude in the gardens.

"You are quick to point out that I am much older than your new friend," said Mouette, nudging him as she spoke, "but have you forgotten that *you* are positively elderly by comparison? I find it shocking that men may pursue females who are young enough to be their daughters without any societal censure."

He blinked and stifled a yawn. "It is the way of nature, as you well know, my lady, no doubt because men do not age in the same way as women."

Unable to help herself, Mouette took the bait. "That is outrageous!"

"Not a bit. We are fertile until the day we die, but women enjoy no such potency."

"If you imagine that protects you from the effects of aging, you are deluded, m'sieur!" Of course, Mouette found Justin St. Briac to be sinfully attractive for a man his age, perhaps even more so because of his weathered patina, but she would never admit it to him.

"I don't think Lady Daphne Leyton agrees with you," he parried.

Justin closed his good eye again and appeared to nap, but Mouette felt as if he might be watching her through his silk eye-patch.

* * *

DOWN A LANE near the village of Bodinnick and overlooking the picturesque River Fowey, lay the rambling stone-and-slate buildings of Trevarre Hall, ancestral home of Isabella's brother Lord Sebastian Trevarre, his wife Julia, and their two children, Cassandra and Lucas.

On this particular afternoon, Isabella was walking with her sister-in-law, Julia, back from the hilltop pasture where the children had been feeding the new lambs.

"Your friend Mouette's sons seem a little lost to me," Julia remarked as they descended into a leafy tunnel that led to the tidal creek of Pont Pill. "I suspect they are missing the security of a real home. I'm glad they came with you today."

"You are right," said Isabella. "They need stability, but also a firm hand. I think Mouette feels guilty that they've lost their father and now their London home. She indulges them too readily. And now she has become entangled in my brother-in-law Justin's scheme to grant his mother's dying wish by finding a wife. He intends to *pretend* to marry, and Mouette is helping him decorate a home here in Cornwall."

"How very intriguing!" Julia said. Then, for several minutes they walked along in companionable silence, listening to the birds and the sounds of the creek at high tide. At length, Julia looked over, tendrils of sable-brown hair framing her face. "I have an idea. Why don't all of you come for supper tomorrow night? I confess that I am very curious to see your brother-in-law, Justin, again. He behaved quite shockingly at your wedding. As I recall, he nearly overshadowed the bride and groom! And now it sounds as if he is at it again, stirring things up."

"It is his way," Isabella agreed with a rueful laugh. "Justin casts a spell on everyone he encounters. I'm not sure he can help himself."

The children were approaching, chattering together as they clambered over the crest of the hill and descended into the sun-spangled greenery.

"Mama!" called Lucas. "Charles discovered two baby fox kits! We think that something has happened to their mother."

Julia shook her head. "You know that your father has forbidden me to bring home more orphaned baby animals since he was bitten by that squirrel last spring."

"But we can't just let them *die!*" protested Lucas. "Camille was weeping at the sight of them."

"Please, Lady Julia!" cried little Camille St. Briac.

"I'll tell you what," she allowed. "Let us fetch Keswick, our stable master, to help you rescue the babies, after he makes certain the mother is truly not coming back." She glanced over at Isabella, smiling. "Your mother and I have a menu to plan for tomorrow night. We're going to have a party and all of you are invited!"

Shortly before their guests were due to arrive, Julia found Sebastian in his bath, washing away the grime of a day spent with the new lambs.

The sun was slow to set on this June evening, and the air wafting in to their upstairs bedchamber was deliciously soft and warm. When Julia came through the doorway, Sebastian put down his soap and smiled.

"Is there time for you to join me?"

Even after two decades of marriage, he could still cause her to blush. "I wish there were, darling, but it wouldn't do for us to be frolicking in the bath together when the St. Briac family arrives."

"If you say so." His dark eyes were on her breasts and she felt her nipples tingle through the thin stuff of her bodice.

"There is a matter I would discuss with you, as you bathe," Julia said briskly. "It's important."

Muscles flexed in his broad shoulders as he washed his hair. "I'm listening."

"Thank you, darling Sebastian." Pulling a little three-legged stool over from the hearth, she perched on it next to the copper tub. "Did you happen to notice the other two boys who were with Izzie yesterday, when she brought the children to the meadow?"

"I was very busy. I barely had time to say hello to my own sister."

"The boys were Mouette Raveneau's sons, Charles and Anthony." Julia paused, watching as comprehension dawned on his handsome face. "Do you remember hearing that Izzie brought Mouette and her sons back from London for a visit?"

"Vaguely."

"Sebastian, do please attend me. I realize that we rarely speak about the special connection you have to the Raveneau family..."

"You mean that small detail about André Raveneau being my true father?" he said in a low, slightly frustrated tone.

"Yes. I know that, when you discovered that Raveneau was your father, you told him you did not intend to share the news with anyone else. That you did not want to intrude on the lives of his legitimate children, especially his son Nathan. That—"

"That it's no one's bloody business but André's and mine," Sebastian supplied. "And yours, of course, my love."

She beamed. "Thank you for that. I am honored to be included in this special secret. And even though you may not divulge your connection with the other Raveneau offspring, the fact is that you are still their brother."

"Half-brother," he corrected.

Julia sighed. "That's the same relation you have to Izzie, and you don't think of her as less of a sister."

"Izzie doesn't know that we had different fathers. Where is this discussion leading? My bath is growing cold."

"Give me one more minute, if you please. I want to

talk about Mouette Raveneau." Julia narrowed her dark-blue eyes. "Just because you have not told Mouette you are her brother, it does not change the fact that you are family. Do you never think about her?"

"I have more than enough to think about without dreaming up new problems." Leaning over, he took his towel from the back of a nearby chair and began to dry his hair.

"Sebastian! I know you better than that."

"All right then, what is it? Look, I'm getting goose-flesh." He pointed to his forearm. "Tell me what is on your mind and let me out of this bath."

"I know that Izzie is worried about Mouette. As you will recall, she is a widow, endeavoring to raise two boys while suffering snubs from the *ton* at every turn."

"And why exactly are we talking about this tonight?"

"Because Mouette will be arriving shortly to dine with us." Julia leaned forward to kiss him, her heart swelling with love. "She is staying with Izzie and Gabriel, and they will be joined, I believe, by Gabriel's disreputable brother, Justin St. Briac. Justin, it seems, is planning a pretend wedding to please his dying mother, and Mouette has undertaken to decorate the pretend home he has purchased."

Sebastian put Julia from him and stood up in the bath, water streaming down his still-powerful body. "Devil take it, I suppose I must listen to all the details of this complicated tale if I am to properly observe Mouette tonight. Kindly enlighten me while I dress." As his wife happily presented him with a fresh towel, he added, "Life with you is never dull. Last night it was or-phaned fox kits, today it's a wayward, secret half-sister."

"Would you have it any other way?" Julia asked.

Sebastian pulled her into his arms, heedless of the way his wet body was dampening her thin muslin gown. "You know the answer, my lady, do you not?"

Passion smoldered in her eyes. "Indeed I do."

* * *

"I THOUGHT JUSTIN WAS ALSO INVITED," Mouette said to Gabriel as she emerged from the coach onto Trevarre Hall's modest drive and looked all around. "Isn't he coming?"

As the children emerged and their bantering voices filled the night air, Isabella went to urge them to exhibit better manners.

"I cannot answer that question," Gabriel said to Mouette. "Have you not observed that my brother does exactly as he pleases?"

She heard the edge of annoyance in his voice. "I have. Yes." Aching a little at the prospect of an evening without Justin's intoxicating company, Mouette regarded Trevarre Hall. It was a mixture of farmyard with an unpretentiously tasteful estate. As she took it in, Mouette realized that Julia and Sebastian were so comfortable in their home that they weren't interested in impressing visitors.

"The last time I arrived at Trevarre Hall, I was attending your wedding," she mused. "Doesn't that seem like a very long time ago? Harry was still alive, though he couldn't be bothered to accompany me."

Gabriel arched an eyebrow. "You and Justin rather stole the show during our wedding, as I recall, with your public row."

"I didn't know who he was." She couldn't help laughing. "He had been terribly insolent to me on the road, when he stopped to help my coachman repair a wheel. I had no idea the rude stranger was your brother until he appeared at the church."

"We were all a lot younger then." Gabriel took Mouette's arm and followed in the wake of Isabella and the

107

four children, walking up the path to the ancient, carved front door. "Had Anthony even been born?"

"No. Not yet." For some reason, her cheeks flamed at his question. Perhaps because she felt embarrassed, thinking about Harry getting her with child again. In the last years of their marriage, it had been increasingly difficult to submit to his infrequent and often drunken advances.

"Ah, there you are!" Julia threw open the door to welcome them. "Isn't it a lovely evening?"

"Where are the baby foxes?" Charles asked without any preamble.

Just then, Lucas Trevarre appeared to take Charles's arm. Mouette was pleased to see that the two boys were nearly the same age, and Charles seemed more relaxed with Lucas than she had seen him for a long time.

"Keswick's made a nest for them in the stable," Lucas announced. "We are feeding them with a tiny sock, squeezing warm milk into their mouths. Do you want to try it?"

Little Camille St. Briac squealed with excitement and ran ahead with the older boys while Anthony and Louise stopped to admire Lord Sebastian Trevarre's rakish portrait, hanging on the wall.

"That's my Uncle Sebastian," Louise said proudly.

"He looks like a real pirate," exclaimed Anthony. "That's what I intend to be when I am grown."

"Uncle Sebastian was a famous smuggler many years ago," the girl confided. "They called him Captain Rogue!"

Mouette saw Anthony's eyes widen in awe. As the two of them disappeared together around a corner, he declared, "That's quite thrilling, but a smuggler cannot compare to M'sieur Justin. He is a *pirate!* He has told me shocking tales that he says would set Mama's hair on fire if she heard them."

Mouette felt Julia watching her and looked over at her hostess with a little shrug. "Justin St. Briac has made quite an impression on my son."

"So it would seem!" Laughing, Julia drew her into the parlor. "We are so pleased that you all could come. How lovely you look. May I call you Mouette? Because of Izzie's affection for you, I feel as if we are already friends as well."

Julia was a few years older than Mouette, but she remained a compelling beauty, confident in the world she and Sebastian had created together. There was nothing grand at all about their home, especially considering the Trevarre family title, yet Julia seemed as proud as if it were a palace.

"You honor me, my lady," Mouette said sincerely.

"My name is Julia," came her firm reply. "Do you remember when we first met, many years ago in London? Your parents welcomed me into your Grovesnor Square home, when Sebastian brought me there soon after our wedding. You were a girl of sixteen then, but no lovelier than you are today. I will always be grateful to the Raveneau family for your kindness at a time when I needed it most."

"I do remember," Mouette said. "And I shall share your kind words with my parents when I write to them."

Just then, Lord Sebastian Trevarre entered, ducking his dark head slightly under the low doorway. When he straightened and smiled at her, Mouette was shocked by the resemblance Sebastian bore to her father, André Raveneau. As he came toward her, she composed herself with an effort.

"My lady," he said, and even his voice seemed to be the same as her father's, except for its British accent. "How pleased we are to have you with us. I hope that you will allow me to address you as Mouette."

"Of course!" she exclaimed. "In fact, I am certain that we dispensed of these formalities many years ago."

"I was very sorry to hear of your husband's death," Sebastian said gravely. "Please accept our condolences. While you are in Cornwall, I insist that you look upon me as a member of your family. Please call on me at any time."

"He means *us*," Julia amended with a fond smile.

"I appreciate that very much," Mouette told them, touched by their kindness.

Isabella came into the parlor, carrying a plush gray cat. "Look! It's Bluebell, Clover's daughter. She is the image of her mother. Clover lives on." Pausing beside her brother, she lifted her face to accept Sebastian's kiss on her cheek. "I'm so glad you two are making Mouette feel at home. She is like a sister to me, you know."

Mouette thought that she saw Sebastian and Julia exchange a glance before he replied, "I'll always be grateful to Mouette and her family for making a place in their home for you after our parents were killed. I was far away with the Royal Navy and George—" Pausing, Sebastian made a disparaging sound. "Our brother George was useless."

"That's not quite true," said Isabella. "He did come to see me at school, when I felt so desperately alone." She paused and sighed. "I still hold out hope that he may return from Europe and redeem his shattered reputation...but I realize that I may be the last person on earth who should speak up for him, considering that he stole Gabriel's treasured Leonardo da Vinci painting."

"And worse," added Sebastian.

Old Mrs. Snuggs, who had once been the housekeeper but now was too frail to do any real work, appeared in the doorway. "Supper be served," she rasped.

"At last!" exclaimed Sebastian. "I am ravenous. Let us go into the dining room."

As the others followed him and began to take their seats, Mouette protested, "But what about Justin? Shouldn't we wait for him?"

Before anyone could reply, a knock sounded at Trevarre Hall's front door and Mrs. Snuggs tottered into the entryhall to answer it.

Mouette held her breath until the old woman appeared again and announced, "M'sieur Justin St. Briac and Lady Daphne Leyton!"

Justin came into view first, filling the house with his energy, scanning the guests until his gaze settled on Mouette. "Ah, here you all are. Thank you for waiting for us!"

Sebastian extended a hand to Justin, and then to Daphne, who followed in his wake looking uncharacteristically uncertain.

Everyone was staring at Justin, waiting, while Mouette's heart beat faster and faster. "I've brought someone to meet you all," he said, bringing Daphne forward. "Allow me to present Lady Daphne Leyton. Because I am seriously considering making her my bride, I thought I should bring her to meet my family and friends."

As Daphne straightened her shoulders, she seemed to thrust out her youthful bosom in a way that Mouette sensed was a taunt. "How do you do?" she said grandly. Her green eyes swept the modest dining room with a touch of disdain. "How pleased I am to be here, among those who most love *my* Justin!"

CHAPTER 12

$\mathcal{M}$ouette felt her cheeks flaming and she sensed that both Isabella and Julia were watching her. It was exceedingly difficult to breathe.

Justin suddenly seemed more potently appealing than ever before. He wore his flawlessly-tailored Parisian clothing as if he'd been born in them. His hair was fashionably windblown and his charcoal-gray eye-patch matched his waistcoat.

Sebastian and Julia had risen to greet the late-comers, offering them wine, welcoming Lady Daphne to their home. Mouette tried to smile, all the while sharply aware that Daphne was young and lovely in a way that she once had been. She wore an evening dress of white lace and satin that was much more elegant than any other female guest's. Ornamented with full-blown roses around the hemline, it boasted a bodice of carnation pink, cut low to display Daphne's high, firm breasts.

"My lady," said Julia, "I must tell you that I am deeply envious of your headdress. May I inquire where you had it made?"

Mouette watched as Daphne touched her white satin toque, ornamented with a cluster of roses on the left side. "You flatter me! As a matter of fact, I had this headdress made by my very own millinery shop. If you would care to place an order, I should be happy to accommodate you."

"A millinery shop!" exclaimed Isabella. "How very… enterprising of you, Lady Daphne!"

As she was being seated, Daphne looked up with a surprisingly shrewd expression. "Enterprising? I suppose so. You see, I had to take action. My brother is on the verge of losing our family estate and all its holdings. I have come to Cornwall to do what I can to stop that from happening, and to look after my own future if he should succeed in ruining our family."

Justin was calmly watching Daphne as she spoke. Clearly he knew all about this and, Mouette guessed, he was endeavoring to turn Daphne's family crisis to his advantage.

"I must admit that I'm a bit surprised to learn about this planned marriage," Gabriel said, his eyes on Justin.

A young kitchen maid was serving a first course of soup and Justin seemed glad for the distraction. "Why are you surprised? You knew I had to choose a bride, for the sake of our mother."

Gabriel's gaze narrowed. "Are we speaking, then, of the same situation?"

"If you mean, the marriage charade that you and I have discussed, the answer is yes. Lady Daphne was quite pleased by my proposal—"

"Pleased?" she repeated. "Such a feeble word. Indeed, I am *enraptured* by the notion of marriage to M'sieur St. Briac, whether real or pretend! I cannot imagine a more beguiling prospect."

Mouette's heart hurt as she watched them, smiling and laughing together, Daphne touching Justin's arm, hand, and even his face. It hurt, too, to realize that she was sitting alone between the other two couples, as if she were a spinster, invited to the gathering out of pity.

Suddenly Mouette became aware that Justin was watching her. When she instinctively looked toward him in response, he averted his gaze. Her heart soared. She couldn't even bring herself to name what was happening, but she realized that he had not forgotten her at all. On the contrary, it was entirely possible that everything he was doing was for her benefit.

She sat up straighter, feeling a glow begin to spread in the center of her being.

"Perhaps we should be married in London," mused Daphne.

"Have I not explained that this wedding is for my mother's benefit?" Justin replied in a low, cool voice. He then glanced around at the others. "I wanted all of you, who will doubtless be guests at the pretend wedding, to have an opportunity to meet Daphne and tell me if you think she can fool Maman."

"I don't know what you are talking about," said Sebastian.

"Yes, you do," Julia rejoined. "I explained it all to you just a short while ago. It's all a charade, to please his dying mother."

"Oh, right." He looked as if he had a headache. "It was such a mad tale that I suppose I thought you must be making it up."

Mr. Snuggs came shuffling toward them, holding a bottle of wine. "Will you have more, my lord?" he inquired in a quavering voice.

Sebastian gave his wife a sharp glance, as if to ask why they continued to employ these ancient retainers. "Give it over, Snuggs, and I will pour. Thank you."

The conversation and the meal continued, with Justin describing his new estate and Mouette answering Sebastian's kind inquiries about her two sons, who were sitting with the other children at a table in the parlor.

At length, Julia turned to Daphne and asked, "I am very curious to know more about your millinery business, my lady. Are your unique headdresses made in London?"

"Oh, no!" she exclaimed, sipping from her third glass of wine. "The work is done here in Cornwall, where I am able to—uh—procure the finest French lace and silk at—well, at an affordable price."

"Are you able to get those items at a lower duty?" asked Sebastian conversationally as he cut a slice of roasted chicken.

For a moment, it seemed that Daphne had dared to wink at him. "You might say that, my lord! Let us agree that I have a very good head for business."

Mouette watched as Sebastian exchanged looks with Gabriel. Was Lady Daphne Leyton implying that she was engaged in *smuggling*?

* * *

JUSTIN WISHED he didn't have these feelings for Mouette Raveneau, but he didn't seem to be able to stop himself. There was a beautiful, young, ripe, eager female sitting beside him, practically throwing herself into his arms, but he realized that his only real interest in Lady Daphne Leyton was to stir up jealousy in Mouette.

It made him furious at himself that he was not in control of this situation—although, thankfully, Mouette had no idea how bad off he was.

Sangdieu, she was an aging widow. She was penniless. She had two rambunctious sons.

And she was not interested in sleeping with him.

If Justin had a grain of sense, he would leave Mouette to handle the decoration of that cursed Pendudwell place while he distracted himself between the sheets with the very willing Lady Daphne Leyton.

Across the table, Mouette sipped from her wine and stared at him for a long moment, something indecipherable smoldering in her beautiful eyes. Was it anger? She had the most luxuriant black lashes he had ever seen, and the irises of her blue eyes were like sapphires when she was emotional.

His cock twitched and stiffened, damn it. It seemed he couldn't control his own body anymore than he could control Lady Mouette Brandreth.

"Will you have orange custard, sir?" a small maid piped at his shoulder.

He blinked. "No." He shook his head.

"Oh, my dearest, do try it. It's quite..." Daphne paused to sensually lick a bit of custard from her lower lip. "Decadent."

Justin stared, willing his body to transfer this ungovernable lust to Daphne. This had never happened to him before. Leaning forward, he gazed at her silver spoon and murmured, "Yes, all right, I'll have some of *yours...*"

* * *

"WHAT THE DEVIL are you on about?" Gabriel demanded hoarsely. "Are you incapable of just enjoying a relaxing meal? Must there always be some sort of drama wherever you go?"

They were standing together in the moonlit terrace behind Trevarre Hall. When Justin had ostensibly come outside to summon his carriage, Gabriel had risen and followed him.

Justin tried to make himself taller than his younger brother, without success. "What business is it of yours?

Just because I'm not content to spend my time nipping the buds off plants—"

Gabriel advanced, clearly furious. "One day, you'll push me too far."

"Fine! Do you imagine that I am afraid of you?" Justin pushed lightly at his chest. "Shall it be swords or pistols?"

"For God's sake, I am perhaps your only ally in this world. You should embrace me."

He stared at Gabriel, breathing deeply in an effort to slow his own heartbeat. Perhaps he'd indulged in too much wine and rich food tonight. "You are right."

"Justin, you have erected so many walls around yourself that no one can penetrate them." Gabriel reached out and put a hand on his shoulder, squeezing it with genuine affection. "It's not a recipe for happiness."

Instinctively, Justin reached for his snuffbox. "What a word—happiness! I'm not certain there is such a thing. It's like witchcraft."

"Listen to me. That woman, Lady Daphne, is not the right choice for this marriage charade you are planning. I realize that you always turn toward trouble, but you don't need more drama when it comes to Maman."

Before Justin could reply, Anthony Brandreth emerged from the lantern-lit stables and ran over to his side. Excitedly, he asked, "Did I hear you say you intend to fight a duel, m'sieur?"

"With my own brother?" He tried to make his tone light. "Never! We may quarrel occasionally, as all brothers do, but he is my greatest ally." Over the boy's head, he met Gabriel's eyes. "Remember that about your brother Charles, won't you?"

The others were coming out into the courtyard, and Justin recognized the form of Mouette, silhouetted in the doorway. His heart hurt at the sight of her.

"Darling Justin," called Daphne, "isn't it a lovely night for a romantic drive along the cliffs?"

Justin felt torn in several different directions. Gabriel was watching him, brows arched, and Mouette swayed slightly in the distance.

"Yes," he said to Daphne, "I will take you home. Let us make our farewells to our hosts."

*　*　*

MOUETTE STAYED AWAY from Frenchman's Lair all of the next day. The thought of seeing Justin, when Daphne's perfume doubtless still clung to him, made her feel sick to her stomach.

Instead, she and Isabella spent the day in the garden with Gabriel, who was especially kind. Later, while Mouette was watching the boys practice their violins, Helivet appeared with a message.

A wagon arrives at Frenchman's Lair with furniture from Leyton Court at eight o'clock tomorrow morning. Kindly arrange to be present.

Yours, etc., St. Briac

His signature was bold, twice the size as the rest of his writing.

Typical, thought Mouette with a wry smile. She looked up at Helivet, who stood waiting for her reply. "Kindly inform M'sieur St. Briac that I shall come tomorrow morning, as he requests."

"*Bien*," the coachman said. "We shall depart at half-after-seven, my lady."

*　*　*

IN THE MORNING, as Helivet drove her to Frenchman's Lair in the little gig, Mouette imagined what she would do if Daphne were still there. What if she had slept in the big mahogany tester bed with him, her naked body entwined with his? What if she came out to meet them, behaving as if *she* were the mistress of Justin's home?

Mouette's stomach twisted at these thoughts. They had descended into the narrow valley, where hedgerows crowded their gig and the lane ahead was dark under a canopy of leafy trees. Then Mouette gulped with relief as they rounded the bend and she glimpsed Frenchman's Lair, standing proudly in a sunlit clearing.

She was surprised to realize that Justin's name for his new estate was beginning to grow on her. And the house itself seemed handsomer, even a trifle arrogant, like its new owner.

Her fingers went up to straighten her pretty plum-colored bonnet. It featured flowers artfully made out of feathers and was lined with white silk. Even though it was two years old, Mouette knew that the hat flattered her and even Daphne, who apparently was a milliner herself, would admire it.

Her walking dress was fashioned of plum bombazine, trimmed with white silk. Knowing that she looked her best, Mouette sat up straighter and took a deep breath. Lady Daphne Leyton could not frighten her. Was she not a Raveneau?

As the gig drew up before the house, the front door opened and Justin appeared, wearing a fine cambric shirt, a striped waistcoat, a snowy cravat, white breeches, and top-boots. The sight of him, coatless and wide-shouldered in the sunshine, was thrilling. His hair was mussed, as if he had just run a hand through it. He wore a smile that held, she imagined, a trace of vulnerability.

The moment Helivet brought the gig to a stop, Justin stepped forward to help her out. Then the

French coachman snapped the reins and the horse started forward.

"Hello," Mouette said primly. It seemed that they were all alone, but perhaps Daphne was just lurking in the doorway, waiting for the right moment to make her entrance.

Justin clasped her hand with his strong fingers and gazed at her under his lashes. Then, slowly, he lifted her hand to his mouth and kissed it.

"Where is the wagon filled with furniture?" she asked.

"Wagon?" He was gazing at her mouth.

"Yes! You wrote to me that a wagon would arrive this morning from Leyton Court and I must be here to welcome it."

"Ah...*oui!* A wagon. I believe it is due to arrive very soon." Still holding her hand, Justin began to lead her toward the house. "But first, I would speak to you on a matter of grave importance."

Mouette's heart was fluttering. When he half-turned toward her, she could see the hard lines of his shoulder muscles through the fabric of his shirt. "But, what about your—fiancée?"

He scowled. "What?"

"Lady Daphne. You informed us all, at Trevarre Hall, that you meant to marry her."

"I did not say that. Perhaps you weren't listening! I said that I was *considering* hiring Daphne to pretend to be my bride, simply to fool my dying maman."

"Justin, that is not what happened!" she protested.

He stopped halfway up the pathway to the front door, holding fast to her fingers, staring deeply into her eyes. "It is what I remember! And now I want to forget about it. I have changed my mind. She won't do."

Mouette could feel her face flush and she knew that her hand was trembling in his. "I see."

"No, you do not." Justin stepped closer, until she could feel the heat of his body through the fabric of her gown. "I have decided that you alone can carry this off. Only you, Mouette. Say yes."

"I'm not certain I understand…"

"I am asking you to be my wife." His tone was utterly compelling.

To her dismay, she feared she might swoon. "I—I—"

Justin took her in his arms and shocked her by bending her backward. Just when she was certain he meant to kiss her, he murmured, "Say yes."

The trees branches that arched overhead began to spin as her better judgment was clouded by sheer intoxication. Was it possible that he was in earnest, that he had kept his true feelings hidden from her? She must be mad, she thought, to believe it even for an instant! Yet, when he was holding her, all the pain she endured during her marriage to Harry seemed to recede into the mist, and only this moment was real.

"Yes," she whispered. "I will be your wife."

Justin's mouth hovered above hers and she felt his warm breath between her parted lips. Her heart was pounding, yearning, but then he straightened slightly and relaxed his hold on her.

"Excellent." He blinked, as if regaining consciousness.

Mouette ached in the secret corners of her being. The conversations they had had about marriage came back to her then in a rush, like dark clouds blotting out the sun. "Justin, did you not tell me that you would never marry?"

"Indeed. But of course, this is different," he said firmly. "Only you are capable of truly fooling Maman. You will make an ideal pretend wife, and of course, you shall be properly compensated for your services."

Mouette felt as if he'd thrown a bucket of ice water on her. Suddenly it all made sense. Why on earth had she imagined, however briefly, that he had suddenly fallen madly in love with her and was proposing marriage?

"It wasn't necessary for you to ravish me, you know, in order to offer a business arrangement," she said, straightening her bonnet as she backed away from him. Her voice sounded a bit sharp and she took a slow breath. It wouldn't do for Justin to guess that her feelings might be involved.

"If you believe I just ravished you, my lady, clearly you have a lot to learn," he said with a lazy smile. "I merely felt an urge to hold you in my arms. Proposing marriage seemed a good excuse to do so."

"Not if your proposal is counterfeit." Mouette started toward the door, wishing to hide from him the telltale spots of color on her cheeks. "Will you give me coffee, m'sieur?"

He was right behind her, and at the door he reached out to touch the small of her back, guiding her into the entrance hall. Mouette felt a little shiver radiate over her bottom.

"Coffee is an excellent idea," he was saying. "I am hungry and Baptiste has baked his incomparable *brioche*."

"And are we alone?" Mouette asked, backing away from his touch.

"What do you mean?"

"Your lover is not present?"

"*Lover?*" A brow flew up over his eye-patch. "What are you talking about?"

"Lady Daphne. Although you may have decided against marrying her, it was clear to everyone last night that you meant to bed her."

He grinned, every inch the wicked pirate. "You are jealous."

"No, *you* are conceited."

Baptiste appeared with a tray. As his eyes darted between Justin and Mouette, he poured two cups of *café au lait* and set down a plate of warm, fragrant *brioche*.

"I want to discuss the terms of our arrangement," Mouette said when Baptiste had disappeared from the parlor.

"That again?" He sighed and buttered his *brioche*, adding a dollop of strawberry jam. "I could swear we have already had this discussion."

"That was when I was being employed only to decorate your home. Now the situation has changed dramatically." She watched disapprovingly as he took a large bite of the *brioche*. "Do you eat pastries every day?"

"Yes, but only the best." He shrugged. "I am French."

"You will be both French and fat if you do not exercise some restraint."

"I have eaten this way my entire life!" As he spoke, he seemed to tighten his stomach muscles. "If this is the way you intend to speak to me during this marriage charade, I must warn you to cease. I won't have you scolding me in front of my mother."

"You are heedless of your health, m'sieur. One day you will regret it."

Justin rebelliously buttered a second *brioche*. "What I am regretting is my decision to hire you as my bride. However, Maman will doubtless rejoice in your overbearing attitude toward me."

"I am not overbearing!" She knew that he was saying these things to stir up her emotions, yet she couldn't help responding. These were precisely the issues that she felt most sensitive about. When Mouette reflected on her unhappy marriage, she secretly worried that it wasn't just Harry who had been in the wrong. Perhaps she had caused her own share of damage, by engaging in behavior that Justin St. Briac referred to as 'overbearing.'

As she brooded on this subject, Justin rose and went out of the room. When he returned, he was holding a sheet of foolscap, an inkpot, and a quill. Mouette watched as he took his seat, dipped the nib in the ink, and began to write.

"Here are the terms you requested," he said. "I shall pay you twice the amount we agreed upon at the outset, when you were only in charge of decorating Frenchman's Lair. In return, you shall sincerely pretend to be my betrothed, and then, my wife." He wrote down an outrageous sum of money and turned the paper so she could see it. "It won't be so difficult, will it?"

Mouette stared at him, and for a moment, they seemed to be alone together in all the world. Must everything in his life be reduced to a sum of money? "There is one very important stipulation that I must insist on."

He cocked his head slightly. "What might that be?"

"This make-believe marriage shall be counterfeit in *all* aspects. To be clear, there will be no consummation."

"No?" For a moment, he looked surprised and even slightly offended, as if unable to accept the notion that she would make a point of rejecting his physical advances. "You didn't need to say it, you know. I had no intention of trying to bed you."

It was her turn to feel a sting of rejection. "Excellent." She pointed to the paper. "Kindly write it down."

Justin blinked, then gave her a smile. "Gladly."

In his bold hand, he wrote in the middle of the page, "It is clearly agreed by both parties that any physical contact in the pretend marriage shall be only what is necessary to fool others. Otherwise, their dealings shall be completely chaste."

Mouette nodded as she read what he'd written, but felt more than a little deflated by the enthusiasm of his agreement. "Yes, that's fine. Perfect, in fact."

"Ah, good." Leaning back in his chair, Justin gave her an irreverent smile. "The question now is, can you keep *your* part of this bargain?"

* * *

No sooner had they finished eating than the wagon arrived, filled with treasures from Leyton Court. Grateful for the distraction, Justin went outside to direct the young men as they unloaded the crates and pieces of furniture.

"Ah, there is my new table," he said, as they handed down the round ebony-inlaid pedestal table from Viscount Edgecumbe's library.

"It will be a perfect addition to the drawing room," Mouette said.

"No." He glared at her. "I have told you that I want it in my study."

Their eyes met and sparks seemed to flash between them. Already Justin was sorely tempted to break his vow of chastity, just to teach her a lesson in submission.

"As you wish, m'sieur," she said sweetly, then presented her slim back to him.

"Follow me," he said to the boys, and led the way into the manor house. When the table was positioned near the window, Justin stood back to appraise it and saw Mouette standing in the doorway.

"It's all wrong, you know," she murmured. "That area needs a desk, preferably the rosewood writing table that was there to begin with."

"It is my study, not your morning room, and I will put the damned table where I please."

"Of course you will."

Remembering the mantelpiece, Justin went back out to the wagon and asked the footman who appeared to be in charge about it.

"Oh, sir, it were far too heavy to bring in this wagon! And his lordship were teary at the thought of letting it leave the manor."

What the devil did that mean? Was Edgecumbe going to try to wiggle out of their bargain, even though he had already been paid handsomely?

"I see. I suppose I will have to arrange for its transport myself."

As they drove away with their empty wagon, he went back inside his house and stared at the ugly old mantel. Mouette glided in, carrying a newly-acquired Wedgewood vase filled with roses that she had coaxed to grow in the garden.

It seemed that she had the ability to divine his thoughts, for she immediately said, "You aren't still hoping to get the Edgecumbe mantelpiece, are you?"

"It was supposed to be on that wagon, with everything else, but now they say that it is too heavy, too cumbersome, and poor Lord Edgecumbe is weeping at the thought of parting with it." Justin reached into his waistcoat pocket, withdrew his snuffbox, and flicked it open.

"He is a sensitive person," she said softly. "No doubt he feels a deep attachment to a part of his home that has so much historic significance."

"Perhaps he should have thought of that before he gambled away his last coin!"

"Yes, it's a pity he isn't perfect, like you."

At that moment, Baptiste peeked around the doorway, eyes wide, then scurried out of sight.

"What's the time?" Justin demanded. Suddenly, he felt an overpowering urge for freedom. "I have an appointment."

"An appointment?"

"With Lady Daphne." When he saw her look up in shocked surprise, he amended, "I have to tell her that I've changed my mind. It's common courtesy, wouldn't you agree?"

Mouette was already on her way out of the room, her lovely head held high. "If you say so," he thought he heard her murmur.

* * *

Justin didn't tell Mouette that his meeting with Lady Daphne would be held at the net loft in Polperro, where she had based her millinery enterprise. The night before, when he'd taken Daphne back to Leyton Court and she had appeared to be so disappointed that he wasn't coming in, Justin had promised to visit her today.

He would have said anything to get away. Why had he encouraged her at Trevarre Hall, eating that bite of custard and acting as if he wanted to nibble parts of her body as well?

Fortunately, Daphne had been happy to let him escape, once she had secured a promise that he would come to the net loft today. She had no notion, however, that he had changed his mind about paying her a great deal of money to be his pretend bride.

Riding down into the valley where the village of Polperro nestled in a rocky bowl on the edge of the English Channel, Justin thought back to the many times he had come there during his smuggling days. There had been a few very close calls, when he and Gabriel had nearly been arrested by the Riding Officers who patrolled the Cornish cliffs. Gabriel had eventually persuaded him to shift into a safer and even more lucrative profession, acting as an agent to other smugglers, but a part of Justin always missed the danger.

Justin had been to the net loft before. Perched on the craggy edge of Peak Rock, at the very edge of the harbor, the slate-and-stone building had always been used to store sails and pilchard nets. As he rode over the steep path from the village and drew closer to the net loft, he wondered how Daphne could possibly be making women's bonnets in such a place.

However, when Justin dismounted, she emerged through an upstairs door that led onto the rocks. As she waved to him, Daphne's pale blue muslin gown was caught in the breeze from the Channel, blowing against her body so that every curve was clearly defined.

"Hello!" she cried. "You've come!"

After tying up his horse, Justin clambered over the rocks to meet her. "How did you choose this place for your business?" he asked.

"It was available. My brother is the owner! He needed more income than the fishermen could provide, as you know, so we are helping one another." She beamed. "Every shilling that I receive from you for our little marriage charade will go into my business. Do come in and see, won't you?"

She took his hand and pulled him along. Behind the net loft, there was a staggering drop to the English Channel.

"This could be a dangerous spot," he remarked, just before Daphne opened the door to the upper floor.

"Dangerous and thrilling," she agreed, looking rather wild.

Inside, Justin noticed the stink of pilchard nets before his eyes adjusted to the shadows and he saw that the upstairs loft was lined with tables where women appeared to be sewing. Not one of them even glanced up when he came into the room.

Daphne appeared to be very proud of her enterprise. She showed him around, explaining that she was able to make bonnets and other headgear in Cornwall for a fraction of what it would cost in London, and then sell them to her wealthy clients.

"They think I have brought them from France," she told him proudly. "And so, of course they expect to pay exorbitant prices."

"Of course," Justin replied, fascinated yet repelled by what he heard and saw.

A closer look revealed that the women who toiled in the net loft were pale and expressionless. Not one of them even glanced up when Justin passed by.

As if sensing his disapproval, Daphne whispered, "They are all very grateful for this work! I've been told that many of their families lost everything in last year's storm."

Justin thought of the lot of Cornish fishermen who nearly starved during bad seasons. And he was reminded that there had recently been a terrible storm that destroyed many houses and boats in Polperro harbor. Perhaps there was truth in what Daphne said about providing work for families that were destitute. But couldn't she improve these conditions?

At the far end of Daphne's workroom, Justin saw the stacks of materials that were used to make the various headdresses she would sell to the London *ton*. There were silks, satins, and velvets of every hue, as well as ribbons, feathers, and other trinkets used to trim the bonnets. One entire table was covered with an assortment of lace that Justin strongly suspected had been smuggled in from France.

"I design the bonnets myself," she told him proudly. "I have a gift!"

"You certainly do."

She drew him with her into the doorway at the far end of the room, so that they could breathe the fresh air and feel the sunlight on their faces. "I mean to save my ancestral home, and make my own fortune in the bargain. You can help me and reap some of the profits for yourself!"

Justin recognized the wild streak in her determination, and he could relate to it. Daphne also looked a bit mad, and he understood that as well. Just as he was on the verge of agreeing to join in her scheme, he remembered his dying mother and the conversation he'd just had with Mouette.

"It's very tempting," he said with a sigh. "But I have other commitments. I actually have come to speak to you about the, uh, arrangement we made last night."

"Are you referring to our betrothal?"

Justin blinked. She was exceptionally bold for a young lady of quality. "It was never a true betrothal, as you were well aware. I was asking you to play a part, in the presence of my mother."

"Is that what you came to tell me?" Her tone was suspicious.

"No. I have realized that my mother would not be fooled by you."

"You cannot simply *change* your mind. We had a monetary agreement," Daphne said sternly.

"See here, I have already given your brother vast payments for a lot of moldering old pieces of furniture—and a mantelpiece he has yet to deliver. Perhaps he ought to share part of those proceeds with you."

"You know better than that, m'sieur!" Daphne came closer and whispered, "Edgecumbe is stony broke. Ruined. Creditors are in line for any funds he receives! No, you gave me your word and I expect you to help me."

"I don't care for your tone," Justin said. "And I also disapprove of your employment practices. Those women are slaving away in that dark, stinking room—"

"They are doing what they must to help their families."

Justin arched a dark brow at her. "That does not absolve you of the responsibility to treat them fairly."

Just then, they both noticed a man approaching from the base of Peak Rock. He was thin and stooped, with wispy fair hair liberally threaded with white. The stranger kept his eyes on the rocky path, as if he were worried about tipping over into the waves that crashed far below. It wasn't until he had climbed the steps to Daphne's workshop that he raised his bespectacled eyes to them.

"Gadzooks!" the man exclaimed, clearly surprised to see Justin.

Daphne hurried forward, putting herself between the two men. "I am afraid you've come to the wrong place," she said. "Perhaps you are lost, sir?"

The stranger began to blink. "Lost?"

Justin thought back to the day he and Mouette had journeyed to Leyton Court, and had glimpsed Daphne sitting in the garden with a man who looked very much like this fellow. Extending his hand, he said. *"Bonjour. My name is Justin St. Briac."*

Daphne tugged on the other man's arm. "I'm afraid you can't stay here. Goodbye."

"Of course. Yes, I must have wandered onto the wrong path," the stranger said. "Pardon the interruption."

Justin watched as he turned and went back down the stairs.

"Poor fellow," Daphne said. "He isn't in his right mind."

"If you say so." He suspected there was more to this scene than met the eye, but found that he had no patience to probe further. "I'll be going as well."

Later, Justin would feel haunted by those last moments outside Daphne's workshop. He could see the shadowy figures of the women who toiled over bonnets for wealthy aristocrats, while Lady Daphne herself grabbed at his coat-sleeve. Suddenly, she looked very different from the ethereal beauty who had appeared before him at Leyton Court.

"You can't just walk away!" she hissed. "I won't let you."

"I'm afraid you have no choice." Justin removed her clenched fingers from his sleeve and separated himself from her. *"Au revoir,* my lady."

CHAPTER 14

*M*ouette had risen at dawn. She had a busy morning planned at Frenchman's Lair, unpacking more crates of valuable paintings, vases, and other fine pieces that Justin had taken from Leyton Court. Now, as she prepared to step from the bath, she felt a little shiver of anticipation at the thought of spending the day with Justin.

In addition to overseeing the decoration of the house, Mouette had also begun the process of hiring more servants. The final decisions would be up to Baptiste, of course, but she sensed that he would accept her guidance. It was exciting to have a goal, preparing the manor house for a future visit by Justin's parents, after their return from Bath.

Perhaps some of the masquerade might even feel genuine.

Before her bath, Mouette had laid out her clothing on the bed: a snowy white cotton chemise and petticoat over which she would wear a fresh sprigged muslin gown with a green satin sash. The choices were simple and functional, yet flattering with her black hair and blue eyes.

Standing up, she reached for a linen towel and

began to dry herself. Sometimes, when she was alone and naked, her thoughts would wander a forbidden path to Justin St. Briac. It was impossible not to think of him, of the feelings he stirred up in her.

Now, as Mouette rubbed the towel over the soft curve of one hip, she caught a glimpse of herself in the looking glass that hung above her washstand. To her surprise, she saw that her breasts were not quite as high and firm as they once had been. Slowly, she turned enough to view her bottom. She had seen how Justin looked at her sometimes, his gaze burning away the thin muslin covering her body. Would he still be attracted to her if he saw that she was no longer as taut as a younger woman...one like Lady Daphne Leyton?

Biting her lip, Mouette quickly donned her chemise, grateful to be spared any further views of her own nakedness. She was six-and-thirty years of age and had given birth to two children. It was only natural that her body would have changed! And for heaven's sake, Justin was considerably older than she. Certainly *he* no longer had the lean physique of a young man. Why did there seem to be a separate, special set of rules for men? Her cheeks flushed as she remembered his little speech about men continuing to be fertile and desirable, no matter how old they were, unlike women who apparently were destined to wither away!

"*Men!*" she whispered heatedly as she finished dressing. "I am better off without one."

* * *

"HIGHER."

Justin wanted to reply that his arms weren't long enough to hold the painting any higher, but perhaps such a declaration would make him appear inadequate, so he tried to make himself taller.

"Hmm." Mouette stood back and tapped one fingertip against her full lower lip. He had dreamed about her mouth last night.

"*Merde!*" Justin exclaimed abruptly. "Make up your mind so I can put this enormous thing down!"

"Oh, I'm sorry." She appeared to be genuinely contrite. "How thoughtless of me to forget that you might be getting tired."

"I was not *tired*," he countered.

"You aren't a young man, after all. I will try to be more considerate in the future! Yes, do set it down for the moment. Perhaps we should call Joseph, the stable-boy, to help you."

Justin felt as if smoke might be coming out his ears. If she were a man, he would be tempted to challenge her to a duel for such demeaning comments. As it was, he thought Mouette had never looked lovelier. Clad in the freshest and simplest of morning gowns, she had also wrapped her ebony curls in a muslin scarf, tying it loosely in front. The effect was exceptionally charming. He had been in a perpetual state of arousal ever since he'd begun assisting with her picture-hanging tasks.

"I don't need assistance from Joseph or anyone else," Justin said darkly.

Just then, Baptiste entered the drawing room. "M'sieur, your brother and sister-in-law are here to see you."

"How considerate of them to send word in advance," he snapped.

It was Gabriel who replied, as he and Isabella came in from the stair hall, "We won't stay. We were just leaving to visit Trevarre Hall when word arrived from our parents."

"Word?" echoed Justin. Suddenly, he felt a dull, disturbing pain in the center of his chest.

Mouette had gone forward to welcome and embrace her friends, offering them refreshment. "Do, please, sit down."

They allowed her to shepherd them over to a new pair of fashionable sofas, upholstered in emerald silk and adorned with gilded paw feet. "Truly, we can't stay," said Isabella. "Sebastian and Julia are expecting us."

In the back of Justin's mind, he realized that Mouette's behavior was perfect. If she were truly his wife, she couldn't have done a better job of papering over his bad manners with her graciousness. Perhaps he could learn from her.

"You're certain you won't have tea?" he heard himself ask as he joined Mouette on the other long, low sofa. "Or wine, perhaps?"

"Look here," Gabriel said, "I don't have the time or patience to sort out your conflicting messages. We've just stopped for a moment to tell you that our parents are returning from Bath."

"Yes," Isabella chimed in. "They write that your mother soon may be too weak to travel, so they hope to be back in Cornwall by week's end."

"Do they?" Suddenly feeling cornered, Justin wished he could sail away to the Indian Ocean with the pirate Surcouf.

"We thought you might like to know so that you can accelerate your wedding plans," said Isabella. "No doubt you'll want to inform Lady Daphne immediately."

Mouette turned her head to look at Justin, waiting.

He coughed. "Ah! Well, I intended to tell you… I've decided Lady Daphne won't do. You were right, Gabriel, when you said that Maman would never accept her as my bride."

Gabriel arched an eyebrow. "What then do you intend to do?"

"I'm marrying Mouette instead." Justin reached over to encircle her waist with one strong hand and felt her stiffen. "It came to me that she would be the ideal choice."

Gabriel and Isabella were both staring, clearly shocked.

"It won't be a real marriage, of course," Mouette assured them. "I would never agree to that."

"Thank God," said Gabriel.

"Have I just been insulted by both of you?" Justin demanded.

His brother stood up and reached for Isabella's hand. "We haven't time to engage in one of your verbal sparring matches."

"Yes, that's right, come in here and deliver your news, stirring everyone up, and then just leave me to sort through the rubble." As he spoke, Justin followed them through the door and onto the front drive.

"I must say goodbye to Mouette," Isabella suddenly announced. She put a hand on Gabriel's arm and added, "I will return momentarily. Be patient, darling."

* * *

MOUETTE WAS STANDING in the sunlit doorway, watching as her friends walked toward their landau. She must remind Justin to purchase a proper carriage, before the return of his parents from Bath. Wouldn't they think it very odd if he continued to borrow Gabriel's landau and driver?

Just then, to Mouette's surprise, Izzie turned and hurried back to the house.

"I cannot go without speaking to you privately," she said in heated tones.

Relieved, Mouette took her friend's hand and drew her into the morning room. The sight of Justin's new

137

table, in the very spot where she meant to place her own delicate writing desk, caused her nose to wrinkle.

"Your brother-in-law is very arrogant," she said.

"How well I know it! Why ever did you agree to en-snarl your life with his?"

Mouette considered that question. She wanted to tell Izzie that she struggled with a swirl of feelings for Justin, but it seemed that such sentiments would not be well-received. "He presented the plan to me in such a way that I felt I couldn't refuse. And, really, why would I? Izzie, he means to reward me very well for helping him in this charade. So well, that I won't have to spend another day as a hostage to bill collectors."

"Oh my dear friend, you must believe that I adore Justin. He is quite irresistible." Isabella averted her face, clearly torn. "But he can also be an expert manipulator. He pursues the things he cannot have, *should* not have. And he is afraid of love. You are like a sister to me, and I don't want you to be hurt!"

"I love you for your concern, but remember that I am a grown woman. My taste for romance was poisoned long ago, by Harry. What I need now is security, and Justin's wealth can provide that." Warming to her subject, Mouette patted Isabella on the shoulder. "I know all about him. We have talked, as friends. I can assure you that I shall not fall victim to the seductive charms of Justin St. Briac!"

Gabriel's voice came to them from the entrance hall. "Isabella! We are very late."

"I am coming!" Adjusting her gold-rimmed spectacles, Isabella looked into Mouette's eyes and sighed. "I will trust you to look after yourself, my darling friend, but if you should find yourself hopelessly tangled in Justin's web, do not say you weren't warned."

* * *

MOUETTE MIGHT HAVE BEEN something of an expert on the proper decoration of a grand residence, but she had a great deal to learn about managing the day-to-day workings of a household. When she was growing up, her mother ran their homes with such quiet efficiency that it seemed she wasn't doing anything at all.

It was only when Mouette was about to get married herself that Devon Raveneau sat her down and tried to explain that she would be in charge of a large household staff.

During her marriage to Harry, Mouette chose to hire an excellent butler and housekeeper to manage the domestic staff. It left her with so much more time to shop for drapery fabric and carpets.

"Baptiste," she said now, approaching with her half-finished list, "could you spare me a few moments of your time?"

"*Mais, oui!*" he exclaimed, as if shocked that she should give him a choice. "How may I be of assistance, my lady?"

She took in the sight of the wiry Frenchman, his sleeves rolled up and a towel tied around his thin waist. He was carrying a bucket of soapy water and a wooden brush. "Will you tell me your title? I assumed, when we first met, that you were m'sieur's valet. Later, I thought you must be the butler, because you were so very knowledgeable. More recently, when I tasted your *brioche*, I decided you must be a chef by training…"

"I am all of those things, if the need arises," Baptiste said proudly. "No task is beneath me! I will do whatever is necessary to smooth the way for my master."

She clapped her hands together, awestruck. "How long have you been with him?"

"*Toujours,*" he replied. "Always, it seems. But especially in Saint-Malo."

Suddenly, the air felt charged with electricity, and Mouette realized Justin must be nearby.

"I can't remember a time when Baptiste wasn't in charge of my home," he said from behind her, in the doorway. "He knows exactly the way things should be. He creates an oasis of calm and order in the midst of my sometimes chaotic existence."

Watching him, Mouette wondered why he didn't seek more calm in his own life. After all, he could choose not to be a pirate or a smuggler—or a libertine. He could bask in a serene existence like the one his brother Gabriel had made, filled with botany, books, gardening, and riding.

And family…

"I was going to speak to Baptiste about hiring more servants," she told Justin. "Now that we know your parents will soon be back in Cornwall, it becomes an even more pressing need."

"You don't need to bother Baptiste with it. You're the expert, after all."

She felt herself flush, which seemed to happen far too often these days. "I never said I was an expert at household management. And why should I be? It is only an illusion in this case, like this make-believe marriage."

Baptiste's eyes widened momentarily before he picked up his wooden bucket. "I shall leave the two of you to discuss this further, my lady."

"No! Please, I'd like to discuss it with *you*, Baptiste." Mouette took a chair at the round, ebony-inlaid table and spread out her list.

"Are you asking me to leave?" queried Justin.

"Surely you have some other mischief to attend to." Without looking his way, Mouette opened the inkpot and readied her quill.

Baptiste watched as his master strode from the

room before setting down his bucket and joining Mouette at the table.

"Will you help me with my list?" she asked. "As you can see, I have already begun with you, Baptiste." Her fingertip moved to his name, beside which she had written, "*Steward.*" It was the most prestigious title, above even a butler, and indicated that he would be in charge of the entire household staff. He would also oversee the accounts and do all the ordering of supplies. "Is it enough?"

He gave a little shrug, looking very French. "It is very grand, but perhaps not quite *enough*, as you say, because I must play other parts as well. M'sieur would never stand for anyone else to be his valet, for he has very precise habits, like the folding of his neckcloths. Nor could he bear it if a strange new butler tried to oversee any of the duties I have always held."

"But it is mad for you to try to do it all. A butler alone works from dawn to dark, overseeing the meals, the guests, so many things! M'sieur can certainly afford to hire more servants, so that you may have a bit of leisure."

"Leisure?" Baptiste pursed his lips and gave a tiny, appalled shake of his dark head. "*Mais non.* I live to assist M'sieur St. Briac in any way possible. That is what makes me happy."

"I find it very curious, but I shall not force the issue."

"*Merci.* Ah, my lady, I wish that you could visit our home in the walled city of Saint-Malo. It is a magical place! And when everything is running smoothly, as it invariably does, I feel a deep sense of pleasure."

Mouette was unexpectedly swept by a wave of longing. "It sounds wonderful."

"Perhaps you will go there one day," he said softly.

"Oh, no, I don't think so. All of this is temporary, after all." Her heart ached as she returned to the list.

"What about a cook? It is impossible for you to continue to prepare the meals, too, once this house becomes busier. After the…wedding…there will be social gatherings. Dinners. Perhaps we will have house guests."

Baptiste squeezed his eyes closed for an instant. "M'sieur has never been one to entertain very much. He likes his freedom, above all!" Then, as if realizing what he had said, he amended, "But no doubt he will adapt, at least for this short time. It is merely a charade, is it not? And as for the cooking, what Cornish cook could possibly make the French foods he likes best?"

"He has a cook in Saint-Malo?"

"*Oui*. But of course, I am in charge of the menu."

"Pehaps we could send for her."

"M'sieur has already told me—" Baptiste swallowed, as if considering his words. "He doesn't want to do that."

Mouette began to wish she'd never started this conversation. "All right then, what about the many other positions? We must have a proper housekeeper, of course. Footmen, an assortment of maids, gardeners, stable boys—and a proper carriage with a driver."

"My lady, pardon me if I am too bold, but if this is meant to be a masquerade, could we not simply engage the services of a few temporary servants? Merely for appearance, you know, until we return to our real life in Saint-Malo."

Setting down her quill, Mouette sat back in her chair. Another wave of emotion that she couldn't quite identify swept over her, and tears pricked her eyes. "Perhaps you are right. Yes. How silly of me!" She took a painful breath. "Your plan makes so much more sense than mine, Baptiste."

<h1 style="text-align:center">CHAPTER 15</h1>

Two mornings later, Justin surprised Mouette by riding over to Elysium and appearing at the family breakfast table.

"Viscount Senwyck is meeting me here," he explained. Before his brother could invite him to sit down, he took a chair next to Mouette. "He has a barouche he no longer needs and has agreed to show it to me."

The table was lined with people, including Mouette and her two children, and they all paused in the midst of eating warm rolls with jam to stare at him. It came to Justin then that he was still holding his riding crop. "I've been a brute again, interrupting your civilized meal. I hope you will forgive me." He met Mouette's faintly sleepy blue eyes and felt an instant throb of desire.

"You must join us," said Isabella as Madame Kerjean appeared to inquire if the rolls were to their liking. When she saw Justin, her withered countenance softened.

"M'sieur, I will serve you myself!" she told him. "Allow me to prepare a *galette* for you."

"Perhaps I would've liked a *galette* as well," muttered

143

Gabriel in mock dismay, but the woman had already hurried back to her kitchen.

"I seem to have that effect on women," Justin couldn't resist teasing his brother. "What can I say?"

Anthony Brandreth, Mouette's younger son, spoke up from his place between Camille and Louise St. Briac. "M'sieur, will you give me another dueling lesson today?"

Justin saw Mouette's eyebrows fly up. How charming she looked when she was in a temper. "Anthony, you will not take *dueling* lessons from anyone," she cried. "Is that understood? Fencing is permissible, but not dueling."

"But of course," Justin murmured to her, amused, "that is what he meant to say."

"Fencing is very dull," countered Anthony. He rolled his dark eyes. "Pirates don't care for such dull pursuits. M'sieur said so."

Across the table, Charles Brandreth watched his brother with narrowed eyes. "Don't you know that pirates are just a lot of unwashed thieves? Stop being ridiculous."

Madame Kerjean reappeared with the steaming *galette*, which looked a hundred times more appetizing than the colorless breakfast the rest of them were pretending to enjoy. How tedious the English were about their food!

No sooner had she set the plate before him than a knock came at the front door. The little red-haired maid, Claire, appeared moments later to announce Tristan Penrose, Viscount Senwyck. At his side was Lord Sebastian Trevarre.

"What a delightful surprise!" said Isabella as she went forward to embrace her brother and his friend. "Will you have coffee, or chocolate, perhaps?"

"It's tempting, but we can't stay," Sebastian replied.

"Julia's favorite mare, Wisteria, is about to foal. I only came along so that Tristan would have a way to return home, if Justin decides to purchase the barouche."

As they stood up to go outside and inspect Tristan's equipage, Justin couldn't help noticing how Sebastian watched Mouette, waiting for an opportunity to smile at her. It was annoying, but soon forgotten as they emerged into the sunlit drive leading to Elysium. Below lay Izzie's painting cottage, its golden stone walls aglow in the morning light.

The children all ran off to play except Anthony, who wore his wooden sword in a makeshift scabbard tied around his little waist, and strutted along between Justin and Mouette.

When Justin saw the barouche, all his other concerns of that morning were forgotten. It was a beauty! Not too big and painted an appealing shade of dark green with black trim, the carriage had a high driving perch in front and a folding hood that was pushed down this morning to reveal the rear seat. The upholstery was immaculate. In addition, the barouche was hitched to a matched pair of striking black geldings.

"Do you like it?" asked Tristan. When he turned to look at Justin, the sun shone on his tousled auburn hair.

"It is absolutely perfect," Justin replied with feeling. "How can you bear to part with so handsome an equipage?"

"My wife is about to give me a fourth child. I'm afraid we've outgrown it."

Justin turned to look at Mouette and saw that her eyes were shining as she regarded the barouche. For some reason, this pleased him immensely. "What do you think?" he asked her.

"I agree that it is perfect! I love the horses, as well."

"Yes." Justin turned back to Tristan. "Will you also sell us the horses?"

The younger man smiled. "Since I understand that you are about to be married, how can I refuse?"

Just then, Anthony spoke up in a loud voice. "I'm going to have a new papa who is a pirate!"

* * *

IT WAS AGREED that Justin would bring not only Mouette back with him to Frenchman's Lair for the day, but Charles and Anthony as well. All four of them would ride in the new barouche.

As Mouette went to gather her things and organize the boys, Justin followed Gabriel to the walled garden to see the pineapples that he was growing in his new pinery. The glass room, attached to a larger greenhouse where orange and lemon trees were grown, boasted several pineapples that were now ripe.

"They are quite impressive," Justin allowed, thinking it bizarre that his brother could prefer these prickly things to the chests of Colombian emeralds that filled the cellars at Saint-Malo.

"It's quite a challenge to grow them," Gabriel said. "They require more heat, but not too much, so my previous experiments have been unsuccessful. Finally, I had to build this separate structure, and put a special flue to the house itself, near the fireplace." He laughed. "And I had to wait until the war ended with France, so I could get more glass at a reasonable price. The tax on it has been prohibitive."

"There are ways around that, you know," Justin said dryly.

Gabriel seemed not to hear him. "I've just harvested the first pineapple. I'll serve it to our parents when they arrive, and then we'll have several more in the centerpiece at your wedding."

"Ah, *oui*—I remember now, they are a symbol of hospitality."

"And so delicious." Gabriel held one of the exotic fruits up for Justin to smell. "Maman deserves a few special pleasures in her last days."

This sentiment caused the pain to return to Justin's chest. Breathing deeply, he took a seat on a nearby bench. "It's warm in here."

"I'll open the door. Are you well?"

"Of course I'm well! What are you implying?" He took out his snuffbox and helped himself to a large pinch, but it didn't seem to help.

"I know you have conflicted feelings about our mother, feelings I well understand. But she is dying and I am proud that you are giving her the experience of watching you marry—and believing that you have found love and will have a family of your own." Watching him, Gabriel added, "And Maman will never know that it was all a charade and you haven't changed at all."

Justin closed his eyes to block out his brother's calm, probing stare. "Fine. It's getting hotter in here, and no doubt Mouette is waiting for me."

"You're certain you are well enough to drive back?"

"What are you implying?" He was on his feet in an instant, shoulders squared. "I'm as fit and strong as you are."

"If you say so." As they emerged from the pinery, Gabriel lightly touched Justin's arm and added, "I realize that you don't have any tender feelings toward Mouette, and that it is only a pretend romance, but I must confess to growing quite fond of her. She has been softened by the pain of widowhood and the challenges of raising two sons on her own, I think, and now she is exactly the sort of woman I might have envisioned for your bride." He gave a little laugh. "Of course, that's nonsense, I know, but I thought I would mention it. And Mouette should be able to fool Maman, which is all that matters—yes?"

Justin breathed in the soft garden air and nodded. "Yes. Of course, that's right."

* * *

WHEN MOUETTE CAME BACK DOWNSTAIRS with her sons, who were quarreling about the merits of pirates, she discovered Lord Sebastian Trevarre, sitting alone at the dining room table.

"I thought you were in a hurry to return home," she said with a smile.

"Ah—yes, I am, actually." He finished his coffee and stood up. "But I wanted to have a word with you first."

"Indeed?" She turned to the boys. "Go outside and look for M'sieur Justin, will you? No doubt he is waiting for us. Tell him that I will be out in a few minutes."

When they were alone, Sebastian said, "Do you mind speaking to me here, where we can be private?"

"Not a bit." Mouette sat down beside him. "I feel very comfortable with you, my lord. Have I ever told you that you remind me of my father? When he was younger, of course."

To her surprise, Sebastian shifted uneasily in his chair and glanced away from her. "Do I? You flatter me. I have only the highest regard for André Raveneau."

"As do I!" Mouette gave a little laugh, hoping to put him at ease. "I miss both my parents very much."

Slowly, he nodded. "I have always felt a special connection to the Raveneau family. And that is why Julia and I would like to invite you and Justin to use our chapel at Trevarre Hall for your wedding."

"How kind of you! But, you do know that it's not a

real wedding—?" Saying the words aloud to him flooded her with strange, conflicted emotions.

"Yes, I understand that you two are pretending to marry, for the benefit of Madame St. Briac. If the idea is to give her pleasure in her last days, an intimate ceremony in our chapel should create the perfect illusion. Don't you agree?"

For a moment, she thought back to the last wedding she and Justin had attended in Sebastian's chapel, a decade earlier. It had also been the day of their first meeting, when sparks had ignited between them that could not be denied.

"Yes, I suppose that would be a perfect setting," she said softly. For one moment, she allowed herself to imagine such a day if she and Justin were in love, if they were truly marrying and had wonderful dreams for their life together. A day that might include her own happily-married parents, and even her sister, Lindsay, and brother, Nathan.

"Are you all right?"

Mouette looked up to see Sebastian watching her, his expression grave. It surprised her so that she blushed and gave a nervous laugh. "Yes. I think I can speak for Justin and tell you we are grateful for your thoughtful offer."

"If you should need assistance of any kind, I hope you will call on me."

From the doorway, a stormy-looking Justin St. Briac interrupted, "Perhaps you would do well to offer your *assistance* to your wife, who no doubt waits for you at Trevarre Hall, my lord."

CHAPTER 16

By the time Xavier and Cerise St. Briac arrived from Bath, Justin's chest pains had worsened, but the thought of confiding in anyone—or seeking out medical advice—was out of the question.

Instead, he rode over to Elysium in his new green barouche, feeling as much on edge as he ever had before a duel to the death.

"It's a fine day, isn't it, my lord?" the new coachman, Will, inquired cheerfully as they set off. He was a slight young man with the look of an elf.

"Fine enough," replied Justin, searching for his snuffbox. When he realized it wasn't in his waistcoat pocket, he nearly ordered Will to turn around. But they were already late, and surely Gabriel could supply him with some snuff.

And a brandy. His *best* brandy, leftover from their smuggling days.

Mouette would be waiting for him there. When he imagined presenting her to his mother, the tightening returned in his chest. He could already see Maman, scrutinizing Mouette, asking questions, ferreting out the truth.

But what the devil was he afraid of? What if she did

discover the truth? It was his life, for God's sake, and he could do as he damned well pleased!

Perhaps he ought to just stride in and tell her the truth outright. What a relief that would be! He smiled, breathing more easily. Was *Deux Frères* still at anchor near Polperro? How soon could he and Baptiste be back in France?

Feeling better and better, Justin reclined against the leather upholstery. They were almost there. The light was softer, almost golden as they neared the River Fowey. His eyelids grew heavy and he began to doze.

"My lord!" cried Will.

"*Mon Dieu*, do you not understand that I am not one of your cursed lords? Do not address me in that manner." Justin sat up with a start. "What is it?"

"A little dog!" Will had the audacity to pull on the reins and stop the barouche in the middle of the impossibly narrow lane.

Justin wondered if he might be dreaming. What was the fellow babbling about? But before he could demand an answer, Will had jumped down from his perch and was running back, behind the coach. Someone must be hurt. Had they struck a person?

"Look, m'lord! I mean, *sir!*" In the next instant, Will was lifting up a scruffy little dog with stubby legs and a fox's face, hoisting him into the air so that Justin had a clear view over the barouche's open hood. The brown-and-white dog seemed to be wearing a big smile. "The little fellow be lost!"

"Are you mad?" came Justin's impatient reply. "The filthy thing doubtless lives at the next farm. Put him down and let us be on our way."

"I can't do that, sir." Will firmly shook his head. "He were waitin' for us."

Certain that he must be losing his mind, Justin stared as the young coachman lifted the smiling dog over the open side of the barouche and put him on the seat. The animal immediately jumped into Justin's arms and buried his dirty face against his snow-white shirtfront.

As the carriage started forward again, Will glanced around from his driver's perch and observed, "I do think he likes you, sir!"

* * *

"I HATE THIS," Justin said to Mouette as they approached his mother's door.

"I realize that." Stopping, she gave him a smile. "Perhaps it will help if you think about your very engaging new dog."

"It is not my dog." Even though he wanted to cling to his dark mood, he felt his own mouth turning up. "I hope that the children take him into the woods and he can't find his way back."

"Oh, I don't think there is any danger of that happening. Did you see the look on Charles's face when your four-legged friend emerged from the barouche? My son has been begging for a dog ever since Harry died. I think he believes his prayers have been answered."

"Excellent. Consider it *your* four-legged friend now."

She gave his arm a little cuff and her beautiful smile widened. "You are incorrigible."

"My parents will agree with you." He stared at the door, then stepped forward and knocked. "I suppose we ought to dispense with this ordeal since there's no getting out of it."

Moments later, his father welcomed them into the darkened bedchamber.

"Papa, why do you insist on keeping all the drapes

drawn?" Justin asked after he had introduced Mouette. "It's as dark as a—" He broke off before the word 'tomb' tumbled from his lips.

Xavier was still holding Mouette's hand, beaming at her like a schoolboy. "What's that? Oh yes, well, your maman can't tolerate very much sunlight these days." He took out a handkerchief and dabbed at his eyes. "I suppose it is part of the *process*, if you take my meaning."

For God's sake, was his father really crying? Before Justin could reply, a thin, plaintive voice rose from the bed that was positioned across the spacious chamber.

"Justin, my dear boy, is that you? Have you brought your future bride to me? Come closer!"

He wished he had a choice in the matter. When he took a deep breath, his heart seemed to constrict. Just then, Mouette reached silently for his cold hand, her own fingers soft and warm. His breathing began to ease.

"*Oui*, Maman. I have brought Lady Brandreth to meet you."

Together they approached the bed, his father trailing behind them. Cerise lay against a lot of pillows, pale and shadowed. She wore a lace cap, tied under her chin, and the blankets were drawn up to her chin.

"Madame St. Briac, it is an honor to meet you," said Mouette, not waiting for him to present her to his mother. To his consternation, she gracefully perched on the edge of the bed. "Justin has told me so much about you."

Cerise peered at her, yet seemed to shrink back farther into the pillows. "Has he, my lady?"

"You must call me Mouette." She was enchanting, he thought, sitting there as if she already shared a bond of affection with his mother. "I understand you have been in Bath, taking the waters. How was your stay?"

Cerise blinked several times, then darted a look toward Xavier. "Well enough," she whispered at last. "Considering that my death is imminent."

"Oh, I pray that is not the case," Mouette replied sincerely.

Justin saw that his mother was watching Mouette with bright eyes. "I have dreamed of this day for years. Years! I thought it would never come. Yet, how could I depart this earth if my first-born son remained alone, with no one to love him and take care of him in my place?"

"Maman, for God's sake, stop!" Justin barked.

Mouette glanced back at him, clearly amused, yet she rose and went to his side. "You do not need to worry about your son," she told Cerise. "He will be fine."

"You will *love* him?" the old woman pressed. "He can be difficult. He is proud, even arrogant, and stubbornly independent."

"Yes, I know." Mouette smiled like a cat with a canary. "I know all about him."

"And you *love* him?" his mother persisted. "I must know that you are marrying him for the right reasons. In order for marriage to succeed for my headstrong son, there must be a great quantity of true love. And passion."

Mouette didn't speak for a long moment, during which Justin heard his heart beating in his own ears. Why didn't she answer? He reached for her hand and found that it was now as damp as his.

"Madame St. Briac, I must tell you the truth," Mouette said at last, in a soft voice. "I am not a young woman. I am a widow with two strong-minded sons. My financial resources are limited. So you see, I really have nothing to offer your son except my heart."

"How touching." Cerise looked at her husband. "Did you hear that, *mon cher*? That is true love!"

As Xavier came to the bedside and embraced his wife, Justin tried to read Mouette's expression. Her words had been spoken so eloquently that it seemed no one else noticed she had not answered the question.

***

"IT WILL HAVE to be a very quiet wedding," Xavier said as he saw them out of the room. "As you can see, my dear wife is very weak."

"Did the waters at Bath not help Maman at all?" asked Justin.

"*Peut-être*." Xavier gave a slight shrug. "It is hard to say. Perhaps without them, she would have already passed to the great beyond."

Mouette saw how Justin recoiled slightly at his father's words, as if he'd been dealt a blow, yet he said, "The Trevarres have offered to have the wedding at their chapel, where Gabriel and Izzie were married. We could have only a few guests. In fact, I would prefer that myself.

"Do you think Madame St. Briac will be able to leave her bed?" asked Mouette.

"*Oui!*" Cerise cried suddenly, from across the room. "For my son's wedding, I would crawl there if necessary."

Before they could respond, Xavier put his hand on the door latch. "It will be good for her, I think."

As the door opened to the hallway, Mouette gasped at the sight of the lost short-legged dog, sitting there before them and wearing an expectant expression.

"Good God!" shouted Justin. "What is that cursed mongrel doing here, putting his mud on my brother's good carpets?"

"Woof!" exclaimed the dog. He then added insult to injury by attempting to jump up into Justin's arms.

"There you are, Robinson!" cried the voice of Charles Brandreth. "We've been looking everywhere!" He came into sight from the stairway and ran down the corridor, attempting to capture the dog.

"Who is Robinson?" asked Mouette.

"Our new dog," replied her son as he wrapped his arms around the struggling animal. "He was lost, like Robinson Crusoe. Isn't it a perfect name?"

Robinson gazed longingly at Justin, wriggling his long, sturdy body in an effort to free himself from Charles's arms.

"I like the part about him living alone on a desert island," muttered Justin. "When does he sail?"

At that moment, Anthony appeared around the corner, running toward them and calling, "There you all are! How thrilling it is that Charles and I will have not only a new papa, but our very own dog!"

* * *

ON MORNING OF HIS WEDDING, Justin stirred in his great tester bed, dreaming that Mouette lay next to him, gazing at him with desire. It was such a lovely dream that, even as he began to awaken, he kept his eyes closed a few moments longer.

"Mmmm." He extended one hand, toward the woman in his dream, and felt something soft.

Like fur.

Justin's eyes flew open and, to his horror, he beheld Robinson lying on the pillow next to him, his brown eyes liquid with adoration. One oversized fox-like ear stood straight up.

"Who the devil let you in here?" Sitting up naked in

the bed, he pulled the sheet to his waist and glared at the dog. "Get out. Now!"

Robinson made a pleased, guttural noise, flipped over on his back and swiveled his body from side to side.

"What did I do to deserve this?" Justin muttered. Getting to his feet, he wrapped the sheet around his body like a toga and stalked over to fling open the door. "Baptiste!"

A moment later, Mouette appeared. "Oh, good morning! Is something amiss?" She was pristine in an ivory morning dress, her glossy hair caught up in a loose knot atop her head. Eying him from his bare calves to his broad chest, she added, "That's quite a costume you've chosen for your wedding day."

"I want this mongrel out of my bed. Now! Did one of your sons put him in here, as a prank?"

"They did come over with me to help Baptiste make your favorite chicken for our wedding meal, but I hardly think they would engage in such mischief." She peeked around him to get a clear view of the rumpled bed, where Robinson now lay on his stomach, all four tiny legs sticking out in a comical fashion.

"Are you trying to get a peek at your marriage bed?" he couldn't resist taunting her.

Her cheeks pinkened. "Hardly, m'sieur," came her prim reply. "You will recall that we struck a very clear bargain regarding the nature of our union."

Justin felt himself throb and harden under the sheet that he continued to clench at his waist. Bending closer, he inhaled the faint scent of lilies of the valley from her hair. "You are a convincing actress," he murmured. What would she do if he released the sheet and brought her into the room, closing the door? This thought brought him to a state of complete, aching arousal.

For one telltale instant, Mouette gazed at his sleep-warm chest and her lips parted ever so slightly. Then she blinked, as if rousing herself, and turned away.

"I shall send Charles up to fetch Robinson. Will is waiting to drive us to Trevarre Hall, where I will dress for the wedding." Clearly shaken, she turned back only long enough to add, "I believe you are in charge of bringing your parents. I will see you anon, at the altar, m'sieur."

CHAPTER 17

Baptiste laid out his master's clothing, one piece at a time, on the giant bed. Behind him, Justin had just finished his bath and was drying off with a succession of linen towels.

"I'll own I never thought this day would come," Baptiste said, sighing.

"No need for tears," came Justin's sardonic response. "It's not a real wedding, you know."

"So you say."

"What's that supposed to mean?"

"The priest will not be authentic? Have you engaged the services of an imposter?"

Justin's brows lowered. "I assume that Lord Sebastian Trevarre has found someone to officiate. An actor, perhaps."

"Ah, *oui*," Baptiste sniffed. "I remember how well your scheme turned out when you interviewed actresses for the role of your bride."

"Perhaps I ought to hire a proper valet after all. One who won't interject his troublesome opinions!" He snatched his freshly-laundered white shirt and put it on. Glancing over at Baptiste, who had clearly gone to a great deal of trouble to find just the right clothing for this occasion, Justin softened. "Of course, I didn't mean that. You know that I would be lost without you."

"I have only your best interests in mind, you know."

"I am grateful for that."

Baptiste handed over his buff-colored trousers, cut in the very latest slim fashion by Justin's longtime Parisian tailor, Rondeau. Although his clothing always drew admiring glances, it was never grand or ostentatious.

"How long has it been since I last wore these trousers?" Justin asked as he put them on.

"Perhaps a season. They arrived from Saint-Malo this past week, in a trunk with much of the rest of your wardrobe." Baptiste cocked a brow. "I realized that we weren't going home quite as soon as originally planned."

Justin tried to button the waistband. "Perhaps they got wet during the crossing and have shrunk." Moving closer to the mirror, he stared at himself. "*Merde*, Baptiste, do you think I am getting fat?"

"*Pas du tout*, m'sieur! You are, perhaps, becoming more robust as you grow older." Baptiste paused, clearly searching for the right word. "More *powerful*, I think."

"You are a very bad liar." Justin turned sideways and scrutinized his profile. Any thickening of his waist would soon be concealed by the layers of his clothing, but perhaps it was just as well he wouldn't be naked with Mouette tonight. "If I don't put a stop to this, I'll soon need a corset like Prinny."

* * *

THE SMALL, centuries-old chapel clung to a gentle hilltop behind Trevarre Hall. Pink and white roses climbed up the ancient slate walls, a few blossoms peeking into a leaded-glass window that was pushed open to let in the soft morning breeze.

Mouette stood near the back wall, waiting to take part in her pretend wedding.

"The chapel was falling down, you know," Gabriel murmured, clearly trying to put her at ease. He stood beside her, ready to escort her to the altar in the absence of her father or other family members. "Even the roof had fallen in. Sebastian and Julia restored it after they married and came here to live."

Mouette nodded. It was impossible not to think of the first time she had come here, to stand up for her best friend, Izzie, when she and Gabriel were married. Sparks had flown between Mouette and Justin that day, to the extent that Julia Trevarre had interrupted the ceremony in order to make them take seats at opposite ends of a bench.

"Who would have guessed that you would be marrying Justin, in this same chapel?" Gabriel whispered, as if reading her mind.

"Well, I'm not really marrying him, as you have known all along." She felt her cheeks grow warm. "You have hired an actor to be the vicar?"

Gabriel shrugged. "It wasn't really difficult to find someone appropriate."

The so-called vicar, who looked impossibly young, had come to the altar, and now Justin strode in through a side entrance. Mouette felt an unexpected surge of emotion at the sight of him. He was ten years older than he had been on that fateful day of their first meeting, but his appeal felt more potent than ever to her. Justin was that sort of man. Yes, he might be brutally handsome, but there was also an irresistible masculine essence that burned deep inside him.

Mouette felt like a moth, drawn inexorably to his flame.

Suddenly, her eyes filled with tears at the realization that her parents were halfway across the world on this day. Perhaps she should have written to her sister Lindsay, imploring her to journey from Oxford to Cornwall. But how could she explain? No, it was impossible.

In truth, Mouette didn't understand herself. This wedding was counterfeit, so why did she long to have her family here?

"I'm sorry your papa is not here to bring you to Justin," Gabriel said as Cassandra Trevarre began to play the violin. The haunting yet hopeful melody filled the chapel.

Mouette looked up at her friend and knew that, in that moment, he must be able to see all her conflicted feelings in her eyes. "Sebastian tells me that Papa has gone to the West Indies to help my brother Nathan with a problem, whatever that means! And even if my parents could be here, I think it is better that they are not."

"Yes, perhaps..."

Mouette's eyes scanned the few assembled guests. There didn't appear to be more than a dozen. Her children were there, whispering with their cousins and Lucas Trevarre. Later, Mouette would somehow have to explain to Charles and Anthony that the wedding had been only make-believe, though she couldn't imagine what they would make of that. She couldn't think about it yet.

Directly in front of the altar, Xavier and Cerise St. Briac sat beside Isabella, while Sebastian and Julia were across the aisle. Viscount Senwyck came in at the last moment, and there were a few Trevarre servants.

"The Banns have been called?" Cerise suddenly demanded of the vicar. Standing on tiptoe, Mouette saw that Justin's mother was in one of the three-wheeled invalid chairs seen so often in Bath. Cerise now sat propped up against a stack of silken cushions, most of her face hidden by an elaborate lace cap.

The young vicar squinted at her, then glanced nervously toward Justin. "Madame, I believe that a common license was procured in place of calling the Banns," he replied, then turned his attention to the Book of Common Prayer. "Shall we begin?"

Although Mouette usually spent far too much time thinking about the clothing she wore, on this important day she had put off a decision until the last moment. Perhaps it was because she had such conflicted feelings about the occasion. Only this morning had she looked into her wardrobe and chosen a pretty, pale pink morning gown of the finest muslin over an ivory sarsnet slip. The neckline was modest, there were lace ruffles at the hem, and she wore pearls threaded through her raven curls.

"I don't know why I feel so nervous," she whispered to Gabriel as they started forward.

"You don't wish it were real...do you?"

Mouette gave him a sidelong glance and shook her head. Yet, as she walked slowly toward Justin and felt his scorching gaze on every inch of her body, she wasn't at all certain what she truly wanted.

* * *

DURING THE BRIEF CEREMONY, Justin felt his mother staring at him, but he found that he didn't care. He was much more interested in Mouette. As the pretend-vicar droned on, Mouette looked up at him with her beautiful blue eyes and he couldn't stop wondering what she was thinking.

There were moments when he swore he felt her hands tremble in his, especially when he repeated after the vicar, "With this ring I thee wed, with my body I thee worship, and with all my worldly goods I thee endow..."

Justin wondered why he had never noticed that wedding vows were so extravagantly romantic. Those weren't words he would ever consider saying to any woman, even in the privacy of the bedchamber, even if he imagined that he might truly be in love. Yet he seemed to have no choice but to utter the entire speech, in church, before a lot of people. Including his mother. Out of the corner of his eye, he saw her watching, listening, judging. Her dark eyes were as sharp as ever.

The sound of Mouette's voice brought him back to the present with a jolt. The cursed vicar was compelling her to repeat a lot of nonsense, too. Yet, when Justin looked into her eyes as she spoke, he could almost believe that she meant every word, every vow of love.

He tried, for a moment, to think of her breasts or derrière instead. To remember that morning, when she had stood outside his door and he had been naked except for a sheet wrapped around his hips. *Any* physically-arousing thought would be preferable to this confounding swirl of emotions.

"In the name of the Father, and the Son, and the Holy Ghost, Amen," said Mouette.

He hadn't expected the marriage ceremony to sound so solemn and real. From a distance, he heard the vicar pronouncing them husband and wife.

"Aren't you going to kiss your new bride?" prompted Cerise St. Briac.

Justin wanted to ignore her, but after all this entire charade had been for her benefit. Soon she wouldn't be there at all.

"Maman," he replied evenly, while slipping an arm around Mouette's waist, "some things are better kept for the privacy of our bedchamber."

"Then, come and kiss your poor maman instead." She looked at Mouette and added, "Both of you, *mes filles.*"

It was Mouette who went first, dropping low on bended knee to kiss Cerise's pale cheek. And Xavier was only too eager to embrace his new daughter-in-law, clearly taking stock of her physical attributes. As annoying as all of this was to Justin, he was grateful for the handful of guests who mingled around them, offering congratulations. Even though most of them knew the truth, they all seemed happy to join in the act.

Feeling a little better, Justin agreed that he and Mouette would stay and partake of some of the wedding meal that Primmie was assembling on tables in the courtyard. Mr. Snuggs, resplendent in his ancient red waistcoat, tottered to and fro, shooing the cats away.

"Mayhap my two boys will bring me in my chair to the garden," Cerise pronounced.

Justin looked at Gabriel and arched a brow. Of course, their mother would love to be the center of attention, especially if both her sons were involved in the scene! Quickly, however, he felt ashamed for his ungenerous thoughts. As they lifted the chair and carried her toward the brick courtyard, Cerise lay back against her pillows and gasped for air, as if she might not be able to draw many more breaths. What if she died this afternoon? Did he want his last feelings toward her to be stained with suspicion?

"Maman, what can we get you?" he asked after they had set her chair down, in a cool spot under a tree.

"I have brought my beautiful bride some sparkling wine from the region of Champagne," Xavier said grandly as he approached with a crystal glass. "No doubt it will restore her."

"Excellent," Cerise approved.

"Wine?" Justin frowned. "Do you think it is wise, Father? I had thought Maman might better tolerate a bit of weak tea."

"If I must die, why deprive myself of this excellent wine?" she argued, bestowing a grateful smile upon her husband as she reached for the glass. "*Merci, mon ange.*"

Had any man ever been burdened with such a difficult mother?

"Woof!"

"Look," cried Charles Brandreth. "It's Robinson, our new dog!"

Justin turned to see the corgi bounding across the courtyard on his stubby legs. He ran right past Charles until he reached Justin, jumping as high as he could, in an unsuccessful effort to land in his arms.

"Down!" Justin ordered. The dog obeyed and sat at his feet. "How did this mongrel get here?"

Mouette came into view, holding a glass of champagne and wearing the knowing smile that he found particularly irksome.

"No doubt Robinson followed you here, my dear husband," she said. "Clearly he can't bear to be parted from you, and who can blame him?"

Charles had joined them by now, with the other children close behind. He attached a thin piece of rope to Robinson's collar and, after giving Justin a disapproving glance, led the dog off to the other side of the courtyard. Even young Anthony wore an expression of disappointment when he gazed at Justin.

"You'll have to do better than that if you intend to be a step-father to those boys," said Xavier.

"Just so," Cerise chimed in. "And soon, no doubt, you and our darling Mouette will be welcoming a babe of your own. That is my dream, you know, to be assured that you will carry on our line after I am gone."

"What?" he exclaimed. "That's nonsense. Gabriel has already done that."

"But it's not the *same*," she persisted. "He is not my first-born son. You will always hold an exalted place in our family, because of that. And Gabriel has *daughters*. Not that I have anything against females..." Cerise paused to chuckle at this sally, and then began to cough. "But you know, there is nothing like a son."

Was she changing the demand she'd made of him? Was it no longer enough that he had agreed to be constrained by the bonds of matrimony?

"Maman," Justin ground out, "you go too far."

As her coughing subsided, Cerise squinted up at Mouette. "You are still able to bear children, I presume?"

"We shall see, madame," came her poised reply.

Sebastian was weaving his way through the guests, all the while gazing at Mouette as if he were her champion. "I have been sent to tell you that Julia and Primmie are bringing the cake."

"How kind of you," Mouette said, smiling. "We can't thank you enough for sharing your home with us on this special day."

"It is our pleasure."

"And you provided the chapel, my lord," Cerise interjected. "That was essential for the union to be legal!"

Justin was contemplating wheeling his mother away from the guests when he was distracted by the sight of a thin, slightly stooped man coming around the side of the house. Where had he seen him before? Glancing toward Mouette, he realized that she was having the same thought.

"I believe that is the man who was in the garden at Leyton Court," she whispered.

Justin nodded, but didn't say that he was also the stranger who had appeared on the steps to Daphne's workroom at the net loft.

Meanwhile, Sebastian's face was going white. And

Izzie was running toward them, her soft summery gown held up in one hand so she wouldn't stumble. Brother and sister were both staring at the uninvited guest.

"Devil take it," Sebastian muttered. "It's my prodigal brother, George!"

CHAPTER 18

This can't be happening, thought Isabella as she rushed across the courtyard. The sight of George, who was not only her oldest sibling but also the rightful Marquess of Trevarre, filled her with mixed emotions. Even though George had done terrible things, and had been in exile in Italy for two decades, she had never given up hope that he might reform one day.

In her quest to help her brother find redemption, Isabella had nearly lost Gabriel. Thank God she had seen the light.... but now, here he was, back in Cornwall for the first time in a decade.

Sebastian reached out to take her hand as she drew near, as if he could read her mind. He had always been much harsher in his attitude toward their older brother. George had gambled away nearly everything that belonged to the Trevarre family, then fled to Italy and left Sebastian to clean up his mess. If not for George, Sebastian would never have chosen to occupy Trevarre Hall, the family's remote and rustic Cornwall estate. He'd been forced to resort to smuggling to restore the place and replenish his coffers, but Isabella suspected that Sebastian now loved it here and wouldn't change his circumstances even if he could.

"Today of all days!" she whispered. "I can't believe it."

"Oh, I can," muttered Sebastian. "Do you imagine that George would behave as a considerate adult?"

Isabella swiveled to search out Mouette. Even though this was a pretend wedding, it certainly felt real enough. Mouette seemed nervous yet radiant, and the effect was charming. Justin kept staring at her when he thought no one noticed. His poor dying mother seemed to be enjoying herself as well. How could George pick today of all days to turn their lives on end?

George was moving toward Isabella, as if he expected her to open her arms and welcome him. But it was Sebastian who stepped in front of her to block George's path.

"You are interrupting a celebration," he said coldly. "I don't know what you're doing here, but I must ask you to go and sit down. I will speak to you after our guests have departed."

"But, Sebastian," he implored, "are you not even a bit pleased to see your brother after so many years? Izzie has assured me that you still carry a torch of filial love for me, no matter what you might say."

Isabella listened in shock to this, remembering the ordeal George had subjected her to in France, and the times she had tried to persuade him to come home to England and make an effort to reform. Perhaps she had even said that Sebastian still loved him, deep inside. But that had been ten long years ago! How manipulative he was to repeat her entreaties now, as if they were freshly-made.

"George," she hissed, "Sebastian is right. You have appeared at a very inconvenient time. We will all talk later."

"Of course." George, the Marquess of Caverleigh, looked around at the curious guests and gave a nervous sniff. "I will wait. I have all the time in the world."

* * *

After a few hours of food, cake, and many glasses of wine, Justin and Mouette were sent off in the barouche, back to Frenchman's Lair and their supposed wedding night. Even Baptiste stood with the other guests to wave them away. When Justin protested that he must also come home, the servant shook his head.

"*Mais non*! Your mother insists that you and the new Madame St. Briac must be completely alone tonight, m'sieur. She invites all of your servants to stay at Elysium, to give you privacy."

How dare she? Justin was about to override this plan when, from the corner of his eye, he felt his mother watching him. She was lying against the pile of silk cushions in the three-wheeled chair, partially shielded from the sunlight by the spreading branches of a great yew tree. Her gaze was razor-sharp.

"You no doubt wish to thank me," she murmured.

His brows flicked upward. Mouette stood by his side, waiting to enter the barouche, and now Justin felt her fingers in his again, squeezing gently. It was just enough to help him pause and slowly inhale.

"How thoughtful you are, Maman," he said.

"One day I will no longer be here to help with these small details. For now, you must forget about me and enjoy your wedding night to the very fullest, *mon cher*."

* * *

As they entered the empty manor house, Mouette set her wedding bouquet and the paper-wrapped layer of her bride cake on a small tripod table.

"I find it very odd, not to have Baptiste appear to offer us refreshment." Justin frowned as he looked around the entrance hall and into the refurbished drawing room. "Have I told you that the house is looking very impressive? You have impeccable taste."

Mouette warmed to his praise. "That's very kind of you, but of course, you've had a hand in it."

"Then we both have impeccable taste." He flashed a grin.

Feeling unaccountably nervous, Mouette said, "I should go to my room and put away my bonnet, then I'll see what there is for us to eat."

"Your room? What room?"

She pulled at the silk ribbons of her bonnet. "When I realized that I would have to stay here now that we are pretending to be married, I claimed one of the bed-chambers for my own." His gaze seemed burn her. "It's a pretty chamber that opens off the morning room. I mean, your *study*."

"You intend to sleep downstairs?" Justin almost sounded offended.

"I thought it would be more proper, since, well—" How could she explain that she was afraid to take the bedchamber that connected to his, where Pendudwell's wife had once slept? Mouette couldn't imagine lying in bed at night with Justin on the other side of a single door, and she wasn't certain either of them could be trusted to keep that door closed.

Justin brusquely interrupted her thoughts. "Show me this room of yours."

Mouette led the way through to the morning room, where the window casements were flung open. It was a lovely late afternoon, and a fragrant summer breeze wafted in from the gardens that they'd begun to tame. A bouquet of roses and lilies, picked and arranged by Mouette that morning, graced the ebony-inlaid table Justin prized.

At the back of the room, a narrow door led to the corridor accessing the servants' quarters. Mouette went through it, followed by Justin.

"You can't sleep back here," he grumbled.

She opened the door to her new room. It was furnished with what had been the housekeeper's bed, as well as a washstand and a bureau. Mouette had chosen a favorite blue-and-white Copeland pitcher and bowl to brighten the space. Still, she wasn't surprised to see Justin's face darken with disapproval.

"You can't stay in here."

"I have to sleep somewhere in this house, and it cannot be in your bed, m'sieur." Her heart was pounding. "Do you recall that we have an arrangement?"

"Ah yes, the arrangement. The one wherein I am forbidden to touch you. It all ends when you receive a small fortune for your time and efforts."

Mouette burned with outrage. How dare he? Now that she had gone through with the make-believe wedding, did he intend to make light of the terms she had set for their bargain?

"Yes, m'sieur, that is exactly the arrangement to which I was referring," she said coolly. He must not suspect that she had felt swelling moments of tenderness toward him today, especially during the ceremony. Moments when she had let herself imagine that the wedding was achingly real, that Justin loved her, wanted to be her husband—and even a father to her sons. "As I recall, the entire plan was *yours*. You begged me to help you, and I generously agreed."

He gave a derisive snort but seemed to stop himself from replying in kind. "It has been a very trying day.

We are both tired. I suggest that we find some food, and then if you wish to come in here, lock the door, and sleep in that miserable bed, so be it."

* * *

JUSTIN TOOK off his charcoal-gray tailcoat and unknotted his cravat. Glancing over at the giant tester bed, he thought of the mean little room Mouette had chosen for herself at the other end of the house. Then, for just an instant, he imagined her lying on his unmade bed, the linens in disarray. Mouette's gleaming black hair tumbled about her shoulders, her lips were parted in invitation, her breasts were swollen with desire, and she was opening her thighs to him so that he could see—

Quickly, Justin stepped closer to the wall and struck his head against it. Hard. What the devil was wrong with him? Perhaps he ought to go into Fowey, or even Truro, and find a whore. But how many times would he have to have her in order to quench this insatiable need?

A moment later came a discouraging realization. Rather than being tantalized by the thought of an anonymous female who would do whatever he bade, he was repulsed. Justin glanced at himself in the mirror on his shaving stand and arched a brow above his eye-patch.

"What do you have to say for yourself?" he muttered.

Just then, Mouette called up from the stairway, "Will you come down and help me with our dinner?" She sounded almost conciliatory.

Justin's heart gave a strange little leap. As he went out the door, he decided it must be because he was so hungry.

* * *

THE SUN WAS BEGINNING to set outside the kitchen window as Mouette cracked fresh eggs into a blue pottery bowl. She had found fresh tarragon, a crock of butter, and ripe tomatoes in the larder. Baptiste's favorite copper pan was heating on a grate set over a low fire in the hearth.

"Eggs? Our wedding dinner is to be *eggs*?"

Mouette's breath caught at sound of Justin's familiar, sardonic voice. She looked up to see his powerful body nearly filling the doorway. He was coatless and the silver strands in his dark hair glinted in the firelight.

And there was something in his gaze that made her feel at once nervous and aroused. "I thought, after the amount of food that was served at Trevarre Hall today, we might both welcome a lighter meal." Pausing, she began to beat the eggs. "And I wanted to practice cooking an *omelette*."

He immediately responded, "What could you possibly know about the art of preparing an *omelette*?"

Mouette felt him beside her, felt the heat of his gaze as he took in the gown she had exchanged for her wedding costume. It was the simplest of muslin round gowns, cut fashionably low to reveal half her bosom, and overlaid with filmy gauze. To her embarrassment, her breasts went rosy under his regard.

"I have been watching Baptiste," she told him, seizing on a topic of conversation. "He has instructed me."

Justin made a dismissive sound. "What does he know about it? I learned to make an *omelette* from Napoleon's own chef." He began to fold up his shirtsleeves. "It is an art."

"So you have said." Unable to stop herself from smiling, Mouette bit her bottom lip.

"Of course, I shall require an assistant." Justin tied a towel around his narrow hips. "Butter, if you please."

She proffered a lump of butter and watched as he put it in the pan and it began to sizzle. Next, the beaten eggs were added. Lean muscles stood out in his forearm as he gently shook and tipped the pan with one hand, cooking the eggs to perfection.

"I'm surprised you have these sorts of skills," Mouette remarked. "I thought you were the sort of wealthy man who employed an army of servants to see to your needs."

Justin deftly tipped the *omelette* out of the pan onto a plate. "Herbs?" He took the dish of chopped, fresh tarragon from her and flicked some of it between his strong fingertips, over the delicately-cooked eggs. "I had to learn to cook when I was very young. My parents were away, as I have told you, playing their love games."

When he said the word *love*, his voice held a disparaging note. Mouette's heart ached, not only for him, but also for any fledgling dreams she might have been nurturing. "Clearly, you are a man of many talents."

"You have only begun to discover them, my lady." Justin arched a wicked brow.

Mouette sliced fresh tomatoes as he made a second *omelette* and uncorked a bottle of Pendudwell's wine. The liquid was darker than rubies as it poured into the glasses. Their plates were beautiful and fragrant.

They took seats there together at the long, rough table, and Mouette sampled the *omelette*. Closing her eyes, she gave a soft gasp. "Oh!"

"I perceive from your expression that you approve," he murmured, amused.

"I don't know if I have ever tasted anything better!"

"You are being kind, I suspect, since I am aware that you have dined in England's finest palaces." Raising his glass, he added, "Perhaps my humble eggs taste especially delicious because of the occasion."

Mouette's heart was beating faster as she raised her own glass and waited for his toast.

"We have not only survived our wedding charade, but my mother was clearly fooled," Justin said. "I deeply appreciate the seeming sincerity of your performance today." He lightly touched his glass to hers. "*Salut.*"

One moment, Mouette was soaring with euphoria, the next moment if was as if he had stolen the air from under her wings. What did it mean?

"I agree that your mother appeared to enjoy the wedding. And was that not your purpose?"

"Just so." He stared at her for a moment. "You are taking a chance, you know, being here with me alone. Unchaperoned."

"Everyone thinks we are married," she replied. Her heart fluttered faster.

"But one day they will know otherwise."

"That's true." Mouette tilted her head, considering his words, and felt a tendril of her hair come loose and fall against her cheek. "But I am not a maiden whose virtue must be protected. And, when this is all over, I shall return to London...far away from Cornwall. I doubt that any gossip about our arrangement will follow me back to my real life."

A faint smile touched his hard mouth. "Tell me more about your *real* life."

"Oh, well, it is as one might imagine. London is quite wonderful, of course! There are endless social engagements, the very best shops—"

"That's not what I mean," Justin broke in. "I know very well what amuses the *ton*. But is that what you really want, when you return to your house in London with the fortune you'll earn for being my make-believe wife?"

Mouette watched as he reached forward to tuck the wayward tendril behind her ear. As he did so, his blunt fingertip grazed her temple and sent a shower of sparks over her most intimate nerves. He smelled of soap and tobacco. She had to bite the inside of her lip to suppress a soft groan. *He sees,* she thought. *He knows what he does to me!*

"That is what I have always enjoyed," she said weakly. Her cheeks were hot. "It shall be a great relief to be able to maintain my former standard of living, without worrying about the bills."

"Ah, yes. And that standard of living will make you more attractive to the sorts of men who might propose marriage. A legitimate marriage, one you deserve." Justin poured more wine for both of them. "What about the cake? I thought we brought some home."

"We did." Mouette glanced at the muscles that flexed in his thighs as he reclined, waiting. She half-expected the aged splat-back chair to snap in two. "Would you care for the lovely iced bride cake, or the dark, dense groom cake?"

"I will have the bride cake." He arched a black brow. "Naturally."

Mouette was relieved to go into the larder, where she had put the cakes to keep them cool. For a moment, she leaned against the stone wall and hoped her own cheeks would cool down. Perhaps it was the wine that made her feel this way, she told herself, all the while knowing the truth.

When she returned to the kitchen, Mouette found Justin absently rubbing his left knee. The moment she appeared, he stopped.

"Doesn't it look delicious?" She set the plate down before him.

Justin regarded the generous wedge of bride cake, a confection consisting of layers of cake and marzipan topped by thick white icing. There were flowers arranged on top, the same pretty violets that had graced Mouette's simple bouquet.

"You brought all this for me? Where is your fork?"

"I have eaten quite enough today," she demurred.

He took a bite, then broke off another piece with his fork. "You are the bride." He held it up, so that the sugary icing touched her lips.

When Mouette opened her mouth, Justin inserted the fork just a bit, so that she could nibble at the cake. Their eyes met as she touched her tongue to the icing. A pulse throbbed between her legs. The cake came in a little farther and she worked at it with her teeth.

Justin shifted slightly in the chair. When Mouette glanced over, she saw his impressive erection, straining against the snug trousers he wore. It seemed that she could feel the heat of his body, even though they weren't touching.

Not quite.

Later, she would wonder what possessed her to lean forward slightly, so that she took the entire bite of cake into her mouth. Her lips closed around the fork. His fingers, so much larger than her own, were so close she could smell him, and his male scent was like a drug.

"Mouette," he said suddenly, drawing the fork out of her mouth. His voice had become a growl. "I am going to kiss you."

Oh, yes, please...

CHAPTER 19

$\mathcal{W}$hen Justin rose to his feet and drew her into his arms, she came up halfway to meet him. There was nothing else in the world at that moment but her need for him.

At six-and-thirty years of age, after a decade-long marriage that ended in a deadening series of betrayals, Mouette had given up on any dreams that she might feel such exquisite arousal. She didn't care about propriety or the terms of their agreement or even her pride. Nothing mattered but that moment when he crushed her against his broad chest and took her mouth with his.

It came to her, dimly, as she opened her lips under his and welcomed his tongue, that his kiss was burningly familiar... Suddenly, Mouette knew that they had been together like this before, but she couldn't think clearly enough to wonder what it meant. She only knew that she needed more.

"*Chérie,*" Justin muttered. He tore away his already-loosened neckcloth.

Mouette sank one hand into his thick, black hair, and touched his neck with the other. As they kissed on and on, she felt drunk on the taste of him. When his tongue moved suggestively, back and forth inside her mouth, her hips suddenly bucked against his erection.

"Oh, I am shameless," she whispered as they stopped kissing long enough to gulp more air.

"For God's sake, don't stop." His tone was tender and rough.

Mouette felt him tugging at her thin bodice, drawing it down from her shoulders. When her breasts were bared, the dark-rose nipples puckered in the lamplight, Justin made a sound deep in his throat. He covered both breasts with his hands, his palms warm against her nipples, and she pressed closer, aching for more and more.

With the side of one forearm, Justin pushed their plates out of the way and laid her back on the table. It was thrilling when he covered her slim form with his bigger, harder body. The heat of him seemed to brand her flesh. Helplessly, Mouette reached down to tug her skirts up, opening her thighs beneath him.

His fingers were deft, lightly pinching and massaging her breasts until her nipples ached and strained. When at last he gave her his mouth, she began to moan. He suckled until she thought she would go mad. She was so wet, unable to stop her hips from seeking him.

Justin raised his head just long enough to stare into her heavy-lidded eyes. "Mouette, it shouldn't be like this—"

"Yes," she insisted, "just like this."

* * *

FOR A LONG MOMENT, Justin gazed down at Mouette. Ebony hair swirled around her on the rough table, her beautiful face was flushed with desire, and her lips drove him mad. As he wondered whether she needed rescuing from this madness, she reached for his hand

and drew it down between her legs. The last of his self-control burned away when he touched her heat, her wet need. Now she was fumbling with the buttons on the flap of his trousers. When she managed to pry them open, his cock sprang into her small, soft hand.

"Oh!" cried Mouette. Her fingers closed around him and he saw stars.

"This is folly." But his fingers told a different story, touching her in exactly the way he knew she needed to be touched.

They were caught up in a voracious tidal wave of need, it seemed, and there was only one escape. They kissed, caressed, licked, stroked until Mouette threw her head back on the table and arched her back, trembling, moaning. Justin had just brought her to a blinding climax, and now she narrowed her eyes at him and guided him between her thighs.

"I can't take you here—" he muttered.

She did not respond, only pushed herself against him so that his sensitized shaft entered an inch or two. She was so slick and ready, yet her channel tightened around him in the sort of embrace men dreamed of.

He reminded himself that she was not some innocent maiden, but a grown woman who had children. What the devil did he think he should protect her from? And wasn't it too late, anyway?

Groaning, Justin bent over her on the kitchen table and cupped her buttocks in both hands. Mouette clasped her fingers around his damp neck, bringing her mouth to his, and their bodies began to fuse, one excruciatingly pleasurable inch at a time. When he was fully inside her, her muscles clenching around him, they began to rock together, faster and faster, until he couldn't hold back another instant.

As his essence poured into her, Justin closed his eyes and surrendered to the searing pleasure.

Nirvana.

There was only one sexual experience in his life that could match this one...

It had been a decade ago, on the night of Gabriel's wedding, when Justin had first met and mated with Mouette—who was then very much another man's wife.

* * *

MOUETTE AWOKE to bright sunlight streaming through the plain, parted drapes that hung at an unfamiliar window. She blinked. What time was it? Where was she?

And, dear God, was she naked?

Lying back, she closed her eyes and let fragmented memories of the night before come together in her mind. Justin, *Justin*. The pace of her heart kicked up just thinking of him. Hot blood washed her face as she forced herself to remember the things they had done. On the kitchen table. And in this bed. She could smell him here. The pillow beside her was creased where his head had lain. And the most intimate part of her body was tender from the utter rapture of their coupling.

Slowly then, Mouette faced the other memories that she had blocked out until the first kiss they'd shared last night. The moment his tongue had entered her mouth and she'd tasted him, the past had come rushing back.

How had she managed to block it out for ten full years?

A potent attraction had kindled between her and Justin the moment they'd met on the road to Trevarre Hall. He had known she was married, yet seemed to sense in some primal way that she not only didn't love Harry, but had never known true fulfillment in her husband's bed.

Both of them had drunk too much wine during Izzie and Gabriel's post-wedding festivities at Trevarre Hall. The next morning, when Mouette awoke in much the same state she was in today, she had not been able to remember what had happened. She told herself she must have been so tired, she hadn't bothered to don a bedgown. She told herself that she may have imbibed too freely, but if it had been anything more, she would surely remember!

Justin St. Briac had sailed away from Cornwall immediately. Before she returned to London herself with little Charles, Mouette heard that Justin had gone not to France, but to the Indian Ocean to fight the British with a famous French pirate called Surcouf.

She had felt changed somehow, yet glad for it. And grateful that she would never see Justin St. Briac again. Some forms of temptation were better off kept at a safe distance.

Mouette hadn't wanted to remember what had happened. And with each passing year, she had continued to cover over any memories that might have tried to stir.

A knock came at her door. "Mama?"

Good Lord, it was Anthony! "Just one moment, darling." She climbed out of bed naked and rummaged through her unpacked valise to find a dressing gown. Donning it quickly, she walked over to open the door.

Her handsome little son was waiting in the corridor, wooden sword in the makeshift scabbard at his side. "Baptiste suggests that it is time you greet the day," he pronounced.

"I—I didn't realize that all of you would be here this morning," she said. "How did you know where to find me?"

"Justin told me. After we arrived, he said that you were very tired after yesterday and we must let you sleep, but now the day is quite advanced." Pausing, Anthony smiled. "Justin said that, henceforth, Charles and I are welcome to address him by his Christian name... although I would prefer to call him Papa. You can imagine how Charles would feel about that!" Anthony rolled his long-lashed dark eyes.

Mouette bit her lower lip. How happy he seemed! Perhaps she didn't have to try to explain the true nature of this marriage quite yet. Embracing her son, she murmured, "Give me a few minutes to dress. All right, darling?"

"All right!" He started to turn away, adding, "I was surprised to find you in this little room, Mama. Shouldn't you be sleeping upstairs, in Justin's grand bed? It's so much better than this one, and just the sort I intend to have when I am a man."

"I have no doubt that you shall have one, Anthony," Mouette said wryly.

***

THE VERY THOUGHT of facing Justin again made Mouette's palms sweat and her throat go dry. But when she came into the dining room, where Baptiste was waiting to serve her breakfast, he was not in sight.

Baptiste said nothing about the late hour as he brought a tray with warm rolls and butter, a pot of chocolate, and strawberries from their fledgling garden. Mouette found that she couldn't look at him without blushing, so she kept her eyes averted and took a chair.

"Were you cooking eggs in my kitchen, my lady?" he asked.

Dear God, that's right—they had left a terrible mess behind! The memory of the food-strewn plates Justin had pushed aside brought hot blood to her cheeks.

What must the kitchen have looked like when Baptiste arrived? "I—yes. I apologize for the untidiness! I grew very fatigued last night, quite suddenly…"

He gave her a quizzical look. "Untidiness? Not at all! M'sieur was washing up when I came in early this morning. The kitchen was scrubbed clean. But he did mention that you had prepared a very fine *omelette*."

As she watched him hurry away, Mouette became aware of the little throb behind her eyes, a reminder of the wine she'd drunk last night. Never again in the presence of Justin St. Briac! From now on, she would be on guard.

"*Bonjour*."

He came into the room like a force of nature. Clad in buckskins, top-boots, and a fresh white shirt with a deftly-knotted cravat, Justin exuded masculinity and self-assurance.

Mouette, meanwhile, felt so desperately warm, she wasn't certain she could speak. "Good morning," she managed to murmur.

"It is midday." He arched a black brow above his visible eye and Mouette momentarily focused on the eye-patch, suddenly wondering if he had removed it in the darkness of her bed. "You slept well?"

She expected see a knowing smile, but to her surprise his expression was serious. "Yes."

Justin took a chair beside hers and reached for her hand. "Mouette, while we are momentarily alone, there is something I must say to you."

In spite of her resolve to resist him, her heart leaped. He sounded so sincere! "I am listening."

"I want to apologize…for last night. I was guilty of breaking our agreement."

Shattering it, you mean, she wanted to say, but instead whispered, "You did not force me."

"That's true."

Mouette looked up and saw the devils dancing in his eyes. The urge to go into his arms and welcome his kiss was almost overwhelming.

"Still, I broke my word," he continued. "I must confess that I have wanted to do those things from the moment we met again, but I should have been stronger. You are a lady. You have another life, in London, as you have told me so often. We had a business arrangement. I—"

"You have another life as well. In France."

"That is so true." He poured himself some chocolate. "Have you been to Saint-Malo, where I live?"

"No, although I have visited many other parts of France."

Justin shook his head dismissively. "No other town in all the world can compare with Saint-Malo. It is magical. You would adore it, I can promise." Then, as if realizing that he was veering into risky territory, he lifted the fragile cup of chocolate. Drinking from it, he grimaced. "This is horrible!" He pronounced the last word in the French way "Henceforth, you should drink coffee."

"You are very arrogant, m'sieur," Mouette said, though she had already planned to ask Baptiste to serve her coffee in the future.

"Don't you think you should call me Justin, after all we have been through together?"

He was staring at her mouth, as if remembering the sinful things she had done with it last night, and Mouette was shocked to feel a rush of arousal. "I don't know what you mean."

"Of course you don't." His eyebrow flicked up again as he rose from the table. "Shall we agree to pretend that nothing improper has occurred between us?"

"Yes, thank you." Then, unable to help herself, she caught his sleeve and whispered urgently, "Justin, I must ask you—was this the *first* time? I have had a memory, I think, but perhaps it was a dream…about something that might have occurred between us on an earlier occasion." She swallowed. Her cheeks were so warm. "On the night Izzie and Gabriel were married. That is—"

"You needn't say more." For one blessed moment, he was serious again, even tender. Tipping her chin up, he gazed into her eyes. "It was no dream, *chérie.*"

* * *

JUSTIN WAS EXCESSIVELY RELIEVED to escape the manor house. Why was it so hard to take a deep breath today? He searched for his snuffbox, deciding that perhaps if he rode hard to the cliffs and could look out at the English Channel, he would feel better. If the sky was clear, he could see the faint outline of the coast of Brittany.

Home.

"Woof!" Something nipped hard at the heel of his boot.

"Robinson!" It was the voice of young Charles Brandreth, calling from the stables. "Robinson, where are you?"

The dog had begun trying to jump up into Justin's arms. "See here, you mongrel, why do you persist in doing that when you know damned well I am not going to catch you? Leave me alone."

Charles and Anthony were racing toward him down the grassy slope, laughing. It was amazing how free they both looked, Justin thought, considering how uncertain and complicated their lives were.

As they drew closer, Robinson ran to meet them, dancing on his stubby hind legs. Good. Perhaps the dog would finally transfer his misplaced loyalties to Mouette's sons.

"What shall we do today?" exclaimed Anthony as he ran right up to Justin and embraced him.

"Perhaps you can spend the afternoon teaching your dog some manners," he said sardonically. Looking at Charles, he added, "If you want him to stay at Frenchman's Lair, he must be kept on a tether, not running loose, putting his muddy paws all over my good floors and fine furniture."

Charles pressed his lips into a line. "Yes, sir."

"Excellent." Justin began to draw on his riding gloves. "I will be away this afternoon."

"Oh, do take us with you!" cried Anthony.

"I don't want to go," said Charles. "Robinson and I have other plans."

Justin looked at the younger boy. "And you must stay here and look after your mama. I have an errand to attend to."

"All right," Anthony agreed. "When you return, will you show me your sword? The one you fight duels with?"

"Perhaps," Justin allowed with a wry smile. Nodding to them both, he started toward the stables. At the top of the hill, he paused and stole one backward glance. Charles had turned away, but Anthony and Robinson sat together, looking bereft as they gazed after him.

CHAPTER 20

Isabella paced to and fro in the dining room at Trevarre Hall while Sebastian and Julia sat at the long table, eating peas and roasted chicken left over from the wedding.

"We really made too much food for such an intimate party," Julia remarked.

"How can you two eat at a time like this?" Isabella paused to readjust her spectacles before continuing to pace.

"Because of George?" replied Sebastian. "I don't understand why you are so overwrought. Haven't you always longed for him to return to England?"

She stopped and stared at him. "Perhaps I did. Once. But it was really more of a *dream*."

"Izzie, come and have some food," Julia implored. "Primmie is cutting pieces of the cake for us."

"I ate far too much cake yesterday." She patted her hips but came to sit next to her brother. "Sebastian, you must understand. I looked up to George when I was young. I have always dreamed he might come home and change, even after he stole Gabriel's Leonardo da Vinci masterpiece."

He snorted. "That was only one of his many trans-gressions. There is a very good reason why he has been hiding in Italy and France for the last two decades."

"I know!" she leaned forward. "I am trying to tell you that I gave up my hope to rehabilitate him long ago. Time and maturity have made me realize that people like George don't change."

"He did some terrible things to you," Julia reminded her.

A voice interrupted from the doorway. "My little sister knows that I love her. I love and understand her in a way no one else ever could."

George stood there, silhouetted against the afternoon light that filtered through the parlor windows. Even though he had apparently slept until noon, he looked very tired.

"Come and sit down," said Sebastian. "You look awful. Eat and tell us why you have come back to England—and what you intend to do now that you are here."

As Primmie brought food for George, Izzie watched him, trying to sort out what was happening. Why had she ever longed for his return? Now that he was here, she felt a deep sense of foreboding.

"Tea?" he was asking as Primmie brought in a fresh pot, with a cup and saucer for him. "Is there nothing stronger?"

The housekeeper glanced toward Sebastian, who merely lifted his brows and said, "If you wish to stay here, George, I'll ask that you not imbibe spirits. Liquor brings you only trouble."

George's haggard face took on new color. "See here! You know nothing about me. I am not the person I once was."

"Are you not? If you no longer have a weakness for liquor, you won't miss it while residing at Trevarre Hall."

"Ale, then," George sniffed, turning his gaze back to Primmie.

"No," said Sebastian.

Watching this exchange, Isabella was struck anew by how little Sebastian and George looked like brothers. George was as fair as Sebastian was dark, and they weren't physically—or temperamentally—similar in any way.

Now, George's nostrils flared, but he refrained from further argument except to grumble, "Strictly speaking, this is *my* house. I am the Marquess of Caverleigh, lord of this manor—"

"And all the other properties you gambled away," finished Sebastian. "Have you forgotten the letter you left with our solicitor, stating that you were running away to Italy forever and insisting that I consider Trevarre Hall as my own? It was bitter consolation, since this place was a disaster when Julia and I arrived."

Julia put a hand on her husband's arm while Isabella watched the blood drain from George's face.

"See here," he croaked. "Are you completely without compassion for your own brother? Are we not flesh and blood?" His voice rose. "Can you not believe in a man's ability to change?"

There was silence for a long moment.

"George," whispered Isabella, "Are you telling us that *you* mean to change?"

"Yes." He grasped her forearms. "Please, give me a chance! Surely I deserve that much."

* * *

JUSTIN RODE HARD across the cliffs east of the tiny hamlet of Lansallos.

A few years before, he had helped a smuggling client bring a cargo ashore in a nearby cove. They'd nearly been discovered by the customs officers, but had managed to escape by traversing a little used path from the beach to Lansallos, while Lieutenant Adolphus Lynton and his men had lain in wait on another route.

A smile touched Justin's mouth as he remembered that perfect, moonless night. The very air he breathed had been charged with danger and excitement, a potent combination that he'd always found irresistible. No doubt that was what he was missing these days. His life was so dull at that cursed manor house, he'd begun to feel like a different person.

That must be the reason he was weakening in ways he had always rejected in the past. There had been moments last night, alone with Mouette in her bed, when he had wondered if he might actually be...falling in love.

Sangdieu! In the bright light of day, Justin could only shake his head at such madness. Next he'd be building a glass room with a special heating vent to grow pineapples. Or feeling so besotted, so unwilling to be parted from Mouette, that he would want to be next to her all day and all night.

Like that annoying dog Charles had adopted.

Pressing his knees into the flanks of his newly-purchased black stallion, Justin leaned forward and savored the feeling of freedom as Hugo galloped hard across the road to Polperro. Below them to the south, the English Channel spread like a glittering blanket of sapphires, sending foamy white-tipped waves crashing against the black rocks and golden beaches. And all along the cliffs, red valerian was in full bloom, clinging in long-stemmed clusters to the stony ground.

Yes, thought Justin, this was the life he craved. Utter and absolute freedom, the freedom to embark on any adventure on a moment's notice, without having to consider the feelings of a woman or—perhaps even worse, children. Wasn't that what it truly meant to be a man?

Even as they paused at the top of a hill that afforded a stunning view out to sea, Justin's pleasure was tinged with unease. Could it be that the pleasures of his youth no longer felt sufficient? Fortunately, he didn't have to ponder this for more than an instant because, just around the next turn, the waymarker for Polperro loomed up before them.

There would be an inn in the village where he could get a pint, though Justin knew he couldn't abide the food they would try to serve him there.

The lane twisted down through the trees, past simple cottages constructed of granite and ships' timbers. Justin was nearing the pilchard-scented harbor when he saw a door open to a dwelling set several steps above the road.

A young woman emerged, her face largely hidden by an exceedingly fashionable veiled bonnet, followed by a tall, thin old man.

Instantly, Justin recognized the lithe shape of Lady Daphne Leyton.

"*Bonjour*, milady," he greeted her, and swept off his hat. Then, taking a closer look, he realized that Daphne was in the company of Zephaniah Job, known as the "smugglers' banker."

The two men exchanged nods. Justin had known Job since the mid 1790's, when smuggling was still a thrilling and very lucrative adventure.

"I was very sorry to hear of the storm that ravaged Polperro's harbor last year," Justin told him gravely. He knew that the hurricane-force winds and the resulting tidal flood had wiped out many of Job's ships, several quays, and even many dwellings within the village.

Zephaniah Job nodded wearily. "Aye. We've come a long way toward repairing the damage and getting our men back to work, but it's been a painful time. Your brother has paid for three new fishing boats to be built, which allowed many men to put food on their tables."

"I'm pleased to hear that, but you must allow me to contribute as well. I'm afraid I was in France at the time of the storm."

"No need to apologize." Job was already turning back inside. "You are only a visitor here in Cornwall, are you not? Besides, the work is nearly finished."

Stung, Justin wondered how the old financier could afford to brush aside his funds. Surely Job had been forced to reach deep into his own coffers to aid in the rebuilding of the harbor, so why wouldn't he welcome Justin's contribution, however belated it might be?

"You can contribute to *my* cause," Daphne called softly to him. As she drew near, she lifted her veil enough to reveal a coquettish smile.

"You should not be walking about unaccompanied," Justin said as he dismounted.

"How gallant you are, sir. I must return to the net loft, and I confess to you alone, there have been men who have looked at me in ways that are improper."

Justin took Hugo's reins and led the big horse as they walked through Polperro's maze of narrow streets. Just as the net loft came into view, high atop Peak Rock, Daphne drew him into a narrow space between two whitewashed buildings.

"I shan't waste your time with polite conversation," she whispered urgently. "I need your help. The Guernsey merchant who has brought my lace and silk from France demands that I come to him to receive delivery."

"That has nothing to do with me." Justin pried her hand from his coat sleeve.

"Your ship is here, anchored just outside the harbor! Would it not be diverting for you to sail to Guernsey and retrieve my shipment?" Daphne pressed herself against him in the tiny space. "As soon as I sell the bonnets, I will pay you a share of my profits."

He shook his head. "I am only in Cornwall for a short time, on other business. I have no time to spare for such an errand."

"Oh, yes, of course. You are newly-*married*, are you not? I know better than anyone what that means to you," she sneered. "What would your poor mother say if she knew the truth about your wedding and your bride?"

Justin drew aside the veil that partially concealed Daphne's face and saw that her beautiful eyes were narrowed. The hairs on the back of his neck stood up. "Is that a threat?"

"Not if you help me. I'll wait for word from you, m'sieur."

With that, she hurried away from him and started up the path leading to Peak Rock. Justin knew a sense of foreboding, but he told himself that there were many solutions to this problem.

The easiest one, of course, would be to sail to Guernsey and smuggle Lady Daphne's contraband lace and silk back into Cornwall...

CHAPTER 21

$\mathcal{M}$ouette stood in the morning room, staring out the window, wondering where Justin had gone and when he would return.

"Mama, what are you doing in Papa's study?" Anthony asked from the doorway.

The unexpected sound of her son's voice made her jump. Pressing a hand to her heart, Mouette took a gulp of air. "Anthony Brandreth, you should not creep up on me that way. And I thought we had decided you would use M'sieur St. Briac's Christian name! Oh, and one more thing. This is my morning room, not his *study*."

The boy strode into the sun-dappled room and stopped beside the round, ebony-inlaid table. "All right, I shall continue to address him as Justin, for now." He pronounced the name in perfect imitation of Justin's French accent. "Charles has already threatened to choke me if I dare to call Justin 'Papa'. He is very devoted to our father's memory, you know."

Mouette swallowed. Of course she knew, and the thought of her older son idolizing Harry, who had turned out to be both dishonorable and false-hearted, made her feel ill. It was painful to think of him learning the truth about his father one day, yet for now, it was equally difficult to endure his protective attitude toward Harry.

"Where is Charles now?" she asked.

"He is outside on the terrace with Robinson, making a little city out of paper. He says he doesn't like this house." Anthony followed behind Mouette as she turned to leave the room. "But *I* like it very much! Justin promised to show me his dueling sword when he comes home today. I am hoping that it might have traces of *blood* on it."

Before Mouette could reply, the knocker sounded at the front door and Baptiste rushed past them to see who was there.

"Good afternoon, Baptiste," exclaimed a female voice. "Would it be terribly rude of me to ask if the newly-married couple is receiving visitors today?"

Mouette felt a surge of joy as she recognized Isabella's voice. She came into the entrance hall with arms outstretched, eager for Izzie's familiar embrace. Moments later, Baptiste had gone to make tea with Anthony in tow, and the two women were seated together on a settee in the drawing room.

"I am delighted by your visit, but what brings you here alone?" asked Mouette.

"I am only now returning home for the first time since your wedding," Isabella replied, removing her chip-straw bonnet. "Gabriel went back to Elysium with the girls last night, but I had to stay at Trevarre Hall. We had a family conference, about our brother George."

"With everything else that happened, I nearly forgot about Lord Caverleigh. It must have been a great surprise to see him again!"

"Indeed." Isabella rolled her eyes. "Actually, it was a shock. You never knew George, did you?"

"Only very slightly, when you and I were young, and our families were neighbors in Grosvenor Square. But of course, my family spent a great deal of time in Connecticut. By the time I was old enough to notice him, George had gone away to school."

"I'm sure you haven't forgotten the terrible things he did after my parents died and he inherited, because that's when your parents took me under their wing." She shook her head. "He has disgraced us all. And poor Sebastian would never be living in Cornwall if it weren't for George, who gambled away everything our family owned except Trevarre Hall."

Mouette considered this. Yes, she had been with Izzie during much of that tumultuous time, but how much attention had she really paid to what was happening in her friend's family? "Sebastian and Julia seem to be happy at Trevarre Hall—now."

"Oh yes, it has all worked out splendidly, but that's no thanks to George. And you must recall the mayhem he caused when he stole Gabriel's treasured painting." Isabella sighed and shook her head. "It's just very hard to have him return to Cornwall, in spite of the dreams I once nurtured that he might reform."

"Yes." Mouette allowed this to sink in. Thinking back to her first visit to Cornwall, at the time of Isabella's wedding, she felt ashamed of her own selfishness. Izzie had just been through a terrible ordeal with George and yet Mouette had been more concerned with the rustic surroundings—and her attraction to the disturbingly attractive Justin St. Briac. "Oh, my dear, I can only imagine how confusing this must be for you. George's reappearance must stir up so many emotions."

"Exactly!" Isabella turned to her eagerly. "How helpful it is to talk about this to a friend like you, someone who really understands and doesn't judge me."

Baptiste entered just then with a tray. It was laden with a tea and a plate of iced cakes decorated with candied violets. After he had served them and soundlessly disappeared, Isabella sampled her little cake.

"How selfish I am to come here on the day after your wedding and speak only of myself," she said with a teasing note. "How do you find married life?"

Mouette flushed. "You know very well it is only a make-believe marriage."

"Is that why your new husband has already deserted you?"

"I know you are being playful, but I must confess to a mixture of feelings today." She let herself look directly at Isabella, whose own gaze had become intent.

"Oh no. I was afraid of this! Justin is very compelling, especially when he chooses to be. Don't say that you've fallen in love with him!"

Isabella appeared to be so alarmed that Mouette could not tell her any more of the truth. Furthermore, she wasn't a bit sure she understood herself exactly what the truth was. "In love? Certainly not." Her laughter sounded rather hollow to her own ears. "You know me better than that. We have a business arrangement, though I will confess that it is easy to like Justin. He is very charming..."

"Yes," agreed Isabella. "Even intoxicating, I imagine." Pausing, she set down her cup and saucer. "My dear friend, you haven't done anything foolish, have you? After all, you two were alone last night."

For a moment, Mouette could feel the rough, hard surface of the table against her bare skin as Justin opened her thighs, touching her in wickedly thrilling ways Harry never had, ways she had only dreamed of before. Remembering how they had shamelessly coupled there, on the very table where Baptiste had prepared breakfast this morning, Mouette caught her lower lip between her teeth.

"What's wrong?" whispered Isabella, alarmed.

"Nothing!" Her heart was racing. Was the truth revealed on her face?

Isabella leaned closer. "My dear friend, you are older than I am and you were once married for several years, but in the event you never—" She paused, her eyes twinkling. "…quite achieved full *satisfaction* in your physical relationship with Harry, I can understand your longings. You cannot shock me!"

"I can't?"

"No! However, if it isn't too late, I would counsel you to exercise restraint with Justin." Isabella paused to lift her eyebrows. "If that is still possible."

Mouette wanted very much to confide in her friend but if she did so, Izzie would know too much when the time came for Mouette and Justin to part. This was, after all, an arrangement rather than a marriage, no matter how confusing it had become.

"I am grateful for your counsel," she said. "You, after all, know Justin much better than I do. I shall endeavor to follow your advice."

"Ah, Mouette, I know that your dear mother would be the first one to tell you that, once this is over and you are able to return to your new life in London, a good man who truly deserves you will come along. Someone who can love you, cherish you, and be a stable father for your boys." Isabella sighed regretfully. "Justin could never be that man. Stability is just not in his nature…"

Just then, Robinson began to bark insistently from the terrace behind the house. Charles could be heard telling the dog to be quiet, followed by a man's voice Mouette didn't recognize.

Rising, she murmured, "Pardon me, Izzie, but it seems we have a visitor..."

* * *

MOUETTE HURRIED through the spacious house with Isabella following in her wake. Who could be outside, talking to Charles? This was such an isolated spot, and they had virtually no servants. What if someone wanted to cause trouble? Just before emerging onto the terrace, Mouette picked up a sharp letter opener.

Robinson came rushing over to her, barking as if to tell her that there was a stranger among them and he had done all that he could to scare the man away. But what Mouette saw did not seem to be anything to worry about.

Charles was sitting on the same bench where Mouette and Justin had drunk wine together during one of their first visits to the manor house. On the seat beside him were what appeared to be three shapes that resembled houses, fashioned from stiff sheets of foolscap. Crouching before him on the flagstones was the thin, round-shouldered figure of a man Mouette immediately recognized as George Trevarre, Marquess of Caverleigh.

"Hello, Mother," said Charles.

"Oh, hello!" George looked up in surprise. Scrambling to his feet, he set down the half-constructed paper building that he'd been holding and introduced himself.

Just then, Isabella emerged from the house and gasped. "George! What are you doing here?"

He shrugged. "I was just passing by." He attempted a hopeful smile. "Darling Izzie, I only want to make amends for the past in any way I can. When I saw your little gig outside, I thought perhaps you might like an escort the rest of the way to Elysium."

"George has promised to make an entire paper city for me!" Charles exclaimed, more animated than Mouette had seen him in a very long time. "There is a town by the ocean in France, he says, completely surrounded by ancient walls."

"Like a fairy tale!" interjected Anthony.

"We are going to recreate the entire city!" Charles continued. "But Mother, we shall have to find a place inside the house to build it, away from the wind."

As he spoke, the breeze picked up one of his new buildings and carried it off. Charles gave a cry of alarm and rushed after it. George, meanwhile, looked at the two women and shrugged.

"My talents are few, but if I can use them to make someone happy, why not?"

Isabella was looking on warily. "What city do you mean? Saint-Malo?"

"Exactly," he beamed. "It's quite magical."

"It's Justin's home, you know," said Mouette.

"Indeed?" He smiled at her. "Then your new husband should appreciate my humble homage. Let us surprise him when it is completed. Perhaps we can include his very house in our model of the city…"

Charles's face lit up. "What a splendid plan!"

"George, you can't stay," Isabella broke in. "Didn't you say you wanted to escort me to Elysium?" Before her brother could reply, she exclaimed, "Oh dear, I've left my bonnet in the drawing room. I'll go and fetch it."

"Yes," he called after her as she went back into the house. "I'll accompany you."

Charles spoke again. "But you'll come again, won't you, sir?"

"Perhaps it would be better for you to visit me at

Elysium, young man." George got to his feet and looked at Mouette again. "If your mother will consent to that."

She didn't know what to say. "I—well, I will consider it."

He finished folding a crease into the roof of one house while gazing into her eyes. "My lady, do you believe in second chances?"

Goodness, it almost seemed that he might be referring to Mouette's own situation. Her heart skipped a beat. "I confess that I do, my lord."

"Please, you must not address me thus. I lost all claim to my title when I abused its privileges."

This frank admission caught her off-guard. "You are very hard on yourself, sir."

"George," he said, coming closer. "You must call me George. And if you believe in second chances, you will understand that during the course of our lives, we sometimes do things that we later regret. We take the wrong path, almost by accident, and it can be an immense challenge to find one's way back. That's what I am endeavoring to do now that I've returned to Cornwall."

"That is very…courageous of you." Mouette paused, sensing that it would mean a great deal to him if she said his name. "George."

"You believe, then, that a person might be capable of real change?"

"I am learning to believe that very thing," Mouette whispered.

"I desperately need a friend. Can you understand?"

Remembering how it felt to be shunned by all her so-called friends in London, she wanted to say that she understood exactly what he meant. "Yes. Yes, I do."

Just then Isabella appeared in the doorway and called a trifle impatiently, "George, are you quite ready?"

"Of course. I am at your service, darling Izzie." He gave his sister a broad smile. "And why don't we bring these two fine boys with us? Charles and I have a city to build, you know."

Without even waiting for his mother to agree, Charles jumped to his feet. "Yes! I would rather stay at Elysium."

Thankfully, Isabella gave George a warning glance and shook her head. "Not today. Charles, you and Anthony would be welcome to visit tomorrow. I hope you will bring Robinson, too. Camille has heard the legend of fairies using corgis as their steeds, and she hopes to make him a saddle."

CHAPTER 22

The sun was setting as Justin rode through the shadowy, green tunnel of trees leading to Frenchman's Lair. When he made the final turn and the manor house came into view, it was as if there were an invisible thread that pulled him closer, back to Mouette.

Slowing his pace, Justin waited to feel his usual, opposing urge to break free and ride away in the other direction. If he did so, he could begin plotting the voyage to Guernsey, to fetch Daphne's cargo of lace and silk.

It was an excellent excuse to escape from Cornwall altogether.

But there was still the matter of his dying mother. After all, that was why he had obtained this house, which he and Mouette had improved so drastically. And that was why he'd pretended to become leg-shackled to a wife.

As he rode up the drive, Justin appreciated for a moment how much it all had changed. The weeds were gone. The trees and shrubs were neatly pruned. And Anthony was tossing a stick for Robinson on the lawn.

It looked like someone's real home.

"You're back, at last!" cried the boy, who had to race the corgi to reach Justin first. "We've been waiting for you all day."

"It's only been a few hours." Justin felt the familiar tightening sensation in his chest. Where the devil had he put his snuffbox? "Will you kindly hold that dog while I dismount? Hugo might be spooked."

As if he were able to understand every word, Robinson politely sat down at Anthony's side.

"Where have you been?" asked Anthony, running along at Justin's side as he led Hugo toward the stables.

"You ask a shocking amount of inappropriate questions." He glanced down toward the boy. "I am a man and, as such, I have all manner of important business to see to during the day. I can rarely be at home. It's just the way of the world."

Robinson was herding them from behind, nipping occasionally at the heels of Justin's very expensive riding boots as he strode quickly up the hillside.

"But Gabriel stays home all day long," Anthony informed him. "He's very busy, growing lots of marvelous and delicious plants. And sometimes he makes us a fort or castle in the garden."

For God's sake, why must he be subjected to this speech from a precocious little boy? This was just one of the many reasons why Justin had no desire for children of his own. *Or dogs!* he thought, as Robinson attempted to bite his left heel.

"If you like my brother so well, perhaps you should pay him a long visit," Justin suggested in an undertone. "No doubt it would be far more entertaining than waiting for me to come home at the end of a long, trying day."

"Look!" Anthony pointed back down the drive, shading his eyes against the setting sun. "Someone is coming."

Joseph, the newly-hired stable boy, came forward to take Hugo's reins, and Justin walked back down the hill to meet the visitor. To his surprise, he saw that it was Helivet, riding a gray gelding and holding a small envelope in one hand.

"I've brought you a message from Elysium, m'sieur," said the Frenchman who had once been a seaman on board *Deux Frères*.

"*Merci.*" Justin accepted the folded parchment with a nod. As Helivet turned to go, he added, "Don't you sometimes miss your old life, Helivet? Remember the feeling of excitement we had when embarking on a new adventure?"

The younger man pursed his lips. "Perhaps I do, on occasion."

"Of course you do! You'd be mad not to."

Helivet sighed. "I've been keeping company with a girl from Bodinnick…"

"See here, I am prepared to give you that life again. Do not be shocked if I send word to you, asking you to meet me in Polperro harbor."

Anthony had come up behind him and pulled at his coat. "If you go away, you must take me, too!"

"Out of the question," Justin replied, sounding more brusquely than he'd intended. As Robinson began to bark and run around them in circles, Justin turned to Helivet. "I am grateful to you for riding out with this message. You should go now, while you still have enough light to guide you back to Elysium."

* * *

THE MANOR HOUSE welcomed Justin with candlelight and wonderful aromas.

"Mama is cooking," Anthony announced as they came into the stair hall.

He blinked. "Is she indeed? Your mother is a woman of surprising talents."

The boy's face shone with pride. "That's true!"

Robinson had pranced ahead of them, leaving a trail of muddy footprints on the priceless Kuba rug that Justin had wrested away from Lord Edgecumbe with no small amount of difficulty.

Turning, he shook a finger down at Anthony. "See here, I wanted no part of that mongrel. You and your brother are responsible for seeing to it that he doesn't ruin the fine things your mother and I have brought into this house." Justin pointed at Robinson, who stopped still and gazed back with wide, innocent eyes. "Take him away, clean his paws, and see to it that he doesn't bother me for the remainder of the evening. Which reminds me of another important thing you should learn. When a man returns home at the end of a long day, he craves a brandy and a bit of peace."

Anthony squared his boyish shoulders and nodded. "Yes, sir! I mean, Justin."

Somehow it didn't sound quite right when the boy said 'Justin,' but what else was he to call him? At the last moment, before Anthony and Robinson went off together, Justin reached out and touched the boy's black curls. He was rewarded by a sudden, incandescent smile.

"Go on, then. Both of you," he ordered gruffly before continuing on through the house, pulling off both doeskin riding gloves as he walked. Usually, he would have gone into his study and poured a large brandy, but tonight he felt curious to see what was causing the tantalizing smells that emanated from the kitchen.

The sounds of low voices and laughter reached his ears as he came into the room. Standing at the same hearth where he had cooked an *omelette* just the night before, Justin saw Mouette, Charles, and Baptiste. His eyes fell on the wooden table and erotic memories rushed back.

"*Bonsoir*, m'sieur!" Baptiste was exclaiming. "Come in. Madame and I are teaching Charles how to make a fine French dish." His black eyes were sparkling. "Napoleon's favorite, Chicken Marengo."

"More importantly, it is *my* favorite." For one long moment, his gaze met Mouette's and he knew that she was thinking about last night, too. She looked enchanting, wearing a borrowed apron that was too large over her charming muslin day gown. Her face was perspiring slightly and several curls had escaped their pins to caress her pink cheeks. When she smiled at him, Justin grew hard with longing. Longing for her.

"I have explained," Baptiste was saying, "that the recipe has been altered since it was originally made by Napoleon's chef, Dunand, just before the Battle of Marengo. They were about to engage in battle with the Austrian army and, of course, there were limited ingredients available in the town, so he was forced to use shrimp and cognac..."

As Baptiste continued to spin his tale, Justin was struck by how much more animated he was than he had ever been in Saint-Malo. Always, this perfect servant had been a model of circumspection, rarely offering more words than were called for in any given situation.

Until now!

"Baptiste, which version of the recipe are we making tonight?" asked Mouette as she poured more wine for the two of them. Nearby, Charles was solemnly chopping mushrooms with his own knife. "I thought Dunand used shrimp and cognac, but we have a chicken in the pot."

"My master prefers it as we are cooking it, with

chicken and white wine." He gave her a knowing look. "And only the finest wine will do."

"That is no surprise," Mouette agreed wryly.

Justin approached the table and inhaled appreciatively. "Ah, I smell the garlic. It is ambrosia." He found the towel he'd used as an apron the night before. After discarding his coat, he tied the towel around his hips and joined the little trio.

Charles watched him warily. "Perhaps I'll go upstairs and read."

"What are you reading?" Justin asked, his tone conversational.

"I told you, remember? *Robinson Crusoe*."

"Charles, you are forgetting your manners," his mother warned.

"Would you punish me by forcing me to stay at Elysium?" the adolescent boy challenged. He chopped harder with his knife. "You know that is where I would rather be."

Justin bristled when he saw the pain and uncertainty in Mouette's expression. Just moments before, she had been laughing, but now, thanks to this insolent young pup, she was unhappy.

"Apologize to your mother!" Justin heard himself demand in a harsh voice.

When Mouette gasped, he realized he had crossed some invisible boundary that had to do with being a parent. It was a right he had not earned.

"You can't order me about!" cried Charles. "You're not my father and you never will be!"

Justin wanted to pick him up off the ground by his collar and shake him, but when he felt Mouette's hand on his arm, a force he didn't understand compelled him to take a step back from Charles. He could hear his heart pounding in his ears.

"Charles," Mouette was saying, "You have been very rude. I must insist that you go upstairs immediately!"

The boy's face was red. He whirled around and ran from the kitchen.

Justin saw that both Mouette and Baptiste were staring at him accusingly. "What is it? You two don't think that was *my* fault, do you?"

"All I know is that we were having a splendid time until you appeared," Mouette said.

Stung, Justin untied his make-shift apron and tossed it on the table. "Why did I ever come in here in the first place?" He knew the answer to that, of course. He had been longing to see Mouette. "I had intended to go to my study and drink brandy, but some foolish impulse brought me here. Why did I imagine any of you might be pleased to see me?"

With that, Justin snatched up his coat and stalked from the kitchen. He expected Mouette to run after him or Baptiste to implore him to stop, but both of them were silent as he retreated down the corridor, alone.

* * *

It was much later when Mouette knocked softly at the double doors leading to her morning room.

"Hmmph," came a muffled response.

Tentatively, she pushed open the door with her hip and entered, carrying a tray. Justin was lying on the chaise she planned to upholster in green silk. A half-empty glass of cognac was positioned precariously in his dark hand, and he had nearly removed his cravat.

"Are you sleeping?" she asked briskly. "I've brought you some supper."

His eye-patch was slightly askew as he pushed himself to a seated position. "I thought you intended to

212

starve me as a means of punishment for my trans-gressions."

"Not at all. However, you are not the center of the universe. I am a mother and I had to see my sons into bed and off to sleep before I could think about feeding the wild, ungovernable member of this household."

A gleam came into his eye. Was it because she had used the word *household*?

"I perceive you are referring to me." He watched her pour a glass of Sancerre wine. "Will you not join me?"

Mouette had set the tray on the ebony-inlaid table and now she laid out his silverware, napkin, and dishes. "I have taken a private vow never again to imbibe in your company, m'sieur."

"A little late for that, is it not?" he teased softly.

She backed away as he approached the table, lighting an assortment of honey-scented beeswax can-dles before taking a chair. "I should leave you to your meal," she murmured. "No doubt you are very hungry."

"I forgot to tell you that Helivet came tonight with a message from Elysium. Don't you want to know what it says? Perhaps it is from your good friend Izzie."

"Oh." She saw him extract a small folded paper from a pocket in his coat. Her lips were dry and she began to lick them before realizing that he was staring at her. "All right. Yes."

Justin shook out his napkin, ate a few bites of the chicken dish with its savory mushroom sauce, and drank from the glass of wine. Finally, he broke the seal on the message and opened it.

"Ah, it is from my brother. Gabriel writes that Maman is worse today and begs that she might visit our home before her life ends." His nostrils flared slightly as he discarded the paper and returned to his meal.

"It is tragic, I think," Mouette said softly. "She

knows that she is going to die, she wants to repair her bond with you, yet it is all an illusion. You are only pretending to participate. Indeed, it seems that you feel nothing."

"Do not imagine that you know my true feelings." Justin surprised her by leaning forward and catching her hand with his lean fingers. "Maman's birthday is one week hence. I propose we invite her, and the rest of my family, for a celebratory party here in our new home. Will you agree to that?"

There was a cynical undercurrent to his voice, especially when he uttered the word *home*, that made the baby hairs on the back of her neck stand up.

"Of course." Mouette had to draw a deep breath before adding, "After all, this is your house, not mine. I have not forgotten that we are engaged in a make-believe marriage..."

"One that will reward you well when it is finished."

How dare he! "Believe me, I will have earned every bit of it!"

"I begin to question my decision to agree to this charade."

"Agree?" she repeated. "It was entirely *your* mad idea, m'sieur!"

"Thankfully, soon it will be ended." Justin glared at her and threw back the remainder of his wine. "Where the devil did I put my snuffbox?"

As he searched through his pockets, Mouette rose to take her leave. From the doorway, she said, "It would be just as well if you never found the thing. Tobacco is very bad for your health."

"My health is excellent!" As he spoke, his shoulders seemed to broaden and his jaw hardened.

"Yes, of course." Unable to resist, Mouette added, "However, you are no longer a young man..."

She had just turned to leave, hoping to have the last

word, when he appeared beside her and caught her wrist in a grip of iron. "My lady, you of all people are *intimately* aware of the splendid condition of my health."

"You are a scoundrel."

"Indeed. That is precisely the reason why I have never allowed anyone to lay claim to my affections." The candle flames sent shadows over his face. "People are changeable. It is wise to keep one's attachments as casual as possible."

*I*t was mid-morning when Justin's handsome green barouche rolled up before Elysium.

"I don't think this equipage was designed for so many passengers," Justin remarked in a tone heavy with irony as Will opened the carriage door and, one by one, Mouette, Charles, Anthony, and Robinson the corgi disembarked.

The two boys immediately rushed off to meet Louise and Camille, who waited under a nearby willow tree. They were surrounded by their own assortment of pets, including two Labrador retrievers, a spaniel puppy, and a rabbit.

Only Robinson lingered, gazing up at Justin with questioning brown eyes.

"What are you waiting for?" he said, and pointed toward the children. "You are a dog. Go and frolic where you are wanted!"

As the corgi reluctantly obeyed, Gabriel emerged from the manor house and descended the steps to stand beside Justin. "Now that you have a family, you may need a larger carriage," he remarked, adding a little nudge of his elbow into his brother's ribs.

Justin felt Mouette watching him. "Very amusing."

"We are honored by this visit, so soon after your wedding," Gabriel said as he kissed Mouette's hand.

"Ah, well, we could only remain in seclusion for a short while," she replied. Dimples winked in her pretty cheeks.

Looking away from them, Justin said, "Where is Maman? I have only come with Mouette so that we might invite our parents to a dinner for Maman's birthday."

"A sort of—farewell celebration, before she leaves us?" his brother inquired, arching a brow.

"I am only doing as you bade in your note. Kindly lead the way to our mother so that I may get on with my other business. Is she still in her bedchamber?"

Justin didn't know why the very air he breathed seemed to annoy him today, but it did. Turning to Helivet, he said, "Wait here for now and keep Hugo for me. I intend to be on my way soon." When he looked back, Mouette had taken Gabriel's arm and they were ascending the stone steps.

He was left to follow behind and then hold the front door for them as they went inside.

* * *

CERISE ST. Briac was not in her darkened bedchamber this morning, but lounging on a chaise that had been positioned in her younger son's beautiful walled garden.

As they approached, Mouette thought that the Frenchwoman looked a bit healthier than she had at the wedding, even though she continued to lie back against a profusion of silk pillows.

"Ah, the lovebirds have come out of their nest," she called as soon as they appeared. Was there a slight taunting note in her voice?

217

Justin came forward to take Mouette's arm. He grasped it just a bit too tightly for her comfort, but when she glanced over to protest, she could read the tension in his dark face.

"*Bonjour*, Maman," he said as they drew near. "Where is Papa?"

"Oh, he has gone to plant something in Gabriel's Italian garden," she replied, waving a hand. "An iris, mayhap. No matter where I want him to be, he is ever elsewhere."

Mouette watched her, fascinated. Cerise St. Briac was still handsome for a woman of nearly seventy years, despite her illness. Her face was elegantly structured and today, her cheekbones seemed to be tinged with color. She wore a charming *toque* of violet-striped silk, set at a rather rakish angle on her head of chestnut curls. And now that she had come out into the sunlight and stopped hiding her face behind shadows and veils, Mouette could see the sparkle in her astute dark eyes that were so much like Justin's.

"You are feeling better?" Justin inquired warily.

"Oh, not really." Her shoulders drooped and she closed her eyes sadly. "Do you not know what is said about the dying?"

"I'm certain you will enlighten us."

"My own dear grandmère always told me that those who are dying revive for a short time…just before the end! Like a candle flame that flickers brighter an instant before it is completely *extinguished*." As she uttered the last word, Cerise gave a little sob.

"I see." A muscle moved in his jaw.

Mouette's hand was curved around his arm and she could feel his muscles harden more with each word Cerise uttered. Clearly the woman hoped to manipulate his emotions, and just as clearly Justin meant to resist.

"Justin," Cerise exclaimed suddenly, "must you wear that dreadful eye-patch? You have always been known for your looks, and now they are utterly spoiled."

Mouette gave a soft gasp. How could the woman say such a thing to her own son?

"Have you forgotten, Maman? You saw my eye. Surely you would not want to inflict the sight of it on others." Justin seemed to take a step back. "As diverting as this conversation must be for you, I must attend to other matters. Mouette and I are here because it has come to our attention that you wish to visit our home. We would like to invite you to a dinner at Frenchman's Lair, for your birthday."

Realizing what an effort this little speech had been for him, Mouette squeezed his arm.

"*Bonté divine!*" Cerise blinked rapidly. "How lovely. It is just what I have been longing for. What a good son you are to have anticipated my wishes!"

"We will give you a proper party," said Mouette, going forward to sit near Cerise. For heaven's sake, the woman might be impossible, but was she not dying? "You must tell me all your favorite dishes."

"Whatever we eat will taste like ambrosia, because I shall be dining in the home of my married son and his wife. My dear girl…" She glanced away as if searching her memory for her new daughter-in-law's name.

"Mouette," barked Justin.

"Ah, yes, such a unique name…" Cerise murmured in a patronizing tone. "Your parents were French?"

"My father, yes," she said.

"How fortunate for you. And now I would suggest that you devote yourself to perfecting your mastery of the French language. It is vastly preferable to English."

Justin's nostrils flared warningly. "Maman, you are absolutely—"

"Correct," Mouette supplied, fearing that he was

about to say things to his dying mother that he would later regret. "French is a beautiful language. Who could blame you for loving your native tongue?"

Fortunately, distraction appeared in the form of Isabella. Holding her sketchbook and crayons, she announced that she was going to draw some of the apricot-tinted climbing roses that had opened against the stone wall. "Mouette," she called, "won't you come with me?"

"I must go as well," Justin said, turning to Gabriel. "But first, might I have a word with you, *mon frère?*"

"Do you all mean to abandon me?" cried Cerise as they began to disperse.

"You must be tired," said Justin. "Close your eyes now and rest. You'll need your strength for your birthday celebration next week..."

Watching him turn away, Mouette felt a pang of sympathy for Madame St. Briac. "Your son is right. Dream of the party we will have." She patted her hand. "I look forward to welcoming you to our home."

"What is it called?" asked Cerise.

Mouette replied with a bemused smile, "Actually, your son has newly christened it Frenchman's Lair."

"How like him," the older woman said approvingly. "It is the perfect name for the home of my splendid first-born son!"

* * *

FOLLOWING GABRIEL INTO THE LIBRARY, Justin was reminded of the day he had arrived at Elysium, only a few weeks ago. The brothers had sat together in this very room, reunited after many years. That day, Justin had hatched his plot to placate their mother with a make-believe marriage, but little had gone according to plan.

"May I offer you refreshment?" asked Gabriel.

"Just a small glass of wine, perhaps. I must leave shortly for an appointment. That is what I must speak to you about."

They sat together in chairs near the fireplace. Justin noticed again how unfashionable the room was, yet now he was also aware of a cozy feeling that overshadowed the need for new furnishings.

"You and Mouette are dealing well together?" his brother inquired.

Justin blinked. "Well enough." To his consternation, he felt his face growing warm. "Though of course, as you know, it is but a charade. Once the birthday celebration is behind us, and Maman departs this earth, I can return to my life in Saint-Malo."

"Ah yes, Saint-Malo." Gabriel nodded.

"What the devil are you smiling about? I have all manner of pressing business waiting for me there."

"And what is it that you wish to discuss with me…?"

"A smuggling venture."

"I suppose this has something to do with Lady Daphne Leyton?" Gabriel put up a hand and shook his head. "I will not be drawn into your mad schemes."

"Kindly hear me out. It is simply an adventure, the sort you and I have always thrived on! You may insist that you don't miss it, but I know better." Justin felt certain he saw a gleam of reluctant interest in his brother's blue eyes. "Lady Daphne has a shipment of lace and silk in Guernsey, waiting to be retrieved on her behalf. *Deux Frères* is anchored just in Polperro Harbor, as you know. Who better than us to slip over to Guernsey and elude the customs officers? It is just the diversion we need."

"Speak for yourself. I am past the need for that sort diversion, or at least I hope I am."

"Can you truly never long for your old life of adventure?"

"Ah, I didn't say that. But there are too many better choices for me to make now." Gabriel paused, considering. "My family depends on me."

"Are you not in need of funds? Lady Daphne intends to share her profits with us."

"*Mon Dieu*, Justin, neither of us need her coin. Your wealth has no limit!"

Justin could see that his brother was losing patience. "Listen to me." Justin took a deep breath and leaned closer. "I feel very restless. Confined. Between the coil with Maman and this marriage charade, I sometimes think I may go mad. There are children running in circles around me, a dog who has decided it adores me, a woman—who—"

"Yes…?"

His chest tightened. God, what if he were dying? "She has put a spell on me, I think."

"Mouette?" Gabriel let out a bark of laughter. "If that is true, you are a fortunate man. Why do you want to run away? Relax and enjoy it."

"Are you mad? Relax?" The constricting pain in his chest intensified. "I swore when we were growing up that I would never allow a woman to lead me on the sort of dance our mother enjoys. She is like a spider who spins an invisible web."

"All women are not like Maman."

Justin shook his head. "You of all people should understand. There were many times when we were boys that it seemed a matter of life and death. Many times, when she ran away and Papa seemed to forget us in his rush to pursue her, I literally wasn't certain they would ever return." He jumped to his feet and began to pace. "You were too young to remember. I was responsible for us!"

"Yes, I see." Gabriel rose and came toward Justin. "You have spent your life avoiding something you perceived to be more dangerous than sea battles or duels… a woman who might cause you to fall in love with her."

"I knew you would understand." As he accepted Gabriel's embrace, Justin found that he could breathe again.

"I understand all too well. My dear brother, you don't have to live this way, constantly guarding your heart." Gabriel stared at him, holding his gaze. "This sense of danger that comes when you begin to love a woman is false. A misbelief."

"False? Ha! It is real enough, I can assure you!" Without thinking, he reached for his snuffbox, only to remember that it was still missing. "Someone has stolen my cursed snuffbox!"

"Sit down for a few moments," Gabriel said calmly. Crossing to the cellaret, he poured a little more wine in both their glasses. "Attend me."

"I must leave very soon." Reluctantly, Justin took his chair again.

"I know that the feelings you have are as old as you are. I know it won't be easy to change them, but I hope you will at least think about what I have to say. I am your brother. I understand you nearly as well as I know myself, and I love you."

As tears threatened, Justin's scarred eye stung like the devil. "Must we do this?"

"In case you have forgotten, we share the same parents. I have had my own defenses against love, but fortunately, you protected me from a great deal—and after I met Isabella, I wanted a life with her enough to gather the courage to be vulnerable."

"*Courage?*" mocked Justin. "More like weakness."

"I know it must feel like it will make you weak, giving in to your tender emotions for Mouette, but in truth it requires great daring. Pirating and smuggling are child's play by comparison. I suggest you stop plotting ways to avoid love and, instead, go forward to meet it."

The steel band squeezed his chest again. "I sometimes think I must be dying. I have this pain…" Justin put a strong hand over his heart. "Mouette tells me that reckless, indulgent living will ruin my health."

"She loves you," Gabriel replied gently.

"Don't say that." He closed his eyes as the pain intensified.

"*Mon frère*, the only part of you that is dying is that boy who feared his own mother didn't care enough to come home to her family."

* * *

AS HE RODE toward Lansallos Cove for his meeting with Lady Daphne, Justin kept hearing his brother's voice.

Plotting ways to avoid love, Gabriel had said.

Good God, it was true. It seemed that Justin had spent his entire adult life doing just that. Perhaps, at eight-and-forty, he was too old to change…

Below Lansallos village, the lane narrowed until Justin was forced to dismount. He led Hugo by the reins under a leafy canopy toward the beach that lay a mile or more south. The path followed a rutted cart track beside a rushing stream, and Justin knew that many a smuggler had transported contraband goods up from their ships along this very route.

The stream ended in a waterfall near an old mill that had fallen into disuse. When Justin paused there to look down at the beach, he saw Lady Daphne Leyton walking among the tall black rocks. She made a striking picture, with the blue English Channel surging in behind her to break against the sand. To his surprise, he saw that Daphne had donned very fashionable men's clothing, including boots, breeches, and an elaborately-knotted cravat. Her fair hair was pinned up, but she carried a stylish man's Parisian hat.

"Are you in disguise?" he called as he and his horse emerged from behind a tall wedge of rock.

She shook her head impatiently. "I could not come here in a gown and slippers, for many reasons. Fortunately, I have a male acquaintance who is nearly the same size."

"I see that you have it all worked out."

"There are many aspects to my work, and I must be prepared to attend to all of them." As she approached him, Daphne seemed to soften, until she was smiling as she came to stand near enough to touch. The breeze loosened some of her curls from their pins. "You see, m'sieur, I am serious about what I do. You are making a wise decision to involve yourself in my enterprise."

"That's why I've come." It was like speaking a foreign language. "To tell you that I won't be able to help you." Justin thought fleetingly of all the romantic adventures he had been at liberty to enjoy throughout his adult life. Could he really change so drastically?

Daphne's smile faded. "I see. How very disappointing."

As she leaned closer, parting her lips suggestively, he considered the notion that his intense longing for Mouette might not be any different, really, than the lust he had experienced for countless women. Perhaps it only seemed different because he was in the wilds of Cornwall, separated from the pleasures of his normal life.

A voice seemed to whisper, *Go on. Kiss her! It's the only way to know the truth...*

Painfully, Justin forced himself to remember what his cursed brother had said about real courage.

Daphne reached for one of his hands and brought it to her breast. Under her man's shirt, he could feel her hardened nipple pressing into his palm. "Have you ever kissed a woman on a beach like this?" she purred.

To Justin's surprise, he felt a sort of revulsion, not so much for her as for himself. It came to him that he shouldn't have come here. Pulling his hand free, he stepped backward. "My lady, I cannot help you—meet any of the needs you brought with you today."

"Not even at the risk that I could tell your mother the truth about your so-called *marriage*?"

"Not at all." He feigned indifference. "Why would she believe you—a stranger—over her own devoted son? If I say that you have attempted to extort a blackmail payment from me, I can promise you that she would have you turned out immediately."

"I do not know if I should believe you." Her nostrils flared. "However, if you will not go to Guernsey for me, you can at least invest in my business! I am well aware that you have very deep pockets, m'sieur."

"Yes, if you mind your own business when it comes to my mother, I might consider it." Turning, he retrieved Hugo's reins and started back toward the cart track, pausing only long enough to add, "But only if my investment would improve the lives of the women who sew for you."

Before Daphne could reply, Justin walked away, behind a broken black cliff, toward the path that would take him back to Lansallos. How long would it take, he wondered, to get back to Elysium, back to Mouette? The thought of her filled him with a longing more intense than any he had ever felt.

What the devil could it mean?

$\mathcal{W}$atching George Trevarre, Marquess of Caverleigh, help her older son to construct a paper replica of the fortified Breton city of Saint-Malo was not the way Mouette had hoped to spend this day.

"He used to make mazes for me when I was a little girl," Isabella murmured, close to Mouette's ear. "Fanciful towns fashioned of folded and painted paper." She gave a little sigh and returned to her paints and easel.

They were seated in Gabriel's glass conservatory, where they could enjoy the pretty day without fear that the wind would carry away George and Charles's creation. The folded paper buildings and walls were carefully placed, as each one was finished, on Gabriel's rough pine planting table.

"Do you see the Holland Bastion?" asked George, pointing to a promontory he'd added in the paper wall. "That's where there used to be a kennel of guard dogs. The dogs were giant mastiffs, and their keepers didn't feed them all day so that at night, after the curfew bell tolled, they would be released on the beach to hunt down anyone who remained outside the city walls."

Charles gasped, clearly thrilled. "That's quite shocking, my lord!"

"Have I not insisted that you call me George?" As he leaned toward the boy, smiling benevolently, Mouette noticed that his cravat was yellowed with wear and some of the buttons were loose on his coat. Poor fellow!

"The dogs are gone now," Isabella reassured Charles. "But it makes for a wonderful story." She gave her older brother a quelling glance.

George beamed back at her. "My dear sister, I find that building a city is thirsty work. Might I beg a drop of whisky from you?"

"I don't think so." Isabella shook her head. "I have not forgotten the conversation we had with Sebastian and Julia at Trevarre Hall, George."

"Ale, then. Surely you can bestow upon a thirsty man a meager draft of ale!" A note of impatience had crept into his voice.

"I fear not," replied Isabella. "I thought to ring for lemonade."

Mouette found their conversation quite curious. Glancing away, she saw that Anthony had gotten up and begun to walk around the conservatory.

"Where is Louise today?" he asked suddenly. "Perhaps she'd like to explore the ravine with me. The rope bridge is nearly finished!"

"You may find her in the stables," Isabella replied, setting down her palette. "The girls were riding with their father, but they should have returned by now."

"Why don't I walk over with you to look for them," said Mouette.

"Mama, do stop treating me as if I'm still in leading strings." He gave her a stormy look. "Robinson will go with me, and we'll be just fine."

"Yes," George chimed in, coming to stand just a bit too close to her. "Do stay here, Mouette."

Her heart hurt a little as she watched Anthony go off with the corgi, who strutted proudly as he led the way. She moved away from George and stood at the glass, watching boy and dog until they disappeared through one of the low, arched doors in the garden wall.

* * *

RETURNING FROM LANSALLOS TO ELYSIUM, Justin rode up the steep lane above Polperro harbor. It was the same hill he had climbed the day he'd first arrived from France, just a few weeks ago. It seemed an eternity.

On that gray, chilly afternoon, he had expected to suffer through a bedside visit with his mother and then sail immediately back to Saint-Malo.

Yet, here he was. Still in Cornwall and not in any hurry to depart. Life sometimes held surprises that were beyond imagining.

As Justin dismounted and began to lead Hugo toward the stables, he saw Robinson running toward him at full speed on his stubby little legs. The dog was barking as if he were sounding an alarm.

Although Robinson had become a persistent irritation in his life, Justin could not brush aside the corgi's clear message that something was wrong.

"Woof, woof!" cried the dog, who ran behind Justin and tried to nip at his heels.

"If you dare to put one tooth on my best boots, you'll deeply regret it," Justin said in a warning tone. "It's quite clear that you want to show me something. Go ahead, lead the way."

He lifted his own pace as they ascended the hill to the stables. His heart began to pound as Robinson grew more insistent. What if something had happened to Mouette? Drawing near, he could hear muffled whimpering from inside the darkened stable.

"Who is it?" Justin called as he entered, looking all around. As his eyes adjusted to the dim light, he scanned the stalls lining both sides of the building. Where the devil was Martin, Gabriel's stablemaster?

"Help me, please," sobbed a child's voice.

Robinson rushed ahead and stopped at the far end of the building, turning his pointed nose toward the hayloft and making warning sounds. Justin then saw Anthony Brandreth clinging to a railing at the edge of the loft, his legs dangling into the air at least five feet beyond his reach.

There was no time even to think. Even as Justin rushed closer, Anthony lost his grip with one hand and screamed. His entire body was swaying high above as he clung to the stone railing with only one hand.

"Don't be afraid!" Justin shouted. "You can let go— I'll catch you."

The child's dark eyes widened with terror and relief when he saw Justin, but the knowledge that rescue was at hand seemed only to increase his tears. "I'm afraid!"

"I will catch you," Justin repeated firmly. "I promise."

Anthony couldn't hold on another moment. It was a terrible feeling to watch as his fingers let go of the railing and he fell through the air. The distance was great enough, and the boy was large enough, that when he reached Justin's outstretched arms, it seemed momentarily that the impact might send them both toppling to the ground.

Anthony was breathing hard, swallowing sobs, his arms wrapped around Justin's broad shoulders. "Thank you..." After a moment, the boy added more softly, "Papa."

"*Pas du tout*," Justin replied with a shake of his dark head. "It was nothing."

"You saved me," Anthony insisted, hugging him tighter. Meanwhile, Robinson was dancing around them in a circle, barking his approval.

"Silence! And sit down," Justin ordered. The dog obeyed instantly, wearing a broad corgi smile. "And Anthony, you were not in any real danger. Even if you had dropped without me there to catch you, you could have weathered the landing."

"No, no, I couldn't have. My foot..." His face turned red and he buried it in Justin's shoulder. "My foot isn't made...correctly. That's why I fell off the edge. I tried to jump over a pile of hay and lost my balance."

"There is nothing incorrect about the way you are made," Justin said firmly. His eyes stung as he added, "You must not believe it! Try to forget any hindrances you've been told that you have. Remember instead how strong you are, how smart and brave and handsome."

"I shall try... Papa." Anthony had buried his face in Justin's shirtfront, whispering the word *papa*, as if for his own ears more than Justin's. "I want to be just like you when I am grown...but you have no physical hindrances!"

Justin set the boy on his feet and dusted him off. "Ah, you are quite wrong about that! Have you not noticed my eye-patch? And look at this knee! It hurts like the devil most of the time." He crouched slightly, smiling into boy's eyes. "However, rather than letting the pain hold me back, I have learned to think of my goals instead."

A voice interrupted them from the entrance to the stables. "Anthony! Are you in here?"

It was Mouette, standing in the stable entrance, haloed with golden sunlight. The sight of her was so welcome, so stirringly beautiful that Justin's heart seemed to catch.

"Mama, I am here," Anthony called. Suddenly, he sounded as if he might begin to sob again.

Justin watched Mouette run toward them, lifting her tissue-thin muslin skirts with one hand. Robinson began to jump up with excitement as she drew near, but one threatening glance from Justin caused him to sit down. Only the softest of yips escaped his mouth.

"Something has happened to you, hasn't it?" she demanded of her son. "I knew I shouldn't let you go off alone."

The boy flushed, but before he could explain, Justin intervened. "Everything is all right. I think he has been perfectly well-behaved. He simply lost his footing in the hayloft, but he was not in any real danger."

"You lost your footing?" Mouette exclaimed to her son. "You should not have been climbing up there by yourself. You know that you must exercise special caution!"

"Papa says I should not think about my physical imperfections."

"Papa?" Color washed her cheeks. "Are you speaking of M'sieur St. Briac?"

Something compelled Justin to say, "Now that we are married, perhaps it is natural that Anthony should call me Papa."

"Indeed? I would suggest that you refrain from dispensing advice to a child when you do not fully understand the circumstances."

"He is fine. I was here to assist him in getting down from the hayloft."

Her eyes flashed with emotion. "You do not understand what it is like to raise two sons. I *alone* am responsible for their safety. For their health."

Justin had that odd feeling again, a sort of fluttering

in the region of his heart. Slowly, he said, "It is true that I have not raised children, as you are doing. I have no previous experience as a father. But I do have experience at being a male, and I can tell you one thing with confidence." He reached across the space between them and took her slim hand. "You cannot protect Anthony from all of the risks and uncertainties of life, Mouette. You must allow him to be a boy."

* * *

A CONFUSING FLURRY of emotions swirled inside of Mouette as she and Justin walked back to the conservatory with Anthony between them. When she looked over to Justin and he sent her a wary yet tender smile, her heart swelled. Moments later, he lifted one strong dark hand to ruffle Anthony's curls.

She knew that she shouldn't allow herself to soften and hope. Yet she did.

When they entered the walled garden, it looked more beautiful to Mouette than ever before. Butterflies flitted among the bright flowers, heedless of Robinson, who chased them. There were thick clusters of lavender in full bloom, and Mouette rubbed the deep purple flowers and brought her fingertips to her nose to smell the fragrance she loved so much.

"Lavender always makes me think of France," said Justin. Then he shocked her by catching her wrist and bringing her hand to his face. It almost felt as if he were kissing her palm as he inhaled. "Ah, wonderful."

"Let me smell, too," begged Anthony, and there was laughter as Justin gave over her hand. "Hmm," said her son, sniffing loudly. "It's all right, I suppose."

Mouette was grateful to see that George was no longer in the conservatory. She wasn't sure how she could explain the Marquess of Caverleigh's involvement in Charles's life. Instead, Louise and Camille were there with both their parents, and Isabella was making sketches of the children as Charles continued to labor over his paper city.

Isabella looked up. "This is a surprise! How did you three find each other?"

Mouette watched as Justin glanced down at Anthony and gave him a smile that seemed to say his secrets were safe.

"Purely by chance, I can assure you," Justin replied in an offhand tone as he approached the table where Charles was folding another rooftop. "What is this you are making?"

"I would have expected you to recognize your own city, m'sieur," said Charles.

"Ah, is it indeed meant to be Saint-Malo? Fascinating." He came closer. "Perhaps I can help you. It's not quite accurate."

"Of course it is!" snapped Charles. "If you don't mind, I would appreciate some privacy to concentrate."

Justin stepped back, his jaw tightening as he glanced toward Mouette. She could see that he longed to reprimand her older son, but he clearly remembered the scene between them in the kitchen at Frenchman's Lair.

"Charles." Approaching the table, Mouette touched his shoulder, noticing again how tall he was growing. "You are not to speak to Justin that way. I don't like the tone you've been taking."

"I am merely being honest."

"I think you mean *rude*, and I won't tolerate rudeness. Please apologize."

Charles took his time folding the roofline, then slowly put the house behind the paper walls. His face and body sent a message that was louder than any words he might speak. "I apologize if I offended you, m'sieur," he muttered, glancing up briefly at Justin.

To Mouette's surprise, Justin extended his hand to her son and smiled. "No offense taken. I clearly remember being your age, Charles. I don't think most adults approved of my behavior then, either, but then I didn't have a mother as wise and devoted as yours."

Charles looked suspicious, but shook his hand. "Well, all right, then."

Mouette was relieved when Justin said nothing more. Part of her was braced for him to say or do something shocking, but it did not happen. Instead, he turned to look directly into her eyes.

"My lady, shall we take these two boys back to our home?"

Home. Justin had said *our home*! His gaze seemed to touch the very core of her, yet what could it mean? Did she dare to allow a tiny green shoot of hope to take root, to discover if it might blossom and grow into something real?

Robinson began to bark, jumping around them, and Charles looked accusingly at Justin. "You forgot Robinson."

"Forgot? Impossible," he said dryly. "Of course, I meant to say 'two boys...and a dog.'"

"There is so much to do before the party," Mouette said, dipping her quill in the inkwell. "I have decided to make a list."

"Have you?" Across the ebony-inlaid table, Justin was surveying the account books. It was difficult to read for very long with only one working eye, and he already felt the beginnings of a headache. "I ought to hire a steward. I have no appetite for managing an estate this size on my own, and I feel guilty allowing it to languish this way."

"I thought you didn't intend to stay here after..." Her voice trailed off.

"After my mother dies?" He wasn't entirely certain how to get out of the conversational corner. "Perhaps she will endure longer than anyone has predicted. I can't just allow Squire Pendudwell's estate to wither away during this interlude."

"I suppose you have a point."

"And speaking of staff, I have arranged for my brother to loan me a few of his servants, at least until after the party. You will meet the new cook today, so that you two may begin to plan the menu."

Mouette looked surprised. "It seems that you have thought of everything. Perhaps I can put away my list!"

"Tell me what you have written."

She moved some of her papers around and shuffled the books that lay open before her. "I've made some notes about the tasks that remain undone in this house, such as finishing the restoration of the stairhall murals—"

"Izzie has arranged for two more competent artists to join the three men who are working on the mural at this moment." As if to confirm his words, the sound of the scaffolding being noisily assembled at the top of the stairs reached their ears.

"Excellent." Mouette nodded. "Henri Franchot, the man I summoned from London will continue to be in charge, will he not?"

"Of course." Justin bowed his head to her with faintly mocking deference. He loved sparring with Mouette, especially now that they occupied the same house and were so often together.

"It's a bit confusing for me to know exactly what my role is now," she said. "Am I the person who oversees the transformation of Pendudwell Manor into French-man's Lair? Or am I the make-believe bride?"

"Both, I hope." He nearly asked if double duties would require him to compensate her twice as much, but something stopped him. Sparring was one thing— reminding them both of their business arrangement was entirely another matter. "Where are the boys? It's very quiet in this house."

"I've given them lessons to write. They are studying in the dining room."

"Lessons? I had nearly forgotten about that. We must hire a tutor!"

Mouette looked back at him for a long moment, her eyes searching his face, before replying, "Unless you know someone locally who would be willing to instruct Charles and Anthony on a temporary basis, I don't think it is practical to hire a tutor who would only have a position for a few weeks, at the most."

"Charles is old enough to be away at school," mused Justin, pretending not to understand her meaning. "But that is a cruel life for a boy his age."

"I agree. I will consider those choices when your mother's birthday celebration has passed." She wrinkled her nose in a gesture he had come to adore. "Soon enough we'll be back in London."

This remark felt like a dagger between his ribs. He reached for the non-existent snuffbox and gave a harsh sigh. Most of the time, he didn't miss the damned thing, but there were moments when he thought it might solve all his problems.

"I've been making lists for our menu," Mouette said, gesturing to the open books. "There are many appealing recipes to be found in these books from the kitchen, but I wanted to show them to you before we settle on final choices."

Still stinging from her remark about London, Justin replied, "You intend to include me in a decision?"

"What is *that* supposed to mean?"

"If you are capable of managing your London home on your own, you can certainly choose a menu without me." He stood up. "I'm going to see to a few of the items on my own list. This is my house, in case you've forgotten!"

No sooner had he strode from the room than he felt a sharp stab of regret. Leaning against the wall near the front door, Justin watched the men who were painstakingly restoring the murals that surrounded the wide staircase. He could hear Anthony and Charles talking and laughing in the dining room. Robinson was lying nearby on the cool marble floor, his legs splayed out and his eyes closed.

Justin knew a warm rush of contentment, followed quickly by the familiar chest-squeezing pain that came when he remembered that soon enough this interlude would end and they would all return to their separate lives.

* * *

IN THE MIDDLE of Justin's sleepless night, it came to him that he had the power to change the course of events. Lying restless and naked on the rumpled sheets, bathed in the light of a full moon, he realized that he had the power to make Mouette stay with him—and even love him.

All he had to do was change himself.

Suddenly, the pieces came together. It was what Gabriel had been trying to tell him. This was an endeavor that would put his very heart and soul at risk, but if he succeeded, he would gain a treasure far greater than all the chests of jewels stored in the pirate cellars beneath his grand home in Saint-Malo.

* * *

WHEN MOUETTE ROSE with the sun, she washed and dressed in a simple, pale blue round gown. Knowing that the day ahead would be filled with party plans and work, she drew her hair back and wound it into a chignon. When the last pin was in place, she paused before the looking glass to survey her face. The soft dawn sunlight that shone through her window illuminated tiny lines that fanned out around her eyes. They crinkled quite becomingly when Mouette laughed, but were a clear sign she was getting older. It was no use pretending otherwise.

Because her modest room was on the ground floor, near the kitchen, she peeked in to say good morning to Margaret, the new cook.

"Good mornin', my lady!" called the apple-cheeked cook. Margaret had labored in the kitchen at Elysium, assisting the dour Madame Kerjean, for five years. She was delighted to have a kitchen of her own, if only temporarily. "His lordship has been askin' for ye."

Mouette had given up explaining to Margaret that Justin was not a lord and she should not address him as such. "Has he? Where might I find him so early in the morning?"

"Our new kitchen maid just took breakfast to his lordship on the terrace."

"New kitchen maid?" Had she forgotten someone?

"Aye, my lady." Margaret continued to bustle around the worktable where Mouette had spread her thighs for Justin not so long ago. "A girl called Jane. And there's now a footman, and a gardener."

"When did this happen?"

"While you were still abed, my lady. Would you like your coffee, fruit, and eggs on the terrace with his lordship?"

Mouette blinked. "I suppose so."

When she emerged onto the pretty terrace behind the manor house, she saw Justin, sitting in a chair with his booted feet propped on a low stone wall. His disheveled dark hair shone in the morning sunlight and his head was slightly cocked as he studied one of the cookery books she had left open in the morning room. The picture he made was so intensely appealing to Mouette that she was swept by a wave of longing.

"I'm sorry," Justin said with a smile. He gestured to the empty dishes. "I couldn't wait. I was ravenous."

"It sounds as if you've been quite busy." She took a seat near him.

"Time is short," he agreed. "And you have been asking for a proper staff for weeks."

Was it her imagination, or did his gaze hold hers a moment longer than usual?"Well, I understood why you hesitated before, given the circumstances of your arrangement here. But now that your parents are coming for dinner, it does seem wise to have servants," Mouette replied. "Are they all borrowed from Elysium?"

"No. I hired them outright. Margaret, too."

It definitely was not her imagination. There was a thoughtful note in his voice that made her heart swell. "How very surprising!"

"I thought of telling you, so that you might approve my choices, but you have had so much to contend with this week…I decided to surprise you, hoping to ease your burden."

A very thin, mousey girl appeared just then, carrying a tray. "Breakfast for my lady," she piped.

"Thank you, Jane," Justin said. Removing his booted legs from the wall, he sat up and helped the blushing kitchen maid set out the breakfast dishes.

Mouette added her own thanks and watched as Justin poured coffee and warm, rich milk together in a cup, adding a spoonful of sugar. As Mouette sipped the *café au lait*, she wondered why it seemed to taste so much better when made by a wickedly attractive Frenchman.

"There is Tom, our gardener," Justin remarked, pointing to a strapping middle-aged man who was crossing the lawn with a large plant in his arms, its root ball wrapped in burlap. "He came to us with a recommendation from Viscount Senwyck."

"Where did he get that plant?"

"It's a gift from Gabriel and Izzie, of course." He watched her eat strawberries for a while before adding, "I know you are probably wondering if Tom means to proceed without guidance from you. I should assure you that is not the case."

Mouette laughed. "You have guessed my thoughts. I actually was thinking that, if you really mean to have a proper garden, your brother should make a plan for it. Don't you think so?"

"Perhaps, though he might attempt impose his vision on us. I will speak to Gabriel, but only if you agree to consult with him, so that he will understand our taste."

Her heart beat faster each time he said *we, us, our*. And yet a wary voice inside Mouette warned her to be careful...very careful.

* * *

THE NEXT AFTERNOON, as the new servants cleaned and polished their way through every inch of the manor house, Justin and Mouette sat down with Baptiste and Margaret to finalize the menu for Cerise's birthday dinner.

"Maman has a special fondness for duck," Justin remarked.

"I propose Rouen Canard a l'Orange," said Baptiste. "It is one of her favorites, as I recall."

Flustered, Margaret exclaimed, "If this be a Frenchie dish, someone must help me!"

"But of course," Baptiste intoned.

Mouette suspected that the Frenchman might be feeling a bit out of sorts since a stranger had taken over his kitchen. Smiling warmly, she said, "Baptiste, you have such a gift for expertly carrying out many tasks at once. I am trusting you to oversee the entire meal, as well as the party as a whole."

"And, of course you have known Maman for many years," added Justin. "Would it be asking too much for you to act as both our butler and de facto housekeeper, at least until after this birthday dinner?"

"You want a man to be yer housekeeper?" Margaret blurted. Turning to Baptiste, she queried, "Do ye not take offense to that?"

He lifted his chin. "On the contrary, I am proud to say I'm proficient in all capacities. I did a splendid job running the kitchen before you arrived at Frenchman's Lair."

"Hmm." Margaret peered over her tiny spectacles at him, clearly fascinated. "Well, I do make very good rabbits on the skewer. And a fine pea soup."

"Ah, now we are getting somewhere," Justin said. "I suggest that you two retire to the kitchen to compose a menu. I have every confidence in your ability to collaborate successfully."

The pair went off together, looking quite congenial. When Justin and Mouette were alone, he said casually, "I wanted to show you my study. I've rearranged things a bit and wanted to get your opinion."

Mouette took a deep breath, smiling. With each responsibility that he lifted from her shoulders, she felt lighter. Rising, she came to stand beside him. "You've rearranged my morning room? No doubt you've added a great male desk with lion's paw feet."

His smile flashed white. "Now *there's* a tempting idea."

The teasing tone of his voice made her feel happy, and as they walked together through the double doors, his hand moved lightly toward her so that his fingers twined with hers.

They came into the sun-filled room that Mouette

had once claimed for her own, and he paused, watching her. She looked all around, her eyes widening, her heart fluttering.

"Justin, what have you done?"

"Go closer and have a better look," he suggested. His husky voice was like a caress.

Slowly, Mouette crossed the Aubusson rug that they had chosen together at Leyton Court and surveyed the room. The round, ebony-inlaid table no longer held a place of honor. He had moved it to another corner, adding a pair of lyre-back chairs on either side.

"Oh, you've moved the table! But that is exactly where I had imagined it would look best. It's a perfect place for a game of cards or chess."

Justin merely nodded, looking mysteriously pleased with himself.

Turning toward the beautiful window overlooking the front drive, Mouette blinked. There, illuminated by a sunbeam, was the graceful rosewood writing table she had admired the first time they toured the house. It was the same desk Justin had disparaged and quickly packed away in the stables, with the rest of Pendudwell Manor's furnishings.

"Is this a jest?" Mouette asked in a small voice.

"*Ma belle*, do you imagine me incapable of sincerity? Welcome to your morning room."

She didn't know what to say. It was hard to breathe as she went closer, taking in the details. On the writing table were a slender crystal vase that held two pale pink roses, a new silver inkwell with an agate lid, fresh quills, and an assortment of writing paper. Angled in front of the table was a chair adorned with griffins, similar to one that Mouette had admired in Thomas Hope's book. The seat was upholstered in emerald-green silk embroidered with gold laurel wreaths.

Mouette turned away from him as tears filled her

eyes and yet she couldn't stop them. Her heart ached. No one had ever done anything so thoughtful, so completely focused on her happiness, before. It was the sort of gesture she had hoped for during her marriage but had quickly learned not to expect.

She could feel the tension of Justin's gaze on her.

"You don't like it?" he murmured at last. "I admit that I am more used to grand gestures, like filling a room with roses, but I had the idea that this was what would make you happy."

"Oh, *Justin*…" Her voice broke as she turned to face him. In an instant, he was beside her, brushing his strong fingers over the curve of her cheekbone, drying her tears.

"Does this mean I've succeeded after all?" He bent to kiss her brow. "Ah, Mouette, don't cry."

She turned her cheek against his palm and closed her eyes for a moment. "No one has ever made so kind and thoughtful a gesture to me."

"*Incroyable*." Justin drew her against him until she could hear the powerful beating of his heart. More softly, he added, "It is high time someone did."

As Justin deftly knotted his cravat of snow-white linen on the night of his mother's birthday party, he stared at his own reflection in the mirror. Would his family perceive that he had changed? True, he looked healthier since he'd stopped taking snuff, drinking too much, and eating rich foods. But it was more than that.

His mind returned, for the hundredth time, to the scene in the study.

Whenever he thought about that moment when Mouette first saw the rosewood writing table in what was now her morning room, Justin felt deeply uncomfortable, almost as if he had a fever. And he didn't seem to be able to stop thinking about it.

It amazed him still that he had been in the grip of tenderness rather than physical passion. Usually when he was alone with Mouette, he had to fight an urge to overpower her with his body, to plunder her mouth with his tongue, to tear the buttons on her clothing until she was naked and he was lying on top of her, touching her, pushing into her—

A knock sounded at the door.

Justin gave himself a mental shake. Good God, now

he was hard and hot again. He glanced down at his snug pantaloons, willing his erection to subside, and called, "Go away!"

"M'sieur, your guests will soon be here," called Baptiste. "Allow me to enter and help you finish dressing."

"No!" He'd said it a bit too forcefully, he realized. "I am a grown man, I can dress myself. No doubt you have more pressing duties on this important evening."

"But I have your polished boots, m'sieur."

Justin opened the door just enough to reach out and take the boots from Baptiste. In that moment, Robinson squeezed through the opening and began to run around the chair beside the massive tester bed, barking.

Baptiste rushed in next, dashing back and forth in an effort to trap the corgi. When Justin swore and Robinson barked louder, the two boys appeared.

"Robinson!" exclaimed Charles. "Have I not warned you about M'sieur St. Briac's temper? Come with me."

The dog scurried behind Justin and sat down.

Anthony said sternly, "Come here this instant, you little rogue!"

"What's all the commotion?"

Justin looked up to see Mouette, standing in his doorway and looking more beautiful than he had ever seen her. He reached around to scoop up Robinson and deposited him in Charles's arms.

"There—all of you, be gone!" As he hustled them out the door, he caught Mouette's hand to restrain her. "Except you, of course."

A soft smile touched her mouth before she addressed her sons. "You are going to spend the night at Elysium while we have a party. Your bag is packed and Will is waiting with the carriage."

To Justin's surprise, Anthony turned back to say, "Goodnight, Papa. I shall miss you while we are away."

"It is just one night." His heart stung for a moment as he touched Anthony's head and then dared to reach out to put a hand on Charles's shoulder. "Both of you, behave yourselves, all right? I'll see you tomorrow."

Alone with Mouette, he drank in the sight of her, so achingly lovely in a simple yet elegant gown of pale azure silk. Pearls and sapphires studded her gleaming black curls, pinned high atop her head. Justin tried not to notice her alluringly subtle scent, the creamy curve of her neck, and the sparkle in her eyes.

"Do you think your mother will approve?" she asked, smiling up at him. "I was careful to choose a gown with only a modest décolletage."

"My parents are French," he reminded her in a low, amused voice. "We French know nothing of modesty."

"I have noticed that." Her smile widened and she came closer, reaching up to adjust his cravat.

Ordinarily, Justin would have been outraged that anyone would dare to touch the masterpiece of neckwear he had just created. Instead, he wanted to reach out and draw Mouette into his arms, to let her untie the damned thing completely if it pleased her to do so.

"You look utterly exquisite," he whispered.

Her lips parted. He could almost taste her but he couldn't think about that because his cock had begun to throb and harden again.

"So will you, once you are dressed." Mouette reached for one of his boots. "Shall I assist you? I think I hear a carriage on the drive. Our guests are arriving!"

* * *

"IT IS A VERY...PLAIN house, is it not?" Cerise St. Briac asked Justin as she entered Frenchman's Lair, pushed in the fancy three-wheeled invalid chair by her husband. Glancing at Mouette, she added, "My son has always

248

had impeccable taste. His home in Saint-Malo is *stunning.*"

Mouette thought that Cerise certainly had a very sharp tongue for a woman who was dying and usually spent her days lying in the shadows, barely able to speak.

"We are so pleased that you were well enough to come tonight," she greeted the older woman, leaning forward to kiss her cheek. "Welcome and best wishes on your birthday."

Justin stood off to one side, brows lowered as if he was about to snap at his mother. However when Mouette reached for his hand, he bent to kiss Cerise before embracing his father and welcoming Gabriel and Izzie, who completed the small circle of party guests.

"We are eager to see the rest of your home," said Xavier. "I'll own I can hardly believe that my libertine son has actually taken a bride and has been able to compromise on the decoration of a home."

Justin frowned. "Have I been insulted?"

Mouette smiled and squeezed his hand. Together they led their guests on a tour of Frenchman Lair's first floor. The newly-restored murals, depicting figures from Greek mythology, drew an approving comment from Cerise.

They proceeded through the dining room, where a new Empire-style mahogany table was set for a candlelit meal with polished cutlery, arrangements of white roses in crystal bowls, and lovely gilded Limoges china. A footman, wearing the new midnight-blue livery Justin had chosen, was standing at one end of the table.

Cerise inclined her head. "Quite nice," she allowed.

The drawing room had been transformed since Mouette's first sight of it, when she and Isabella had happened by en route from London. She had personally seen to every detail on this evening, making certain that the beeswax candles were lit, the Aubusson rugs were taken outside and beaten, and every surface was polished. The new furniture was in the latest sleek and classical Empire fashion. The walls were freshly-painted a soft shade of ivory and much of the plaster-work had been replaced. The overall effect was one of restrained, inviting elegance.

Cerise St. Briac's critical black eyes swept around the room, lingering on the new crystal chandeliers and each vase and side table. Just when it seemed that she would voice her approval, her gaze settled on the fire-place surround.

Mouette felt Justin go tense beside her. They had always agreed that the plain bolection moulding was all wrong for the new style of the house, but their view-points had diverged after that. Justin had been deter-mined to purchase the priceless granite mantelpiece from Leyton Court, over her emotional objections to removing the historic piece from its home.

"*Eh bien*, how can you bear to look upon so horrid a piece as that?" Cerise exclaimed.

"Your son has already chosen a replacement," Mou-ette replied, bristling. "It is a grand fireplace surround that was constructed centuries ago, from the stones of Restormel Castle."

Madame St. Briac arched a brow. "Indeed? Now, that sounds more like my son." She swiveled to look at Justin.

"In truth, after considering the matter, I have changed my mind." His tone was offhand. "I decided that so historic a piece should remain in its original home, no matter how foolish the lord of the manor might be."

A great wave of emotion washed over Mouette. Tears burned her eyes, but she could not possibly weep in front of their guests. Instead, she looked up at Justin and saw the compassion in his expression.

"How fine a man my husband is," she said softly.

"My girl," Cerise said, arching a brow, "clearly you are blinded by love."

Justin seemed not to hear his mother's remark, but turned toward the next set of double doors. "Before dinner is served, I should show you Mouette's morning room."

As they entered the room, which was now filled with artfully-arranged vases of flowers from the gardens, Mouette's face lit up. She still found it hard to believe that this was her private refuge from the world.

"Oh," cried Isabella, "this is just the sort of room I have always dreamed of having!" Turning to look at Gabriel, she added, "My husband has his library, but I have been forced to put my writing desk in our bedchamber."

"*Chérie*," rejoined Gabriel, "have you forgotten that you have an entire cottage of your very own, as your painting studio? I had it built for you."

Isabella looked charmingly embarrassed. "Oh, that's true! How silly of me."

Mouette couldn't resist showing her friends the little drawer in her desk, where she kept paper, quills, and nibs. However, when Justin glanced over at the drawer, she remembered that there was something in it he must not see. Her heart raced as she quickly closed the drawer and turned away.

As they started back to the dining room, Cerise reached out to grasp Mouette's hand, drawing her down until their eyes met.

"I perceive that you love my son," she said. "He is not an easy man, but if you can win his trust, he'll be an ardent husband."

Mouette was taken aback by the emotion in the

Frenchwoman's voice. "I believe that, too. Thank you."

* * *

THE DELICIOUS MEAL was served by Baptiste's carefully-trained new staff. As each glass was poured, the candle-light seemed to grow brighter and the guests more festive.

There were moments, as Justin watched Mouette laughing with his father or Gabriel teasing their mother about an episode from their childhood, that he felt something very much like contentment. Or at least, what he imagined contentment must be like.

"You look bemused," said Isabella with a trace of mischief. "Are your plans getting away from you?"

"Izzie, I want to apologize for all the trouble I caused before you and Gabriel were married," he said, surprising himself.

"You are forgiven." She beamed. "My dear Justin, I think you may be falling in love!"

"Does it feel like dying? If so, you may be right."

After everyone had enjoyed a festive birthday dessert of strawberry trifle, Isabella suggested music in the lovely drawing room. Xavier, an accomplished violinist, volunteered to play for the two younger couples as they waltzed.

When Justin took Mouette in his arms, he felt the tension of the evening drain away. "Finally, he whispered hoarsely.

"Have you been longing to dance that much?" she teased.

"I've been *longing* to hold you in my arms." He drew Mouette's alluring body closer, until her breasts brushed his chest. "I must confess, I want to kiss you. Badly."

Her blue eyes twinkled. "In front of your mother?

Besides, we have an arrangement. Remember?" Her tone told him what she really thought about that arrangement.

Justin glanced toward his mother, whose special chair was positioned next to Xavier and his violin. To his surprise, he saw that she was smiling and nodding in time with the music.

In that moment, Justin felt grateful for both his parents, and he glimpsed a future that was quite different from the independent life he'd always clung to. Gabriel and Isabella were waltzing next to them, laughing together, and Mouette was beaming up at him. Even Robinson had come into the drawing room and was curled in his new wicker basket near the sofas.

"Mouette, about that arrangement, I wonder if we might talk later—" he began.

Just then, a loud knocking came at the front door.

"Who could it be at this hour of the night?" Gabriel said.

"I don't know. Perhaps I should see, in case it's someone who needs help." Justin bent to kiss Mouette's hand. "Wait for me, won't you?"

Walking into the entrance hall, Justin beheld Baptiste opening the door to a portly, older man he'd never seen before. He wore an old-fashioned cape and his cravat was tied in a voluminous style that Justin hadn't seen for two decades.

"Good evening," he greeted the stranger. "How may I assist you?"

The man was ruddy-cheeked and his smile was contagious. "Ah, you must be the Frenchman to whom I've let this estate!" He put out his hand. "I'm Reginald Pendudwell. I was just visiting the area after an extended sojourn in Bath. As my carriage passed by here, I noticed all the windows were ablaze with light. Can't tell you what pleasure it gave me to see my tired old house come to life again. I thought, after my dear wife departed this earth, that this place might become my tomb. Fortunately, my son saw the problem and persuaded me to come away." He coughed. "So sorry if I'm intruding!"

Justin noticed that the squire was craning his neck in the direction of the music.

"You aren't intruding in the least, sir. I'm gratified to meet you at last. I will confess that I've become quite attached to… Pendudwell Manor."

"Have you indeed? Truth be told, I am considering selling. Perhaps you'd be interested in making this your *permanent* home?"

The familiar band squeezed Justin's chest at the prospect of such a commitment and what it would mean. However, when he took a deep breath and thought of Mouette, it eased. "That's a very intriguing offer. Meanwhile, I would invite you to come in and join my family. Have you eaten tonight? Yes? A glass of wine then."

Baptiste took the squire's cape and Justin guided him toward the drawing room.

"How different everything is!" Pendudwell marveled, looking all around. "And how warm and festive the house feels. I scarcely recognize it as my own."

As they came into the drawing room, the music stopped and everyone looked up, clearly surprised by the sight of an unexpected guest. Justin led Pendudwell toward an empty chair, performing introductions as he went.

"I am already acquainted your brother and his beautiful artist wife. We were once neighbors," the squire said, nodding with pleasure. He stopped then, at the sight of Cerise St. Briac.

Justin was surprised to see that his mother had taken the edge of her shawl and held most of it over her face. "Pardon me," she piped in an odd voice. "I am feeling very ill."

"Madame?" Pendudwell leaned down to get a closer look. "Can it be?"

"You must be mistaken," said Justin. "This is my mother."

"Oh no, I am not mistaken. I would know this vibrant and beautiful lady anywhere!" The squire reached out to take both her hands, as if he might draw her out of the three-wheeled chair and onto her feet. "Your mother was my dancing partner at the Bath Assembly Rooms, once my attack of the gout subsided and I was up on my feet again! Others might grow tired and take a seat, but never Madame. Ah, she was a woman of mystery, never doing me the honor of divulging her name...but that only added to her allure in the ballroom."

"I'm certain you are in error," Justin told him firmly, thinking that the old man must be demented. "My mother is extremely ill. She only went to Bath to take the waters, hoping to extend her life by a few weeks." For emphasis, he gestured toward her reclining wheeled chair. "You see, she is unable even to walk, so she certainly couldn't have *danced* with you."

Squire Pendudwell continued to shake his head. Turning to Xavier St. Briac, he appealed, "M'sieur, kindly tell your son the truth! Surely you remember the evening when you grew fatigued and went to the card room, begging me to stay and dance with Madame?"

Justin felt his world tilt wildly, and then it all began to come horribly clear. He saw his mother's guilty expression, the way she was trying to hide from the squire behind her pathetic shawl, the way his cowardly father averted his eyes.

"*Sangdieu.*" Justin muttered, fearing that he might be sick. "I have been a fool."

CHAPTER 27

Justin felt all the blood draining from his face. He seemed to go numb, and yet there was a white-hot searing pain in his brain, in his heart.

"What is it?" It was Mouette. She had come to stand beside him and was reaching for his hand. "Are you ill?"

He looked around the room as the fragile structure of this new life seemed to crumble away to dust. "It's much worse than that."

Squire Pendudwell, meanwhile, was chattering on to Cerise, oblivious to the drama that was playing out around him. "God's teeth, who would've ever thought that you could turn out to be connected to me, Madame? That your very son could be living in my home?"

Justin saw his father coming closer, looking very nervous and uncertain. "I should take your mother away, I think."

"You certainly should." Justin heard his voice shake even as his younger brother appeared in their midst. "Preferably this instant."

"Squire, I fear that our mother is not well," Gabriel

said. "I hope you will understand that this is not the best time for us to entertain a guest."

Justin managed to bid Pendudwell good night and waited while Gabriel saw him out. When he heard the front door close, Justin turned back to his mother. He could scarcely bear to look at her.

"You have deceived me," he ground out. "And I will never forgive you. Get up out of that ridiculous chair and leave my house."

"Oh, *mon fils*," she implored, wild-eyed. "Do you not see, everything I have done was for your own good. Do you think it was easy to pretend to be dying?"

"You are utterly mad!" he shouted.

Sensing danger, Xavier tried to take Justin's arm as he soothed, "Perhaps your mother has been misguided, perpetrating this little charade—"

"*Little charade?*" He repeated, acid dripping from each word. "She plotted to change the course of my entire life! A life I had created over decades and was perfectly *happy* with! And do not imagine that you can escape accountability, Father. You were her willing accomplice, lying to your own son, stringing me along as if I were an idiot, incapable of making my own choices, charting my own course—"

He broke off as his blood thundered in his ears. Gabriel and Isabella were getting their mother out of the chair, Xavier was packing up his violin—and Mouette was backing away as if he had become a monster.

"We're going," his father said. "Of course, you are right. But do not forget that we are still your family."

"*Oui*," exclaimed Cerise, who was walking without assistance, her head high. "And I will always be your *maman!*"

As they took their leave, those last words rang in Justin's ears like a curse.

* * *

"I MEAN to find my snuffbox tonight if it's the last thing I do!" Justin thundered, once they were alone.

Mouette felt dizzy with emotion. Her world seemed to have spun off its axis. Part of her wanted to weep because the scene of happiness that had existed just minutes before was now in ruins. And although her heart ached for Justin's pain, she was also instinctively afraid of him.

"Your snuffbox will not change what has happened," she told him softly.

He seemed not to hear her. Stalking to the wide doorway, he discovered Jane, the painfully thin kitchen maid, hovering there.

"My lord, be there something you need?" she queried.

"Yes! Where is my cognac?"

The girl's light gray eyes widened, as if she'd seen a ghost. "I b'lieve the cellaret with all the spirits do still be in yer study, sir." Swallowing visibly, she amended, "Oh! I mean, in her ladyship's *morning room.* I nearly forgot yer instruction about the room's new name."

A chill ran down Mouette' spine when Justin replied harshly, "You were right the first time. It's my study. Now go away. All of you, make yourselves scarce!"

The maid scurried away and Mouette watched as Justin turned and started toward her morning room. He was like a jungle cat that appeared tamed, but now, having been provoked, reverted to his natural wild state.

It occurred to Mouette that she should heed the command he'd issued to everyone else. She should stay far away from him, but it was impossible. By the time she reached the morning room, he was at the cellaret, pouring himself a cognac. He drank it down, stripped off his coat, and turned to stare at her.

"If you are wise, you'll go to your room and lock the door."

"Justin, please—" The thought that everything they had made so painstakingly together had now been shattered because of Cerise St. Briac's deceit was unbearable to Mouette. It was like being sucked back into the dark chasm of her past betrayal at the hands of Harry. She understood the shield Justin kept around his heart, for her own first instinct was to protect herself from pain again. "All women are not alike, you know."

"Are they not? What I *know* is that I was right all along. My mother proved that tonight. Love puts on a mask, waiting until its victim begins to trust, but something dark and manipulative lurks in its depths."

"I am not like that." Mouette didn't seem to be able to stop herself. As she watched him begin to look around the bookshelves for his snuffbox, it came to her that she must clear the air between them or else he would think her as controlling as his mother. "In fact, I have a confession to make."

"I am busy at the moment, searching out my snuffbox."

"That's what I need to tell you." Crossing the room to her new rosewood writing table, Mouette opened the single drawer. "I want to dispell any secrets that might exist between us. I hid your snuffbox because I was worried about your health."

As she held out the object that had once seemed a part of him, Mouette saw Justin go pale for the second time that night.

"*That* is what I glimpsed in the desk earlier tonight! When I looked over, I had a moment of recognition, but you were very quick to close the drawer." He came closer, looming over her. "Give it over."

Mouette felt sick as she put the agate snuffbox in his strong, elegant hand, the same hand that had caressed her back when they'd danced tonight. Clearly such moments of tenderness were a thing of the past.

"Justin, I only hid the snuffbox from you because I knew it was harmful to you. Because I cared about you—and I knew you didn't really need it."

"*You* knew, did you? Next you'll say that you did it for my own good!"

"Well, yes, that's true…" As she spoke, Mouette covered her mouth as she remembered that Cerise had spoken the same words to him tonight.

The scar on Justin's face whitened with rage, but his voice was deadly calm. "I can assure you that you are not the first woman who set out to domesticate me, and you doubtless won't be the last. But none of you will succeed. You can plot and scheme, but I enjoy being wicked and reckless."

"I can see that." Mouette desperately wished that she could stop caring.

"I will never sell my soul for *love*." As if to emphasize his point, Justin took snuff, snapping the agate lid closed and returning it to his waistcoat pocket. "I've suspected all along that love is an illusion, and the events of this evening proved that once and for all."

"I have never asked for your love! In case you have forgotten, we have an arrangement." The words, filled with pride, seemed to burn her throat. "A business arrangement! What conceit causes you to believe I want anything more from you?"

He stared at her and for an instant, they silently acknowledged the truth about the yearnings they'd begun to nurture together.

"*C'est vrai*," Justin said hoarsely. "A loveless arrangement. And it is just as well, for there are only two things I can freely give you."

Mouette knew an involuntary rush of forbidden arousal. Over the beating of her heart, she whispered, "And what are those?"

His hands reached out to grip her shoulders and it came to her that he could easily snap her in two. "Wealth." He pulled her roughly against him, adding, "And *this*..."

Mouette felt the full, pulsing power of his erection through the clothing that separated their bodies. She knew she should push him away, but she wanted the same thing he did.

She burned for him.

This time, Justin didn't ask her if she wanted him to stop. He lifted her off her feet and kissed her in exactly the way she had dreamed of during so many nights alone. His tongue plundered her mouth and she greeted it, returning his kiss with equal passion, sinking her fingers into his hair. How she had hungered for him! Every nerve in her body was on fire for this powerful, untamable man.

He was the man she loved, but could never claim.

Boldly, Mouette reached for his hand and brought it to her breast. The mere thought of his wet tongue on her aching nipple intensified her arousal. He squeezed the fullness of her breast, then pinched her nipple through the thin muslin of her gown.

"Yes," she heard herself murmur shamelessly.

This time, Justin didn't warn her. He swept her up into his arms and carried her out through the formal rooms, where guttering candles marked their progress to his bed. As he started up the stairway, neither of them noticed that a pale girl with light-gray eyes was watching with interest from a dark corner of the entrance hall.

* * *

MOONLIGHT SPILLED through the leaded-glass window at the top of the stairs. It was all the illumination Justin needed to find the way to his bedchamber.

When he set her down beside the curtained bed, Mouette came back into his arms, kissing him. It was a forbidden fantasy come true. How many nights had he lain there, in that great, ugly tester bed that offended his sensibilities, and imagined that Mouette was there in his arms, whispering to him in the darkness, telling him that she loved—

Forget about that. This is all that matters!

His heart raced as he stripped away her fragile gown. He expected her to change her mind, to back away, but instead she dropped her head back, as if reveling in the moment. *Mon Dieu*, she was drawing off her own chemise, until all that she wore were gossamer-thin stockings and garters.

Her breasts were those of a woman, full and soft, her rosy nipples puckered in an invitation. Her hips were full and there was a faint swell to her belly, a reminder that she had borne children. Helplessly, Justin dropped his gaze to the dark curls at the apex of her thighs. His cock swelled, burning for her.

He felt consumed by the need to claim her, to devour her, to be inside her.

Mouette reached up to tug at his neckcloth. Only moments later, it seemed, they were both naked, falling back on the big bed, their sins hidden behind the heavy drapes. Justin pinned her beneath his weight, kissing her until they were both drunk on desire. His long fingers found the secrets of her body, first holding a swollen breast so that he could lick and then suckle it until she was panting, opening her thighs beneath him.

He kissed and nipped his way over her shoulders, tasting the edges of her ears, the sweet curve of her throat. And all the while, he grew harder, until it seemed he would burst with the need to be inside her. His fingers caressed the small of her back, the swell of her bottom, the shadowed indentation there. Mouette made a soft mewling sound.

She was touching him, too, which was torture. He wanted to tie her wrists to the bedposts to make her stop. She managed to lap at his nipples, to run the edges of her nails down his broad back, to squeeze his buttocks when he was lying on top of her. And then she bucked against his cock and he felt how wet she was.

That did it. He caught her hands and held them at her sides. Her knees opened further, until he could see the pink glistening of her womanhood.

"Brazen wench," he grunted.

Her only response was a small, seductive smile that only inflamed him further.

Justin kissed her navel, and then deliberately nibbled his way toward the core of her. Mouette squirmed. Just as her hips came off the bed in a silent plea, he touched her there, just once, with his hot tongue. A low, primal sound came from the back of her throat.

Justin fastened his mouth on her then, swirling his tongue around the bud of her desire, suckling harder, softer, harder, as Mouette tossed her head back and forth on his pillows, gasping, panting, until he brought her to a shuddering climax. Unable to wait another moment, Justin rose up and pushed inside her as her sheath continued to contract around him.

Mouette's slim legs encircled his narrow hips. She clung to his shoulders, her face buried in his neck as he thrust into her body, again and again. The immense power of his own need was something he didn't understand or question. Deeper, harder, and still it was not enough.

When Justin at last found his own scorching release,

it seemed to be wrung from his very depths, a place beyond his heart, discovered for the first time tonight.

Dimly, it came to him that his eye-patch had come off during their heated coupling, and Mouette was gently kissing his scarred eye. Both their faces were wet...with tears, it seemed.

CHAPTER 28

When Mouette awoke in the dark, curtained bed, it seemed she must be dreaming. Where was she? Then she heard Justin's strong heartbeat and the events of the past few hours came rushing back.

She was curled in his arms, her cheek resting on his broad chest, in some sort of mockery of a loving, intimate embrace. Slowly, she registered the distinctive scent of their coupling in the air, on their bodies. Justin had thrown off the covers and, as Mouette's eyes adjusted to the darkness, she slowly raised her head to look at his proud face.

The eye-patch was gone, lost in the heat of passion. The sight of his disfigured eye, slashed through with a long scar, was shocking but not a bit repulsive to Mouette. She wanted to hold him, to tell him that this wound only made her love him more.

But such tender moments could only exist in her fantasies. Tonight, she had realized that she must accept him as he was and let him go. How many times did he have to tell her that he intended never to marry, never to have children, never to be restricted by commitments to a family, before she would believe him?

And now that they knew Cerise St. Briac was not dying, there was no further reason to continue with their make-believe marriage.

Tonight he had stormed at her that he would not be domesticated. Woe be to the woman who tried! After the agony of her marriage to Harry, Mouette didn't intend to knowingly attach herself to a man who would bring more pain and disappointment to her and to her sons.

Mouette carefully disengaged from Justin and crept to the edge of the feather mattress. Sliding down to the floor, she stood there in her bare feet, praying that he wouldn't awaken. She couldn't bear to face him now.

Donning her chemise by moonlight, Mouette knelt to retrieve her gown. But where were her stockings? She saw one then, peeking out from the bedhangings. Very carefully, she drew back the curtain with one hand and reached for the stockings with the other.

And then she saw Justin's foot. His dark, muscular left leg was thrown across her side of the bed and now his foot was illuminated by a silvery moonbeam. Her heart seemed to stop as she saw the impossible.

His second and third toes were fused together.

Mouette had only ever known one other person born this way...her own son, Anthony.

* * *

"It is well past midnight and I should take my leave," said Lady Daphne. "My brother might well fear that I've been set upon by highwaymen."

George stared at her from the other side of the little table in the cottage he had hired from a fisherman in Bodinnick. Outside the ancient, deep-silled window, the River Fowey glimmered in the moonlight. "Why leave? Your coachman has no doubt fallen asleep by now."

"I'll rouse him, then. I can assure you, I will not share your bed, marquess or no," she said haughtily. A lone candle flickered unsteadily between them as she sipped a glass of wine. "I only came so that we might discuss our plans, but you've had little enough to offer me."

"I'm waiting for that girl Jane to come, the one I hired to be St. Briac's kitchen maid. There was a party there tonight and I am hopeful she will bring us news." Just then, as if on cue, a knock sounded at the door. "There, you see!" George exclaimed as he hurried to open it.

Standing outside was thin little Jane Padstow, holding the reins to a horse that was too big for her. George squeezed through the doorway so that the girl wouldn't see Daphne. Once outside, he peered at her in the shadows. "At last! What has taken you so long?"

The girl had a timid look, but now she narrowed her pale-gray eyes at him. "It were not easy to get here, milord. 'Twas lucky the stableboy believed my tale of needin' to visit my sick aunt, or I wouldn't have a horse."

"Fine, fine. What can you tell me?"

As if realizing that he didn't mean to invite her inside, she put out her hand, palm up. "It be information you'll value."

He rolled his eyes and went back inside, returning with a pouch of coins. After pressing a crown into her hand, he demanded, "Go on!"

"Something's amiss. The Frenchman's family went off in a huff, and then they do have a great row."

"They?" His heart began to race with excitement. "St. Briac and—his wife?"

"Aye, milord. He shouted at us to leave the house, but I hid myself away to watch. There were more shouting, 'tween them, and he did carry her off, up the stairs. I were almost afraid for her ladyship!"

"I *see*." Eyes narrowed, he stared off into the distance. He was already closing the door on her as he added, "Good night then."

"Did you hear that?" George exclaimed, hurrying back to the little table where Daphne had poured herself more wine. "They've had a terrible row. I have a feeling *this* will be the time that Mouette sees the light and flees back to London. I must go to Elysium, so that I can determine what has happened and, I hope, intercede...on our behalf."

"But what am I to do in the meantime?" fretted Lady Daphne.

"Trust me! I shall drive a wedge between those two once and for all, and then St. Briac and all his wealth will be yours for the picking." Suddenly he straightened. "Didn't you mention that you had received an invitation to the Countess of Finchley's annual masquerade ball?"

"Yes, but it merely languishes in my reticule. What hope have I of getting to London by Friday?"

"Give it to me." He held out his hand. "It may be of use to us."

"Gladly," beamed Daphne. "And if you succeed in keeping them apart so that I may take advantage of Justin in his time of need, I will generously share the spoils. Rumor has it that he has a cellar filled with pirate's treasure beneath his Saint-Malo home."

For a moment, George looked dreamy. "When this is all behind us, perhaps you'd like to come with me to Italy. I intend to live out my days in splendor, selling off St. Briac's priceless jewels, one by one..."

* * *

MOUETTE WAS numb as she packed a small valise with all that she could fit inside, scrawled a note to Justin, threw a dark cloak over her gown, and started toward the door. To her surprise, she saw Robinson the corgi, sitting on the stairs and watching her as she passed by.

Although Mouette knew that her sons would be outraged by her decision, her choice felt very clear. Pausing for only an instant, she leaned over to pet the dog's head, whispering, "You must stay here, Robinson. Your master needs you, now more than ever."

With that, Mouette opened the great door and slipped out of the manor house, into the night. Deciding it would be better not to leave behind any clues to her whereabouts, she avoided the stable and set off on foot for Elysium, where her boys were staying with Gabriel and Izzie.

As the barest hint of dawn began to lighten the sky, Mouette emerged from the dark tunnel of trees leading to Frenchman's Lair. She couldn't help glancing back, one last time, at the plain manor house that she and Justin had transformed so completely in the space of a few weeks. Even Squire Pendudwell himself had felt the magic, because it went far beyond interior decoration. It had to do with the warmth and spirit of a new family.

Tears spilled onto her cheeks, yet she drew a deep breath and went on. If life had taught her anything it was that she could survive whatever crossed her path— and eventually emerge stronger.

* * *

A HALF-MILE down the narrow lane, Mouette reached the junction with Raphael Road. The hedgerows were high on either side, blocking her view, and she was grateful for the full moon to light her way. If someone should come along she would be easy prey...but it seemed that all of Cornwall was asleep. The moon and stars provided the only source of light and the only sounds were the whoosh of an owl, swooping over the fields, or the rustle of a badger in the bushes.

As if in response to her thoughts, Mouette heard the sound of hoofbeats in the distance, followed by the distinctive shape of a gig approaching on Raphael Road. Her throat went dry.

There was nowhere to go. All she could do was flatten her body against the stony, foxglove-studded hedgerow and pray the occupant of the gig didn't notice her.

"Who goes there?" called a male voice, even as the small equipage slowed to a stop. "Make yourself known to me! I warn you, I am armed!"

Mouette went forward, praying that the man would not turn out to be a dangerous villain. "I am a gently-bred female, sir, bound for the home of friends."

"Madame St. Briac? Is that you—Mouette?"

As he leaned forward, she gave a small exclamation of surprise. "George?"

He clambered out, looking as if he'd dressed very carelessly, without even bothering to tie his neckcloth. "Gadzooks, m'lady, this is a great surprise! Were you walking to Elysium?"

She nodded, forcing back an urge to weep, and let him take her bag and hand her into the gig. "Yes. I would be grateful to you for delivering me there."

* * *

MOUETTE DIDN'T TELL George what had happened at Frenchman's Lair to cause her to flee in the middle of the night, and he didn't ask. Instead, as they jounced along the bumpy road toward Elysium, he carefully inquired about her plans.

"I am going to collect my sons and then we will return to London. Immediately," she said.

"Indeed?" He drew out the word, as if he were immensely curious but too much a gentleman to press her. "And how do you plan to make this journey?"

"I—I am not certain. I suppose I shall ask Gabriel for advice." Mouette thought about the vast sum Justin had promised her in return for her masquerade as his wife. She found that she could no longer imagine accepting any remuneration for what they had shared, yet for now she was virtually penniless. "No doubt there is a stagecoach from Truro to London."

"Out of the question!" he declared, puffing himself up. "I will take you there myself."

"Oh, I could not possibly—"

"I insist. As it happens, I am bound for London myself, on a matter of business. I was on my way to procure a coach for the journey."

Suddenly, Mouette felt exhausted. All the recent events, including the days of preparations for Cerise St. Briac's birthday dinner, seemed to rush toward her in a wave.

She didn't have the energy to argue with him, and in fact, found his offer highly appealing. Perhaps they could depart before she even had to try to explain to Izzie and Gabriel…

* * *

BECAUSE GEORGE'S sister was the mistress of Elysium, he was permitted to come and go at will. The stablemaster thought nothing of it when George appeared near dawn with the gig and requested a post-chaise in its place, with two fresh horses.

Mouette, meanwhile, went into the house, which was utterly still and welcoming. As she walked through the big, cluttered rooms on the ground floor, she felt ashamed for the rather disparaging thoughts she'd originally had about her friend's home. Now she ached with longing at the sight of children's shoes pushed under a frayed ottoman, a pair of Izzie's spectacles lying on an open book, and two wineglasses waiting next to a sofa so worn and outdated that Thomas Hope's hair would stand on end if he saw it.

The appeal of Elysium, Mouette realized, had nothing to do with fashion or style, and everything to do with love.

Her bedchamber upstairs was still filled with many of her things. She went there first, knowing that she would find a small trunk that George had assured her would fit in the carriage. When she had filled it halfway, she decided to go and get the boys' clothing from the wardrobe they shared. Dawn was beginning to break as she turned toward the doorway.

"What's happening?"

Mouette jumped at the unexpected sound of Izzie's soft voice. "Oh!" Whirling around, she saw her friend, clad in a soft muslin dressing gown, her golden hair spilling loose over her shoulders. "I thought you were sleeping."

"I have an instinct for sensing when someone is abroad in this house," Isabella said gently, as she crossed the room. "I confess I expected to find one of the children indulging in mischief by moonlight—not you, my dear friend."

Mouette was relieved to share her story with someone she could trust. "I had to go, Izzie. You saw him last night. It's simply impossible and I must accept that."

"But you love him." She made it a fact, not a question. "I suspect you fell in love with him on the day you two met, at my wedding to Gabriel. Sparks were flying all around you, that day in the chapel."

Mouette blushed at the mention of that long ago day, when she'd been unhappily married to Harry and aspiring to the shallow standards of the London *ton*. She and Justin had verbally sparred by daylight, imbibed too freely, and eventually shared a midnight interlude of unbridled lust. Her heart clenched anew at the realization that Anthony had been conceived that night.

Was it any wonder she had blocked out the memory of that night for a full decade?

"I—I really can't talk about my feelings for Justin. It is too painful," Mouette said, her voice breaking. "And I cannot stay here. I am taking the boys back to London, back to our home."

"Your home that has no furniture or servants?" Isabella asked, arching a brow.

"I will work that out when I return. I believe there are still a few fine pieces I can sell." Turning back to the trunk, she refolded a chemise and added, "George has offered to take us. Apparently he is bound for London himself, on business."

"George?" Isabella's voice rose. "I cannot approve of that plan, and I know Gabriel will not."

"It's not up to you two." Turning back, Mouette stared directly into the eyes of her closest friend. "I am no green girl, but a woman grown. If any good has come from this...*adventure*, it is that I've found the power to claim what is mine." It was more true than she could say, for she had reveled in last night, taking her own pleasure as surely as Justin had claimed his. And she didn't regret it for a moment.

"Mouette, my dear, will you not listen to reason?"

"I fear not." With a wistful smile, she embraced her friend. "I am going to go with George, no matter what you or Gabriel say."

CHAPTER 29

Justin opened one eye and quickly closed it again. The curtains were completely drawn around the monstrous bed and he hoped it might still be the middle of the night.

His head throbbed, his mouth was dry, and there was an odd burning sensation deep in his nose that he'd nearly forgotten about. Groaning, he flipped over on his belly and buried his face in the pillow.

Then, like a river overflowing its banks, memories of Mouette came rushing into his consciousness.

Mouette, naked, submitting to him and yet also welcoming her own fulfillment. Mouette, shuddering as she climaxed against his mouth. Mouette, holding him, rocking with him as he pushed into her body, weeping with the power of her emotions, kissing his scarred eye...

Unable to bear another moment, Justin jumped up and thrust the bedhangings apart. To his shock, sunlight spilled into his bedchamber and Robinson was lying on the carpet bedside his bed.

But where was Mouette? His heart pounded as he thought of the things he had said to her last night. The way he had captured her in his arms and forcibly carried her away up the stairs to his bed. She had seen a side of him he'd managed to keep hidden from everyone else. All his barriers, erected over a lifetime, had fallen away and now she knew the horrible truth.

He was unlovable.

Standing there naked, Justin caught a glimpse of himself in the mirror. His body, though still powerful, was older. His hair was disheveled, his face dissipated, and his uncovered, scarred eye was all the more shocking because he knew Mouette had seen it, too. How could he ever face her again?

And yet he was utterly desperate to do just that.

"Woof!" cried Robinson, standing at alert. He came over then and leaned his solid, short-legged body against Justin's calf.

Something compelled him to bend down and pet the dog. As he did so, to his shock, an involuntary sob rose in his throat. He had to dress, to get out of this room. Looking around, Justin saw pieces of his clothing scattered around the bed, where they had fallen when Mouette helped him undress.

The memory of those moments brought a fresh wave of pain. He ached to see her, to hold her, to hear one word from her that would relieve his fear that he'd ruined everything.

A knocking came at his door. "M'sieur?" called Baptiste. "You have a visitor."

Justin threw open the door. "Help me find something to wear, will you? Buckskins. Boots. You know."

Baptiste entered and his eyes widened when he saw Justin. "M'sieur, what have you done to yourself?"

"I'm not certain," he replied with heavy irony. "Attempted suicide, perhaps."

Baptiste quickly brought him a fresh eye-patch from a special drawer in his armoire. Once that was in place, Justin felt better. Quickly, he dressed, splashed water on his unshaven face, and followed Baptiste down the stairway with Robinson at his side.

To his surprise, he beheld his brother Gabriel, sitting in the dining room and drinking coffee.

"What are doing here?" he asked, even as Jane came rushing in with coffee, milk, and sugar for him. "And where is Mouette?"

Gabriel stood up and came forward to put a hand on Justin's shoulder. He looked as if he were about to tell him that someone had died. "I've brought you some bad news," he said with a sigh. "Mouette has gone back to London, with Charles and Anthony."

The steel band was back, tightening once again around Justin's chest. For a moment, he couldn't draw a breath. "*Vraiment?*" he said at length. "And when will she return?"

Gabriel slowly shook his head. "Never, I'm afraid."

* * *

As Gabriel explained what little he knew about Mouette's movements that day, Justin drank *café au lait* but could not eat. He was sickened by the thought of food. What he really wanted was to go into Mouette's morning room and drink an entire bottle of cognac.

"You look terrible," Gabriel said suddenly. "How could your appearance deteriorate so rapidly since last evening, when I observed your health to be vastly improved?"

"Maman happened, that's what," came his dark reply. He took out his snuffbox and inhaled a pinch from the anatomical hollow at the side of his wrist. "I had every right to be enraged by her plot to deceive me."

Gabriel nodded slowly, leaning back in his chair. "True, but what about your own manipulation? You and Maman were doing the same thing. Can you not see the irony in that?"

"Do you have the audacity to compare me to our devious mother?" he demanded, outraged.

"I do. I think the similarities are quite obvious."

Justin's head was pounding like the surf on the Cornwall cliffs. "You are supposed to be my ally."

"Do you want my help?" inquired Gabriel. "Do you want the truth?"

"What I want is to see Mouette again." He knew he was exposing himself, yet the words came nonetheless. "But if you will help me, I'll hear the truth."

"Perhaps you already know, but won't admit it. You are in love with Mouette, have been in love with her for quite some time, yet you've kept various avenues of escape always open."

"Escape?" Even as he spoke, Justin knew exactly what Gabriel meant.

"Pretending to be married, but knowing that it wasn't real was a very convenient means of tasting what you hungered for without becoming vulnerable."

"I despise that word." He thought of all the other ways he had discouraged Mouette from expecting a commitment, and the discomfort intensified around his heart. "Have I told you that I think I might be dying?"

"You did mention it, that day at Elysium, when we last spoke of Mouette." Gabriel appeared unconcerned. "You and she seemed to be dealing rather well together recently, while you were preparing for our mother's birthday party. Did you have those pains during this past week?"

Justin arched a sardonic brow. "Perhaps not."

"Then, as I have said before, you are not dying. Once you surrender to love, I can promise you the pain will disappear."

He took a deep breath. "Surrender is not in my nature."

"Fine. Go on that way. See where that leads you." Gabriel stood up, looking bored. "No doubt you'll be departing soon for Saint-Malo, where you can carry on as before?"

"No, wait. That is not what I want." Justin stood up as well. "I must find Mouette. Will you help me? With the boys in tow, it will take her at least four days to reach London. We could find her at one of the coaching stops."

"Of course I will help you," Gabriel said. "But Mouette has not traveled by public coach. My brother-in-law, George, has taken her to London."

Justin's first impulse was to go to Charles's bedchamber and smash the paper model of Saint-Malo that George Trevarre had been helping him to construct, but instead he clenched his fists. "I see. Then there is no time to lose! We must depart immediately."

* * *

"Mama, when can we stop?" demanded Anthony. "And when are we going home?"

"Darling, we are nearly there. And we *are* going home, don't you remember? We are in London." In the crush of horse-drawn equipages that crowded London's Great Russell Street, Mouette too had begun to wonder if they would ever reach Bedford Square.

He shook his head. "No, I mean to Frenchman's Lair, of course!"

Mouette felt another sharp pang of guilt over the fact that she had taken the boys out of their beds at Elysium and bade them travel back to London with her, without any plausible explanation or the opportunity to say goodbye to Justin. This was one of the best reasons why it was advisable to remain free of amorous entanglements until her sons were fully grown. It wasn't fair for them to suffer for her romantic mistakes.

"Boys, you know we couldn't stay in Cornwall forever," she said, thinking that she must begin to break the news to them about Justin and the make-believe marriage. Perhaps tomorrow. "We had to come home, back to Bedford Square, to look after the house."

"Ah, here we are," interrupted George, who was riding on the box with Helivet, the coachman Gabriel had been good enough to send with them.

Mouette was startled to see how narrow and staid her townhouse appeared. Could it be that she had come to prefer the green countryside and larger manor houses of Cornwall? She sighed. Perhaps it was simply that she had been away for so long…

Charles, who had been reading Gulliver's Travels, closed his book and sat up straight to look out at the home where he had been born. "It seems smaller than before. Is that possible?"

"I miss Robinson," mourned Anthony. "And Jus—"

Mouette, feeling her heart clench, spoke before he could finish the word. "I think the house looks wonderful! Let us go in, shall we?"

Soon enough, with Helivet's assistance, the band of travelers were coming into the entryhall. Of course, there were no servants to greet them, and Mouette saw the surprise on George's face.

"Gadzooks, it's like a tomb!" he exclaimed, looking around. "Where are the furnishings?"

"Oh, Mama disposed of those, one by one, a long time ago," Anthony said.

"Yes," Charles agreed, "we couldn't invite any of our friends to visit because our home was quite bare."

"That's not true," Mouette protested. With that, she

went ahead of them and opened the double doors to the sitting room, the one room she'd kept intact, in case of visitors. "You see, isn't it lovely and inviting?"

George began wandering around, poking his head into her morning room. Her small desk sat in the great empty space and there were shadowed spaces on the walls where paintings had once hung.

"What's this all about?" he cried. "This is Bedford Square, after all! I thought your husband was a bloody baronet!"

Mouette refused to flush with embarrassment or shame. Instead, she stood up straighter and met his eyes that were blinking with curiosity. "My lord, I would ask you to moderate your tone in front of my sons."

"Never mind," said Charles. "We'll go to our rooms. I have forgotten if we still had beds." He paused, as if trying to think what he would do with himself. "My paper city was left behind in Cornwall. I rather wish I had stayed behind with Robinson while you made this journey. I was beginning to like it there."

Anthony started to follow his brother but turned back after a short distance, his dark eyes sparkling with emotion. Now that Mouette knew the truth, she could see all too clearly how much her son resembled Justin.

"What is it, sweetheart?" she asked.

"What *about* Robinson, Mama? Why didn't we bring him with us?"

"Because...then Justin would be all alone. The thought of that made me sad."

Both boys seemed to consider this for a long moment, and Anthony replied, "Yes, I think Papa needs company more than he knows. And perhaps now he will finally allow Robinson to sleep on his bed!"

Mouette waited for Charles to protest that Justin was not their papa, but he only nodded his agreement.

* * *

GEORGE HAD FOUND the cellaret and was peering inside. Mouette braced herself for his reaction when he saw the meager supply of spirits.

"What?" Incredulous, he held up a single decanter of brandy. It was two-thirds empty. "Surely this cannot be everything."

She watched as he poured most of the contents into a crystal glass and drank it down. "I'm afraid so. As you can see, we had fallen on hard times. I could not entertain, and thus did not regard wine and spirits as real necessities."

George sidled over to her and smiled. "What about your *husband*? I understand that he is richer than Croesus."

It came to Mouette that George somehow knew the truth about her marriage to Justin. How he knew, she couldn't say, but he did. "I would rather make my own way in the world."

"That is ridiculous. Why should you refuse a chest of jewels from a man who has an entire cellar of them in France? It is rumored that St. Briac has Colombian emeralds the size of your fist, more of them than he can count. And if that seems excessive, you might settle instead for gold coins." He paused, drank down the brandy, and then added boldly, "No doubt you have earned a share of his wealth, one way or another."

"My lord, if I may be so bold, I feel that you are speaking out of turn. I appreciate your kindness in bringing us to London, but—"

"Have I offended you?" George quickly put down his empty glass and took her hand. "I assure you that was not my intention, my dear. On the contrary, I was merely hoping to offer a rather obvious solution to your problems. If I were a man of means, I should step forward to lend financial assistance, but I fear that I only can give you my *self*."

There was something about the pressure of his rather damp hand that made her nervous, especially because they were alone in the house, except for her sons. "You have been more than kind, and I am more grateful than you know..."

George stepped closer just as a knock came at the front door.

"Who in the world could that be?" exclaimed Mouette. "No one knows I am here!"

CHAPTER 30

ouette hesitated to open the door, since most callers were either bill collectors or members of society she wanted to avoid.

"Perhaps I should see who it is?" asked George, as the tapping at the continued.

"No! I will go."

Was it possible that Justin might have followed her? Her heart lifted slightly as she opened the door. To Mouette's utter shock, there on the doorstep stood her mother.

"Mama!" She blinked as if fearing that she beheld a mirage.

"I am quite real, darling." Devon Raveneau said, reaching out to embrace her oldest child. "And look who is with me."

Mouette looked down to see a beautiful, strawberry-blond toddler holding on to Devon's skirts. "Oh my, this must be Bridget. She looks like you, Mama! I couldn't be more thrilled or surprised. You must come inside and tell me how you came to be in London."

She brought them into the pretty sitting room and settled her mother on a blue-striped silk settee, with little Bridget snuggled on her lap. In her surprise, Mou-

284

ette had temporarily forgotten about George, but now he came up beside her.

"Ah, is it my great honor to make the acquaintance of Madame Raveneau?" He bowed low before Devon. Grasping her hand, he kissed it. "Your celebrated reputation precedes you, Madame."

Devon arched a brow and glanced toward Mouette who forced a smile. "Allow me to present George Trevarre, Marquess of Caverleigh." Turning to George, she added, "You do indeed have the honor of meeting my mother, Devon Raveneau, as well as my niece, Bridget Coleraine."

Mouette desperately wished he would go. There was so much she wanted to discuss with her mother! Thankfully, there was no more brandy for George to drink, so she suspected he would soon be on his way.

"Mama, tell us how you came to be in London. I had heard that Lindsay intended to visit you in America."

As Mouette perched on the edge of one of the Adam chairs across from Devon, George was taking another look inside the cellaret.

"Oh, it is a long story and I wouldn't want to bore his lordship. Suffice it to say that Lindsay had a last-minute change of plans, so I came to them."

"Well, you and Papa have ever been at ease sailing across the ocean," said Mouette, nodding.

Devon smiled. "Once I arrived, I encouraged Lindsay and Ryan to go away for a few days so that I might bring Bridget with me to stay at our house in Grosvenor Square. We were passing by here, rather by chance, when I saw movements inside your windows! As you might imagine, I had to investigate."

"Madame, you were taking a risk," said George, suddenly attentive to their conversation. "What if we had been footpads, lurking about in this empty house?" Before Devon could reply, he sat down on the other Adam chair and leaned toward her. "You mentioned that you were on your way to your home in Grosvenor Square. Perhaps you were aware it once belonged to me...?"

"I am indeed." Her alert blue eyes seemed to read his thoughts. "I am aware, of course, that we originally purchased the house because you were in...financial difficulties."

Mouette watched her mother in admiration. What a little spitfire she was! Of course, she was referring to the fact that George had gambled away nearly the entire Caverleigh estate. The Raveneaus, friends of the Trevarre family, lived across Grosvenor Square at the time and acquired the home with the intention of treating it with respect. André Raveneau had even offered Sebastian the opportunity to repurchase it if he one day had the means and desire to do so.

"I can only say, in my own defense, that two decades have passed since that rather unfortunate chapter in my life. And, as your daughter and I have agreed, people are capable of change." He stared into Devon's eyes. "Are they not?"

Mouette was certainly grateful to him for bringing them safely to London, and attempted a friendly smile when George put his hand over hers. But something about his behavior didn't feel quite right. Why was he so determined that she should accept financial assistance from Justin St. Briac, and how did he know so much about the extent of Justin's wealth? Furthermore, why was George so interested in the Grosvenor Square home he had once casually gambled away? He almost sounded as if he had designs on it again.

"Yes," Devon was saying, her tone polite yet faintly skeptical, "people certainly are capable of change, but only if they produce actions to accompany their words."

George thrust out his jaw and stared longingly toward the empty brandy decanter. "How very wise you are, Madame."

"At my age, I have learned that promises are easily made but frequently abandoned," Devon replied sweetly. She set Bridget down on the Axminster carpet and watched as the infant toddled off, the ribbons on her miniature muslin round gown fluttering behind her. "Mouette, do you imagine that there is any tea in the house? No, it is likely stale, I suppose. Why don't we pack up the boys and all go to Grosvenor Square, where a proper household is in place?"

Before Mouette could reply, George exclaimed, "A brilliant plan, Madame! And I shall go to my lodgings. However, I have just remembered that I am in possession of an invitation to a glittering masquerade ball that will be held this very night at the Countess of Finchley's home. It is an annual affair. Perhaps you have attended?"

"No, but I am aware of Lady Finchley's ball. How fortunate you must feel to have received an invitation."

He colored slightly, but took the folded parchment from inside his coat and waved it in the air. "Indeed I am. Of course, we are very old friends. Emily was over the moon when she learned that I had returned to England to reclaim my position."

Mouette exchanged a brief glance with her mother. "Clearly you have more important matters to attend to, your lordship, so we won't keep you..."

"Now, Mouette, have I not given you leave to call me by my Christian name?" He reached over to touch her back. "And I would not have mentioned the ball if I were not intending to invite both of you to accompany me!"

Devon arched a delicate brow. "How kind you are to ask, but of course I will be occupied with my grandchildren. It will be the first time I'll have all three of them together!" She looked toward Mouette. "Darling, you must go if it would please you to do so. Masquerades have fallen out of favor, since so many of them have taken on a disreputable air, but I'm quite certain Lady Finchley's ball remains above all that."

Mouette knew what her mother meant. Masked balls had become quite lascivious, and these days they were often hosted by courtesans. However, everyone was aware that the Countess's masquerade was different. It was a tradition among the *ton*…and part of her did want to go. She was desperate for anything that might distract her from the pain she felt whenever she thought of Justin.

What was he doing at that moment? It took an act of will to keep from imagining where he might be, what he might be thinking, during every waking moment of her days. Mouette could clearly see Justin in her mind's eye. She could lose herself in the contours of his brutally handsome face, the shape of his fingers, the husky sound of his voice. She hoped that Baptiste was taking care of him, that Justin was not abusing his health with too much rich food and drink. She hoped that he would hold Robinson and let the dog love him.

It seemed at times that Mouette might drown in heartache, but she was determined not to. *I am stronger than that. And my boys need me!*

"I would like to attend the masquerade with you, my lord," she said to George. "And I appreciate the invitation."

"Yes," her mother agreed. "It will be good for you to put a toe back into society, especially in a setting where few people will know you are there. You can safely practice being back among the *ton*."

"How wise you are, Mama," Mouette said warmly.

"It's settled then," pronounced George. "Excellent!

Shall I collect you at the Grosvenor Square house? I can assure you, I know my way there *very* well!"

* * *

WHEN GEORGE HAD GONE, Mouette sat down on the settee and tried to coax Bridget to sit on her lap. Devon, meanwhile, went to the window and looked outside.

"My carriage is waiting," she said. "Shall we call the boys so that we can go to a house where there is food to eat?"

"I remain the greatest failure among your children," said Mouette with a sigh. "I am thirty-six years old and I can't even manage to provide a home with furnishings and a stocked larder."

"You've been away, darling."

"So have you, Mama. I think you know what I mean."

"You are understandably tired and worried about how you will navigate the future." As she spoke, Devon squeezed in beside Mouette on the small settee. "But what I think we should talk about now is the state of your heart. What has happened in Cornwall? Lindsay had a letter from Sebastian—"

"Do you mean Lord Sebastian Trevarre?" Mouette said in surprise. "He wrote a letter about me?"

"Well, yes." Color washed Devon's cheeks. "He is very good about keeping in touch. We've grown quite close to him over the years, as you know."

"What did he write?"

"Of course, we knew you were going there, to stay with our Izzie, but he did mention in his letter that you were entangled in a situation with Justin St. Briac. He said that it was a business arrangement on the face of it, but he felt that it might be involving your heart." Devon took Mouette's cold hands in hers. "And he was concerned."

"I don't see that it is any of his affair," protested Mouette.

After a moment, Devon said, "I know that, if your father were here, he would be immensely grateful to Sebastian for looking in on you. But that is not the point, my dear. I hope you will tell me the reason for these shadows under your eyes."

"Shadows?" Mouette wrinkled her nose. "Old age, no doubt." When her mother did not deign to reply to that, she sighed. "You are perceptive as always, Mama. I am nursing a broken heart."

"I am so sorry."

As her mother embraced her, Mouette felt something crack open inside her and she began to weep. "I thought—after Harry—that I would never again love or desire a man. But with Justin, I discovered that what I knew with Harry was only a weak imitation of passion…"

Devon's eyes widened. "I *see*."

"Have I shocked you, Mama?"

This evoked a bubble of laughter from her mother. "On the contrary. I am very pleased for you! Now, do tell me what ensued between the birth of this great passion and the shattering of your heart."

"Justin is—" Struggling to find the words to describe him, Mouette sighed. "Oh, he is magnificent and ungovernable, wicked, extravagant, manipulative and *wildly*—" She paused, blushing.

"Never mind, I can imagine," Devon said dryly.

"But there is no future for us," Mouette said. "Even if I could bear to take such a risk again, Justin has demons that he cannot banish. Perhaps more to the point, he has vowed repeatedly never to marry or have children, and he means to return to his libertine's existence in France."

Devon was silent for a full minute and Mouette imagined there were many things she wished to say, but was holding her tongue. "Well then, you are doing what you think is best, for yourself and for the boys," she murmured at length. "And I applaud your courage. No doubt you must feel you have more control over the outcome now."

"That's very cryptic."

A smile spread over her mother's face. "I have had a bit of experience with a Frenchman like your Justin."

"Do you mean Papa? Oh no. If you should ever meet Justin, you will see that he is quite different."

As Bridget climbed back onto Devon's lap, she said, "It is growing late and we all need sustenance. Let us repair to Grosvenor Square and get everyone fed and settled before Lord Caverleigh arrives. I have remembered that there is a beautiful old gown of mine, packed away there. It would be perfect for a masquerade ball!"

When they arrived at the Raveneaus' grand home in Grosvenor Square, Mouette felt grateful for its secure embrace, yet also discomfited that she still needed to be rescued by her family.

"Don't worry, you'll be back in your own home in no time. Helivet has driven Mrs. Butter over to do a bit of housekeeping and to put some proper foodstuffs on your shelves," said Devon, referring to her own long-time housekeeper. "Tomorrow you can go home, if you wish, but there's no shame in accepting help from your own parents."

"Perhaps, but it seems to be a recurring theme in my life. At this age, I should have a secure home of my own." Watching as servants prepared a hot bath for her boys, Mouette sighed again. "It's certainly not the life I envisioned for myself when I was young."

"No," agreed her mother with a trace of irony. "I think you intended to marry a prince."

"In theory, perhaps, but certainly not the Prince of Wales," laughed Mouette. "I doubtless aspired to become a duchess."

"Yes… I think you supposed that wealth and a castle

decorated in the current style would bring you happiness. But perhaps you have learned differently?"

As Anthony and Charles climbed into their baths, Mouette stood across the room and sipped from a small glass of wine. "Although I intend to continue using my skill for interior decoration to earn a living, I confess that I do not place the same importance on material possessions that I once did. I have discovered that the pursuit of the latest fashion is an empty diversion." She wrinkled her nose. "In truth, it is but a distraction from life's real treasures."

When her mother came closer and wordlessly embraced her, Mouette was swept up in a wave of deep contentment. Tears filled her eyes.

"I am very proud of you, my darling daughter."

"Thank you, Mama. I am trying."

Distraction arrived in the form of Devon's lady's maid, who slipped into the room to tell them that she had located her mistress's ballgown, and it was ready for Mouette's inspection. After that, Mouette was spared any more probing questions from her mother.

She had a hot bath of her own and nibbled at a tray of food as two maids spread out Devon's beautiful gown. Mouette remembered seeing it when she was a little girl. She'd thought her mother was a princess when she'd worn the creation of ivory satin embroidered with blood-red roses on swirling green stems. Froths of lace trimmed the low, curved bodice and the edges of the elbow-length sleeves.

Dressing was a lengthy process, complete with a ruffled chemise, corset, and panniers that held the gown out from Mouette's body. Once the maid had fastened the last tiny button, Mouette twirled around in delight.

"It is so perfectly old-fashioned, like something Marie Antoinette would have worn at Versailles!"

"I have never felt so old before," Devon said with mock sorrow. "My favorite gown is a museum piece."

They laughed together as they artfully applied white powder, rouge, and an assortment of patches to Mouette's face. Her hair was piled high atop her head, with a cluster of long curls spilling down in back.

"No one will recognize you!" Devon proclaimed. She held one of her own silk masks in front of Mouette's face and they laughed together. "All that is missing are some well-chosen jewels."

Mouette felt herself go pink when her mother produced the very same collarette of rubies she had dreamed of selling to raise money just a few short months ago.

"Oh, Mama, I think it is too beautiful for such a frivolous occasion."

"Nonsense." Devon stood behind her and fastened the clasp herself. "You see, the rubies are perfection with your black hair. I've sent my sapphire necklace to your brother Nathan, as a gift for the woman he will one day marry, and I want you to have this piece, Mouette."

Tears burned her eyes and for a moment, Mouette couldn't speak. "I am indeed fortunate to have such wonderful parents. Thank you, Mama."

"I believe I hear sounds downstairs. Perhaps your escort has arrived. Shall we go and see?"

A short time later, Mouette had kissed her sons good-night and was greeting Lord Caverleigh in the entrance hall. To her surprise, she saw that he had gone to great pains to achieve an impressive costume for the ball. From his tricorne hat and brocade waistcoat to his fancy walking stick and red-heeled shoes, he was every inch a Georgian popinjay.

"George, how splendid you look!"

He struck an attitude, preening. "You're looking

magnificent as well, my lady! And so is my Caverleigh House, I must say." Glancing toward Devon, he flushed under the paint covering his face. "But I suppose it ain't Caverleigh House any more, eh?"

"Yes, many years have passed since your family lived here," she agreed. "I can imagine that you might feel a bit sad to be in this house again."

"Sad? No, I rather think this might signal the beginning of a splendid new chapter in my life!" Turning back to Mouette, George bowed. "Your carriage awaits, my beauty. Shall we embark upon a night of adventure?"

* * *

"Now what do you suggest we do?" Gabriel St. Briac demanded of his brother.

Justin stared at the darkened townhouse facing Bedford Square. "There's not even the flicker of one candle. Where the devil can she be?"

"If you intend to take that tone with Mouette when you do find her, we might as well go back to Cornwall right now. I would suggest you begin practicing something called *contrition*."

"I can assure you, I know how to handle Mouette." Justin swung down from Hugo's back and rubbed his aching knee.

"Ah, right. That's why she ran away."

"Do you take me for a fool? I can assure you that I have given this a great deal of thought." The truth was, ever since he'd awakened in that hulking bed without Mouette, he had done nothing else but think of her and all the unforgiveable mistakes he had made.

Just then, a muffled "woof" came from the one of the saddlebags and a head like a fox's poked out.

"I still cannot believe you brought that dog with us," said Gabriel.

"I share your disbelief, yet it is true." Because of the late hour, Bedford Square was quiet. Justin lifted Robinson from the leather saddlebag and set him on the cobbled walkway so that the dog could relieve himself. "Somehow he gives me hope that this will all end well."

Gabriel leaned down to put a hand on his shoulder. "I suggest we find lodgings and fortify ourselves with food and sleep. Perhaps tomorrow you'll be able to learn Mouette's whereabouts."

Justin wasn't a bit hungry or tired himself. In fact, food and sleep felt like boring distractions that would only slow him down. But what alternative did he have at nearly ten o'clock at night?

"*Capitaines?*"

Justin and Gabriel swiveled in unison to see Helivet's moon-silvered figure waving to them from the driver's box of an approaching carriage. As he brought the vehicle to a stop in front of Mouette's townhouse, a plump old woman pushed open the passenger door and descended unaided to the ground.

"I'll require your assistance," the woman called to Helivet.

"Yes, Mrs. Butter," he replied in French-accented English.

When he scrambled down to carry some chests of provisions into the house, Justin followed them inside.

"Helivet, I must speak to you," he called as the two servants disappeared in the direction of what he supposed must be the kitchen. "Make haste!"

The entryhall was so dark, he couldn't even discern the furnishings. Eventually, as candles were lit in the kitchen, faint light began to flicker toward the part of the house where Justin stood.

Suddenly he felt very curious to see this house, decorated by his talented Mouette during her marriage. How many times had she said that she couldn't wait to get back to Bedford Square and her *real* life, once the charade of their make-believe marriage was concluded?

As his eyes gradually adjusted to the shadowed interior, Justin realized that the narrow entry was virtually bare. An unimpressive mirror hung on one wall, nothing more. Odd! Turning left, into the morning room, he blinked. Where were the furnishings? Only a small writing desk and a satin-upholstered side chair were positioned in the window facing the street. Otherwise, the room was empty.

His heart began to pound as it came to him that Mouette's financial situation had clearly been much worse than she had admitted. He could imagine how many fine paintings and pieces of furniture she had sold from this very room, and how painful it must have been for her to part with each one. No doubt they had been sold to pay for food, clothing, and lessons her sons required to become proper gentlemen.

More quickly, Justin crossed to the sitting room. When he saw that it was fully and impeccably furnished, the situation became even clearer. Mouette had kept this one room for entertainment, so no visitor would guess the extent of her shame...her ruin and betrayal at the hands of Sir Harry Brandreth, her own husband.

Justin's heart hurt for her, even as his love deepened.

"There's not a stick of furniture in the dining room or kitchen!" declared Helivet as he reappeared. "And not a servant to be found. How can her ladyship expect to live here?"

They went outside together, back to the carriage where Gabriel was waiting. Grasping Helivet's arm,

Justin queried, "You brought Lady Brandreth and her sons to London?"

"*Oui, Capitaine,*" he replied, glancing at Gabriel.

"I wanted them to travel safely, with a good carriage and driver," said Gabriel.

"Yes, yes." Justin tightened his grip on Helivet's arm. "Where is she?"

"Her ladyship's mother, Madame Raveneau took them to her home in Grosvenor Square. And then she bade me bring this woman here to clean and stock the kitchen."

Nodding as he absorbed this information, Justin released him and lifted Robinson back into the saddlebag. "Gabriel, you must take me there, now."

"Are you mad? Who will open the door to you, a dangerous-looking stranger, at this late hour? Come with me to an inn, where we may have a meal, a bath, and some sleep. Then, refreshed, we can go there together in the morning."

"That's very sensible...but don't you see, I *cannot* wait." He was in the saddle again, his left knee in agony, his heart soaring with hope that he might set eyes on Mouette again before this night ended.

* * *

"You must come with me," Justin whispered urgently as he dismounted in front of André and Devon Raveneau's home in Grosvenor Square. "Madame Raveneau knows you!"

"All the more reason for me to wait at a distance, in the darkness," said Gabriel. "I would prefer to protect what remains of my good name."

Moments later the two brothers were standing in front of the elegant front door. Justin shifted Robinson in his arms as he lifted the lion's-mask knocker. His

298

heart pounded as he imagined that Mouette might be on the other side of the door.

Instead, when the door swung open a short distance, he saw a very tall butler who eyed them with polite suspicion.

"How may I help you gentlemen?"

Clearly the man believed they were lost. Or had evil intentions.

Robinson chose that moment to bolt from Justin's arms into the entrance hall, running straight ahead. Barking loudly, he dashed up the stairs on his stout little legs.

"Please accept our sincere apologies for that unruly dog," Gabriel said to the butler. "If you will allow us to pass, we shall quickly retrieve him—"

No sooner had they taken one step forward, in unison, than the butler extended a long arm to stop them. "I'm afraid not," he intoned.

It came to Justin that the old man must think this was all a ruse simply to gain entrance to the mansion and wreak havoc on its occupants. Robinson's plush backside, meanwhile, was disappearing around the corner at the top of the stairs.

"Come back here, you little fiend!" he couldn't help yelling after the dog. "Is this how you repay me for bringing you all the way from Cornwall?"

A moment later, Justin heard the cries of Charles and Anthony. They came running down the steps in their bare feet and nightclothes, chasing Robinson, while a lovely woman with hair the color of sunset followed in their wake.

"Papa!" cried Anthony, and promptly threw his arms around Justin's waist. "I knew you would come!"

Even Charles looked pleased to see Justin and Gabriel. "Thank you for restoring Robinson to us," he said. "I don't suppose you've brought my paper city with you...?

Justin bent to embrace Anthony and drew Charles near as well. "I have never been so glad to see the two of you," he said with only a trace of irony. "Where is your mama?"

The titian-haired woman was coming toward them, smiling radiantly. "Gabriel St. Briac, is that you? I have not seen you since we all were together in Roscoff, many years ago."

Gabriel went forward to kiss the woman's hand, then turned back to extend an arm toward Justin. "Madame Raveneau, allow me to present my brother—"

"Oh, I know all about Justin." She stepped forward and extended a hand in welcome. "I have heard a great deal about you, m'sieur."

"Madame," Justin said harshly, "I find it impossible to engage in polite conversation tonight. I have come to find your daughter." Out of the corner of his eye, he glimpsed his reflection in a gold-framed mirror flanked by candlelit sconces. He looked utterly lawless—disheveled, unshaven, and travel-stained after three days of hard riding and little sleep. The eye-patch only added to his disreputable air. "Please do not be alarmed by my appearance. I have come on an errand of honor —to deliver the payment I promised Lady Brandreth for assisting with the interior decoration of my home in Cornwall. I cannot sleep until this debt is paid."

"Goodness, how businesslike you are when it comes to my daughter. I know better, however." Devon gave him a wide smile, pausing for effect before she added, "Mouette has gone to a masquerade ball...with Lord George Caverleigh."

"*Sangdieu!*" swore Justin, forgetting himself. "How could this have happened? How could you let her go off to one of those licentious entertainments, especially with that weasel?"

"Charles and Anthony, will you please take your dog upstairs?" said Devon. When the trio had taken their leave, she returned her attention to Justin. "M'sieur, surely you are aware that my daughter is a woman grown, not a girl for whom I could presume to make rules. She will do as she pleases. Why should she not go out and enjoy a bit of frivolity, especially after all she has been through recently?"

"What do you mean by that?" He felt himself frowning. "Are you referring to our marriage?"

"Marriage?" Devon lifted an eyebrow. "Is that what you call it?"

"Do not disparage it!" He wanted to force her somehow to tell him what he wanted to know, but summoned instead the courage to reveal his feelings. "I love your daughter. *Mon Dieu*, I love her with every fiber of my being and I want to be a husband to her. I am dying without her. Madame, I beg you to help me."

"Of course I shall help you." To his surprise, she put her arms around him and rested her face on his chest for a moment. "And now that you have won my trust, I have a small secret to share with you."

Although Justin wasn't certain if he could stand one more revelation, he nodded bravely. "I am listening, Madame."

"Our family has had a letter from a very close friend, Lord Sebastian Trevarre. I believe your make-believe wedding was held at his estate?" Devon's smile was almost mischievous as she glanced toward Gabriel. "When he wrote, Sebastian confessed that he and your brother were in agreement that you and Mouette were meant to be together, even though you could not yet see it yourself."

Justin slanted a suspicious look at Gabriel. "What is this all about?"

"We couldn't tell you until you discovered the deeper truth yourself, *mon frère*," Gabriel said as he draped an arm around Justin's shoulders. "You see, the vicar we hired was not an actor at all…and your make-believe wedding was quite real."

"It's really just a detail, after all, but I thought that tonight of all nights, you might like to know." Smiling, Devon stood on tip-toe and kissed her son-in-law's cheek. "Welcome to the Raveneau family, my dear."

onveniently, Finchley House was located on the other side of Grosvenor Square. Thanks to Devon Raveneau, Justin was holding an invitation to Lady Finchley's annual masquerade ball when he and Gabriel ascended the wide stone steps. Their progress was illuminated by countless chandeliers, spilling golden light from the windows, out into the night.

Two liveried footmen stood guard in the massive doorway. The smaller man regarded Justin's invitation through his spectacles.

"You are M'sieur Raveneau?" he intoned, clearly suspicious.

"That's right."

"And who is this?" The footman gestured toward Gabriel. "Not *Madame* Raveneau, we can see. Only one of you may enter."

"Go on," Gabriel urged him. "As you know, I'm exhausted. Perhaps Devon will allow me to have a nap on one of her fine sofas."

As Justin entered the mansion with its marble floors and sweeping staircase, he felt relieved that Gabriel wouldn't be present to implore him to exercise restraint. He was in no mood for restraint.

More servants directed him upstairs, where two sets of double doors were open to a glittering ballroom. White-wigged footmen glided discreetly around the edges of the room, bearing trays filled with goblets of wine. Justin accepted one and drank it down, scanning the masked guests for any sign of Mouette.

Soon, he noticed that many of the sumptuously-garbed revelers were staring at him with a mixture of curiosity and trepidation. His mother-in-law had outdone herself with this costume, he thought with a grim smile.

When the dancing began, Justin moved back toward a doorway, watching behind his mask. He passed over Cupid, a milkmaid, Red Riding Hood, a horned Centaur, and a harlequin, until at last he saw an ebony-haired beauty wearing an old-fashioned gown of ivory satin embroidered with blood-red roses on swirling green stems.

* * *

"I don't like the look of that fellow," George muttered, inclining his head toward the doorway. "I'm surprised they allowed him in."

Mouette, who had been momentarily cheered by the music and dancing, forced herself to turn her head and look. In the open doorway, among the throngs of costumed guests, she saw the disreputable-looking, solitary guest George referred to. And for a moment, her heart seemed to stop.

It must be my imagination, playing tricks on me again!

The man seemed to be costumed as a threatening highwayman from another age. He wore tall black boots and a tricorne hat. Lace frothed at his neck and over the backs of his hands, contrasting with the heavy fabric of his long greatcoat. Both a sword and a flintlock pistol were visible under his midnight-blue coat. Most intriguing of all, his face was virtually hidden by a black silk mask covering his eyes and a black kerchief that was drawn up over his mouth and nose.

MOUETTE IMAGINED she could feel his eyes, burning her flesh. How many times had she seemed to see Justin since they'd left Cornwall—on the street, in a passing carriage, and now at Lady Finchley's ball? But it was impossible.

Impossible.

"Why is that scoundrel staring at me?" complained George. "Let us go out onto the terrace for a bit of air, shall we? It's frightfully warm in here."

Mouette found that she didn't have the will to refuse. She had hoped that this evening might lighten her mood and distract her from her heartache, but it was not to be. Perhaps it would help to be outside, where she could breathe freely and see the stars.

George took her elbow and guided her along the edge of the crowd and out through a pair of glass doors.

The torch-lit balcony that overlooked a garden and mews was surprisingly large. There was another couple in one corner, fumbling with one another in the shadows, but George drew Mouette to the opposite side.

"It is very grand, don't you agree?" He came closer to her as he spoke. "Mouette, my dear, don't you see that you and I could enjoy social events like this as often as we please if we were...together here in London. We already have a connection, of course—"

She stared at him, genuinely confused. "A connection?"

"Why, yes! Your family has been living in my ancestral home. Don't you see what a triumph it would be for all of us if we could join our two lines. Of course, I mean to restore my fortunes completely, to make my title respected and celebrated once again."

"Perhaps I am dull-witted after all the events of the past days, but I do not understand. Join our two lines?"

Now he was pressing her back against the stone railing. "I would make you Marchioness of Caverleigh, my dear. Can you *imagine?* It would bring you a position at the very pinnacle of London society! I would regain my home, sharing it of course with your family, and together—"

"George, please stop this. Even if this were possible, I would never ask my parents to share their home with us. Also, you have nothing to bring to a marriage except your title, and I have even less!"

"We shall have a *fortune*," he argued. "I have plans that I cannot reveal, not yet, but even putting those aside, you are entitled to a portion of that St. Briac fellow's wealth. He owes you that much after all that you did for him—and he has riches beyond our imagining!"

As George went on, Mouette began to struggle, but he tightened his grip on her arms. "Stop this, please. You are mad!" she cried.

"You are shockingly ungrateful, after all that I have done for you." Now he was gripping her soft upper arms, bending her back over the railing until she feared he might push her over the edge. His mouth stabbed at hers, too awkward to engage in a real kiss.

Just then, George seemed to sail up into the air, away from her, until she saw him land in a heap on the stone floor of the balcony. Then she saw the highwayman, his face still obscured, standing over him.

"Get up," the man growled in a low voice. It sounded as if he had some sort of accent.

"I beg your pardon!" cried George. "You are

speaking to the Marquess of Caverleigh, you knave. I demand satisfaction!"

The highwayman gave a grunt of laughter and gestured inside his coat, to the two weapons he wore. "I accept. Swords or pistols, my lord?"

Horrified to see George clambering to his feet, Mouette cried, "No, this is madness!"

He didn't seem to hear her as he brandished his walking stick. "Swords!"

And in the next instant, George grasped the cane's engraved gold knob and swiftly withdrew an evil-looking sword that had been hidden inside. Without waiting for his opponent to arm himself, George lunged forward with his blade and thrust it into the man's chest, ripping his heavy coat and piercing his flesh. A moment later, a bloodstain blossomed in the vicinity of the highwayman's heart.

* * *

"*Sangdieu!*" Justin swore, forgetting to disguise his voice. He pulled down the kerchief that had covered his mouth and nose. "You puny, cowardly rodent of a man!"

George was dancing around the balcony, jumping back and forth from foot to foot, as if he were engaged in a fair fight. It was almost too easy. A familiar thrill coursed through Justin's body, and it was like being back on the deck of a ship, fighting pirates or the crew of a British merchantman alongside the great Surcouf.

Of course, this was child's play in comparison. Drawing his sword from its scabbard, he brandished it in the torchlight, as he had taught Anthony to do. George hopped faster from foot to foot.

"Justin," cried Mouette as she pulled off her mask. "Do you not see me? Stop!"

"*Chérie*, of course I knew it was you. Why else would I be here?" He sent her a dashing smile. Then he advanced on his opponent, flicking a button from George's brocade coat with his sword tip.

"Justin," Mouette exclaimed again, "you are bleeding!"

He spared a glance for the stain that was spreading across his dark coat. Even his white lace jabot was turning crimson. "It's nothing. Worry not, my love."

It was exhilarating to be holding a sword again, to be on the verge of dispatching a dastardly opponent. This was what he was best at—adventure, danger, risk. And yet, the expression on Mouette's face reminded him that he couldn't have those things and be a husband, too.

At least, not a husband worthy of his exquisite Mouette.

"My bride," he called to her, "I will be brief. *Regardez.*"

George and his sword-cane were no match for Justin, even in his wounded state. With just a few deft thrusts, he struck George's weapon from his shaking hand and had him lying on the balcony floor, on his back.

"Have you no mercy, St. Briac?" the nobleman cried as Justin touched his sword point to his prominent Adam's apple.

"*Mon Dieu,* you are a pitiful creature." The coward had attacked him first, drawing blood when Justin was unarmed. If he killed George, who would blame him? Yet it came to Justin that this was the brother of Mouette's dearest friend, and Gabriel's brother-in-law as well. He might be detestable, but he was still a part of Justin's own extended family.

And family had come to mean more to him in recent days than he could have ever imagined possible.

"Get up." Justin averted his own blade and kicked George's sword-cane toward Mouette, who picked it up and held it behind her back. "I have seen you with Lady Daphne, and I can easily imagine what you two have been plotting. I will allow you to go, but only if you leave the country with all possible speed."

"I will! I promise!" George was on his hands and knees, trembling, and then slowly pushed up to his feet. "But I have no *means*."

Reaching into his pocket, Justin brought out a gold guinea. He tossed it to George, saying, "You don't deserve this, but you are Isabella's brother. Use this coin to finance your journey back to Italy."

Pale and sweating in the moonlight, George glanced over toward Mouette. "I will bid you farewell, if that is your wish."

"It is indeed. Goodbye," she said firmly.

As he saw her coming toward him, Justin felt a powerful surge of hope. "Mouette, you cannot know...how desperately—"

It was like a dream. He felt her embracing him, saw the tears on her cheeks, heard her saying, "I love you. I should have said it sooner, Justin. I love you with all my heart, no matter what happens."

Her face blurred before him and his legs went weak. Pure joy, both sought and feared for so long, was just beyond his grasp.

Perhaps he really was dying, after all...

<h1 style="text-align:center">CHAPTER 33</h1>

One fist pressed to her mouth, Mouette stood in the corner of a spacious bedchamber in her parents' Grosvenor Square home. Her heart was clenched with fear that Justin had sustained a mortal wound and his life might be ebbing away with each passing moment.

Across the expanse of a blue-and-ochre Kuba rug, Justin lay motionless on the bed, his disheveled hair pushed back from his brow. His clothing had been cut away so that his tanned, bare chest contrasted with the snow-white bandages. He was so still she wasn't certain if he were breathing.

"Madame St. Briac?"

It was the portly physician, turning toward her and peering over his spectacles. For a moment, she didn't understand that he was addressing her.

"Oh, yes! I am Madame St. Briac." Mouette lifted the skirts of her mother's old-fashioned ballgown and hurried to Justin's bedside. "I beg you to tell me that he will recover. I will do anything."

At that moment, her make-believe husband's mouth quirked slightly and he whispered, "Anything?"

Mouette gasped even as her heart lifted. Was it possible that he could manage, even on his deathbed, to be wicked?

The physician was putting his implements and bandages away, but he glanced up long enough to say, "Oh, he will recover. Although the slash made by his opponent bled a great deal, it was little more than a flesh wound, thanks to that heavy coat he wore. If you can keep your husband quiet and change his bandages every few hours, he should be up and around tomorrow."

Mouette barely noticed when the physician gathered up his things and left the room. She couldn't take her eyes off Justin.

"Look at me," she said.

He obeyed, his gaze soft. "With pleasure, dear wife. I told him not to give me laudanum. I didn't want to miss a moment of this night. I don't want to die—before I tell you..."

"What is it?" Could the physician have been mistaken about the severity of his wound?

"Ah, Mouette...*I love you.*" When the words were out, he arched a brow, looking bemused. "That wasn't as difficult as I expected. What the devil was I so afraid of?"

Mouette's tears were flowing in earnest now. She ached to hold him, to kiss him, but the sight of his bandaged chest held her back. "And I love you. Quite desperately, in fact."

"Are you certain? I don't deserve it. But if I live, I mean to be a true husband who is worthy of you."

"You are going to live! The physician said it is only a superficial wound."

Relief washed over his face. "Ever since I awoke and found you had fled, not only from my bed but from Cornwall, I have feared that it might be too late. That I had ruined everything with my temper and stubbornness. That I might die before I could tell you how..." Justin brought her hand to his mouth and kissed it. "How very precious you are to me."

"I cannot believe you are truly saying these things." Her heart ached with joy. "Your mood was so black, so angry, I was certain there could be no future for us."

"I was a fool." Justin turned her hand over and pressed his lips to her palm, sending a thrilling current of arousal to the most intimate corners of her body. "But I have changed profoundly, and I will demonstrate that to you every day that we have together. Henceforth, I will be a different man."

Mouette laughed softly and touched her fingertip to his mouth. "Do not say so, m'sieur. I love you exactly as you are."

"I have too many reckless qualities."

"I love them all."

"But then why did you hide my snuffbox if you don't want me to change?"

She flushed. "Ah, *touché*. I surely should not have done so. I may worry that some of your habits are harming your health, but those are choices only you can make."

"Yes, we must trust one another. No more secrets." His gaze wandered to her breasts, swelling above the lace-edged bodice. "There is one wicked pastime I wish to continue to indulge, my lady. I suggest that you disrobe, slowly, and join me."

"Justin, you are hurt. You cannot—"

"Perhaps not tonight," he allowed, "but I can hold you." His brow arched. "And we can touch..."

A keen edge of happiness rose up inside her. Was it possible that they might make a real marriage together? It was a dream that had always seemed just out of reach, yet now felt close at hand.

Then, as Mouette began to unfasten her bodice, she

remembered Anthony and her breath caught in her throat.

If she chose not to tell Justin the truth about Anthony's parentage, she would be keeping a secret of monumental proportions. Yet how many times had he said he had no desire for children? It was perfectly understandable, given the fact that his own childhood had been stolen from him. Wasn't it enough that Justin now had changed regarding romantic love and marriage? Surely it would be easier for him to adapt to having stepsons than to the revelation that one of them was his son by blood—a son who already longed desperately for a father's love.

"What's amiss?" Justin had pushed up on his elbows, so that he was leaning back against the pillows. "You look worried."

She licked her lips, which suddenly felt very dry. "You said that we must not have secrets, and so I realized I have something to tell you."

"I'm listening."

Seeing how serious he looked, Mouette felt clammy all over. "I am afraid."

"Then you had better get it over with." Justin was clearly nervous, too, but he took her hand and held it tightly.

"It's about Anthony." Mouette glanced down to see Justin's foot on top of the sheets, the two fused toes clearly visible. She took a deep breath. "I know that you remember that night ten years ago, after Gabriel and Izzie's wedding."

"I do," came his husky reply.

Then, before Mouette could speak again, the door opened and Robinson ran in at full speed. Anthony followed close behind, calling, "Papa, you're back!"

Horrified, Mouette jumped up. "Anthony, you know you must not enter a room without knocking, especially in the company of that unruly dog!" She held out both hands in warning, as much to Robinson as to Anthony. "Wait! Justin has been hurt. You must stay back."

"Hurt?" Alarmed, Anthony turned to Robinson and commanded, "Sit!" When the corgi had obeyed, he looked at Justin. "Please, if I promise not to jostle you, may I sit on the edge of the bed?"

Mouette was elated to see Justin's expression soften. "*Bien sûr,*" he said, and patted the spot where Mouette had perched moments before. "I'm not really hurt. It's just a scratch."

Relief flooding his small face, Anthony climbed up onto the Empire-style bed next to Justin and folded his legs. "I was too excited to sleep, knowing that you had come to London for Mama—and us, of course." He was looking at Justin's bandaged wound as he spoke. "Were you in a real *duel*, Papa?"

Every time her son said *Papa* it made Mouette start slightly, but Justin didn't seem to mind.

"Yes, I was forced to draw my sword tonight," he said, laughing. "Of course, it wasn't a proper duel because the villain decided to attack me without warning, which is the only reason he managed to inflict this minor wound. Ah, you should have been there, Anthony. You would have loved the part where I cut the button right off the front of his coat—just before I knocked his weapon away and pinned him down on his back." Justin held an arm out, pantomiming the flick of his wrist.

"Lud!" Anthony's dark eyes were big as saucers. "Can you teach that to me?" In his excitement, he squirmed a little and his bare foot brushed Justin's arm.

Mouette held her breath, watching as Justin glanced over. After a moment, his big hand closed around the little boy's smaller foot.

"Of course I shall teach you." Gently, he touched

Anthony's two fused toes and rubbed them between his thumb and forefinger. "You told me that your foot was not made correctly. Were you speaking of these toes?"

Anthony wrinkled his nose and nodded sadly. "Yes. My...*other* father told me they are a deformity."

"Ridiculous!" He bent his strong left leg and displayed his own toes for Anthony to see. "You see, I have them, too! They are perfectly normal—even special. I doubt whether I could have ever become a pirate if not for these toes."

Watching them, Mouette felt more tears come. Anthony was staring in wonderment, as if Justin had just performed an impossible magic trick. "Mama," he exclaimed at last. "Look, Papa has toes just like mine! Wait until I show Charles."

"For now, why don't we keep this between us," Justin murmured. "Toes are a rather private business, don't you agree? And we don't want Charles to be jealous."

Just then, the door opened again. A startled Robinson let out just one bark, stopping immediately when Justin sent him a quelling glance.

"What's happening in here?" It was Charles, looking annoyed. "Aren't we ever going to go to sleep?"

"Papa was hurt in a duel!" Anthony rose up on his knees and pointed to Justin's bandaged chest.

Justin motioned for the older boy to come over and he shared with him the story of the sword fight at the masquerade ball. "I had to rescue your mother, of course, and now that I have, and we are all reunited, I propose we declare ourselves a true family."

Standing there in his nightclothes, Charles looked wary and vulnerable. "A family? Are you quite serious?"

"I've never been more serious than at this moment," Justin assured both boys. Reaching out a hand to Mouette, he drew her next to the bed so they were all together. "Charles, I know I can never take the place of your father. But I love all three of you and I hope that we can make our own special family. We can only succeed if we all try."

Mouette thought for a moment that she saw the glint of tears in her older son's eyes. "Yes, I think I'd like that," he said. "Are we going to live at Bedford Square or Frenchman's Lair?"

"Oh, Frenchman's Lair, don't you agree?" Justin's voice held only a hint of the relief and joy she sensed he was feeling.

Mouette suggested playfully, "Now that you have proclaimed that we are a family, perhaps we should change that name. Don't you agree that *lair* has a rather sinister ring to it?"

"You have a point." Arching an eyebrow, Justin looked at both boys. "Any ideas about this, lads?"

"What about… Frenchman's *Den?*" cried Anthony. "Robinson would like that, I think!"

Justin gave an amused laugh. "Hmm. I am not certain about that. Climb in here with your mama and me, you two," he said, gesturing to Charles, who had remained by the bed, "and let us ponder the matter as we fall asleep."

And so they did. Mouette took off her mother's ball gown, blew out the candles, and climbed into bed wearing her petticoat and chemise. She lay on one side of Justin while the boys happily snuggled in on his other side. Even Robinson managed to jump up onto the bed, where he burrowed into the satiny covers and made a nest for himself.

Just as an utterly blissful sleep overtook Mouette, she felt Justin reach for her hand under the sheet. He brought it up to his mouth and kissed her fingers.

"I have it," he whispered, sounding bewitched. "Our

home will be a haven. *Frenchman's Haven*, don't you agree?"

Before Mouette could reply, she heard the sleepy voices of her sons rise up from the other side of the bed.

In unison, Charles and Anthony said, "Yes!"

EPILOGUE

October 1819
Frenchman's Haven, Cornwall

"We can't," Mouette whispered.

"You know better than to say those words to me." Justin's tone was amused, but he seemed to mean what he said. He rolled her over on their new Sheraton bed, held her head still with his strong hands, and began to kiss her.

Soon, Mouette's will melted away. She tingled all over, lost in the inevitable intoxication of Justin. She was kissing him back, squirming to bring her mound of Venus in contact with his manhood.

"Well, we *shouldn't*," she panted between kisses.

"But we *must*." He nibbled at her ear lobe, despite the fact he knew this drove her mad.

"It is the middle of the day. We have children! And guests arriving soon..." As she spoke, she urgently worked at the buttons on his riding breeches. "Perhaps we should go away somewhere. To a cottage at Land's End..."

"You know I have promised the boys that we will never leave them alone." His hand found its way between her legs. She was already wet and she felt him grow even harder when his fingers began to explore. "They must always know that their parents are close by, watching over them, loving them."

"And loving each other?" She already knew the answer to that question. When they were together like this, it was always a firestorm that surpassed mere physical arousal. She ached for him. As his kiss deepened, his thumb grazed her bud, rhythmically teasing, taunting, until she felt the shuddering waves of her climax begin.

"Please—oh!—for God's sake, Justin, let me..."

"I thought you said we shouldn't." He freed himself, groaning when her fingers closed around him.

"Do not tease me," Mouette begged. She brought him between her thighs, lifting her hips in welcome, answering his thrusts. She was shameless, never able to get enough of him, but of course he was shameless, too. Sometimes, in the afterglow, they laughed about it together.

Just as she saw the muscles in Justin's jaw tighten and a second wave of contractions began at her own core, Mouette heard something.

"Is that crying?" Instinctively, she cocked her head.

Justin was making that low, animal sound that signaled the peak of his orgasm. His face was buried in her neck and she knew he was nearly insensible.

"Justin, do you not hear it?" she whispered.

His full weight still upon her, his head reluctantly came up, eye-patch rakishly askew. She loved the way his hair stood out in silver-flecked disarray when he was completely spent.

"Ah, *oui*." As she separated their bodies, he groaned and fell back on the pillow. "How cruel you are."

Sunbeams shone through the sapphire silk drapes that graced their new bed as Mouette looked down at the fragile bodice of her gown. There was a damp spot over her left nipple.

"You see? Just the sound of that cry tells me it's time to feed her."

Mouette started to rise, attempting to rearrange her clothing, but Justin was quicker. In one movement, he swung both legs over the side of the bed, stood, and pulled on his breeches. Crossing the room, he opened a door that had once led to Mistress Pendudwell's bedchamber, but now connected to a nursery.

Mouette settled herself against the pillows and freed her swollen left breast, anticipating the sight of Justin returning with their child in his arms.

"Someone is looking for her mama," he said as they rounded the corner of the Sheraton bed. The sight of the soft, innocent baby girl in the arms of this powerful man with a scarred chest made Mouette's heart turn over.

She reached out with both hands to receive their three-month-old baby.

"Hello, Emeline."

Watching fondly as his raven-haired daughter turned her head and began to suckle, holding Mouette's breast with both tiny hands, Justin observed, "The young lady lacks manners."

"Just like her papa." Mouette beamed. They shared a look of profound understanding, and it came to her that no one in the world had ever understood her deepest longings in the same way he did.

* * *

AN HOUR LATER, dozing contently on the sunlit bed with Mouette and Emeline, Justin heard the sound of carriage wheels on the gravel drive.

"Oh, goodness!" Mouette said. "The first of the family must be arriving. And your mother was going to make some sort of Breton butter cake with Baptiste..."

"I will go down and greet them," he said, though at that moment he didn't want to. "Don't be long, my beauties."

After splashing water on his face, Justin put on fresh clothing and went downstairs.

It always surprised him to see what a hive of activity the house had become. Charles and Anthony were inevitably busy with some activity, ranging from chess to croquet. Today they were in the drawing room with their cousins.

"Papa," called Anthony, "we are showing our guests the special terrestrial globe!"

The boy, now ten years of age, was standing in front of the shelf where Justin kept the valuable globe. Charles stood nearby with Lucas Trevarre, while little Camille knelt on the carpet, endeavoring to fit a reluctant Robinson with a "fairy saddle" made of ribbons and flowers.

"Do not forget that the globe is very old and fragile," Justin said as he came into the room. All four children watched as he walked over and put a hand on Charles's shoulder. "I know I can depend on you to see that the globe is treated with care."

"Of course," Charles answered, smiling shyly as he added, "Father."

By the time Justin left the room, they were all talking at once, pointing out the various countries and touching the raised mountains.

Through the windows at the back of the house, he

could see Gabriel and Isabella outside on the terrace with Sebastian and Julia. The women were arranging china plates on a long table while Gabriel walked in the garden, doubtlessly pointing out to Sebastian where he thought Justin should plant fruit trees. It was his favorite subject when he visited. Never mind that the brothers didn't agree about it; Gabriel seemed to feel that he should have the last word because he fancied himself a botanist.

"Can you not indulge him and follow his advice?"

Justin turned to see his father, walking up behind him with a knowing smile.

"It is not his place, you know. Mouette and I may have different tastes," Justin replied. But, as they watched his brother walking back and forth, gesturing and smiling, he remembered that Mouette had once suggested Gabriel might make a plan for their garden. "I will, however, hear him out."

"*Merci*," Xavier replied. "Do not let him know I have told you, but I think he intends to make a gift to you and Mouette of several special trees he has grown himself, from seeds."

Justin didn't particularly like the part of himself that had instinctively minimized Gabriel's accomplishments since he'd married, left their smuggling business, and settled in Cornwall. Perhaps, as Mouette often suggested, this was an area where Justin might try to improve.

"*Eh bien*, Papa. I will consider what you have said."

Just then, Devon and André Raveneau came toward them. They had been in Cornwall for several days, but were staying with Sebastian and Julia at Trevarre Hall.

"Hello!" Devon greeted him with a warm smile. "We've been admiring your home, Justin. Every time we visit it is more lovely and welcoming."

André Raveneau was nodding, though Justin sensed that he still was not entirely certain he approved of his daughter's husband. "It is a fine estate, and Mouette's influence is very evident. However, I confess that I would not have chosen the wilds of Cornwall as a place for her to settle."

"So you have previously mentioned," Justin said evenly. "But perhaps we can find a reason for you to spend more time in Cornwall. I have an investment proposal for you."

Devon tactfully wandered off, chatting with Xavier, as Raveneau repeated, "An investment?"

"Perhaps you have heard that there was a terrible storm in Polperro two winters ago?" When his father-in-law nodded, Justin continued, "Now that I have settled in Cornwall, I'm exploring projects that will help to restore Polperro's economy. The harbor has been rebuilt, but there remains a great deal of work to do. Many fishing vessels were lost, and with them went the livelihoods of entire families."

"I would hazard a guess that your notion of 'help' involves providing employment through new smuggling ventures?" mused André.

"Once that would surely have been the case, but not any longer," Justin assured him. "Last year, I purchased the net loft that sits atop Peak Rock and entered into an agreement with Lady Daphne Leyton, who now works for me, overseeing the millinery enterprise that operates upstairs. I have raised the wages and improved the working conditions of women who labor at hat-making. Most of them had to seek employment to keep food on their tables, due to the storm's damage to the village fishing industry." Justin paused, noting with pleasure that Raveneau seemed to be genuinely interested. "Now I want to bring more fishing vessels to

Polperro, so more of the men can work again. I thought you might like to join me in this venture?"

"A very interesting proposal," André said thoughtfully. "Perhaps we can discuss this in greater depth tomorrow?"

"Excellent. Shall we go outside and find our wives? I believe that a simple meal is to be served shortly."

They went past the kitchen in time to hear voices being raised. Justin put his head in the door and saw Baptiste, Margaret the cook, and his mother all standing around the work table.

"Madame," implored Baptiste, "I assure you that I can guide Margaret as we finish the *kouign amann*. You must remember that I too am French."

"I am quite certain she did not put enough salt in the butter," complained Cerise. "It is the secret to a perfect *kouign amann*, you know. And look there, she is not mixing the dough properly." Waving her hand in front of Margaret, she added, "Use your fingers, my girl!"

"Maman, come with us," Justin said firmly. "You have already made enough trouble for one day."

Cerise put her nose into the air but obeyed, sweeping from the room like an empress in her fashionable, high-waisted gown of sage-green gauze. She emerged into the corridor just as Mouette came to join them, carrying little Emeline.

When the baby saw her father she immediately began to make urgent sounds of longing with her little rosebud mouth. Everyone looked at Justin and he laughed.

"What can I say? I am irresistible to women." Before Mouette could put the baby in his arms, he shook his head. "Do you know, I sense that she would prefer to go to her grandfather today."

André Raveneau looked momentarily surprised before he parried, "It is true that I've perfected an excellent technique for holding babies." He took his granddaughter and held her close to his wide chest. Gazing down at her irresistible little face and raven curls, he said, "She is the image of Mouette, who was already at sea at three months of age!"

"I hope we will be able to say the same for Emeline," said Justin, "though I suspect her first voyage will be across the Channel to Saint-Malo. We want all our children to feel a part of France as well as Britain."

The little group continued out onto the stone terrace where nine-year-old Louise St. Briac was placing little squares of hand-lettered parchment on each plate.

"I have been put in charge of the seating arrangements," she said with a shy smile. "You see, I have made a special card for each guest."

Justin walked over to admire the precisely-made cards, noticing that Louise had placed Charles's name next to her own seat. The children were starting to come out of the house, and when Charles saw Louise, his face lit up.

"Hello," he said, coming around the table to smile first at Justin, then at Louise. "I've brought one of the new houses from my model of Saint-Malo to show you."

Out of his coat pocket, he withdrew a small wooden house, part of the elaborate model he and Justin had been constructing together for the past year. The house featured painted windows, a door, and shingles on its sloping roof.

Louise's eyes shone behind her spectacles. "Oh, I love it! I will add it to the map I am making. Uncle Justin, you must provide the address for me." She paused to wave at Gabriel. "My papa will love to see this!"

"I think that all of us should plan a family journey to Saint-Malo in the spring," Justin said. "There is plenty of room for everyone in our home there. Then you can verify the locations of all the buildings on your map."

Glancing toward Charles, Louise smiled. "That sounds like a grand adventure!"

Isabella was approaching with a beautiful vase of pink hydrangeas mixed helter-skelter with red valerian and daisies. She put it in the center of the table and beamed. Justin was struck by a moment of perfect happiness as he took in the scene...the last roses of the season climbing up the nearby wall of the manor house, the smiling faces of family and friends who were completely comfortable together, the delicious fragrance of food as Margaret carried dishes out from the kitchen, and Robinson in pursuit of a red squirrel that frolicked across the lawn.

As the family gathered around the table and everyone found their chairs, Mouette moved the cards around so that she was sitting next to Justin.

Leaning over, she whispered in his ear, "The scent of you is on me."

Justin made a growling sound under his breath and they beamed at one another, holding hands under the table.

"*Pardonnez-moi*! I should like to say something," announced Cerise. She sat nearby, between Gabriel and little Camille. Baptiste and Margaret had just placed a platter of sliced, roasted pheasant on the table, and now they stepped back, waiting.

"We are listening, Maman," Justin said with a note of irony. "Not that we have a choice."

His mother pretended not to have noticed his barb. Raising her glass, she sat up straighter and looked at him. "*Mon fils*, I know that you were shocked and angry at my *petite charade* last year." Cerise paused, allowing her words to sink in. "However, time has passed. Perhaps you now can see that I deserve your *gratitude*. If it were not for me, you would still be seeking one more reckless adventure—and Mouette would be trying to keep up appearances in London." She made a sweeping gesture with one be-ringed hand. "Look around you! Only I could have caused this contented home to come into being."

Justin felt his brows fly up in utter disbelief. "Maman, you are absolutely—"

"Correct!" Gabriel interrupted. Justin could scarcely believe it when his brother raised his own glass. "To our mother...the only person who could have carried off so brazen a plan and guided it skillfully to fruition. *Salut*, Maman."

Justin was incredulous. Was his mother actually taking credit for the home he and Mouette had created, by bravely opening their hearts to love?

"She does have a point," Mouette said under her breath.

It struck him then, as he looked down this festive table lined with family and friends, that it was true. Their home was a place of love and laughter, where everyone's heart seemed to stretch a little more each day...and it would not have come into being without his outrageous mother's scheme.

Across the table, André Raveneau was cradling Emeline in his strong arms. His silver hair shone in the late afternoon sunlight as he met Justin's gaze and arched an eyebrow.

Feeling one more barrier give way inside, Justin laughed. He and Mouette raised their glasses and he addressed their guests.

"*Salut* to all of you. We are grateful to you for being here." Then he met Cerise's dark eyes that were so much like his own and flashed a rakish smile. "And to you, Maman, I say *merci*."

Turning back to his wife, Justin felt tears burn his

eyes. When one slipped from under his eye-patch and Mouette reached up to touch it, he saw that her eyes were also wet.

"Tears of joy," she whispered, smiling.

"I thank God for them, *ma belle.*"

~ THANK YOU ~

Also on Facebook: I post "Behind the Book" tidbits and news about my research, family adventures, and crazy pets at https://www.facebook.com/ cynthiawrightauthor
Or friend me at:
https://www.facebook.com/cyntha.wright.98

You can also follow me on Twitter @CynthiaWright1 and on Instagram

If you enjoyed reading this book, please consider posting a brief REVIEW. It's the very best way to say thank you to an author, and your review will help other readers make a choice.

HIS MAKE-BELIEVE BRIDE is Book 6 in
Rakes & Rebels: The Raveneau Family:

1 – SILVER STORM (André & Devon)
2 – HER HUSBAND, THE RAKE (André & Devon)
a sequel novella to SILVER STORM
3 – SMUGGLER'S MOON (Sebastian & Julia)
4 – THE SECRET OF LOVE (Gabriel & Isabella)
5 – SURRENDER THE STARS (Ryan & Lindsay)
6 – HIS MAKE-BELIEVE BRIDE (Justin & Mouette)
7 – HER IMPOSSIBLE HUSBAND (Justin & Mouette)
8 – HIS RECKLESS BARGAIN (Nathan & Adrienne)
9 – TEMPEST (Adam & Cathy)

The *Raveneau Family* series intertwines with
Rakes & Rebels: The Beauvisage Family:

1 – STOLEN BY A PIRATE (Jean-Philippe & Antonia)
a novella prequel to RESCUED BY A ROGUE
2 – RESCUED BY A ROGUE (Alec & Caro)
3 – TOUCH THE SUN (Lion & Meagan)

4 – SPRING FIRES (Nicholai & Lisette)
5 – HER DANGEROUS VISCOUNT (Grey & Natalya)

You can access a complete list of all my series at the end of this book.

A fantastic audiobook of HIS MAKE-BELIEVE BRIDE is available, and I know that you will love Tim Campbell's inspired performance! Tim has already brought the St. Briac brothers vividly to life in his performance of THE SECRET OF LOVE. You can listen to samples of my audiobooks and order your copy HERE.

I have just finished a new novel featuring Justin and Mouette – and their growing children! HER IMPOSSIBLE HUSBAND is set ten years later, when our favorite couple are facing strains on their marriage and are challenged to deal with unfinished business from the past. What will happen when Justin tries to navigate life among the London *ton*? You are invited to read an excerpt after the Author's Note and order your copy of HER IMPOSSIBLE HUSBAND today.

If you haven't yet read SILVER STORM, the bestselling romance of Mouette's parents, André and Devon Raveneau, you can download your copy now at a special price and read the Raveneau series from the beginning.

Once again, my heartfelt thanks for your support, interest, and encouragement for my books. I welcome your comments and suggestions, and I hope that you'll write to me at Cynthia@CynthiaWrightAuthor.com. I promise to reply!

Warmest wishes,
~ *Cynthia*

When I was writing THE SECRET OF LOVE, my husband and I traveled to Saint-Malo, France to do research. That's where Justin's character was born. I even found his home there. He went from being mentioned in SMUGGLER'S MOON to nearly taking over THE SECRET OF LOVE to having his own book in HIS MAKE-BELIEVE BRIDE…and now I confess I find it a bit difficult to let him go.

When we were on our latest research trip to Cornwall, Alvaro and I got lost walking on a remote country lane. We came into a dark, magical tunnel of trees and it was truly like going back in time. When we emerged, we saw a stately home sitting quietly all by itself, no sign, no cars, no people. It could have been 1818 and Justin and Mouette might have been inside, bickering about furniture. That house immediately took root in my imagination and became the inspiration for Pendudwell Manor.

After I wrote HIS MAKE-BELIEVE BRIDE, I took a break from Cornwall and the 19th century and traveled to Scotland to research three books set in the 16th century. Now they are part of a wonderful 5-book series, *Crowns and Kilts*. I hope you'll read and enjoy AB-

DUCTED AT THE ALTAR, RETURN OF THE LOST BRIDE, and QUEST OF THE HIGHLANDER!

In 2021, I returned to the Raveneau series and have just finished a brand-new novel featuring Justin and Mouette, HER IMPOSSIBLE HUSBAND. It is set in 1829, after they have been married a decade and face new challenges in their relationship. When Mouette has an opportunity to return to London and finally repair her broken reputation, she agrees to go for the sake of her grown son, Charles, who aspires to a position in the *ton*. But Justin has issues of his own and no wish to mingle in London society. It's a test for this passionate couple...and a chance for us to get to know their older children, including Anthony, who is now a student at Cambridge.

Please page ahead to read the first chapter of HER IMPOSSIBLE HUSBAND. As always, Justin may be impossible, but he is also irresistible!

Thank you again for reading my books and letting me know your thoughts. I appreciate every one of you.

Warmest wishes and thanks to you,

~ *Cynthia*

HER IMPOSSIBLE HUSBAND

RAKES & REBELS: THE RAVENEAU FAMILY, BOOK 7

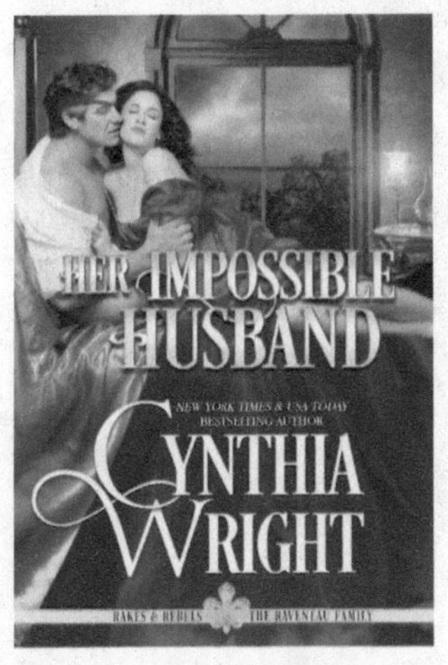

Please enjoy this sample chapter…

CHAPTER 1

Saint-Malo, Brittany, France

April 1829

"M'sieur," called Baptiste, Justin St. Briac's devoted manservant. "Might I remind you of the time?"

Justin paused at the top of narrow steps leading down into a labyrinthian cellar, where all his treasures from years on the high seas were stored. Even though he now lived in Cornwall with his wife and children, he would always feel a mystical attachment to this three-story mansion in the walled city of Saint-Malo. Facing the ramparts, Justin's grand residence was part of Corsairs' Row, an impressive series of homes overlooking the sea, built by the ill-gotten gains of pirates. Here Justin had long enjoyed the reckless, splendid life of a smuggler and corsair, amassing wealth, legendary adventures, and enough lovers to keep him from the altar until he was forty-eight years old.

Every year, Justin brought his family across the English Channel to Saint-Malo. For a several weeks, he could pretend to turn back the hands of time...a fantasy that appealed more to him the older he became.

Turning now to Baptiste, he challenged, "Stop scolding me. It is noon, is it not? My meeting with Giles Taureau is not for another hour. I am taking Anthony down to my secret storeroom to search for a particularly wonderful relic of the past."

Just then, his tall, broad-shouldered son came into the room while adjusting the cuffs of a snug forest-green coat. Something in Anthony's expression suggested that he was about to beg off the excursion to the cellar, so Justin started purposefully toward the steps.

"Follow me," he said, gesturing with one dark hand. "We have not visited the storerooms lately, and you should view the riches that will one day be yours."

Bending slightly, Justin led the way down the darkened stairway. Father and son continued on through a maze of vaulted stone tunnels, where lanterns were hung at intervals. Occasionally, Justin glanced back to check on Anthony. Noticing that the youth risked striking his dark head as they passed under an arch, it came to Justin that Anthony might now be even taller than he was.

Yet, had it not been just a brief season ago that the little boy had begged for dueling lessons, declaring that he wanted to be a pirate when he grew to manhood? Justin's heart clenched as he absorbed the swift passage of time.

"It's thrilling down here, don't you agree?" he asked his son. It wasn't really a question, for surely the answer was obvious.

"Indeed," Anthony replied after a moment, polite yet hardly enthusiastic. "Thrilling." They came into a gloomy storeroom stacked high with ornate furniture and other forgotten treasures, and he blinked. "But...what do you mean to do with all this?"

"Do?" Justin echoed, wondering if he should take

offense at Anthony's question. He unhooked a lantern and brought it forward to spill golden light over a lifetime of memories. "Perhaps you've forgotten our past visits to these rooms, when you begged me to regale you with tales of my adventures with the great corsairs of Saint-Malo! Every item you see in this cellar is infused with history and meaning." He paused to let his words sink in before adding, "One day it will all be yours."

"Ah." Anthony looked around, brows lifted, and raked a hand through his fashionably disheveled black hair. "Right. I do remember."

Justin pointed toward a carved, thronelike chair, its worn ochre velvet upholstery now spotted with mildew. "That piece once belonged to Robert Surcouf himself, the greatest Malouin corsair of all! Can you not hear it whispering to us? You used to stand on the chair seat as if it were a quarterdeck, waving your wooden sword and proclaiming that one day you too would sail to the Indian Ocean!"

Anthony looked pensive. "When I was young, I think I lived for your smiles. Making you shout encouragement felt like a great accomplishment." He paused, as if transported back to his childhood, then flashed a reassuring smile. "What a magical adventure it was, being your child."

Justin frowned. "I'm not dead, you know."

"Of course you are not." The youth glanced away. "It's just that...it feels like a bit of a fairytale now, that's all."

"Indeed? I can assure you, it has been quite real for me, and remains so. In fact, I came down here to look for something that once belonged to the corsair I am going to meet with today." He handed the lantern to Anthony and advanced toward the jumble of furniture and other goods. Just as the object Justin sought came into focus, Anthony spoke.

"Papa, you call your friend a fellow corsair...but isn't that all in the past?" He paused. "I mean, since you married Mama and we began a new life in Cornwall, you have changed, haven't you?"

"I would have wagered that you, of all people, would not wish me to forget those glorious exploits!"

Anthony rubbed long fingers against the side of his jaw. "I suppose I thought of it all as a part of your past, a wonderful story, but then it seemed you have chosen to have a family instead."

Stung, Justin chose a cutlass from the assortment of goods and returned to display the savage weapon in front of Anthony. "This belonged to my comrade, Giles Taureau. Do you see, it is designed especially for daring hand-to-hand combat on the deck of a ship, where space is limited and a longer sword could easily become tangled in the rigging." Justin gestured toward the short, broad blade, the faded red sash tied around the scabbard, and the initials "G.T." carved with a flourish near the hilt. His voice deepened as he added, "Once a corsair, always a corsair! It is in my *blood*."

Anthony was regarding him with concern. "Are you feeling quite well?"

"Never better. In fact, I have an idea. Giles has written to ask that I meet him on the ramparts of Saint-Malo at one o'clock. Why don't you come, too! Wouldn't you enjoy hearing bold tales of our life upon the sea from one of the bravest corsairs of them all?"

There was a pause. "Do you mean today?"

Before Justin could reply, he glimpsed a movement in the doorway, and Mouette came into view. As usual, the sight of his ravishing wife made his heart beat faster. If not for the glints of silver in her ebony curls, it would be hard to believe she had recently celebrated her forty-seventh birthday. Clad in a geranium-tinted morning gown with a tulle-edged stand-up collar, Mouette looked fresh and delectable.

"What are you two doing down here?" she inquired, scanning the cluttered room. Her thick-lashed blue eyes soon settled on the cutlass.

"Anthony is always eager to see the fruits of my labor, as you well know, *ma belle.*" Of course, this wasn't quite how it had happened, but Justin had always enjoyed a fluid relationship with the truth. He heard his son exhale, but thankfully he did not correct him. "We were just admiring my comrade Giles Taureau's very fine cutlass."

He held it toward Mouette, and her nostrils flared. "It is a gruesome thing, and that *sash* he has tied to the hilt - " She finished the sentence with a disgusted grimace. "It is filthy. I suspect some of those stains may be blood!"

"You are quite right." Justin gave a firm nod of approval. "Can you not envision the scene of battle on the deck of Surcouf's own *Revenant*? In those moments, a man feels truly alive!" He glanced toward Anthony. "More alive than you can possibly imagine."

Mouette was clearly making an effort to hold her tongue, while Anthony leaned against a stone pillar and watched his parents. For an instant, seeing him grown nearly to full manhood, Justin was transported back to a long-ago day, when they were newly-acquainted. They had been in a tangled Cornwall garden, and young Anthony was begging for a fencing lesson. He had danced about, holding a wooden sword, thrilled to be in the presence of a true corsair.

Justin hadn't known then that they were father and son, that Anthony had been conceived during one wildly sensual night following too many glasses of wine at the wedding of Justin's brother, Gabriel to Mouette's dear friend, Isabella. In the morning, Mouette had hidden from Justin, then taken her young son, Charles, and hurried back to her husband in London. A decade would pass before a widowed, destitute Mouette would return to Justin's life, shaking its very foundations. Anthony had adored Justin on sight, copying his every gesture, proclaiming, "I want to be a pirate when I grow up. Like you!"

By the time they had all surrendered to being a family and Emeline was conceived, Justin wondered what he had been struggling against all his life. By God, he was *happy*! Sometimes he could even forget about the deep antipathy he'd always harbored toward marriage, spawned by a lifetime of witnessing the manipulative relationship between his own parents.

The love of a good woman had healed even Justin's deepest scars, it seemed. Most of the time, he could believe it...until someone didn't behave as he expected. For instance, why wasn't Anthony responding to Justin's utterance with a grin, or at least a nod that would let him know they were of one mind. Instead, he went to his mother and kissed her cheek.

"You know how Papa is," he murmured dryly, and Mouette replied with a faintly amused smile.

What the devil did Anthony mean by that? Justin scowled. Hadn't father and son always been in league together? "I think Cambridge is making you soft. Come out with me to meet Giles Taureau, so you can observe a real man who truly knows how to live."

"All this talk of pirates makes me wonder if you are suffering some sort of crisis." Mouette's tone was deceptively light.

"What does that mean?" he demanded.

She smiled sweetly. "Oh, you know, the kind of distress older men endure when they realize they will never be young again."

Justin could only swivel slightly to send her a warning stare. Before he could say something he would doubtless regret, nine-year-old Emeline appeared in the doorway behind her mother. Every time he saw their daughter in recent months, Justin was struck anew that she had begun to cross the bridge from childhood to adolescence.

"Hello!" She smiled at Justin before turning her attention to Anthony. "I've been waiting for you upstairs. Are you ready to go?"

"Go?" echoed Justin. He wished his enchanting Emmie would rush into his arms when she saw him, as she had done for so many years. He would stroke her soft black curls with his big hand, loving her so much it hurt...but these days Emeline seemed to have more important concerns than her papa. "Where are you going?"

Anthony cleared his throat, looking uncomfortable. "As it happens, Papa, I was just about to explain that I cannot go with you to meet your friend because I have promised to take Emmie to the beach to hunt for fossils."

Fossils. Justin clenched his teeth to stop himself from protesting, "*Mon Dieu*, not those again."

* * *

Mouette watched with interest as Emeline crossed to her brother's side and grasped his forearm. "Yes, we must leave, Anthony," the girl exclaimed. "The light will fade if we delay."

"There are no fossils on the beaches here," Justin declared with a note of finality. "I would have seen them long ago."

Mouette tried not to smile. Did he really think anything he could say would change Emeline's mind? She was every bit as hard-headed as he was.

"Papa, perhaps you might acknowledge that you are not an expert on this subject," Emmie dared to assert. "Villers-sur-Mer may be the superior beach for fossils in Brittany, but we don't have time to travel there. Therefore, I hope to astound the geologists by discovering something wonderful, like a *trilobite,* right here in Saint-Malo!" She tugged again at her brother. "Really, there is no time to waste."

Anthony, who grew more handsome by the day, threw his father an apologetic look. "I did promise Emmie earlier this morning. Perhaps I can meet Giles Taureau another time? Even next summer."

With that, the siblings took their leave. Justin stood alone in the cellar room, holding the terrible cutlass with its stained, threadbare sash. Mouette's heart went out to him. Justin was used to exerting a magnetic power over his family, and while the children were young, that had been easy enough. However, they now had strong minds of their own and thought nothing of challenging the authority of their parents.

"Next summer?" he muttered under his breath. "Can he not fit me into his social calendar before then?"

"Our time here is ending. Tomorrow we must begin packing to return to Cornwall, remember?" Mouette reminded him. "The Michaelmas term at Cambridge has already begun."

"I never imagined my own son would choose to spend entire *years* at a stuffy university when he could be out in the world, taking hold of life with both hands, plunging into adventures while he is young, strong, and..."

His voice trailed off, and Mouette narrowed her eyes. "What were you going to say? Virile?"

"Perhaps." Justin shrugged, but his expression was challenging. "What is wrong with that? He is coming into the prime of life."

"Oh, for heaven's sake. I have no doubt that Anthony is perfectly capable of becoming a rake, if he so chooses, whether he is studying at Cambridge or standing on the deck of a pirate ship." Sometimes it was difficult to indulge Justin's flinty moods, but Mouette loved him enough to try. Crossing to his side, she rested a hand on the sleeve of his flawlessly-tailored, midnight-blue coat.

Although Justin could be impossibly arrogant and stubborn, age had not dimmed his masculine aura. Even the silk patch that slanted rakishly over his right eye added to his appeal, Mouette thought. Glancing down at her, he remarked, "I never knew it could be so difficult to be a father. No wonder I avoided it most of my life."

"You might turn your attention to other concerns," she suggested, forcing herself to look past him to the assortment of old furniture, books, paintings, and other memorabilia from the past. "Why not begin to sort through some of these items?"

Justin looked suspicious. "To what purpose?"

She couldn't help herself. "Well, do you truly need any of this? The first time you brought me to this house, these pieces were here, but ten years have passed, and I do not recall you ever reclaiming any of them."

"Reclaim them?" A storm cloud passed over his face. "Why should I do that? These are not mere *things*, but valuable artifacts!" Drawing back, Justin added, "You, more than anyone, should understand that."

"Of course I understand, darling," she soothed. *Really, though, what value could these possessions hold?* "But I also understand that you are a very meticulous person.

Every detail in our homes must be perfect or you are not satisfied, and all our servants know it. You insist on flawlessly made clothing and furnishings that reflect the latest fashions and the best of taste."

"*Oui!* Of course I do," he growled. "What is your point?"

"Only that I find it hard to reconcile this musty clutter with the man I just described."

Justin walked away from her, staring at his hoard of memorabilia. "Many of these pieces were accumulated before I knew you, when I was a free man, engaging in outrageous adventures as smuggler or sailing with legendary corsairs to defend France in the Indian Ocean." He picked up a large compass in an enamel case and blew away a layer of dust. "This belonged to Surcouf himself. The very sight of it takes me back to our time together in his cabin on board *Revenant*, as we planned our secret attacks on British ships in the Bay of Bengal. He was vibrantly alive." Justin paused, then added hoarsely, "We both were."

Mouette's eyes stung in sympathy. Last year, when their family arrived in Saint-Malo for their annual summer visit, Justin had gone off as usual to visit Surcouf and had been stunned to find his old friend on his deathbed. She knew this blow had meant not only the loss of a comrade, but also a stark reminder of Justin's own mortality. Surcouf had died at age fifty-four, suddenly an old man, ravaged by a wasting disease...yet Justin himself was even older. Mouette knew better than anyone that her husband resisted letting down his protective shield and becoming vulnerable to pain, but she should not encourage that resistance.

"I know how hard it has been for you, losing your friend, Surcouf," she whispered. "Yet we cannot turn back time."

Gesturing toward the ramparts that lay beyond the

windowless cellar walls, Justin demanded, "Perhaps you would have me build a great bonfire on the beach and burn everything from my past?"

Mouette knew she had pushed him far enough. "Of course not. I only ask that you think about what I've said." Embracing him, she leaned against his broad chest. The scent of Justin's warm, powerful body stirred her senses, as always. Suddenly, Mouette was hungry for him, and it came to her that they might make love in one of the ancient chairs. It was a long time since they'd done something so wickedly arousing. "I must admit, this cellar does feel like a place out of time... Perhaps we might pretend that you are a corsair and you have captured me from an enemy's ship." Even as she spoke, heat coursed through her body and she slipped her hand between them, fitting it to his crotch. Her nipples grew taut as she imagined sitting on his lap, her bodice undone, his warm mouth working its magic.

Justin made a low, primitive sound and hardened against her palm, but in the next moment, he abruptly stepped back, eyes flashing. "I do not need to *pretend*. I will always be a corsair. And now I must go to meet Giles Taureau." He picked up the old cutlass and started to turn away.

"Will you not kiss your wife before you leave?" As intended, Mouette's tone held more of a challenge than a plea.

"As you wish, *chérie*."

When he caught her against him with one strong arm, the years melted away. His mouth covered hers, burning, and Mouette responded as passionately as ever. Then, just as quickly as the flame ignited, her husband snuffed it out.

"I must go," Justin said, stepping back to brandish

the cutlass with its bloodstained sash. "Giles is not a man to keep waiting!"

Order HER IMPOSSIBLE HUSBAND today at your favorite online retailer! (publishing January 7, 2022)

See all of Cynthia Wright's titles here:
http://cynthiawrightauthor.com/books.html

~ MEET CYNTHIA WRIGHT ~

Cynthia Wright is the *New York Times* and *USA Today* bestselling author best known for her *Rakes & Rebels* series, 13 intertwining historical romances starring the irresistible Raveneau and Beauvisage families. Her other acclaimed series are *Crowns & Kilts* and *Rogues Go West*. Romantic Times Magazine hails Cynthia's novels as "Romance the way it was meant to be."

Cynthia lives in northern California. She enjoys riding a tandem bike and taking road trips in an airstream trailer with her Colombian-born husband, Alvaro, and their corgi, Watson. She is also devoted to her two loving grandsons who live nearby.

You are invited to visit Cynthia's website (where you can sign up for her newsletter and peruse the Books Page):
http://cynthiawrightauthor.com/

You are invited to join Cynthia's private Facebook reader group here:
https://www.facebook.com/groups/986064468145940/

View her "Behind the Books" boards on Pinterest:
http://pinterest.com/cynthiawright77/

~ BOOKS BY CYNTHIA WRIGHT ~

Rakes & Rebels

THE RAVENEAU FAMILY
SILVER STORM
HER HUSBAND, THE RAKE
SMUGGLER'S MOON
THE SECRET OF LOVE
SURRENDER THE STARS
HIS MAKE-BELIEVE BRIDE
HER IMPOSSIBLE HUSBAND
HIS RECKLESS BARGAIN
TEMPEST

THE BEAUVISAGE FAMILY
STOLEN BY A PIRATE
RESCUED BY A ROGUE
TOUCH THE SUN
SPRING FIRES
HER DANGEROUS VISCOUNT
~
Crowns & Kilts

THE ST. BRIAC FAMILY

YOU AND NO OTHER
OF ONE HEART
ABDUCTED AT THE ALTAR
RETURN OF THE LOST BRIDE
QUEST OF THE HIGHLANDER

~

Rogues Go West

BRIGHTER THAN GOLD
IN A RENEGADE'S EMBRACE
THE DUKE AND THE COWGIRL

~

Boxed Sets

RAKES & REBELS: THE RAVENEAU FAMILY 1
(Silver Storm, Her Husband, the Rake)

RAKES & REBELS: THE RAVENEAU FAMILY 2
(Smuggler's Moon, The Secret of Love, Surrender the
Stars)

RAKES & REBELS: THE RAVENEAU FAMILY 3
(His Make-Believe Bride, His Reckless Bargain,
Tempest)

THE RAVENEAU FAMILY IN CORNWALL
(Smuggler's Moon, The Secret of Love, His Make-
Believe Bride)

RAKES & REBELS: THE BEAUVISAGE FAMILY 1
(Stolen by a Pirate, Rescued by a Rogue)

RAKES & REBELS: THE BEAUVISAGE FAMILY 2
(Touch the Sun, Spring Fires, Her Dangerous Viscount)

CROWNS & KILTS: COLLECTION 1 – CROWNS

(You and No Other, Of One Heart)

CROWNS & KILTS: COLLECTION 2 – KILTS
(Abducted at the Altar, Return of the Lost Bride, Quest
of the Highlander)

ROGUES GO WEST
(Brighter than Gold, In a Renegade's Embrace, The
Duke and the Cowgirl)